Praise for *Honeysuckle Season*

"This memorable story is sure to tug at readers' heartstrings."

—*Publishers Weekly*

Praise for *Winter Cottage*

"Offering a look into bygone days of the gentrified from the early 1900s up until the present time, this multifaceted tale of mystery and romance is sure to please."

—New York Journal of Books

"There is mystery and intrigue as the author weaves a tale that pulls you in . . . this is a story of strong women, who persevere . . . it's a love story, the truest, deepest kind . . . and it's the story of a woman who years later was able to right a wrong and give a home to the people who really needed it. It's layered brilliantly, and hints are revealed subtly, allowing the reader to form conclusions and fall in love."

—*Smexy Books*

Praise for Mary Ellen Taylor

"Mary Ellen Taylor writes comfort reads packed with depth . . . If you're looking for a fantastic vacation read, this is the book for you!"

—*Steph and Chris's Book Review*

"A complex tale . . . grounded in fascinating history and emotional turmoil that is intense yet subtle. An intelligent, heartwarming exploration of the powers of forgiveness, compassion, and new beginnings."

—*Kirkus Reviews*

"Absorbing characters, a hint of mystery, and touching self-discovery elevate this novel above many others in the genre."

—RT Book Reviews

"Taylor serves up a great mix of vivid setting, history, drama, and everyday life."

—*Herald Sun*

"A charming and very engaging story about the nature of family and the meaning of love."

—*Seattle Post-Intelligencer*

THE WORDS WE WHISPER

OTHER TITLES BY MARY ELLEN TAYLOR

Winter Cottage

Spring House

Honeysuckle Season

Union Street Bakery Novels

The Union Street Bakery

Sweet Expectations

Alexandria Series

At the Corner of King Street

The View from Prince Street

THE WORDS WE WHISPER

MARY ELLEN TAYLOR

This is a work of fiction. Names, characters, organizations, places, events, and incidents are either products of the author's imagination or are used fictitiously.

Published by Montlake, Seattle

www.apub.com

ISBN-13: 9781542018395
ISBN-10: 1542018390

Cover design by Amanda Kain

Printed in the United States of America

THE WORDS WE WHISPER

CHAPTER ONE
ISABELLA

Rome, Italy
Friday, August 13, 1943, 11:45 a.m.

Nothing ever ends as we would expect.

The birthing was no exception. It was going badly, hours longer than it should, and the young woman's thin body, pear shaped with a distended belly, refused to release the child. Screams reverberated in the small upstairs room, as to the east, near the rail yards, bombs shook these medieval walls, rattled arched windows, and kept the pendant light above my head swinging.

"I can't do this anymore," the young woman said, her voice a hoarse whisper.

"Mia," I said firmly. "You must push again." Mia had labored with this child for nearly eighteen hours, and she was growing weaker by the minute.

"I can't," she whimpered. "It hurts."

Our landlady, Signora Marcella Fontana, hurried into the room with more towels tucked under her arm and a clean white porcelain basin filled with water. "The doctor is not coming," she said. "The city is exploding. The Allies are bombing the rail yards again. No one can be bothered with a simple birth."

There was nothing simple about this birth, but saying so or cursing the doctor, the Allied planes swarming the skies, or the Germans crowding Rome's streets would not bring this child into the world. That task rested solely on the three of us.

I placed my hand on Mia's drum-tight belly. Her normally vivid brown eyes were watery, and her blonde curls were plastered by sweat to her pale forehead. "Mia, it's just us now. Only you, me, and the signora can bring your child into the world."

"Where is my brother, Riccardo?" she wailed. "He said he would not abandon me."

Mia's brother had vanished six months before. Some said he had joined the Resistance, and others said he had hidden like most of Rome's men, avoiding conscription. There were also rumors he had been transported to a labor camp. Or perhaps he could not bear the shame his wild younger sister had brought upon the family. "He does not matter now. Only you and the child." I smiled but feared the expression was far from soothing. "Don't you want to meet your baby?"

"No." Tears rolled down her cheeks as another contraction tightened her belly. "Her father abandoned her, so she's better off not coming into this world."

"But she must." My voice sharpened like a knife fresh off a whetstone. "Signora, get behind Mia, and push her forward. We must do this. Now."

Another explosion rocked the area near the rail yard ten blocks from our home in the Monti district. Signora froze and looked toward the open window as fresh black smoke rose above the buildings.

In July, the Allies had hit the San Lorenzo railroad marshaling yards. The BBC had reported no civilian casualties, but, of course, that was not true. The news accounts failed to mention the destruction of the little shops containing the baker who gave his day-old bread to hungry children, the umbrella maker who kept five cats, or the watchmaker who always said, *"Grazie mille."* The news reports did not speak of the children whose laughter had gone silent, the damage to the Basilica di San Lorenzo, or the homes reduced to rubble that crushed and buried the occupants.

The heavy lines on Signora Fontana's face deepened as she met my gaze. When her husband, a well-known shoemaker, had been killed by the Fascists in the late 1930s, she had begun renting out rooms to earn money. I had first arrived on her doorstep in 1941 hoping for a new life away from the war. The signora was a kind soul, generous with the children when they came looking for food, and she was always willing to offer a bed to those in need.

Last year, the signora had gladly welcomed Mia, a young seamstress who, like me, was from Assisi. The girl claimed to be twenty, but I was twenty, and in some ways she was so young for her years. Mia had always hungered for a bigger life than her small home city offered and had arrived in Rome starving for adventure. I often acted more as a mother than friend or coworker, but if I had been a true mother, she might have heeded my warnings about the temptations of Rome.

"Signora, do not worry about the planes!" I ordered. "There's nothing we can do about the bombs."

Months of strict rations, no milk, looting, and soldiers on the streets had taken its toll on all of us. But the old woman shook off her shock and moved behind Mia, then hefted up the girl's slight frame, now laid bare for the birthing.

"Take a deep breath, and push, Mia," I said. "You must be brave a little longer."

"It hurts."

"I know. The signora knows. But there is no other way."

The girl's gaze fastened on mine, and for a moment I thought she could not summon any additional strength. But somehow she tapped into my will and drew in a breath. Closing her eyes, she pushed hard, and I pressed on her belly as the signora urged her with kind words.

The child would be born. Death could not have this soul. The seconds stretched, and her body strained to rid itself of the child.

The baby's head emerged, and I reached in the birth canal and grabbed hold. I pulled. Mia screamed louder, but this time the little infant, who had been fighting entrance to this troubled world, slid out.

Mia collapsed against the pillows, and Signora Fontana pressed a damp towel to her head. The moment of victory and elation vanished when I saw the perfectly formed face tinged in an ominous shade of blue. After picking up the baby by her ankles, I rubbed my knuckles hard between the shoulder blades, but there was no sound or twitch of a muscle. There was no struggle for breath, no will to live.

I laid the child on her side on the bed and cleaned out her mouth before I pressed my lips to hers and blew in a breath.

"The baby," Mia said. "She's too quiet."

I did not dare meet her gaze as I continued to breathe life into the tiny lungs. But the stubborn creature would not cry or draw a breath. I don't remember how long I worked on the child, but finally the signora touched my arm, her eyes reflecting disappointment.

"It's done," Signora Fontana said.

"It cannot be. We've worked so hard," I said.

"She's gone," she whispered.

I stared at the perfect little face framed by dark curly hair and was overcome by overwhelming disillusionment. The weight of thousands already lost in Rome dropped onto my shoulders.

Raising my gaze to Mia's, I found her staring at me with an anxious intensity.

"She's so quiet. Is she all right?" she asked softly.

"No."

Tears welled in Mia's eyes as another bomb crashed into the city. Finally, she closed her lids and fell against the pillows. "It's for the best. This is no world for a fatherless child."

Signora Fontana came around the bed, looked at the infant, and slowly crossed herself. "What will we do?"

"I'll take her to Padre Pietro," I said.

"He won't bury her. The child's father did not acknowledge her," the signora said gravely.

"The priest and God will," I said. "I'll beg if I must."

Despite my bold words, I was not sure what the priest could do. My shoulders deflated slightly as I cut the cord. Then I removed the afterbirth and wrapped the child in a blanket. After disposing of the afterbirth, I carried the infant toward the washstand, poured water into the basin, swirled my hands in the cool water, and wished it were warmer.

Carefully, I unwrapped the blanket and stared into the perfect face that even death could not rob of its beauty. I lifted the small body, amazed that the infant's head fit in the palm of my hand. Cradling it over the water as I had my own child two and a half years ago, I hummed a lullaby my mother had sung to me when I was a child. Gently, I scooped the water in my hand and let it trickle over the dark curls.

When she was clean and her skin dried, I clipped a piece of her hair and wrapped it in unblemished muslin before I dressed her in a small white gown I had sewn for her christening, and then I swaddled her in a crocheted blanket. "Mia, would you like to see the baby?"

"No." Mia rolled on her side and wept. "No, I can't bear it."

"You'll always wonder if you don't," I said.

"Please take her away." As Mia cried, the signora gently stroked her hair.

With the babe in my arms, I went to my room and laid her on my bed. After moving to the washstand, I cleaned my hands, scrubbing away all traces of blood, and then checked my face in the mirror.

Satisfied there were no tears, I removed my apron and rolled down my sleeves. After combing my hair and repinning it, I draped my head with black lace and then cradled the child close to my breasts.

By the time I descended the rear staircase and exited the kitchen door into the alley, the bombing had stopped. I had no idea how long this respite would last, so I moved quickly through cobbled alleys filled with smoke. All around I heard the rumble of tumbling stones, the shouts of men, water rushing from broken pipes, and, oddly, the sound of a violin bow straining over strings from a distant apartment.

Suddenly I resented the Fascists' violence and grift, Mussolini's unholy bargain with Germany, and the Allies' determination to bomb us until we were dust.

I hurried past a boarded-up carpenter's shop and along the piazza toward the steps leading up to the modest church of Saint Luca. I raced inside the building now filled with women and children seeking shelter. The women whispered the prayer "Ave Maria, gratia plena, fa'che non suoni la sirena," their hushed tones drifting to the vaulted stone ceiling. Several of the young priests administered last rites to the injured while nuns tended to the earthlier needs of water and food.

I never considered asking for permission as I normally would as I rushed down the side aisle to Padre Pietro Franco's closed office door and pushed it open. I found the priest sitting behind a carved desk that dated to da Vinci. He looked solemn, and his expression was tight with concentration as he spoke to a tall man wearing a dark suit of moderate quality. They both turned to me, the priest's face telegraphing shock while the stranger regarded me with suspicion.

Padre Pietro's long face had thinned, and his dark hair now was feathered with gray. "Yes?"

"I am Signora Isabella Mancuso, and I attend services here."

"Yes, I know you. You work in the dress shop on the Via Veneto and deliver clothes to the children in the ghetto," Padre Pietro said.

I wasn't surprised. The priest knew this city well. "Yes."

The stranger tensed, watching me closely, his keen gaze outwardly absorbing a thousand little details, as if he were determining whether I was a threat.

I stepped forward so they could both see the still babe in my arms. The priest removed his glasses, as if he needed a moment. He looked older, more fragile, without the lenses. "Mia Ferraro gave birth to a child that never drew a breath."

The stranger's expression shifted, his interest piqued. I could not tell if he was annoyed by the intrusion or sad for the loss. "I'll leave you." His accent was distinctly Roman, but he had the air of a man who traveled. "We will speak later, Padre Pietro."

"Yes, of course," the priest replied.

The man nodded slightly as he passed me. "Signora."

When the door closed behind the man, the priest focused his attention on the child. "I haven't seen Mia in months. I had heard she was in Assisi with her aunt."

The last six months in Rome had been chaotic as the city's population had swelled with refugees, deserters, spies, and more Germans. A girl hiding out to keep her pregnancy secret was an easy detail to overlook.

Padre Pietro slid on his glasses and thankfully regained some of his vigor as he rose. Stone dust smeared his dark cassock, and blood-soaked dirt smeared his hands. I imagined him with his flock, trying to dig out the survivors from the rubble.

"Let me see," he said.

I drew back the blanket and revealed the child's angel face. Ivory skin was offset by dark curly hair, and her bow lips, though pale, were perfectly formed. Perhaps if the child had been born in a hospital or if Mia had not been riddled with worry for the father, the child would have lived. But she had not survived, and now there was only her eternal soul to consider.

Padre Pietro made the sign of the cross over the infant. "I am sorry to hear this. How is Mia?"

"Physically she appears to be fine."

A bitter smile tugged at the edges of his lips. "It's a blessing she will recover."

"Will you bury the child on consecrated land?" I asked.

"Who is the father?"

"Mia never said."

There was little Padre Pietro did not know about in this part of Rome. "They did not marry?"

This familiar story had become more common in the last year. "No."

Padre Pietro absently rubbed his raw knuckles. "Has the father acknowledged the child as his own?"

"Mia assures me that he would if he could."

The priest sighed. "You're asking much, Isabella," he said, moving toward the sanctuary of his desk. "The church does not accept children such as this one."

"How could God not accept such a pure soul?" My voice rose above a tense whisper, and for the first time, outrage threaded through my words. I stepped closer to the priest. "You must do this for me."

"I am sorry, Isabella. I have a church full of the injured and dying."

"I've seen you break rules before, Padre. I know you've looked the other way when Resistance fighters hid in the church or Jewish refugees sought sanctuary. You have connections on the black market. How is helping this child so different?"

He leaned against his desk, as if the weight of my request was too much. "The child cannot be welcomed into holy ground. That is not my rule but God's."

"Tell me where God is now, Padre. Tell me if he heard the screams of your parishioners when the bombs fell or when the secret police took them to their headquarters on the Via Rattazzi? If you believed so fully in God's will, why would you bloody your hands removing stones trapping the fallen?"

"God helps those who help themselves."

"We've kept the child's birth a secret from everyone. No one will know you've administered the sacraments but you, me, and God."

The silence trailing my words grew heavier until finally he nodded slightly. It was as much of an acceptance as I would get. "Wait here," he said.

When he left the room, I sank into a chair. I tenderly rearranged the blanket swaddled around the motionless child. A ticking clock mingled with the prayers of another priest and children scurrying in the hallways. "He will take care of you, my love."

When Mia had first told me she was pregnant, I had not been entirely shocked. She was a lovely girl, with blonde hair, fair skin, and pouty lips that men adored. Soon after her arrival in Rome, she and her brother began going out to dinners and cafés, and she often arrived home late and unescorted. Signora Fontana and I argued with the girl, but Mia would smile, produce a handful of flowers or chocolates, and somehow alleviate our concerns.

And then she came to me in June, weeping and confessing her secret as she opened her robe and showed me her rounded belly. I was angry and worried. This was not the time for a baby, and with no father present, the outcome promised to be dire. After the shock eased, we made a plan. She stayed sequestered in her rooms, and I told our employer, Signor Sebastian, that she had traveled to Assisi to visit a distant aunt.

Despite all the reasons to resent the child, I found my excitement for the birth growing. Signora and I sewed outfits and blankets and crocheted hats as I once had for my child. I had believed that Mia's darkening mood would lift once the infant was born.

"I am sorry," I whispered. "You deserved better."

A knock on the door had me rising to face a young altar boy, who could not have been more than ten. His name was Carlo, and he had dark-brown eyes, thick ink-black hair, and a solemn expression common in Rome now. “Come with me,” he said.

I embraced the child and followed him along a corridor that led to a small private cemetery bathed in bright sunshine. The light was an affront to us all. The windless azure sky should have been blocked by dark clouds and rain weeping into water-soaked land. Life should have halted, but the world spun as it always did and in time would grind the pain to dust.

As I crossed the threshold into the courtyard, the warm sun brushed my face but did not penetrate the chill settling in my bones. I was certain I would never feel warmth again as birds tweeted and a soft breeze stirred the tops of olive trees rimming the courtyard. I followed the stone path until I saw Padre Pietro standing in his dust-stained cassock and a bright stole.

I approached him and saw the very small hole scored in the earth. Padre Pietro looked at me. “What is her name?”

“Gina,” I said easily. Mia and I had never discussed names, but it had been my daughter’s name, and it seemed fitting the two angels share it.

“Very well.” He began the service, his deep voice reciting the prayers of the dead. The words floated around me as I silently begged God to accept this child in his loving arms. I would gladly trade my life or fulfill any of his wishes if he would spare the girl’s soul.

The priest rushed the sacrament, as if he feared we would be seen. Finally, he made the sign of the cross in front of his face.

“You may lay Gina now in the cradle of God’s arms,” he said quietly.

I kissed Gina on the forehead and then made the sign of the cross over her brow before I covered her face with the blanket. I knelt and then laid her on the soft soil.

I removed the crucifix that had been in our family for generations and tucked it in the blanket. Very slowly, I fisted handfuls of dirt and sprinkled it over the small body, gradually covering every inch until she vanished from sight. The child's loss would forever cast a deep shadow on Mia, whether she now realized it or not.

Standing slowly, I sensed someone in the shadows, watching, but when I turned, I saw no one. "Thank you, Padre."

"Isabella," Padre Pietro said softly. "I may need a favor from you."

God was already calling. "What is it?"

"We will not speak of it now, but soon. Go home to Mia, and tend to her."

Of course, I could not deny him anything. He had saved the child's soul.

CHAPTER TWO

ZARA

Present Day
Saturday, June 5, 2:00 p.m.

Zara Mitchell had discovered more about death in her twenty-nine years than most learned in a lifetime.

As she held the small, trembling Chihuahua, Little Sister, close to her body, she leaned against her van warmed by the afternoon sun. Because of Little Sister and her two dogs, she was parked twenty feet away from the grave site, but she had a clear view of the military color guard as they slowly lifted the flag from the cherrywood coffin and folded it into a crisp, precise triangle. The motions of the uniformed soldiers were practiced, almost meditative, and everyone in this crowd watched.

The triangle settled into the white-gloved hands of a soldier barely old enough to shave and certainly not worldly enough to have such a solemn and stoic expression. He walked toward the white-haired woman sitting in the front row of folding chairs and handed the flag to her. There was sadness in her gray eyes but also relief and a sense of gratitude for the well-lived life of her husband, Colonel Harvey Wallace, who had passed at the age of eighty-two three days ago, in his bed, with Little Sister at his side.

Zara was a hospice nurse, and she had been to twelve funerals in the last seven years. Some were like this one, a final chapter, a closing of the hymnbook, so to speak. But others were so ripe with sadness the air curdled with a choking grief, making it impossible for mourners to draw in full breaths or speak without their voices breaking. Those funerals left a somber aftertaste that never really rinsed away.

Riflemen raised their guns toward the blue sky and fired. The pup in her arms looked up at her, whimpering. The dog shook more with the second and then third gun blasts and finally buried her head into the crook of Zara's arm.

"It's okay, Little Sister," she said. "It's almost over."

A dog's deep woof had Zara turning toward her van, where her two dogs, Gus and Billy, watched from their windows. She had left her engine running and the air-conditioning blasting, but the pups were restless.

Gus was a large, wiry terrier-lab mix with a stout body and long legs. Gray covered his dark snout as he looked to her for an explanation regarding the noise and, more importantly, the reason for the delay of their morning walk. Beside him sat Billy, a mutt with a short body and legs.

"It's okay, fellas," she whispered. "Like I told Little Sister, it's just noise. We're going to the park soon."

At the mention of *park*, a staple in their lexicon, the big dogs wagged their tails. Her pups had traveled all over the country in her van. They had explored more parks than she could remember, but they all agreed walks in the woods restored the soul.

Knowing her boys would start making a fuss, she reached in her pocket and pulled out biscuits for both. They gobbled them up. She offered one to Little Sister, but the dog turned her face away.

Zara understood Little Sister was mourning as sharply as the humans dressed in black for her late owner. Likely more so, for now she worried over her uncertain fate.

The colonel's youngest granddaughter had pledged to take Little Sister after the funeral to her home. So once Zara saw the dog safely placed, her duty to her client would be complete.

"Then it's off to the park, boys." Both wagged tails and nosed her hand, a signal they wanted head rubs.

If anyone understood Little Sister's plight now, it was Billy and Gus. Both had been much-loved pets of Zara's former clients who had left the earth before their times. Billy's owner, Burt Thompson, had been a gentleman who had made a good living selling cars until ALS had wrecked his body. Gus's owner had been a young attorney, Catherine Bernard, who had passed two years ago from ovarian cancer. She'd been thirty-two, and her untimely death had devastated too many lives. Neither dog had had anyone who was fit to take them, so she had.

When the colonel's ceremony ended, the mourners stood around the grave, talking and sharing stories. Finally, a midsize blonde always filled with nervous energy approached Zara. She was the colonel's granddaughter, Kelly Decker.

"Thanks for coming," Kelly said. "It would've meant a lot to Granddad."

"He was a great guy," Zara said. "I took Little Sister for a walk, so she's ready to go."

"Hey, about Little Sister," Kelly said. "What about you taking her? I mean, you're great with dogs, and it's pretty clear she loves you."

"You told your grandfather you were taking her."

"Yeah, well, I didn't want to upset him. And you didn't know him before, but he could get really upset if he didn't get what he wanted. That's why I said I'd take the dog."

Zara's work had taught her that families were complicated. As death neared, the cracks often widened, and loved ones lied to each other in the name of kindness, peace, and harmony.

"I was talking to my husband, and our life is so crazy. We have the twins, and our youngest isn't out of diapers. I don't know what we'd do with a dog."

Three dogs.

"I'll pay you," Kelly offered.

"It's not about the money," Zara said. "It's about having three dogs."

Kelly scratched Little Sister on the head, but the dog only burrowed deeper. "She's small and will be easy to take care of. Besides, she's ten, and how much longer can she live?"

Zara had taken the dog on enough walks to know she was strong and healthy, and given her size, Little Sister had another five to eight years in the tank. *Three dogs.* She would officially be the leader of a pack.

Gus and Billy woofed. She was not sure if that was a yes or no vote as she tightened her hold on the dog. Most motels tolerated two animals, and though she sometimes fudged on the boys' weight, they were quiet and could be trusted not to chew furniture. Three dogs would cement her in a no-man's-land of campgrounds, drive-through restaurants, and limited job opportunities.

No sane woman would take a third dog while balancing her crazy life. "Okay. I'll take her."

The woman's relief was palpable. "There'll be a bonus in your last check."

"It's not necessary."

Kelly brushed aside a curl and looked eager to return to the lingering crowd. "We really appreciate what you did for Granddad."

"That's what I do."

"Where do you get the patience? How do you spend so much time with the dying? It would make me so sad."

Zara remembered how Kelly had always vanished when her grandfather had become ill and needed cleaning up. She called people like Kelly *runners*. "I appreciate life more when death is close."

"Yeah, like a reminder to us all to seize the day," Kelly said, more to herself.

"Basically."

"Sometimes that's easier said than done. Everyday life makes it hard to stop and smell the roses."

"All the more reason," Zara said.

"You don't have three kids and a husband," Kelly challenged. "My life is not my own."

"Then whose is it?" Zara asked.

"You don't get it."

Zara let the silence linger between them.

Kelly's brow knotted. "Well, thank you for all you did and for accepting the job as mom to Little Sister."

"Sure."

As Kelly turned and all but ran away, Zara looked at the dog. "You can stop hiding now, Little Sister. She's gone, and you're part of the pack."

The dog looked up.

"That's right, girlfriend. You're a free spirit like the rest of us." Little Sister weighed well under ten pounds, so tossing her in the back seat with the boys did not make sense. Until she decided where the pup fit in this new pack dynamic, Little Sister could get trampled. "Looks like you're riding shotgun."

Zara moved around to the driver's side, slid behind the wheel, and grabbed a blanket from the back, arranging it on the front passenger seat. She settled the dog in the center of the threadbare blue blanket. "I hope you can read a map. That's the navigator's seat."

The dog glanced at the pilling fabric and immediately pawed it, as if she were intent on digging a hole.

Zara's phone rang, and she stared at the screen displaying the name of her older sister, Gina. Families were complicated. "Gina."

"You have to come home." Her sister's annoyingly upbeat tone had hardened.

Zara leaned against the headrest. "I was home at Easter, and I'm scheduled to be there in late July."

"Easter was two months ago, and July will be too late."

Gina lived with their ninety-seven-year-old grandmother, Renata Mitchell, in Richmond, Virginia.

"What's going on?" Zara asked. "Is Nonna okay?"

"She's dying."

"She's been dying for years. You know how she gets worked up. She likes the attention."

"No, it's for real this time," Gina said. "The doctors are giving her six weeks. Her heart is failing fast."

Nonna had been a fixture in all their lives for so long Zara could not imagine the world without her. "Have you spoken to the doctor, or is this what Nonna is telling you?"

"I spoke to the damn doctor. She's failing fast." Gina's voice turned uncharacteristically sharper.

Zara had planned a couple of days at the beach before visiting her grandmother. And given the addition of Little Sister, they were basically the kind of traveling circus that her grandmother hated.

Zara had moved in with Nonna and Papa when she was twelve. Her father had died seven years earlier in a car accident, and her mother had basically drunk herself to death. Her mother's family did not really want the moody twelve-year-old Zara, but Nonna and Papa, already in their eighties, welcomed Zara into their home. Gina, the product of their father's first marriage, was twenty-four when Zara moved into her grandparents' house but still lived with Nonna and Papa under the guise she was saving money for graduate school. Gina's relationship with her own mother had always been problematic, and she had been living with their grandparents for a year at that point.

Whereas Nonna was close to Gina, Zara always gravitated to her quiet, well-read grandfather, John Mitchell, who took her with him during her summer vacations to Washington, DC, to visit old associates from his time in the army. Whereas Nonna never spoke of the war, Papa enjoyed talking to his friends about their time in the army. Even after he opened a successful law practice, Papa still loved to travel, and each summer he would pack up Nonna, Gina, and Zara, and the four would take a road trip somewhere in the United States. The car rides were always an adventure and a study in patience. For every historic site Papa had seen, Nonna had taken time to visit a thrift shop, and by the time they'd returned to Richmond, the trunk had been full of historical books and vintage clothing. Zara supposed she had inherited her wanderer tendencies from her grandfather.

Gina and Nonna had both shared a love of fashion and had always enjoyed each other's company. Zara had been a kind of odd man out in their trio, and she had never wedged a place in their lives. When her grandfather had died seven years ago, her last solid link to the family had vanished, and she had taken the traveling nurse job. Seeing Gina and Nonna at Christmas, Easter, and Nonna's birthday had become a kind of middle ground that suited them all.

Tiny paws stepped onto her lap, and she watched Little Sister circling and looking for a comfortable spot. She rubbed her head.

"I'm in North Carolina," Zara said. "I can leave in the next couple of hours, but I won't be there until very late."

Gina's relieved sigh cut across the line. "Fine. As long as I know you're coming."

Little Sister yipped, reminding Zara of her promise to take them to the park.

"Is that Billy or Gus?" Gina asked. "He sounds funny."

"That's because that's Little Sister."

"Who?"

"Little Sister. I now have three dogs." She glanced in the rearview mirror at the boys and smiled as she rubbed Little Sister's head.

"Shit, Zara. Three dogs. Is that really wise?" Gina asked.

"It's not, but that's never stopped me before."

"You're there for everyone," she said quietly. "Now you need to be here for us. I can't do this alone, Zara."

She stared out the van's front window toward the mourners as they dispersed. It was one thing to walk strangers through the process of dying, but it was another to apply the lessons to family.

She thought back to their own father's funeral, when she had been five and Gina seventeen. The reception had been at Nonna and Papa's house and had included a collection of family friends, her father's work associates, and several former girlfriends. Gina's mother had attended, but she and Gina had soon been fighting. Zara's mother had refused to attend and had told Papa if he wanted Zara there, he could come and get her. He had.

The funeral had been grim, and Zara had felt out of place and lost until Gina had grabbed the keys to Nonna's car and found five-year-old Zara sitting alone at a folding table, pushing around a plate filled with casseroles and fruit salads.

"You want to blow this party, kid?" Gina asked.

"Can we?" Zara asked.

"Sure, why not?"

Zara looked up into her sister's eyes, reflecting the anger and frustration mirroring her own heart. "Nonna will be mad if we leave."

"We'll get her strawberry ice cream while we're out. She'll get over it. Come on, kid."

Zara followed her big sister to the car; sat in the front seat, something she had never done before; and clicked her seat belt in place. Gina cranked Hootie & the Blowfish's "Let Her Cry" on the radio, slid on her white-rimmed sunglasses, and revved the engine. "Hang tight, kid."

For the first time in weeks, Zara was hopeful.

"Hang tight. I'm on the way, Gina," Zara said.

CHAPTER THREE

ZARA

Richmond, Virginia
Saturday, June 5, 8:00 p.m.

The drive should have taken five hours. But big dogs had big bladders, and little dogs had tiny little clocks in their bodies that went off about every two hours, requiring additional pee breaks. And once you let one dog out, the other two were not going to be left behind, so every two hours, they stopped, peed, received a snack, and walked around.

It was eight when Zara pulled into the driveway of her grandmother's house. Made of white stucco, it was one story and crafted in a Mediterranean style of the 1920s. When her grandfather had died, his will had stipulated that his wife would remain in the house until her death, and after that the house would be jointly inherited by Gina and Zara.

Out of the car, she lifted a sleeping Little Sister and attached her leash to her pink rhinestone collar. Next, she hooked the boys' leashes and grabbed a plastic bag tucked in the door pocket. Then the four of them walked the tree-lined street toward the small park that stretched along the James River.

The evening breeze had thinned the humidity, and the air had softened. She had often jogged or biked this trail as a kid, and it reminded her that belonging somewhere did have perks from time to time.

The boys tugged on their leashes with their noses pressed to the ground. Little Sister walked at a slower pace and was more particular about where she peed.

It took fifteen minutes before everyone was ready to return, but Zara kept walking, needing a few more minutes of peace before the inevitable.

A man rode by on a bike and paused to look at her, and she stood a little straighter. He was midthirties, attractive, and fit, looking like he cycled a lot. There was interest in his gaze, but it quickly dwindled when he inventoried all the dogs. He pedaled faster.

"That's right; crazy dog lady has come home," she said.

Shifting Little Sister to her left arm, she turned around, and the four of them strolled along the winding path. At the van, she caught a glimpse of her reflection in the driver's-side window. Her hair was sticking up, her mascara was smudged, and her favorite T-shirt, which she had changed into in the rear of the van after the funeral, was inside out.

She poured water into each of the boys' bowls as well as into Little Sister's pink rhinestone-studded dish, which she had snagged from the colonel's house before the funeral. She had expected the bowl and the dog would be staying with Kelly, but here they were. The trio lapped up their water, and then each accepted a small piece of a Slim Jim she had bought at a gas station an hour ago.

"Ready or not, here we go."

With Little Sister tucked under her arm and the boys following, she walked up the brick herringbone sidewalk toward the large arching front door painted a dark green and adorned with a bullnose door knocker. There was a time when she would have pushed through the door and made herself at home, but since her grandfather's death, she had drifted so far away she did not feel like she belonged.

She rang the bell.

Nerves jangled in her belly, jacking up her adrenal system. Her heart beat faster. "This is silly," she said to Little Sister. "We've nothing to worry about."

Inside, the click of Gina's high heels echoed in the foyer. The sound reminded her of the younger version of their grandmother, who had worn heels until the orthopedist had exiled her to flats ten years before.

The door opened to a flutter of green fabric mingling with the soft scent of expensive Italian perfume. The perfume's name escaped Zara, but the sweet, faintly spicy scent was her sister's trademark. Gina had cut her blonde hair into a stylish pixie cut and had accented her green eyes with black liner and mascara that transformed pretty eyes into mesmerizing.

When Zara had been in high school, she'd had her share of boyfriends, but Gina, then in her late twenties, had had the ability to hypnotize all males the instant she walked into a room. Gina was never coy about her sex appeal, but to her credit, she embraced it, and the woman worked it.

Gina's A-line dress nipped at her narrow waist, and the off-the-shoulder sleeves drew attention to milky-white skin that she relentlessly protected with sunscreen and umbrellas. The heels were black leather and, naturally, Italian. Again, the brand escaped Zara.

"You made it," Gina said. "I was worried."

"Traveling with three dogs takes longer than I figured. Sorry about that. I like the haircut."

"Thanks. Needed a change." Gina leaned in to kiss Zara on the cheek, only to have Little Sister growl softly. Her sister straightened, shooting the dog a disapproving look. "The newest of the pack?"

"Her name is Little Sister. And you can't tell me anything I haven't already told myself. It's a little excessive."

Gina reached to pet Little Sister, but the dog growled. "She has an attitude."

"She's had a rough couple of days. Lost a family, gained a pack of traveling companions. She's on edge."

"Little Sister and I should start a club," Gina said. "It's been no picnic here either." She stared at the boys. "Have they done their business?"

"Yes."

"Because the oriental rugs in this house are handmade."

"I remember. It's why I could never have a dog as a kid."

"The carpets are works of art, not scattered newspaper."

"You sound like Nonna. And the pups will be fine. Where is Nonna?"

"She's in her bed, sleeping."

"Good, that will give us time to talk about her, because when I spoke with her three nights ago, she was fine."

"You know Nonna. She's always fine. But she hasn't been for a long time."

The pups and Zara followed Gina through the house, and a couple of times the boys paused to sniff. She coaxed them along, knowing the last thing they all needed was a hiked leg and a puddle.

The kitchen was large, and though it had not been renovated in twenty-plus years, it had an old-world charm, including a large brick fireplace, a white AGA stove, and a large rustic wooden table that could seat ten. The floor was made of wide-plank hardwoods, well worn by years of foot traffic. The sink was white porcelain and the backsplash handmade yellow-and-blue Italian tile, and in the center of the long farmhouse table sat a large wooden bowl filled with red apples and lemons.

"This hasn't changed. Thank God," Zara said.

"The world might come to an end one day, but this kitchen will remain untouched. Too many good memories in here."

Their grandfather had been a talented cook, and the family had shared endless meals around the big table. Papa had always sat at the head and Nonna at the opposite end. Gina had taken the east side, closest to the kitchen, and Zara had sat across from her. She smoothed her fingers over the table's polished wood and was certain she could not enjoy a meal at the table unless she sat in her chair. The universe would basically be unbalanced.

Gina rested a large brass teakettle on the stove burner and set out two porcelain cups.

This was all very civilized, and each was pretending that the world was not shifting. But it was all changing. Nonna's dying meant the last of their family was crumbling.

The boys settled on the floor. Each was clearly glad to be free of the van and sitting in one stationary place. Little Sister closed her eyes, and her head drifted against Zara's chest.

"What did the doctor say about Nonna?" Zara asked.

"She has advanced heart failure." Gina carefully laid a tea bag in each cup.

"She's ninety-seven and has had to be mindful of her activities for years. That's nothing new."

"It's more than that. She has twenty percent heart capacity, and that's not going to last. The doctor has given her a few months."

"You said six weeks."

"Six or twelve weeks," Gina said, shaking her head. "Basically, she's running out fast."

Nonna had been the rock of their family. Always unflappable, weathering the storm of her son's passing and then the arrival of his two daughters. Nothing had seemed to trouble her until their grandfather had died. Then the foundation under her feet had crumbled. Nonna had grown angry and bitter after her husband's death, and it seemed only Gina could charm her out of her bad moods.

"Is Amanda still coming in and helping?" Zara asked.

"Yes. She's still here from eight to two, and she'll return in the morning. But Nonna is requiring more care at night."

"If you need more in-home medical care," Zara said, "I can get top-notch nurses in here."

"Nonna doesn't want a home nurse. She likes Amanda, but she wants you in charge of her care."

"Why would she want me? I irritate the hell out of her, Gina. She makes that clear every time I call."

"She wants you home."

"I'll stay, but it's not going to last. She's going to get pissed off at me, her blood pressure is going to spike, and then it'll be a 911 call and off to the hospital."

The kettle whistled, and Gina poured the hot water into the cups. She stirred the tea gently and dropped a sugar cube into each. "Believe me; I tried to tell her that. But she won't listen."

"I'll be nice. I'll try not to ruffle her feathers."

Gina set the teacup in front of Zara. "Good."

Zara sipped the tea, wishing it had a shot of whiskey. "How is the shop?"

Their grandparents had wished for more children, but their hopes had never been realized. Nonna had become restless and bored when their only child had entered middle school, and it had been their grandfather who'd suggested Nonna open a dress shop. She had been working in a couture salon in Rome in the 1940s when she'd met their grandfather, who had been serving in the US Army. The way they'd told it, it had been love at first sight, and they'd met and married immediately. Zara's father had been born in 1945.

Gina and Zara had often pressed their grandparents for details about their love affair, but both had never really answered their questions. The local dress shop, Renata's, had opened in 1957 and had been a staple for women who liked vintage and couture fashion. Hers was a small, exclusive clientele.

"We've several commissions for spring weddings. And the vintage items always sell well." Her grandmother had taken Gina and then Zara to several estate sales, searching for vintage designer dresses. Whereas the fashion gene had skipped Zara, Nonna and Gina lived and breathed Valentino, Saint Laurent, and Prada. "I've been ignoring the shop badly lately. And I really need to spend more time there."

"I get it. It's my shift now. I have it covered," Zara said.

Gina smiled, and for the first time Zara noticed her makeup was not quite hiding the shadows under her eyes. A bell rang from the other room, and the boys raised their heads and barked. Little Sister's head popped up, and before her eyes were fully open, she was also barking.

"Please," Gina said. "Can you stop the noise? It cuts through my head."

"They're dogs. That's what they do," Zara said. She never yelled at her dogs, knowing each had endured enough trauma. She reached in her pocket and handed treats to them all.

"Now you're encouraging the behavior," Gina said.

"They're quiet. Goal achieved." Zara handed Little Sister to Gina. "You hang out with the guys, and I'll go talk to Nonna. Better to introduce the crew slowly but surely."

Gina held the little dog out, as if she had been handed a live hand grenade. "Does she bite?"

"Only exquisitely dressed women who smell nice."

"Then you're clearly safe."

Chuckling, Zara waved away the retort and headed toward her grandmother's bedroom. She paused and looked in the room that had been hers for ten years and noted since Christmas it had been stripped of her furniture and turned into a storage room for gowns. Down the carpeted hallway, she noted the other spare room was also packed with gowns. However, Gina's room was as she had left it.

"That's right; erase Zara," she muttered.

She reached the last door and pushed it open. For a brief second, she was twelve years old, and she could hear her grandmother singing as she sat in front of the window. Yards of lush fabric had draped her lap as she'd sewn one of the many thousands of gowns she had made in her life.

Today, the blinds were drawn, and her grandmother lay in the center of her four-poster bed. She looked small and fragile and was buried under a mountain of quilts. The room was warm, but a constant chill was the sign of a failing heart. Nonna's body was not pumping enough blood to her extremities. Her grandmother's face was pale, and her hair was as white as the lace pillowcase. The lines in her face, traces of a life well lived, were deeper and more pronounced.

Everyone died. Everyone came to this earth with an expiration date. Zara counseled her patients about this moment and warned them about the stages of grief. But in this instant, all her wise words sounded empty and did nothing to change that this sucked.

"Nonna, it's Zara."

Silence hovered in the room, and her grandmother did not open her eyes. Her breathing was so shallow it prompted Zara to move closer. Jesus, had the woman died? Panic swelled.

"Nonna!" Zara took her thin wrist, held two fingers against the pale-blue lines, and searched for a pulse.

Nonna's eyes remained closed, but finally she drew in a deep breath. "I am not dead yet."

"Damn it, Nonna. You scared the hell out of me."

"Language, please, Zara."

Zara laid her grandmother's wrist on the soft bedsheet. "Sorry."

Nonna's eyes fluttered open, and sharp brown eyes stared at her. Slowly a thin pale brow arched. "My God, girl. What happened to you?"

"What do you mean?" Zara asked.

"I thought perhaps you'd been ill or attacked by a band of marauders. And what is that smell?"

When Zara's patients became ill, their loved ones often treated them differently. They patronized them, agreed when they normally would have argued. People were trying to be kind to their loved ones, when all the dying wanted was to hang on to the last shreds of normalcy left on this earth.

Zara owed it to Nonna to treat her as she always had. "Ah, Nonna, an insult about my appearance. Now I feel like I'm really home."

CHAPTER FOUR

ISABELLA

Rome, Italy
Friday, September 17, 1943, 1:00 p.m.

There is value in illusion.

Used correctly, a designer can brandish silk, as a magician employs a sleight of hand, to make a woman appear to be the woman she dreams of being rather than who she is. Prime Minister Badoglio's new government had employed this technique to sell the idea that the dangerous deal his predecessor, Mussolini, had struck with Hitler would not cost us so dearly, which of course it would. The truth was the war raging to Rome's north and south could no longer be veiled by patriotic speeches or empty promises.

In the center of all this was Salon Sebastian, the couture shop in the fashionable Via Veneto district, blocks from the Spanish Steps, the St. Regis Hotel, and the opera house, where the Wehrmacht trucks now routinely parked in the prized piazzas.

The owner of Salon Sebastian, Antonio Sebastian, was a master of artifice. He had become adept at maneuvering the difficult climate and somehow remained in business despite never joining the Fascist party.

Not surprising, in this time of great troubles, the shop was quite busy. Most of our regular clients from Roman royalty still had a taste for fine dresses, though most were not as quick to pay. If they did remit, it was with goods from their country estates, including bottles of olive oil, sacks of flour, fine wines, or cured meats. Sebastian's office at times resembled a grocer's storeroom.

The customers with real money were the wives and mistresses of the German officers, who, upon arrival in the Eternal City, readily embraced Italy's couture fashions, which were less rigid than their German counterparts. Most importantly, these new clients had the gold to pay for the work we did. Instead of decrying the tenuous relationship with Germany, Sebastian embraced it and was keeping all of us employed and fed.

The shop's basement workroom was long enough to accommodate eight sewing machines and seamstresses, who all wore white smocks. The women ranged in age from fifteen to sixty. At the front end of the room, there was a twenty-foot table, which I used for cutting patterns and laying out fabric.

I stood at the worktable, supervising a young woman, Maria, who was cutting out silk fabric to be used to make an evening dress. Maria had been hired a year ago and had recently married a cook who worked at the St. Regis.

"Go slower," I said. "Once it's cut, it's cut."

"Yes, Signora."

"Full, even cuts with the scissors. No small choppy cuts."

"Yes, Signora."

"Isabella," Sebastian said. He was a midsize man who always wore a black suit equipped with a vest that stretched over his rounded belly and displayed a gold pocket watch. He oiled his overly black hair and sported a neatly trimmed mustache.

"Yes, sir."

"Signora Bianco is here. She has requested you."

One of my favorite clients, whom I had served for two years, Signora Margherita Bianco was the widow of a World War I hero who had made a fortune in banking. For more than twenty years, they had lived in a comfortable apartment near the Spanish Steps overlooking the Forum and the Piazza del Campidoglio, fashioned in the style of Michelangelo.

"Of course." I drew my finger across the fabric, showing Maria precisely where she must cut. "If you're unsure, then stop. I'll help you later."

"Yes, Signora."

I adjusted my white smock, retying my cloth belt tighter around my waist, and followed Sebastian up the rear staircase.

"Isabella, you said Mia is returning soon?" Sebastian asked.

"In a couple of weeks. Her great-aunt is recovering." The lie had been awkward at first but now slid off my tongue easily.

"Tell the girl to hurry. I can't hold the job much longer."

"She knows this and is grateful you have been so generous."

He huffed. "I give you too much latitude. I should fire you both."

"I am the best seamstress and designer you have ever had," I said.

"Maybe, but everything has its limits."

"Have I fallen behind on any of my orders?"

As he matched my quick pace, his tone became breathless. "No. But if you continue disappearing, it's inevitable."

I turned to him and smiled. "I have never let you down, have I?"

He frowned as we reached the top step, which fed into the back room, next to the customer's salon. "Isabella, Signora Bianco still has a balance due on her account," he whispered.

"She has always been good about paying, no?"

"True. But given her situation, it might be wise to collect the balance due as quickly as possible. I have heard some talk among the clients."

"Such as?"

"The Jews are now required to register. And there is talk of a gold ransom the Jewish community must pay."

Signora Bianco was Jewish, a member of an ancient family that could trace their lineage more than two thousand years. Though her late husband's reputation and money had shielded her from Mussolini's disenfranchisement of the Jewish community, most of her brethren lived in the densely populated, flood-prone ghetto along the Tiber River.

Despite Signora Bianco's wealth, men like Sebastian saw her as different. He never would have pressed a member of the Italian royalty for money. We had served only a few Jewish clients since I had arrived in 1941, and they had dwindled as the war had intensified. Signora Bianco was his last.

"I'll speak to her," I said.

"Collect the money today, or select a time when I can send a boy to her apartment." He dropped his voice a notch. "She, like many of her kind, could vanish without warning."

"Have you spoken to her?"

He arched a thick brow. "It'll be less crass if you two speak about it privately in the dressing room."

"As I handle all the delicate cases."

"Exactly."

"Consider it done."

When I entered the showroom, Signora Bianco was sitting on a Louis XIV sofa positioned in front of eight-foot mirrored cupboards. A soft carpet covered the marble floor, and heavy velvet curtains bracketed a window overlooking the busy street and the manicured park beyond.

Signora Bianco was a tall, elegant woman with thick gray hair swept into a chignon. On her jacket, she always wore a large emerald encased in a gold setting. The broach had been a gift from her husband years before.

"Signora Bianco," I said. "This is a lovely surprise."

We kissed each other on either cheek. Her eyes reflected warmth born out of shared respect. Few knew a woman as well as the woman who dressed her.

"Your recent delivery of children's clothes was much appreciated."

"It wasn't much."

"The kindness was appreciated."

"I'm glad. My landlady and I will have another delivery soon."

"Excellent."

"What brings you here today?"

"I require a very special dress," she said. "My grandson is getting married, and I want to look my very best."

"When is the wedding?"

"October tenth." We had worked together long enough for her to look a bit apologetic over the rushed request, even if she was not. "I understand it's a lot to ask, but I want this family gathering to be as special as it can be."

"Of course." The request would mean many hours of work. "It'll be my pleasure. I would love to show you some sketches."

She settled on a velvet couch as a young girl appeared with a silver tray sporting a teapot, china cups, and candied nuts. She accepted a cup of tea.

"Who is your grandson marrying?" I asked. "You have never spoken of him dating any young woman."

"They've known each other for only three months. Normally, I would complain, but in these times, I cannot protest."

I laid my sketch pad on the small table in front of her and flipped to a suit that nipped at the waist and skimmed above the knees. "Of course, I would drop the hem for you."

She lifted the pad and regarded it with a critical eye. "If my legs were like yours, I would gladly wear the shorter skirt. But it would be too risqué for me now." She set down the pad. "What else do you have?"

I turned the page to a dark cocktail dress. It had a high collar and a fitted bodice. It was not the latest of styles, but it would suit the signora's tastes. "It would highlight your broach."

"Yes," she said thoughtfully. "However, I was hoping for something different. The bride's grandparents are longtime friends of mine, and I don't want them to see me as an old woman. I want them to see the young girl I was when our husbands served in the Great War."

I had learned that though all women aged, the young woman still lived inside each, and sometimes she needed to be remembered. "Perhaps I could create a V-neckline. I could add lace so your skin would be covered, but the sheerness would add a bit of daring."

"I don't feel as if I care so much about propriety now." She lifted the sketchbook and studied the image. "I'll let you do as you wish with the lace, Isabella. I trust you."

"I'll take care of it," I said. "Can you return for a fitting?"

She laid the sketch on the table. "I would rather you use the dressmaker's form you have for me. I am avoiding the streets these days."

All our regular clients had forms made to their measurements so a seamstress could fit a garment even if the client was not available. "Certainly."

"The times are changing, Isabella," she said, more to herself. "All my friends are either dead, in hiding, or leaving. The Jewish elders and rabbis assure us once the gold ransom is paid to the city, there will be little to fear from the Germans. Like good sheep we're minding our manners and hoping the wolf does not attack."

"Perhaps a short trip would be in order for you after the wedding. I hear Switzerland is lovely."

A smile tipped the edges of her lips as her gaze grew distant. "I have thought of it often, but my absence would be noticed by the police. I think a trip to Switzerland for the young couple would be lovely."

"Excellent idea."

"Their travel papers will have to be sorted first. That hideous letter *J* stamped on their identification card restricts their movements."

As the old woman rose, I steadied her with a hand under her elbow. "There is a priest in the Monti district. His name is Padre Pietro Franco. He knows many people in the city."

She tugged on a glove. "Does he?"

"They say he has connections around the world."

"That is good to know." She patted my hand. "I knew there was a good reason I came to see you today. When will my dress be ready?"

"If I can get the fabric easily, ten days if I hurry."

"Perfect. I'll pay a handsome surcharge."

"Thank you."

"Perhaps when you deliver the dress, we can talk more about this priest."

"Of course." I took her hands in mine. "I'll make you the finest dress you have ever worn."

She smiled. "I know you will."

Behind the curtain Sebastian coughed.

"About payment," I said.

"I'll pay my account in full when you deliver the dress."

"Thank you."

I watched Signora Bianco leave the shop, and her driver opened her car door. She settled inside without another glance in my direction, and the car left.

Across the street a column of German soldiers gathered, which they now did with annoying regularity. Boots hammering on cobblestone mingled with a guttural rhythmic chant.

"She will pay?" Sebastian asked.

"When I deliver the dress, I'll collect the money myself."

He grinned. "She has gold. Money."

"Yes."

"Make this dress a priority. Sooner is better than later."

"Of course."

That evening, when the clock chimed six times, I was the last in the salon. I could have stayed a few more hours, but with the evening curfew looming, I needed to leave. I had chosen a midnight-blue silk for Signora Bianco's dress and had cut the fabric myself. Most of the shop's projects were well on their way to being finished, and it could all wait until morning.

Out in the warm fresh air, I hurried along the streets, crossed the cobbled piazza in the graying light, and strode past the shops. A man whistled at me. Annoyed, I kept walking south toward the Monti district and a favorite café where friends met for a drink and news of the war.

The rusty clay building had arching windows and doors surrounded by thick potted ferns and vines of ivy that coiled up to the terra-cotta roof. Though the café's front door was closed, soft jazz music and laughter drifted out to the street. It drew me closer, and for a moment I remembered the young girl I had once been in Umbria and the day I had met my Enzo.

I had been no more than seventeen when I'd traveled with my parents from our farm in Perugia to Gubbio for the Festa dei Ceri. The small medieval village had filled with brightly colored revelers dressed in red, yellow, or black. They had come to celebrate and see the young men race with thirteen-foot wooden candles sporting the likenesses of saints. We drove north to the small village in the north of Umbria to celebrate not only the saint but my father's new position at the university.

Childish excitement fueled me, and I ran ahead among the tightly packed bodies controlled by horsemen. When my legs and lungs finally forced me to stop, I looked up and saw Enzo standing in the crowd, watching the race. My heart stopped, and I could not take my eyes off him. As if sensing me, he had turned and smiled.

A fresh burst of laughter inside the café pulled me from my memories, and I spotted Mia through the café window. Smooth skinned, Mia wore a red dress that skimmed her already flat belly, and heeled shoes elongated her calves. Silky blonde curls framed her face and emphasized plump, moist, red-tinted lips men adored.

She was standing by a man dressed in a dark suit, smiling and flirting with him. I knocked on the window, and she looked up, grinned broadly, and hurried across the crowded room and opened the door. "Isabella, have you come to scold me? You are always so serious."

Belladonna drops widened her pupils, creating a stunning effect. "I thought you were home, sleeping."

"I have slept enough." Her breath carried the strong scent of wine. "It's time for me to get back to my life."

"Are you sure that is wise?" I asked.

Mia curled a blonde strand around her finger. "Have you come to take me home and remind me of what good girls do?"

"What has come over you?" I asked in a low, desperate tone. "It's been only a month."

"I can't stay in that dreary room another minute. All day long I hear the men moving rocks and debris. Thump. Thump. Thump. Too much death. It's too much."

"Your body and mind need time."

"Look around. We have no time." Mia grinned broadly. "Let me introduce you around. I have some very delicious men for you to meet."

She hooked her arm in mine and led me to a table sporting several bottles of wine. She poured a glass and handed it to me. "Drink it while it's here. It won't last."

"Leave with me now."

"Drink the wine first."

The Castelli wine had a fruity flavor with a significant kick. "It's good. Now can we go?"

"Not the best wine, but beggars can't be choosers." She refilled her glass to the brim. "I need to finish my glass first."

Mia reminded me of a tightly wound bowstring ready to snap. Instead of insisting she leave, I shifted tactics, hoping she might calm and see reason. "Who bought the wine?"

"A young soldier. Very attractive. I don't know his name. But you know how I have a weakness for uniforms."

I scanned the collection of people, who were already pairing off into couples, and they seemed unconcerned by the German manhunts and Allied bombs. The war, now at Rome's doorstep, had heightened the quiet desperation sweeping the city, and everyone here seemed determined to have fun or at least pretend. They drank, ate, and romanced as if the world would end tomorrow.

"Mia, who are all these people?" I asked. "They can't be your friends."

She ran her fingers through her hair. "Some I know. Most I don't. Does it matter?"

"This is Rome, and this is a dangerous time. You need to be more careful."

Mia waved her hand to a man, as if I had not spoken. "Aldo! Come here this instant."

When the man in the dark suit turned and approached us, his expression was ominous. I immediately recognized him. He had been the man in Padre Pietro's office four weeks ago. As before, he did not strike me as handsome, but his penetrating gaze and strong bearing created a masculine air that was attractive. Perhaps a decade older than me, he was doing a poor job of hiding his annoyance.

"Aldo, I want you to meet Isabella Mancuso. She's the top seamstress at Sebastian's. Very in demand by all our clients. She's booked months in advance." Mia grinned. "Isabella Mancuso, meet Aldo Rossi.

He's a businessman and most adept at finding wine and port." She held up her glass. "He brought several bottles with him tonight."

An imperceptible change in Aldo's expression told me he recognized me. He nodded. "It's a pleasure, Signora Mancuso."

His voice was deep and rich, and it hinted that his nerves were also strung to the breaking point. "Signor Rossi," I said. "It's a pleasure to meet you."

Neither of us acknowledged the circumstances of our first meeting, and that seemed mutually suitable. "You'll call me Aldo, and if you're not opposed, I'll call you Isabella. Foolish to waste time on formalities."

His thick Roman accent sounded slightly different. He had the air of a man who had lived many places and had been exposed to multiple dialects.

"Aldo, you should ask Isabella to dance," Mia said. "I must find my new friend."

As she darted into the crowd, Aldo watched her for a beat and then dutifully asked, "Would you like to dance?"

The record player stopped, and another lively song was selected. "Certainly."

He held out his hand, and I took it. His grip was stronger than I'd anticipated, and when he pulled me close, an undercurrent of energy radiated from him. He smelled of Italian tobacco and a faint cologne that was rather pleasing.

"How long have you known Mia?" he asked.

"Two years. We work at the same shop. She and I are both from Assisi, so it was natural for us to be friends."

"It was her child you carried that day," he said.

"Yes." As we moved around the dance floor, I added, "Do not judge her too harshly. She's young and grieving."

"She does not look upset."

"I assure you grief shows itself in many ways," I said.

"If you say so." He maneuvered our bodies around several giddy and laughing couples. "You said you were from Assisi, but your accent is hard to place."

"My father was a language professor at the University of Perugia until the midthirties. He taught me a great deal."

"And he teaches at university no more?"

"No."

He, of course, would know that to hold any university position required a loyalty to the Fascist party. My father's support had waned by 1935, and when he had refused to endorse the party, he not only had lost his new position but had been fired. Luckily for the family, he had not been arrested but had been allowed to retire to his farm, where I, his only child, had become his sole pupil.

"Do you speak other languages?" he asked.

"A little German, English, and French."

He stared at me with renewed respect. "Are you fluent in any of the languages?"

"No," I lied. "You ask a lot of questions."

"It's my nature. And you're the most interesting woman in this room."

"Tell me about yourself," I said. "Have you always lived in Rome?"

"All my life."

This I did not believe, but lies in these times were a matter of survival. "And you're a businessman. What does that mean?"

He had the look of a man connected to the black market. "As all men in business, I dabble in many things."

The song ended, and before I could press for details, Mia returned to us with a tall broad-shouldered man with a stout body, blond hair, and warm blue eyes. His stiff bearing reminded me of the Germans I had seen in Munich when my father had taken the family there in the summer of 1930 to study.

"Now, Isabella must dance with Hauptmann Karl Brenner," Mia said. "He's from Germany, newly transferred here, and we must make him feel welcome."

I turned to thank Signor Rossi for the dance, but he had already shifted his attention to the bottles of wine. Seemed I had not made as big an impression on him as I'd thought.

Hauptmann Brenner was an attractive man in his early forties, and he fit the mold of the ideal German. His bearing suggested he was accustomed to wielding authority, but when he pulled me into his arms, his hold was tentative and respectful. "You're very beautiful, Isabella." His Italian was flawless, but I heard hints of his native Munich.

"Thank you."

The phonograph played a song too slow for my tastes, but I allowed Hauptmann Brenner to draw me deeper into his embrace.

"Where are you from?" I asked.

"Munich," he said easily. "But I suspect you know that."

"How would I know?" I asked.

"You've a keen eye. You sip your wine carefully, and you have been studying the room since you arrived."

"I don't go to many parties. It's a curiosity to me."

He did not pull me closer, but his grip remained firm, like Germany's was on Italy. Drawing away from him would have been difficult and awkward. As if sensing my thoughts, he released his hold a fraction.

"Mia must have many friends?" he asked.

"Yes, she has always been popular."

"I shall be seeing Mia again," he said. "I find her entertaining and a joy to be with. She says I must get your approval."

"I am not her mother."

"But she values your opinion."

"She's young. And fragile. I would rather she focus on work."

Even white teeth bared into a smile. "Spoken like a practical woman. I admire that about you, Isabella. Do not worry. I'll treat Mia with utmost delicacy."

Mia's laughter rang out above the crowd, and when we turned, she was holding up a glass of wine.

"But I would also add, she's not as fragile as you might think," Hauptmann Brenner said. "I'd wager she's tougher than us both put together."

The wildness in Mia was far from tamed, and nothing I could say to her would keep her away from him. "Be careful with her."

His smile broadened as he moved me around the dance floor. "Of course."

When the dance ended, I withdrew a step. Mia approached us and slid her hand into the crook of Hauptmann Brenner's arm. "What did you think of this nice man, Isabella?"

"Very charming." But charming hid many sins. "The curfew approaches. Mia, will you walk home with me?"

"Hauptmann Brenner has offered to escort me," she said.

"The curfew does not apply to the Germans," he said.

Swallowing bitterness, I smiled. "May I have a word with my friend?"

"Of course," he said.

I pulled Mia to the side of the room, searching for a spot we could speak privately. "You need to come home with me."

"I have done all that you've said these last four weeks, and now I am healed. I won't wait in that room for a bomb to land on my head."

"Grief does not go away so quickly."

She drew in a breath. "It has for me. Besides, the way this war is going, we might all be dead by spring, and I refuse to face death sober and bored."

I glanced around and then whispered, "Who is this Karl Brenner?"

"He's in the police," she said.

"The German police. Is he with the SS? The Nazis?"

"I suppose."

"Do you know how dangerous he is?" I asked.

"That's what makes him interesting, no? When he asks for anything, he gets it. And I like being around that kind of power."

"Mia, please. Come home with me."

"Enough," Mia said. "I must go. Hauptmann Brenner will not wait forever." She kissed me on the cheek. "You're sweet, and I love you for it. But I am not you, and I don't follow the rules as well as you."

She brushed past me and went straight to Hauptmann Brenner, slipping her arm in his. He tugged her closer and kissed her lightly on the lips.

A new song began, but I had no more interest in the music and moved toward the door. Out on the street, the night cooled my hot, flushed skin. The sky was clear and the stars bright.

As I started to walk, I heard, "I'll walk with you."

I turned to see Aldo Rossi leaning against the wall, smoking a cigarette. He dropped the butt and crushed it with a Capri shoe, which struck me as slightly out of sync with his suit.

"I am not that far from home," I said.

Aldo pushed away from the wall and moved toward me. "Still, a few blocks can be dangerous. You did not convince Mia to leave?"

"No, she's an independent spirit."

"And she thinks you are far too serious?" he said lightly.

"I am afraid so." I wished at that moment I was not responsible or worried about the unfinished dresses that needed to be completed tomorrow. For once, it would have been nice to be the foolish one. But we were who we were.

We walked under the moonlight, along the stone streets. "You live near Padre Pietro's church," he said.

"Yes, in the Monti district," I said.

"How did your house fare in the bombings?"

"It was not damaged, but many were in San Lorenzo. The war has reached Rome."

"It's been here for some time."

He was right, but in the dress shop, surrounded by the fashionable ladies, it was easy to pretend. Now there would be no ignoring it.

The hard thud of soldiers' steps startled me, and as they approached us, Aldo pulled me into an alley. I followed without resistance because any confrontation with so many soldiers could end badly. He pressed my body against the wall and used his own to block me from any bystander. We stood close, listening as the marching grew louder until the battalion passed by.

"There are more and more patrols in the neighborhood," I whispered to him. "They say they are keeping the peace."

Aldo's jaw tightened a fraction, but he said nothing. "Time to get you home."

As we moved quickly along the sidewalk, the rubble from the bombing grew more pronounced. Buildings as ancient as the Roman Empire had been crushed, and my resentment for all our troubles grew.

We arrived at the indigo-blue *porta* of Signora Fontana's house. "It was a pleasure, Isabella. You're a very interesting woman."

Aldo took my hand and kissed it, sending an unexpected rush of heat into my face. It had been three years since Enzo, and I'd missed the feel of a man's body against mine. "Interesting?"

That prompted a slight smile. "It's not bad."

"If you say so."

"We'll see each other again, Isabella. This I know."

CHAPTER FIVE

ZARA

Richmond, Virginia
Saturday, June 5, 8:30 p.m.

"Gina tells me you're dying," Zara said.

"Still direct," Nonna said.

"Did you think I might have changed?" When Zara saw her grandmother struggle to rise up, she automatically moved the pillows up behind her and helped her to a sitting position. She noted the glass of water on the nightstand and held it up to Nonna's lips. The woman drank thirstily.

Nonna gasped in a breath. "I had hoped you had not changed too much."

"Why is that?" Zara set the glass on the table and pulled up a wooden chair. "You always said I was too bossy."

"You were, and I can see you still are, but I need someone like you. Now is not the time for the weak."

"I can care for you and keep you as comfortable as I can. And I know doctors who might offer a second opinion."

"More doctors are not necessary. I am dying. I accept that, but in the time that I have remaining, there are tasks that must be done. Gina is not up to the job."

"She's done well."

"She's a nervous wreck," Nonna said. "She smiles all the time because she thinks smiles hide everything, but they do not."

"What is she hiding?"

Nonna shrugged and fussed with her sheet. "How would I know?"

"You know everything."

"You overestimate me."

Zara regarded her grandmother. "Well, then you're in luck, because I don't smile much."

"No, you do not." She smoothed out the wrinkles on her sheet. "I need the attic cleaned out before I die."

"The attic? That's it?"

"I want to make sure that all my belongings are disposed of properly."

"You can't go up in the attic?"

"No, of course not, but you can. You can assist me as I go through what's up there."

Zara supposed this change had to do with her health. "You always said that I shouldn't worry about what was up there. That it was junk."

"I said that so you would not snoop."

Zara shrugged. "Smart play. If not for the lock on the door, I'm sure I would have been up there rooting through the junk."

"Why do you think there was a lock?"

"What are you looking for?" Zara asked.

"I'll know it when I see it."

"You have the sharpest mind of anyone. You don't forget anything. You know exactly what you want."

"You give me too much credit. And now I am old, and I have forgotten. I need help remembering."

Zara nearly called her out, but something in Nonna's tone backed up the words. Nonna would be ninety-eight on her next birthday, and it was possible the memories were scattering.

In Virginia's June heat, the attic would be sweltering most of the day, limiting her work to the early morning hours. That was just as well. It would give her time to care for Nonna.

"I'll pay you, of course," Nonna said.

"Excuse me?"

"I know this is what you do for a living." She waved her lined hand, as if searching for the words. "You shepherd the dying."

"I've never heard it put that way."

"It's true, is it not?" Nonna asked.

"I suppose."

"Well, I am dying, and I would like to be guided through these last days."

"Wouldn't you rather do something fun? I know that sounds trite, but you used to love clothes and the feel of good fabric. You and Gina could design a piece together like you did when I was a kid."

"I don't want another dress. I want my life in order. And I expect you to do that."

"Your life is not the attic," Zara said.

"It is." She allowed a tired breath to leak over her lips. "Don't argue, Zara. I do not have the will."

With dying came extreme fatigue and a narrowing of life. Life's broad spectrum of colors faded and then tapered to a pinpoint. That was where Nonna was now.

"Okay, I'll start on the attic in the morning."

"Why not now?"

"It's ninety degrees outside and a hundred and ten in the attic. This is going to be an early-morning gig."

"Very well. But do not throw out any item until I have inspected it."

"I'm a pretty good judge of junk."

"I must see each piece." Her voice was trailing and her body slipping into a deep sleep.

"Understood."

Zara tugged the blanket up over Nonna's chest and tucked it close to her chin. She smoothed her hand over the old woman's thinning white hair. This was the first time in years she had not seen Nonna made up with her hair styled. Zara used to tease her grandmother about being so pulled together, and now that she wasn't, it bothered her more than she could have predicted.

She left the room and closed the door behind her. She found Gina in the kitchen, sitting at the table, legs crossed, Little Sister in one hand and her teacup cradled in her other. The boys slept on the kitchen floor and barely looked up. "How is she?"

Little Sister whimpered when she saw Zara, so she took the dog from Gina's arms. "She wants me to clean the attic out."

"The attic. Good God, who in their right mind would spend their last days cleaning out that bird's nest?"

Zara sat across from Gina and sipped tea that had now grown cold. "I don't know. Maybe if I can clear out a little, that will appease her."

Gina extended her hand and studied her manicure. "Don't count on it."

"I need a bedroom," Zara said. "Looks like you and Nonna turned mine and the spare room into storage."

"You weren't here."

"I'm not placing blame," Zara said tersely.

"Don't you sleep in your van?" Gina asked.

"I do when I have to, but I don't have to now. There's room in this house for me."

"And the dogs?"

"They'll sleep with me."

Gina sighed.

"What's with the attitude? You called me," Zara said.

"I shouldn't have had to call," she said.

"Why not?"

"You should have checked in more."

"I call twice a week," Zara said.

Gina shook her head. "Never mind. There's nothing you can do." She rose and picked up the cups.

"I know you've taken care of a lot for me over the years, but this I can do. So I'm going to do it."

The cup rattled on the saucer. "You should have checked in more."

Zara stabbed fingers through her hair. Gina had always acted like a mini mom to Zara, and that had worked when she was a kid. But she was an adult, not a frightened orphan. "I'm here now."

Gina planted her hand on the counter and leaned into it. Her sister's skin had always been milky pale, but today her pallor was sallow. "Yes, you are."

"Are you feeling okay?"

"I'm tired. And there's an air mattress in the closet of your old room. It should do the trick. Push the clothes aside." The dogs whined, and Gina shot each a warning glance. "Do they need something?"

Zara grabbed the dogs' leashes, hooked each up, and snatched one of the disposable bags she kept in her back pocket. Then she and the three dogs headed outside for a walk.

The air had cooled, and the sky was clear as they strolled toward the collection of rocks on the river. Called Pony Pasture, it had been a favorite hangout of Zara's when she had been a teenager. No better place to sneak a cold beer on a hot day.

Whenever she and the dogs walked new territory, the dogs were alert and engaged, determined to study, sniff, and pee on every patch of ground. They ambled for a half hour before Gus started to slow. Zara had heard in his puppy days he could run for miles, but these days the arthritis in his hips limited him.

They made their way to the house, and as they approached the van, the dogs wagged their tails. "I suppose you're right," she said. "This is home."

She opened the side panel, pulled out the dogs' bowls, and filled three with kibble and the fourth with water. As they ate, Zara rolled out a six-by-eight carpet and set up a folding chair. She grabbed a soda from the small refrigerator, popped the top, and sat. The trick to living on the road was creating home wherever you were.

Zara stared at her grandmother's Mediterranean home and thought about the Sunday and Wednesday evening calls she always made to her grandmother. Lately, she'd listened while Nonna had talked about Papa and her son and how much she missed them. It was not like her grandmother to be nostalgic. But lately, the past had drawn Nonna more and more.

An older man dressed in ironed khakis, a crisp white shirt, and sturdy athletic shoes strolled along the street. She recognized Mr. George Harper, who had practiced law with her grandfather for forty-plus years. He had been a solemn, stoic figure at her father's and grandfather's funerals.

"Zara," he said.

She rose, left her can in the chair's cup holder, and crossed and hugged him close. "Mr. Harper. How are you?"

"I'm well. How is your grandmother?"

"Not well."

"I thought as much when I saw your van."

Some of Zara's clients remarked that Death rode shotgun with her in the van. "You've been talking to Gina?"

"I try. She's a little scattered."

"I'll take that blame," Zara said. "I should have come home sooner."

"Your job has great meaning, and you can't walk away from an assignment like other people." He scratched each of the dogs between the ears. "Are you staying for long?"

"For the duration," Zara said.

"Good. Renata is in good hands."

"Thanks." Zara looked around for his black Lincoln. "Where's your car?"

"I had the Uber bring me."

"*The* Uber. You're not driving?"

"Naw, gave it up. My eyes aren't what they used to be."

Mr. Harper lived ten miles west of here in a quiet suburban neighborhood. When he and his wife had bought their house in the midsixties, the houses had been cheap and the lots big. His wife, Stacey, had died a couple of years before Papa. Zara remembered that her grandparents had all but adopted him, having him to dinner several times a week for a couple of years. She envied the deeply rooted friendship the three had shared.

"You still look pretty fit to me," Zara said.

"I am," he said with a grin.

"Are you going into the office each day?"

"I am. Just for a few hours."

"Keep the young ones on their toes?"

He winked. "That's exactly right."

"Hey, I'm going to cook dinner as soon as I can get my grandmother and sister settled. I'll call you, and you can get yourself an Uber and come? Can't guarantee that Nonna will be up and about, but you never know. It would do her good. By then I'll have some of the stuff cleaned from the attic, and we can play Giveaway and Keep."

"The attic?"

"It's Nonna's only request. She wants me to clean it out."

Nodding slowly, he looked up at the house toward Nonna's window. "That sounds nice. I'd like that. Call me when the ladies are up to it."

"Great."

A black SUV pulled up in front of the house, and Mr. Harper jabbed his thumb over his shoulder. "That's my ride. I always get dropped off and picked up here."

His way of checking in. Zara leaned forward and kissed him on the cheek. "See you soon."

"Looking forward to it."

She walked him to the car and closed the door when he was settled inside. Standing on the sidewalk, she watched the car drive off and vanish around the corner.

"Nonna, you aren't sitting in that bed for the rest of your days. That I promise you."

From the van, Zara grabbed one of her empty notebooks she used for her clients, and she and the pups closed up the van and went inside. She found Gina in the kitchen and spent the next half hour going over Nonna's medications and making meticulous notes. She documented her grandmother's schedule, her latest dietary preferences, and her sleep schedule. "When does she go outside?"

"She hasn't in weeks," Gina said.

"It'll be a shame to waste these early mornings and evenings."

"She sleeps a lot."

"Do you have a wheelchair?" Zara asked.

"It's in my room. She refuses to use it. She doesn't even want to look at it."

"Okay. I'll put it in my room."

"She won't use it," Gina insisted.

"We'll see." Most of her patients came to the end of their lives kicking and screaming and desperate to hold on as tightly as they could. Wheelchairs and walkers became a necessary evil.

"I'm going out tonight," Gina said. "I need a break."

"Take all the time you need. I have this."

"Are you sure? You won't forget the pills?"

"I do this for a living," Zara said.

"I don't know how you do it. These have been the most depressing days of my life. Dad and Papa were here one day and gone the next. But this slow walk to the light is agonizing."

"I know it can be very difficult."

"But how do you do it?" Gina searched her sister's face, as if hunting for the secret.

"I find the joy," Zara said simply.

Gina shook her head. "There is no joy, Zara."

"That's not true. Less time can magnify the good in the remaining days."

Gina grabbed her small black leather clutch purse, snapped it open, and removed a mirrored compact and lipstick. She freshened her rose-tinted lips. "I'm going to find some real joy. He's tall, good looking, and serves a mean gin gimlet at Red's bar."

"I tried to sneak in there with a fake ID once. And the bouncer caught me and was going to call the cops."

"And you called me, and I talked him out of it right over the phone."

"You're kryptonite to men, Gina. They cannot ignore you."

That prompted a smile as she dropped her gaze to her phone. "I know. Speaking of which, I'm heading in that direction now."

"Have fun."

"You know it."

A car parked in front of the house, and she left. When the front door closed, a thick silence settled over the house. The grandfather clock ticked. Zara set up the dogs' beds in the kitchen and checked in on Nonna. She was sleeping soundly, but her face still had a troubled expression. She always worried. About Papa, the shop, her son and granddaughters. She always feared that if she took her eye off them, they would be gone.

Zara closed the door softly, climbed the stairs to the second floor, and opened the door leading to the now-unlocked attic. It was going to be hot as hell up there, but Nonna had never once mentioned the attic in all her years. And now she needed it cleaned ASAP.

Her curiosity overriding potential discomfort, she opened it and was slammed by the day's pent-up heat. After flipping the switch, she climbed the wooden stairs toward the lone bulb that spit out a faint ring of light on the wall-to-wall clutter. There was not a square inch of the attic that was not packed full of every piece of furniture or lamp that Nonna and Papa had ever purchased and then set aside.

Sweat beaded on her brow and between her breasts. The heat in the attic gave hell a run for its money.

"And so the adventure begins."

CHAPTER SIX
ISABELLA

Rome, Italy
Saturday, September 18, 1943, 11:43 a.m.

I was pinning together the muslin pattern of Signora Bianco's gown on her mannequin when the air-raid sirens wailed. Seconds later the first bombs exploded. The building shook, and as the next two bombs detonated, the lights blinked on and off and then went out completely.

Each of the girls stopped work and looked up toward the window overlooking the street level. I could see people running past the shop, hear screams mingling with the rumble of German vehicles grinding through gears as they drove faster. The building rattled, and crumbling stone fell to the street.

Sebastian stared toward the ceiling, and with each new explosion his face grew paler. Several girls looked to him for leadership, but he did not seem to notice them as he wrung his hands.

"Ladies, let us go upstairs," I said.

Mia stared out the window. "They won't hit this area. They have vowed not to bomb this part of the city."

"Have you spoken to the Allied pilots today?" I asked. "Of course you have not. Go upstairs. Sebastian, follow us."

Sebastian, always so sure and confident, suddenly aged, and for the first time I realized the toll this war was taking on him. Though the bombs sounded as if they were hitting outside the city, there was no guarantee the bombers would not shift directions.

The women were eerily silent as they quickly gathered their purses, jackets, and hats and climbed the rear staircase to the alley. Outside I looked up toward the azure sky and saw the precise formations of planes flying east. Running toward the street, I tracked the planes and guessed they were hitting the airport to the south.

"It's the Americans again," Mia said. "Karl said there would be more bombings."

"Hauptmann Brenner knew about this bombing?" I asked.

"Not this one exactly. But we're the enemy to the Allies," Mia said. "It was a matter of time."

Mia had returned home late last night, well past the curfew, thanks to her captain. Last night, I had sat up late waiting for her, determined to make her see the folly of her actions.

"What do you think will come of this?" I demanded.

"It's fun. And that's all that matters!" she shouted. She held up her hand so I could see a diamond bracelet winking in the light. "He gave me this."

"He barely knows you. Why would he give you such an extravagant gift?"

"He likes me."

Shaking my head, I did not bother to hide my disgust. "I would have thought you learned."

"I have learned to be more careful. There will be no baby this time."

"How can you be sure?"

"I won't allow it."

The arrogance had astounded me, and we had argued for another fifteen minutes until she had finally stormed off to her room.

More explosions followed in rapid fire, and as I looked for the billowing black smoke, I found its dark tendrils rising in the south near the airport.

I thought of Padre Pietro's church in the district and the apartment buildings filled with people. I thought of Signora Fontana in her kitchen. She was but ten blocks from the rail yards and the switching stations, and there was no guarantee that the area was not on today's target list.

The skies filled with scattered black puffs of flak as the Allied planes moved like birds of prey in wave after wave.

Several of the women wept and screamed for family and friends. "I need to get home to my husband," Maria said.

"You must wait for the bombs to stop," I said. "Mia is right. So far this area has been untouched by the bombs, and we must hope it remains that way. We must survive."

"But he could be dying," Maria said.

"There is nothing you can do for him or anyone else if you're dead. Stay here."

"What do we do?" Sebastian shouted.

"We wait," I said in a firm voice. "Everyone, sit close to the walls."

"How will the walls keep us safe from the bombs?" he demanded.

More explosions rocked the ground under our feet.

"Sit now!" I ordered.

Sebastian and the women complied, as if my sharp order was their refuge from danger. I stood, staring toward the skies, my anger toward our attackers growing. I refused to imagine the anguished shrieks mingling with the explosions.

In less than a half hour the skies went silent, and the flak finally thinned. The acrid scent of smoke thickened the air as the fire brigades raced through the city, their sirens blaring.

None of us moved, fearing a second wave, but when the skies remained clear, I said, "Go home and see to your families."

I clutched my purse close as I looked at Sebastian. "I must check on the people in my neighborhood. I'll return as soon as I can."

"We have work to do," Sebastian said. "What about the dress for Signora Bianco?"

"I have plenty of time." The comment sounded almost comical. "It'll get done. But not today. Mia, you'll come with me."

"I need to find Karl." Her voice had taken on a childlike quality.

"There'll be time for that. Now we'll check on Padre Pietro and Signora Fontana."

"It won't be safe," she said.

"We're in a war, Mia. No one is safe."

I took her by the hand and pulled her past the growing crowds of people who hurried around dazed and confused. The walk normally took twenty minutes, but today it took us an hour to push through the people. Some were crying, looking helpless and lost; some were taking advantage of the confusion and rushing from markets with eggs and chickens; and others stood in stunned silence.

I was relieved to discover our area had not been the bombers' target today. The people moved about the streets, shocked and nervous, chatting to each other and sharing cigarettes, all the while glancing toward the skies.

After pushing through the front door, I hurried toward Signora Fontana's kitchen. I found her by her stove, stirring a pot of stew.

"Signora," I said.

She stood still, her gaze on the polenta, and as I approached the stove, I could smell the burned cornmeal. I pushed the pot off the burner and took the spoon from her hand.

"Signora."

She looked at me, her face pale and drawn, her gaze vacant. "Isabella."

"Come. Mia, pour us all some wine."

Mia moved to the corked bottle and filled three glasses. The three of us sat at the table. Mia greedily drank her wine, but the signora simply stared.

"Drink," I ordered, pushing the glass toward her.

She complied, her hands trembling. "When the bombs started to fall, I was certain I would die."

"You did not die," I assured her.

"So much noise. My ears still ring with the blasts."

"They must have been going for the airport," I said.

"I may have burned the polenta," Signora Fontana said.

"It's okay. I'm sure your burned polenta is better than most." Even if it was not, we would still eat it. In these times, nothing went to waste. "Mia, I want you to sit with the signora."

"I want to see Karl," Mia protested.

"You'll not leave tonight," I said. "It's too dangerous. You'll know soon enough how your new lover fared in the morning."

"How can you be so cruel?" Mia asked.

"Go to your room," I said. "It'll do Karl no good if you're accosted on the street. Think of him."

"He could think I'm dead!" Mia shouted.

"He knew you would be in the Via Veneto and that it was untouched today." All the German vehicles parked near our shop, the most affluent portion of town, and so far they had rightly guessed that areas like that would be spared.

A fist pounded on the front door, and I hurried toward it. I was surprised to see Aldo Rossi standing on our doorstep. He was wearing a dark suit dusted with powdered concrete. "I was in the neighborhood. I came to see that you were all right."

"We're fine. What did they bomb this time?"

"Judging by the sounds, the Ciampino Airport. The Allies are finished with us today."

Mia was running her fingers through her hair as she approached. She glanced at Aldo and then to me. "I need to find Karl."

"I have said no." My voice had turned harsh, frayed by shattered nerves.

"You're being so cruel," Mia said. "I won't stand for it."

"You can, and you will," I insisted.

"I'll take her to find Brenner," Aldo said. "She won't give you any peace until she knows."

"She belongs here," I said.

"You need rest," Aldo said. "I'll look after Mia."

"I can go by myself," Mia said.

"No," I said through clenched teeth. "Mia, tell Signora Fontana you're leaving. As a guest in her house, you owe her that much."

Mollified, the young woman returned to the kitchen.

"She's young," I said by way of apology.

"So are you," he said. "Be careful. The Germans will be on high alert, as will the Roman police. Stay clear of them all."

"All the more reason Mia should stay."

"The girl will sneak out," he said. "She'll be safe enough with Brenner."

"I don't know why she's so obsessed with that man. It'll come to no good."

Aldo frowned. "Let us hope not."

When Mia appeared with her purse, the two left, and I locked the door behind them. I glanced out the window and saw Aldo reach for Mia's arm, but she jerked it away. They were speaking to each other, and I could tell by their expressions that they were fighting. "Mia, do you have any sense?" I returned to the kitchen and found the signora back at her stove. "We must put you to bed, Signora Fontana."

"The polenta."

"I am sure it's salvageable. Do not worry."

I guided her into her bedroom, and when she sat on her mattress, I pulled off her shoes. She reclined and stared up at me. "It'll be all right, Isabella."

Smoothing my hand over her forehead, I smiled. "Of course it will."

After selecting a light quilt folded at the end of the bed, I covered her and gently tucked the soft folds around her before I kissed her on the head.

When I reached my room, I crossed to the small washstand and poured water into it. I dunked my hands and watched the dirt taint the clear water. I scrubbed, thinking of the two girls named Gina and the other children I had seen over the last few weeks searching the rubble for belongings and loved ones.

As I raised my gaze to the small mirror, I looked into bloodshot eyes ringed with dark circles. I washed my face, trying to forget the scenes of the day. I thought of my father and mother, who had both passed last year, and was glad neither was here to witness this destruction.

Squaring my shoulders, I reached for a towel and dried my face. "We will endure. All of us."

CHAPTER SEVEN
ZARA

Richmond, Virginia
Sunday, June 6, 5:30 a.m.

Zara woke before the sunrise, filled her travel mug with coffee, and walked her dogs along the James River. The early-summer drought had left the rocks exposed and the river hungry for water.

She had forgotten how pretty this area was and what a treasured childhood she and Gina had enjoyed here with her grandparents. Despite their age, her grandparents had sacrificed their retirement for parent-teacher meetings, soccer practices, and endless hormonal moody days. Nonna had been the disciplinarian, setting curfews and insisting both girls worked in the shop to earn an allowance. If Zara had a dime for all the garments collected from the changing rooms and rehung, she would have been rich. "You'll appreciate the money more if you've earned it," Nonna had often said.

Papa had been the soft touch. He had always found a way to charm his wife and get her to soften rules about dating or driving. "Renata, remember when you were that age?"

That had always prompted a raised brow and then a "Very well, Zara, you may have the car until . . ." They had been more like parents to her than her own parents.

When she and the pups returned, she doled out food to each dog and stood between them, watching as Billy gobbled his food and then stared at Gus, who never rushed a meal. When Billy shifted his gaze to Little Sister, she stepped away from her bowl.

"Nope, big fella. Let her eat." She guarded the little dog. "Keep eating."

Little Sister continued to nibble as Billy glanced between Zara and the other dogs' food, as if he were somehow being cheated. When the trio had finished and each had lapped up water from the big bowl, she walked to the phone and the stack of envelopes.

They were all addressed to her grandfather, as all the bills had been. When he had passed, Nonna had seen no reason to change the accounts. The bills ranged from the electric company to the water and various other services that her grandmother had employed to keep this house running. The postmarks on the stack were several weeks old. She opened the first and found the red past-due stamp at the top. The next three bills were also overdue.

"What the hell, Gina? Why aren't you paying the bills?"

She replaced the invoices in the envelopes and walked her trio to the garage and opened the door. She backed Gina's blue Mercedes out and parked it on the street. Next, she pushed the trash cans and the unfilled garden pots to the side.

Looking toward the ceiling, she thought about the cramped, growing-hotter-by-the-moment attic space. "Can I trust you three to stay put?"

Gus sat and closed his eyes. Billy did the same, but Little Sister, not used to the nomad life, appeared confused. "You and I don't know each other that well yet. But sometimes you need to be quiet while I work." The day would come when her ties ended here, and she would move on to the next job. The thought gave her no joy, but it was her reality.

The dog cocked her head, and Zara saw a challenge. Zara grabbed one of her longest leashes, hooked it to Little Sister's collar, and looped it around the base of a planter. She set a big bowl of water next to the dogs. "I've about an hour to work this morning. Stay tuned."

On the way to the attic, she passed Gina's room. Her bed was neatly made, suggesting she had not come home last night. "You'd better come back."

Zara and Gina's father had never stayed in any relationship long. He had left Gina's mother when Gina was seven. Apparently, there had been several women between his first and second wife, who had been Zara's mother. From what she remembered, her parents had never had a charmed marriage. The fights, the slamming doors, the empty bottles of wine piled in the trash all foretold of the divorce that her mother always claimed she'd never seen coming. Her father moved out when Zara was four, and ten days after his divorce from her mother, he'd died in a car accident.

Papa had driven to Raleigh and picked up Zara so she could attend. They left Raleigh immediately, rain beading against the windshield for nearly the entire drive. Papa did not try to cheer her up, but he was a steady presence that made her believe she was safe.

By the time they arrived in Richmond, snowflakes fell thick on the brick sidewalk from a gray sky. It was past midnight, and cold had sharpened the air. Papa carried her inside and laid her in Gina's double bed, and her sister hugged her close.

The next morning, when Zara woke, she was confused and did not remember where she was.

"It's okay," Gina said, half-asleep. "Let's find Nonna. She always gets up early."

After taking Zara by the hand, she led her into the warm kitchen filled with the scents of cinnamon and sugar.

"Girls, are you hungry?"

"I'm starving," Gina said.

"I made a pot of oatmeal, and there's fresh bread. I don't think I've made bread since I was a girl. We'll see how much I remembered, eh, Zara?"

"Where's Papa?" Zara asked.

"He's taking care of a few details." Later she would piece together that he had been making the funeral arrangements.

Nonna opened her stove. "You'll be hungry, of course," she said.

The bread, along with soft butter and a cold glass of milk, had been a welcome relief from the fast food and convenience-store chips and candy that her mother loved.

"Has Momma called?" Zara asked.

"No dear, not yet," Nonna said. "She knows you're in safe hands."

Zara's mother did not call for a week, and then she had shown up and told Zara it was time to leave. Zara had lived with her mother for the next seven years, and though Papa had sent a monthly check, they'd always seemed to have little money. Zara would spend summers with Nonna, Papa, and Gina, and their five-bedroom house seemed like a mansion compared to the two-bedroom apartment she shared with her mother.

Of the two Mitchell sisters, Gina was most like their father. She could never stay in one relationship long, and she was forever casting her gaze to the next horizon.

"You'd better come back, Gina," Zara whispered. "I'm not doing this alone."

She checked in on her grandmother, who lay on her side, sleeping. She crossed the room, confirmed she was breathing, and tugged the blanket up before she slipped out of the room.

Zara opened the attic door and climbed the stairs. The heat had abated since yesterday, but it would soon reach one hundred–plus degrees. That translated into surface-of-the-sun kind of hot.

The first few items included a broken lamp, stacked Christmas wreaths, and boxes of red, green, and blue lights. She settled the items in the garage and returned to the attic. Next came several broken tables, boxes containing bolts of fabric, wrapping paper, glass vases once filled with flowers likely delivered after her father's or grandfather's deaths, a cane chair with a worn-out seat, three different Christmas trees (green, silver, and pink), and a few small rugs that had been rolled up.

Within an hour, half the floor space of the garage was filled, and she was covered in sweat. She checked her watch, hurried into the kitchen, and assembled her grandmother's morning meds. As she walked to her grandmother's room, her phone dinged with a text from Gina.

Gina: Amanda running late. There by ten.

Zara: Where are you?

Gina: About to do unspeakable things to the man beside me in bed.

Zara: Have fun.

Gina: Always.

"Nonna, it's time to get up," Zara said, pocketing the phone.

"What time is it?" she asked.

"It's almost nine."

"Good Lord, why didn't you wake me earlier?" she snapped.

"You were sleeping well."

"I'll be sleeping forever very soon, so I'd rather not do it now." She sat up as Zara propped pillows behind her.

"Sleep is good for us all." Zara handed her three pills and a glass of water. She watched carefully as her grandmother took each. Experience had taught her that not all patients were compliant. As death grew near, some resented the meds and the daily regimen. The fact that her grandmother was still accepting hers without a fuss was a good sign.

"What about my attic?" Nonna asked.

"I spent the last hour cleaning the first section out. There's a lot more to do, but I put a good dent in it."

"You haven't thrown anything out, have you?" she asked.

"None of what I removed is worth saving. It's a matter of trash versus thrift."

"I am to make those decisions," Nonna said. "I must see each item."

"I can do this for you."

"I do not wish you to do it for me. Now I must get up and get dressed. Where is Amanda?"

"Running late."

"And Gina?"

"She's out right now."

"Where? She helps me in the morning when Amanda is running late."

"And now I will." Zara removed her covers and brought around the walker. "Let's get you in the shower."

"You know nothing about hair and makeup."

"Maybe you can teach me a few tricks. You said enough times I should start trying."

Her grandmother eyed her. "You don't smell too good."

"That would be because I've sweat my butt off cleaning out your attic."

Nonna cocked an eyebrow, followed by an imperceptible lift of her shoulder. In the old woman's world, that amounted to an acknowledgment that Zara was right.

The bathing process was fairly smooth, and within a half hour, her grandmother was clean, dressed in a fresh gown and a soft yellow bed jacket. As Zara brushed her hair, she noted all traces of Nonna's signature blonde hair dye were gone. "Your hair is lovely."

Her grandmother raised her gaze to the mirror and smoothed her hand over wrinkled skin. "I have not had it properly colored or styled in months."

"Would you like your hair done?" Zara asked.

"I don't have the energy to go to the salon. Gina does a good job but not like my hairdresser."

"Who does your hair now?" Zara said.

"Her name is Delores. You do not know her."

"At the Church Street Salon?" Zara squirted styling gel in her hand and rubbed it into her grandmother's hair.

"Yes."

"You've been seeing her for years."

"Of course. She's good."

"I'll call her."

"Why?"

"To see if she can come here."

"That's unnecessary," Nonna said. "It's a great deal of fuss."

"You like it done properly, so it's necessary. Live a little, Nonna."

Zara used a hair dryer to get the moisture out and add body to Nonna's hair. She rubbed cream into her grandmother's skin and added hints of blush and then eyebrow pencil.

Her grandmother regarded her image. "Thank God I'm not going anywhere today. People would think I'd been run over by a truck."

"I think you look pretty good."

Nonna regarded Zara's sweat-stained shirt and tangled hair. "That is not saying much. Call Delores. Tell her it's an emergency."

Zara grinned. "Will do. Ready to see the garage, or do you want your coffee first?"

"The garage and then coffee."

Using the walker, they made their way very slowly through the house, and Zara guided Nonna to the garage entrance. She pulled a chair from the kitchen and settled her grandmother on it. "We'll call this game Giveaway and Keep, round one."

Nonna adjusted her bed jacket. "This is not a game, Zara. It's my life."

"Our *things* are not *us*," Zara said.

"Of course you believe that. It's the nomad in your blood."

"I travel to work. There is no wandering in my blood."

Nonna shrugged. "You never know."

Zara held up a Christmas tree with a broken stand. "Trash?"

"It can be fixed," she said. "It needs the bottom repaired."

"How long has it been broken?" Zara asked.

"That does not matter."

And so it went. Every item, no matter how bent, twisted, or broken, could be fixed, still had a use, or should be put aside for another day.

By the end of round one, the score was Giveaway: zero and Keep: fifty-two. "I need to clear out the garage so I can refill it tomorrow."

Zara's phone buzzed, and she glanced at the screen. Nicolas Bernard. She had not seen the name in two years and automatically glanced to Gus, wondering if he had decided to reclaim his late wife's dog. He had dutifully sent money to cover Gus's vet bills but had never sent a text or note asking after either dog. Instead of answering the call, she let it go to voice mail.

"Let's get you to bed."

"What are you going to do with all this?" Nonna demanded.

"I'll handle it." She helped her grandmother stand and guided her to her room. Within fifteen minutes, her grandmother was seated in her bed, a tray with her small espresso on her lap and *The Price Is Right* on the television. "Our next adventure is going to be in that wheelchair."

"No. Absolutely not."

"You fall and break a hip, then it's game over."

"You don't know that."

"I've seen it too many times. I'll make sure your new ride is ready to go in the next hour."

"Bossy."

"Wonder who I inherited that from?"

When Zara returned to the garage, she looked at all the junk. There was no point returning it to the attic, and there was no room for it in the house. She called the local junk-collection service and arranged for it to be picked up.

"She's going to kill me," she said to Little Sister.

The dog licked her face as Gus let out a loud woof. He rose up off the cool concrete floor, his tail wagging.

A light-blue four-door sedan parked in front of the house, and Amanda got out. Amanda, who had worked for her grandmother for fifteen years, was in her late forties and wore her brown curly hair in a bun, a navy-blue T-shirt, jeans, and white tennis shoes.

"I'm sorry I'm late," Amanda said as she raced toward Zara. "Car trouble."

Zara hugged her. "It's okay. It's all under control."

"I am so glad you're here. I've been telling your sister for weeks it's time to get around-the-clock care."

"The cavalry has arrived, but Nonna's not too thrilled."

Amanda smiled. "Your grandmother shows her love by bitching and complaining."

"Well, then I am adored."

Amanda patted Zara on the shoulder. "Let me get to the kitchen so I can figure out what I need to buy at the grocery today."

"Thanks, Amanda. What's the deal with the bills? They aren't being paid."

"I've mentioned them to your sister several times, and she said she would take care of it. The checkbook is in your grandfather's desk."

"I'll dig into them."

"Glad to have you back, Zara."

As Amanda vanished into the house, a Jeep pulled up. At first Zara did not recognize the guy with shoulder-length hair, deeply tanned skin, and a faded T-shirt and board shorts. But when he raised his gaze to her, she knew him instantly. It was Nicolas Bernard. He was or had been a corporate lawyer, and his late wife had been one of her patients two years ago.

As soon as Nicolas approached the garage, Gus looked up and immediately ran toward him, his tail wagging. Nicolas scratched the dog at the base of his spine, near his tail. Gus bared his teeth in a smile and whimpered with happiness as Nicolas said, "Good boy. I've missed you, pal."

Billy, not to be ignored, followed and nudged Gus aside. "Billy, how are you, pal? Been a while. Both you guys are grayer." Little Sister wiggled to get down, and when Zara set her on the floor, she ran toward Nicolas. "And who are you?"

"That's Little Sister. She's new to the pack," Zara said.

Nicolas rose as the trio of dogs circled around him. "I should have waited for you to call, but I was in the area."

"The area? Last I remember, you lived in Atlanta."

"Job interview with the Washington, DC, branch of my father's firm. Time to rejoin the world."

Nicolas had hired Zara two and a half years ago, when his wife, Catherine, had been diagnosed with terminal ovarian cancer. Zara and Billy had parked in their driveway and for the next five months had been daily fixtures in Catherine's, Nicolas's, and Gus's lives. And when Catherine had passed on a day in July, Nicolas had quit his job at his father's law firm and asked her to take Gus.

"I'm such a shit for giving him up," Nicolas said. "But I can barely take care of myself now."

"He'll be fine with me," Zara said.

Bloodshot eyes rose to hers. "Catherine said not to trust him with anyone else but you while I'm traveling."

Zara could minister to the dying, but she had little luck counseling the ones left behind. When her parents and then grandfather had died, she'd discovered there was no path back to normal. It was a matter of stumbling around until the pieces reassembled into the next version of life.

"I thought you didn't want to work for your father's law firm," Zara said.

"It's what I know. And I'm good at it. Plus, he's getting older and needs the help."

Loyalty ran deep in Nicolas. Few spouses had been as devoted. "I'd give you a hug, but I've been cleaning out my grandmother's attic. Smelling a little ripe right now."

"You look good," he said.

There was a warmth softening the words, and she supposed he was glad to see an old friend who had seen him at his worst and stuck by him. "So do you. How did you find me?"

"You listed this place as your permanent address for your taxes. I took a chance."

"You're clever. And if you've come to take my dog, you can't have him."

CHAPTER EIGHT
ISABELLA

Rome, Italy
Thursday, October 7, 1943, 7:00 a.m.

As the sun rose, Romans gathered as they now did each day, with shovels and pickaxes to clear rubble. The Germans were taking up what remained of the rail yards and, I was told, were shipping the iron to Germany. We all had taken to hiding our valuables, carrying little cash, and wearing gloves to hide rings.

I ate a quick meal of polenta while Signora Fontana stood by the stove, cutting an onion and carrot that would be combined with overripe tomatoes for tonight's sauce. There was no meat to be had, and these vegetables were a luxury.

I tied a scarf around my neck and made sure my chignon was smooth. Sebastian's clients were not interested in seeing me disheveled or sad. Appearances mattered.

Mia entered the kitchen. Though she had washed her face and combed her hair, her eyes were red and puffy. She had not been sleeping well for months, and last night was no exception. She crossed to the stove and poured herself a cup of coffee before she kissed the signora on the cheek.

"You came home," I said.

"Why wouldn't I?" she asked.

"You've not been here much the last few weeks."

"I've been with Karl."

My disapproval must have been etched in my features, because the signora moved between Mia and me. "You look tired."

Mia smiled as she always did. "I'm fine."

"You're getting too thin," the older woman said.

"And here I was thinking how Paris chic I looked," Mia said.

"We must be leaving soon," I said. "Sebastian will be worried about the day's work."

"He's always worried," Mia said as she raised her cup to her mouth.

"Without him we would not eat," I said.

"We would be fine," Mia said.

"Don't be so sure," I warned as I gathered my purse. "Let us go."

"If we must." She gulped the last of the weak coffee and, after grabbing her gloves and purse, followed.

On the street, the scent of smoke dangled heavily in the air, and all around us we heard the clink of shovels against stone. As we passed the church, the young altar boy who had assisted Padre Pietro with the funeral was waiting for me.

When he saw me, he hurried down the stairs. "Signora Mancuso, the father would like to see you."

I considered the time but also remembered my promise. "Mia, you go on into work, and I'll be right behind you."

"What could he want?" she asked.

"Likely he needs vestments repaired."

Mia regarded me and then shrugged. "Very well. Sebastian will be shocked I beat you to work."

"Tell him I'll be there shortly."

When she rounded the corner, I followed the boy through the church's side door and to the priest's office. This time, I knocked and waited for him to say, "Enter."

There were two young men, perhaps no more than fifteen, standing across the room, each holding their hats in their hands. Their clothes were threadbare, and both looked too thin.

"Padre, you wanted to see me?" I asked.

"Isabella, I knew you would be passing by about now. You are very reliable."

The predictability of my daily pattern worried me, and I vowed to change it tomorrow. "What can I do for you?"

"These two young men, Marco and Gino, need a place to hide for several days. I'm trying to arrange transport out of the city, but it'll take longer than expected. They're hiding from the forced labor camp roundups."

The priest's tone was firm and held no hints of a question. He was not concerned that the house where I lived was not mine or that it would be dangerous to be caught hiding these boys.

"Of course." I did not have to ask if his request was illegal. It was. And we all could go to prison for it. "Marco and Gino and I must go now. I need to get to work, or questions will be raised."

The priest's eyes brightened with satisfaction. "Excellent."

"There is a rear exit to the church, if I'm not mistaken," I said.

"I'll show you the way," the priest said.

Nodding, I motioned to the boys. "Follow me."

I trailed the priest along the long corridor toward the cemetery. Searching for the tiny grave, I said a prayer for the child. At the back gate, the priest removed a key from his pocket and unlocked the door. "Thank you, Isabella."

"Of course."

As soon as we were on the street, the three of us moved quickly along a side alley. A window opened above us, and I saw an old woman reaching for her laundry line. She saw us and simply nodded as we hurried along until we reached the back entrance to Signora Fontana's house.

"Let me do the talking," I said.

Both boys nodded.

Inside the house, I told them to wait and hurried into the kitchen. "Signora, the priest has asked a favor of me which I cannot refuse. There are two young men we must hide from the labor camps."

She had poured her vegetables into a large cast-iron pot and was stirring them. "Where are they?"

"Waiting by the door."

She carefully lifted the spoon to her mouth and tasted the broth. "You know better than to leave a guest standing. Bring them in here. I know they must be hungry."

"Thank you," I whispered.

"There is nothing to thank me for. I'll feed them and then put them in the small room at the end of your hallway."

The third-floor room came equipped with a closet that had a false wall. The signora had once explained it was there to hide her valuables, but I suspected the room had been for her husband. Like me, she was a Catholic who had married a Jew, and as I well knew, it was a decision that often invited trouble.

I kissed her on the cheek. "You're a blessing."

"Go on with you," she said gruffly.

I found Marco and Gino and brought them into the kitchen. They stared at the old woman, who pointed toward the table. "Sit. I have polenta. No bread yet, but later today perhaps." When they hesitated, she said in a sterner voice, "Sit. You both look like skin and bones."

The boys sat like all good obedient Italian boys, who always minded their mothers.

"Sebastian has a storeroom where he keeps meats and cheeses clients give him," I said. "I shall see what I can find for supper."

"Bring whatever you can. Now that we have boys to feed, the soup will need thickening," Signora Fontana said.

"Again, thank you," I said.

She waved me away. "Nonsense. Go."

I dashed out and circled around the block before heading toward the shop. When I arrived, Sebastian was there, waiting.

"When you're late, it means the world has truly gone mad," he said.

"You have only just noticed?" I asked.

That prompted a small smile. "Go on. Signora Bianco's dress must be finished. Can you get by to see her today?"

"It'll have to be today. Yom Kippur approaches. She will be with her family."

"Celebrating quietly, I hope," he said. "Not wise to flaunt their religion now."

"Knowing the signora, she'll have a lavish dinner for her family tonight."

I quickly hung up my jacket and changed into my work smock before tackling the finishing touches on the dress. At nine o'clock, I hung the silk gown up and gently skimmed the soft fabric. It was indeed some of my best work, and I was honored Signora Bianco would be wearing it.

"Isabella," Sebastian said. "We have a new customer, and I need you to attend to her. She'll be here at nine thirty."

"So early? Is she Italian?"

"Her name is Frau Greta Brenner," he said. "She's new to the city."

More and more German soldiers had moved to Rome, and the arrival of wives suggested they intended to stay for some time.

Frau Brenner entered the shop at precisely nine thirty. She searched the salon, curiosity sharpening her hazel eyes as she carefully removed her white gloves. Blonde hair, milky-white skin, and a sturdy figure were classically German, but there was something tentative about her as she approached one of the full-length mirrors and regarded her reflection.

Each time a new client arrived at the shop, Sebastian turned it into a sort of small production. He entered the stage first and fawned over the client for a set amount of time while I waited behind the curtains.

As he did so, I stepped back from the curtains, turned to a small oval mirror, straightened my collar, and smoothed down a few flyaway strands of hair. My expression reflected a sourness that would not do, so I forcefully softened it.

"Let me introduce Isabella Mancuso, the most talented seamstress in Rome."

I pushed through the curtains and found Frau Brenner standing by a satin chaise, her back now to the mirrored cabinets. "Welcome," I said in German.

The sound of Frau Brenner's native tongue seemed to relax her rigid stance a fraction. "You speak German?"

"Very little," I said. What I never shared was that I was fluent, but I had never spoken more than basic sentences in Rome, sensing it was best everyone assumed I understood less.

Sebastian continued in German, explaining that we were the finest couture shop in Rome, and he was pleased to help her. Her expression remained cool, but under the stony reserve brewed some anxiety and self-consciousness. She might have the means to shop here, but I sensed she had not grown up with money.

I took her jacket and hung it on a hanger and then placed her hat on a small table. "Lovely," I said as I ran my hand along the fine stitching.

"Thank you," Frau Brenner said. "I had a young Jewess in Munich who sewed for me, and unfortunately she's no longer available. A pity."

My expression remained blank as Sebastian translated all but the part about the missing Jew. "What is it you need?"

"I need a dress. I have a very important function to attend that will reflect on my husband, Hauptmann Karl Brenner."

Karl Brenner's name caught my ear. He had been the man at the party who had danced with me but had been enthralled with Mia. He was not the first man in Rome to keep a wife and mistress.

"If you'll allow us, Isabella will take your measurements, and then she and I will show you sketches," Sebastian said.

"Very well."

I opened the door leading to the large mirrored changing room that was furnished with several chairs and a wooden box for the client to stand on while I took measurements.

Frau Brenner stepped into the room, again studying her reflection with a critical eye before she looked away. She set her purse on a small table, sat, and then unlaced her shoes. I accepted her silk blouse and carefully draped it over a chair as she shimmied out of her skirt.

I studied her figure with a critical eye. Like all women, it had its flaws and advantages. "Signora," I said, indicating she stand on the box. "Please."

She stepped up and tugged at the slip that gathered at her slightly rounded belly as I removed the measuring tape from around my neck.

"I've had no one sew for me since Miriam," Frau Brenner said in Italian. "I'm a bit nervous."

"There's nothing to worry about. I'll take good care of you."

I spent the next several minutes measuring, knowing she was watching my expression closely in the mirror, as if searching for hints of disapproval. But I had learned long ago to hide all but the happiest emotions from my clients.

"Very good," I said as I scribbled the last measurement on the scratch pad. "Dress, please."

We rejoined Sebastian, who had laid out a series of sketches for Frau Brenner to review. He had also set out a silver tray with tea and cookies. He was an expert at wooing women into buying clothes.

We sat, and I listened as he showed her the sketches of our most conservative designs. But as I watched her expression, I could see she was not pleased. She, like many women new to Rome, wanted a different life.

"One moment," I said. I rose, walked to the back room, and selected several designs that were more adventurous. I set them on the table over the others. "These."

Frau Brenner's eyes widened with shock and then curiosity. "That seems rather wanton."

Her tone had softened, and I realized I had captured her interest. "Sebastian," I said in Italian. "Tell her I would like to make this dress for her. She has lovely shoulders, and the plunging back will be quite attractive."

"Isabella, are you sure?" he asked.

"I know women," I said. "I understand."

He translated, watching Frau Brenner closely as she studied the off-the-shoulder dress cinched at the waist. The garment would create a stunning silhouette that would highlight her shoulders and lovely skin.

"It's too daring," she said.

"Perhaps a bit," he said. Even he realized we had captured her interest. "If you wish to be noticed, then you must be a bit bold."

I rose again and hurried downstairs and selected the dress I had made for Signora Bianco and carried it upstairs. "I think this type of fabric."

She gently fingered the midnight-blue silk, and I motioned for her to stand and face the mirror. I held the dress up in front of her. "Of course, yours would be different. Our dresses are one of a kind. But it'll give you an idea."

She fingered the fabric. "It's lovely."

"Yes," I said. "Perfect for you."

Frau Brenner stared at her reflection. I collected the soft folds, which allowed the fabric to shimmer in the chandelier light. "Look," I said, nodding.

"I would buy this dress," Frau Brenner said.

"That is not possible," Sebastian said. "It's for another client."

"I'll gladly pay more," she said.

"That is not possible," Sebastian said. "And the V-neck would not be to your advantage. As Isabella said, an open back."

Isabella had dressed enough women to know when they liked what they saw. "It's Rome, no?"

"Yes, it is." Slowly a smile curled the edges of her lips, and the light of the girl that was inside all women glistened. "But perhaps raise the back up."

"You wished to be noticed, correct?" Sebastian said.

"I want my husband to be proud. It's important that he make an impression with Hauptmann Dannecker."

I had not heard of Dannecker. "An important man, no?"

"He's SS and the Jewish expert," she said proudly in German. "He only arrived in Rome. I trust you have no Jewish clients." She looked at me, and for a brief moment her gaze lingered, as if she realized I had understood. Quickly, I recovered a pleasant but blank expression.

Sebastian smiled, as if she had not spoken. "If your husband has red blood in his veins, he'll be proud of you," Sebastian said.

The comment drew Frau Brenner's attention to the dress. "Does it make me look younger?"

"It does," he said. "Even with the higher back."

Sebastian could easily push aside politics as he calculated the cost of the rich fabric and my time sewing the dress.

"My husband has a weakness for beauty," Frau Brenner said more to herself.

"You're beautiful, Signora," Sebastian said.

A glimmer glistened in her eyes, and I sensed she was comparing herself to the young woman she had once been. "What jewelry should I wear?"

"Diamonds," he said. "Perhaps pear-shaped earrings."

"I have a striking pair."

"Then you are ready."

Frau Brenner lifted her gaze to mine and then to Sebastian's. "If all goes well, I'll return for more dresses. My husband tells me we will be doing much entertaining in the coming year."

"So your stay will be extended?" he asked.

"We could be living here forever."

I carefully removed the fabric and refolded it as Sebastian calculated the cost of the dress. If the Germans stayed and continued as they had in Europe, this city would indeed change more.

After I was dismissed, I returned to Signora Bianco's dress and spent the next several hours finishing the detail work on the gown. When it was completed, I wrapped it in a linen cloth bag. Next, I dashed into the storeroom, where there were stacks of onions, sausages, cured hams, bags of pasta, rice, and good wines. I took a ring of sausages and a wedge of cheese and shoved both in my bag. Barely able to close the purse, I realized I needed a larger handbag.

With the dress draped over my bulging purse, I hurried along the cobbled street past a procession of Wehrmacht trucks and armored cars. I hurried south toward the Biancos' beautiful apartment near Trajan's Forum. Their building, which dated to the time of the Renaissance, maintained its crumbling elegant beauty in a section of Rome where one could believe that there was no war.

At the front entrance, I presented myself to the porter, who opened the door. After exchanging greetings, I climbed the one hundred marble steps to the signora's floor and knocked on her apartment door.

Her manservant, a tall elegant man with black eyes and graying hair, greeted me with a somber smile. "She's in the sitting room and would like to see you."

"Of course." I followed him past Renaissance paintings that included a Leonardo da Vinci, a Raphael, and a Botticelli. There were also statues, gilded furniture, and rich tapestries. Signor Bianco had a reputation as an art collector, but I had not realized how truly extensive his collection was.

I found Signora Bianco sitting by an arched set of glass doors that opened onto a small balcony overlooking the Roman ruins of Trajan's Forum. The stunning view was marred by the not-too-distant destruction of the San Lorenzo district, and I wondered what Signora Bianco had thought when the horizon had exploded with bombs in July and August.

"Signora Bianco," I said. "Would you like to try on your dress?"

She smiled and bade me to sit. "No, I am sure it's perfect. You have never made me a dress that was not. Have a seat, Isabella."

I carefully draped the dress over a chaise and perched on the edge of the seat at the small table. She filled a china cup with tea for me. I accepted it, feeling a little guilty that my client was serving me.

"How do the girls in the shop fare?" she asked.

"Most lost someone they knew in the bombings. But they are back to work."

"Work is the best remedy in times like this," she said. "It diverts the mind from sadness."

"Yes."

"I watched the bombs drop in July and August. My heart went out to the people's suffering, but I was also glad."

"Glad?"

"The Germans will never leave on their own. They'll have to be brutally forced out."

"We see more and more German clients," I said carefully. "They have plans to stay for some time."

"Is that so?"

"Is the wedding still in three days?"

She smiled. "We held it last night."

"What? Why didn't you send word? I would have brought your dress."

"It's a small detail now. The young couple is safely wed, and that is what matters."

The dress had cost a small fortune. For her to consider it unimportant said much to me. She was very aware of the dangers facing her family. "May I again suggest that you take a trip after the wedding? Perhaps Switzerland."

"Because of the Germans."

"Yes."

"The Jewish community paid its ransom to SS Obersturmführer Kappler. There is an understanding between the Jews of Rome and the Germans."

"And you believe this? I hear a Hauptmann Dannecker has arrived in the city. He's the Jewish expert."

"Other warnings of trouble have reached me, and though the rabbis said there was nothing to worry about, I do."

"It would not hurt to hide what you can and take that holiday along with your grandson and granddaughter-in-law."

The old woman smiled at me. "You have taken a risk telling me this."

"Yes."

She was silent a moment. "I fear these bones are too old now to travel far. And this apartment is filled with too many memories to abandon. But I understand your meaning. I have already spoken to my banker, and he's made arrangements to transfer monies to Switzerland."

"I'll help you in any way I can."

Signora Bianco regarded me closely. "Perhaps, if the need should arrive, my grandson and his new wife can visit your Padre Pietro. Perhaps you and he will be able to give them shelter if the time should come."

"I will do the same for you."

"No. As I've said, I don't need help. What I need is to enjoy this marriage, which I'll do if I know my children can turn to you."

"If that is what you wish."

"It is. Thank you, Isabella." She reached in a side drawer and removed a bag of coins. "For Sebastian."

"Thank you."

She handed me a second bag. "And for you."

"I don't want your money."

"Money can buy a lot of food, and you never know who you will have to feed."

She was right. If circumstances continued, there would be more people to hide. "Thank you."

When I left her apartment, I made my way to the church and found Padre Pietro standing in the center of the church, talking to one of the nuns. When he saw me and met my gaze, he seemed to sense my worry and moved away from the nuns. "Are you here for confession, Isabella?"

"Yes, Padre."

I ducked into the confessional and waited until I heard him sit on the other side and open the small window between us. "What can I do for you, my child?" he asked.

Leaning toward the grate between us, I whispered, "I have a new client. She's German."

"Is that so?"

Until today, I had never once whispered a word of gossip about a client. It was one of the reasons I was so highly regarded.

Padre Pietro did not respond, as if he understood his silence would coax out the words.

"My German client has ordered a dress. She wants to impress Hauptmann Dannecker."

"I have heard of him," he said gravely.

"My client believes she'll be here for a long time to come."

"This client speaks Italian?"

"It's not as good as my German."

"How good is your German?"

"Very."

The seat creaked as he leaned forward. "This client will be returning?"

"Yes." I drew in a breath, absorbing the deeper meaning of what I was about to say. "Would you like to be kept informed of our conversations?"

"I would," he said. "I would very much."

"Then I'll return in a couple of days after her fitting. Now I must get home."

"Of course."

My heart beat quickly as I stepped into the sanctuary and studied the faces of those kneeling in prayer, searching for any sign I had been overheard. An old woman, sensing my gaze, looked up at me before returning to her prayers.

My heart racing, I hurried out of the church into the fading light. When I arrived at Signora Fontana's residence, there was a man standing in the alley beside the house. I paused, very aware of the young men hiding in the upstairs apartment. There were many willing to spy for the Fascist police as well as the SS.

As I moved to open the door, he approached me, causing me to grip my purse filled with stolen food and the pouch of coins. "Can I help you?"

He removed his hat. "Signora, I am looking for someone."

Again, I thought about the boys. "Who?"

"A young woman. Her name is Mia Ferraro. She's my sister."

I studied his sharp features closely and saw faint traces of Mia in his face. Whereas she was slight, he was tall, perhaps naturally broad with a thick bone structure and large hands. His suit was well worn, but his tie was straight and his coat buttoned. "You're Riccardo Ferraro."

He bowed slightly, relieved to be recognized. "Yes, yes, I am. And you?"

"Isabella Mancuso. Mia lives here, but I'm not sure if she's home."

He held his hat close to his heart as he stared at my face a beat too long. "Can you check? I will wait outside."

I hurried inside and found Signora Fontana at her stove. "Is Mia home?"

The old woman did not raise her gaze from her pot. "No. I haven't seen her since this morning."

"Riccardo, her brother, is outside."

Signora Fontana muttered a curse under her breath. "So he's not dead."

"It seems so."

"And now he's here for what? He's not contacted Mia in nearly a year." She shook her head. "He should never have left her alone."

"Why haven't I met him?"

"I only met him once shortly after Mia moved into my house. He's charming but a little too arrogant and so certain of himself. Mia clearly looks up to him. Like my husband, God rest his soul, he'll come to a bad end because he believes he's the David to slay all the Goliaths preying on Italy."

"He's with the Resistance?"

"It's not a question to ask a man these days."

Dropping my voice, I asked, "Where are the boys?"

"Sleeping," she said. "They were exhausted."

I opened my purse and gave her the cheese, sausage, and bag of coins. "That should hold them. And the money will buy more food."

She hefted the bag of coins, judging its value by its weight. "Where is this money from?"

"A grateful client. How are the boys?"

She stirred her pot, smiling. "They eat as if there is no tomorrow."

Looking toward the front door, I said quietly, "Make sure they stay upstairs and do not make a sound. I don't know this man beyond what he has said about Mia."

"Mia said he's good and honest, but now I am not so sure I believe her."

I tore off a sausage link.

"What are you doing?"

"If he's with the Resistance, then he'll need more than our prayers."

Signora Fontana shook her head. "You're too generous, Isabella."

I opened the front door, where Riccardo patiently waited. "She's not here."

The expectant glimmer in his gaze faded. "Do you know where I can find her?"

"No."

His fingers tightened around the brim of the hat dangling at his side. "Would you tell Mia that her brother stopped by?"

"Of course."

"Thank you, Signora."

I should have let him go on his way, but there was something about him that I could not leave alone. I handed him the sausage. "You need to eat."

"That is very kind, but no. I'll not take your food."

"You're clearly underfed."

Pride had him lifting his chin. "I'll be fine."

"Ah, there is that word again. *Fine.* It does not mean much to me anymore."

He tossed me a curious sideways glance. "Why is that?"

"It's the word we use when we're not fine but are embarrassed to admit it."

He grunted, and a faint hint of a smile tipped the edges of his lips. "How is it that you know Mia? You're not like my sister."

"We work together." There were plenty of times I had wished I were more like her. I would worry less and have more fun.

A German truck filled with soldiers passed, and both of us immediately stepped into the shadows and waited for them to move along.

"Go home, Isabella."

"Take the sausage, or I'll be greatly offended."

"You don't take no for an answer." Amusement mingled with annoyance.

"That is correct."

"Very well. But just this once," he said. "And one day I will return the favor."

"I'll tell Mia you were here."

"Grazie." And with his word of thanks, he darted into the shadows and was gone.

Catherine Bernard's Bucket List for Nick

~~Hang glide off a Hawaiian volcano~~

~~Climb Mount Kilimanjaro~~

~~Swim in the Aegean Sea~~

~~Visit the northern tip of Scotland and then ferry to Norway~~

~~Toast the sun as it sets on Key West~~

~~Race a car on a NASCAR track~~

~~Eat cake every night~~

Take Zara out to dinner

CHAPTER NINE
NICOLAS

Richmond, Virginia
Sunday, June 6, 9:00 a.m.

"Zara, I'm not taking the old guy from you," Nicolas said. "It wouldn't be fair to him."

"Seriously?" Zara asked.

"Yeah."

As Gus rubbed against him, Nicolas scratched along his spine and then Billy's and Little Sister's. "They look like they're doing well."

"We do okay."

"Catherine and I used to take Gus for long hikes in his younger days." He was not sure if he was proud or saddened that he had spoken his late wife's name with only a slight hesitation. Her death had gashed his heart and left the wound open and weeping. The last time Zara had seen him, he'd been so angry that he could barely speak to anyone.

"We still do our share of hikes, though they're a little shorter," Zara said.

"How's his hip?"

"I give him joint medicine for it daily, so he does well. The rain and cold make it worse, so I've been taking jobs farther south. Thanks for the checks to cover the vet bills. They were really generous, and I haven't spent it all, so I opened an account, and I'm saving it in case they get sick."

"Good. I don't ever want him to go without." He had never thought of Catherine as a job to Zara, but of course that was exactly what she had been. "How is the work going?"

"It's always there."

"Life marches on, and so does death."

"Yeah."

His wife's passing had been the most devastating moment in his life, and here Zara had dealt with a series of deaths in the last two years. And though all endings came with challenges, he had seen how Catherine's death had taken a toll on Zara.

"I'd never planned on needing Zara." Catherine's hair had thinned so much she wore a blue headscarf all the time now. "The plan was for me to beat this cancer and go on with my life. The plan was for it to be an unfortunate blip and then happiness." Her blue headscarf stood in stark contrast to her pale skin, sunken eyes, and thin lips. "This is the first time I've ever failed."

Nicolas wanted to point out that Catherine had lived two years longer than any of the doctors had originally imagined. He wanted to tell her she was brave and inspired anyone who met her, but Zara entered the room carrying the vase of daisies he had brought Catherine.

"Nicolas brought you some lovely flowers," Zara said.

"He does that every couple of days. They're always whisked away before I can see them fade. I suppose he thinks I can't bear to see death."

"He loves you very much."

Catherine met his gaze. "I love him very much." Tears welled in her eyes, and when they spilled, she carefully swiped them away. "I need your help, Zara."

"Nicolas, could you excuse us a moment?" Zara asked.

"Is she all right?" he asked.

"As my nonna always said, a lady likes to keep a few secrets from her husband."

He cleared his throat and stepped out of the room but paused on the other side of the door. He leaned against the wall, the grief pulling him into a crouch.

He was not sure when Catherine had made the bucket list for him or how she had come up with such random ideas, including seeing Zara again. But he was grateful she had done it. It was the last thing they'd shared.

"You're returning to your father's law practice?" Zara asked.

"Where else would I go?"

"You didn't discover any other passions these last two years? Catherine had hoped her list would show you a world beyond the law."

"Which items did you put on the list?" he asked.

"It was all Catherine. I was a sounding board for her. Making the list turned into great fun. We would brainstorm ideas."

"She certainly picked the most challenging."

Zara shook her head. "She knew you liked adventures."

"Did you see the final list?"

"No. That was Catherine's doing."

When Zara smiled, her eyes brightened, and the constant hum of tension straining his muscles eased. She was a lovely woman. Not like Catherine's classic beauty, which was refined and cool. Zara always reminded him of a nomad with her gusto for travel and unwillingness to put down roots.

"Then how do you know what's on it?"

"Did you run with the bulls? Or did you climb Mount Everest? I'd have to say no on the second, because that takes too much time."

"No, neither of those was on the list."

"The general idea was to give you a sampling of the world."

So why see Zara again? "Mission accomplished."

"Then she achieved her goal."

He shook his head. "I'm sorry it's almost over. I liked checking items off the list."

"What was your favorite?"

"I enjoyed and hated something about them all. The people I met were interesting. We were all much the same. Searching. It was a challenge carrying a cake up Mount Kilimanjaro. I had to ration it so I had enough for each night."

"What flavor was it?"

"I paid a local baker to make these little half cakes. They're kind of like a doughnut."

"Clever."

"In your travels, did you find what you were looking for?"

As Nicolas looked at Zara, desire kicked him in the gut. He slid his hands into his pockets, realizing he was treading in dangerous waters. Catherine had sent him to Zara for a reason, but he doubted it was to get laid. "I realized it's time to move on with life."

"And the law firm?"

"Work is life."

"It's part of it," Zara said.

"You've worked nonstop for a few years."

She chuckled in a way that softened the bindings around his heart a little. "Do as I say, not as I do."

"Meaning you'll be looking for a new job soon."

"I'll be here for my grandmother as long as she needs me."

"And then?"

She laughed. "I suppose I'm like you. I'll default to work and keep trudging forward."

"While I'm in town, would you like to grab a bite to eat?"

"I'd love to, but it's kind of hard for me to get away. Nonna's pretty sick, and I don't want to stray far."

"Sure, I get it." The stab of disappointment surprised him. "Mind if I visit again and check in on Gus? It's nice to see him."

"Sure, come back anytime."

A bell rang several times and echoed throughout the house. "Sounds like you're being summoned."

"That would be my grandmother. She'll be curious to see if I've tossed what I pulled from the attic this morning."

He looked around at the collection of odd, broken, and discarded items. "I'll bet she has a story attached to every item in here."

"I know she does."

"You're still not one for hanging on to much."

"No." For some, accumulating everyday collectibles created a sense of security. If physical items could anchor memories or keep them alive longer, he would still be in the house he'd shared with Catherine in Atlanta.

"I've never been a believer in hanging on. It's all baggage for me."

"Be careful what you toss away," he said. "There are times I wish I'd held on to more."

As the bell rang louder and faster, Little Sister rose and whimpered. Gus and Billy chimed in with barks. "They need a walk."

"I'll take them," he said. "I remember the times I used to walk the boys. I think they kept me sane."

She handed him the leashes. "I should return in about twenty minutes."

He hooked the leashes on each collar, and Zara handed him a couple of plastic bags. "We'll take our time as long as it doesn't get too hot. Gus still hate the heat?"

"He does. Thank you."

"My pleasure."

Zara found her grandmother sitting on the side of the bed, straining for the walker intentionally kept out of Nonna's reach so she would not try to walk. "Don't try to stand up by yourself."

"I've been ringing for hours and hours. I thought you left."

"I was in the garage. I'm still cleaning out your attic," Zara said.

Nonna raised a brow, regarding her granddaughter. "Yes, you look like it."

"What do you need? I don't have time for insults right now."

"Very cheeky of you," Nonna said.

"What do you want?"

"I need to freshen my makeup."

Which was code for a bathroom break. "We can do that, and then you can meet a friend of mine. He's walking the dogs now."

"You have a man in your life?" Her astonishment was evident.

"No, and don't sound like it's an impossibility."

Nonna shrugged. "You don't dress to attract a man, so it makes sense you would not have one."

Zara looped a wide cloth safety belt around her grandmother's waist and, gripping it, helped her stand. The trip to the bathroom went easily enough, and fifteen minutes later Nonna had on fresh lipstick. "Now the wheelchair."

"No," Nonna said.

Zara pushed the chair in the room. "Yes."

"It's for old women."

"It's for women who don't want to fall in front of our guest."

"Is he handsome?"

"Yes."

"Very well, but just this once."

Zara locked the brakes and helped Nonna into the chair. Once her feet were on the footrests, Zara unlocked the brakes and wheeled her around. "Not bad. Easier than walking."

"No comment."

Zara pushed the wheelchair through the door leading into the garage. "That was smooth, wasn't it?"

"It was fine."

The sound of her barking horde echoed down the street. Until Little Sister, the boys had been fairly quiet. No longer.

"What is all the noise?" Nonna said.

"My dogs."

"Good Lord," she said. "My neighbors will complain."

"Sorry about that, Nonna, but I'm all they have."

Nonna lifted her gaze to her granddaughter's, and as she stared at her, Zara had the sense she was not seeing her but seeing someone else. "Perhaps neighbors can be overrated."

"I thought you liked your neighbors."

"I enjoy their company, but they're not family, and it's wise not to trust."

"I've never heard you talk like that before," Zara said. "I thought you liked everyone but me."

"I've never been dying before. And it's not the neighbors that are forcing me into this chair and fixing my hair in the most appalling way but you." She spoke with a flourish that would have made any actress proud.

Smiling, Zara patted her grandmother and accepted what sounded like a thank-you.

Nicolas came around the corner with the three dogs pulling. He released the chains, and the dogs ran into the garage toward Zara and Nonna.

"The crew has been returned," Nicolas said.

"Thank you," Zara said. "Nicolas, I would like you to meet my grandmother, Renata Mitchell. Nonna, this is Nicolas Bernard."

Nonna looked up at him, and her eyes brightened with appreciation as she extended her hand.

Nicolas took Nonna's hand and carefully shook. "It's a pleasure to meet you," he said.

"And you as well, Mr. Bernard," Nonna said.

"Please call me Nicolas."

A smile curled her lips as she nodded toward him. "And you may call me Renata."

If Zara had not been watching, she would not have believed her grandmother could still blush.

He grinned. "Looks like Zara has been busy this morning. You have quite the collection of memorabilia here."

Nonna pulled her gaze from him and regarded the collection of boxes and broken bits of this and that. "It's a lifetime."

"Amazing how it gets distilled to the simplest items," he said.

"That's a very wise comment for a man so young," Nonna said.

"I'll take that as a compliment," he said.

Zara moved to a round box covered in satin. "I found this after our morning attic review. I missed it. It's a hatbox, I think."

"Of course," Nonna said.

Zara lifted the top and carefully fished through the brittle tissue paper. "It's a white hat."

Nonna's gaze grew distant. "I wore that on my wedding day."

"Really? How did it end up in the attic?"

"We had to clean out many closets when we did the bathroom renovations twenty years ago. I suppose it was moved and forgotten."

Zara handed her the delicate ivory hat, embellished with small pearls and a layer of netting that draped over the face. "It's lovely."

"I found it in a small shop in Assisi, Italy. When your grandfather proposed, there was no time to plan a big wedding, but a bride wants something special on her wedding day. I saw this in the shop and knew it would be perfect. He bought it for me, and I wore it that afternoon when we went to the church."

"You were engaged and married on the same day?" Zara asked.

"It was Italy, and the war had just ended. After too many years of hardship, we were both ready to get on with the business of living our lives."

"How did you meet Papa? You've never said."

She traced the netting. "At a party."

"You had parties during the war?" Zara asked.

"Life goes on whenever it can," she said.

"Would you like to put the hat on again?" Zara asked.

"I don't think so."

"Why not?" Zara asked. "I'd like to see you wearing it. There are no pictures of your wedding day."

"I'd like to see it." Nicolas's smile was so genuine it was touching.

"If you insist," she said.

"Is it getting too hot out here for you, Nonna?" Zara asked.

"I am in air-conditioning all the time. It's refreshing."

"Let me know if it's too much." Zara took the hat and carefully settled it on her grandmother's white, thinning hair.

"It feels as if it's too low," Nonna said. "I need a mirror."

Zara found the broken makeup mirror that had been Gina's in high school. She held it up, and her grandmother adjusted the hat forward and cocked it slightly to the left. Carefully, she pulled the netting, made brittle by age and heat, over her eyes.

She studied herself with a critical eye, but there were hints of appreciation as well.

"Tell me about your wedding day." Zara realized her grandmother and her life in Italy were shrouded in too many decades and were on the verge of being lost forever. She had never thought much about Nonna's past beyond the day she had moved into this house.

"It was a lovely day in September. The sky was a brilliant blue and the clouds white and plump."

"What was Papa wearing?"

"He was wearing his uniform, of course."

"US Army?" Nicolas asked.

"Yes. By then he was a major, and he moved with the confidence of a man twice his age. Of course, many of us grew up fast in those days." She closed her eyes as she gently fingered the netting brushing her face. "He was such a handsome man. Dark hair, a thick coarse beard that required regular shaving. Not pretty but rugged. At first glance he looked Italian, but he wasn't emotional and didn't allow his feelings to rule him. He guarded his thoughts closely, but he possessed a directness that was very American."

Zara listened as her grandmother's voice grew stronger, as if she had returned to the woman she had been. "I've never heard you talk about him like this."

"It's not easy to remember now that he's gone," she said.

"That I understand," Nicolas said.

"You have lost?" Nonna asked.

"My wife. Two years ago. That's how I know Zara. She was Catherine's nurse."

"My Zara is a good nurse."

"I'll remember that," Zara said.

"It does not mean you're in charge of me," Nonna said.

"Maybe not all the time," Zara said. "But sometimes."

Nonna shrugged. "Is it easier if I allow her to run my life and my death, Nicolas?"

"None of it's easy," he said carefully. "But it's nice to know you aren't doing it alone. That's worth more than I can say."

Nonna lifted the hat from her head, set it in her lap, and smoothed the white flyaway strands of her hair. The flush from her face had faded, and the underlying fatigue that was always there emerged.

"How about I get you to your room?" Zara said.

"I'm fine," Nonna said.

"Remember, I'm the good nurse," she said. "Rest now. And we'll look through memories later."

Nonna looked at Nicolas. "Was she this way with you and Catherine? Always bossing?"

He nodded solemnly. "She was quite the tyrant. I learned Zara Mitchell is not a woman to cross."

"She was like that as a child, you know. Always controlling."

"Not much has changed," he said easily.

"I'll rest for a bit, but, Nicolas, you must promise me you'll return and have tea with us. There might have been a time when I would have left an invitation open ended, but time is not on my side. Shall we say tomorrow morning at eleven?"

"As long as Zara okays it."

"I think tea would be lovely. Maybe we can find another hat for Nonna to wear."

"I have a few hats," she said to Nicolas. "It's a weakness."

He grinned and winked. "Secret's safe with me."

Zara helped Nonna to her bed, set the hat on the dresser so she could see it, and carefully tucked her under the covers. She kissed her on the forehead. "Sleep well."

"You must wear lipstick when Nicolas comes tomorrow."

"Why?"

Even with her eyes closed, Nonna managed to look annoyed. "Zara, there is so much I must teach you. For now, promise to wear lipstick."

"I promise."

Zara found Nicolas still in the garage with the dogs. "Thank you," she said. "That's the happiest I've seen her in a long time."

"Glad I was here." He scratched Billy between the ears. "I'll be in town for a few days. If you change your mind about dinner, let me know. You taught me that the caregivers need a break too."

"That's nice. Thank you. But I doubt I'll be able to get away anytime soon. Nonna is expecting you for tea tomorrow."

If he was disappointed by her refusal, he gave no hint of it. "I'll be here at eleven sharp. What can I bring?"

"Nothing. What I don't have, I'll get my sister, Gina, to scrounge up for me." Assuming she could find and convince her to return.

"Great. See you tomorrow, Zara."

As Zara watched him stride away, she remembered an old ache that had bottled up in her chest when she had seen Nicolas with Catherine. It was a kind of love that touched the hardest of hearts.

As "Stand by Me" played from Zara's phone, Nicolas pulled Catherine's fragile body from the wheelchair. The bright-blue kerchief made her head look larger and disproportionate with her rail-thin body. She leaned her head on his shoulder, and he banded his arms around her body. He held her close, but Zara could see the terrified caution rippling through him. He was afraid of hurting her.

"I won't break," Catherine said.

"You're the toughest person I know," he said.

"I wish I'd been a little tougher," she confessed.

He tightened his hold a fraction, cradled her head, and kissed her on the lips.

Catherine had died three days later. That kind of love came around once in a lifetime. No woman would take Catherine's place.

Every woman who came after would be a pale comparison.

CHAPTER TEN
ISABELLA

Rome, Italy
Friday, October 8, 1943, 6:00 a.m.

When I woke the next morning, my first thought was for Riccardo. The man's uneasy gaze still bothered me. He would not have returned to find Mia if he had not cared for her. He had not inquired about a baby, so he was either being discreet or did not know.

I knocked on Mia's door, and when she did not answer, I opened it and found her bed made. Had I not heard her rise? I was a light sleeper, and I could not remember a day when she'd woken before me. Then it occurred to me that she had not come home last night.

Descending the stairs, I found Signora Fontana in the kitchen, stirring a very large pot of polenta. She was humming and looked as if she had lost ten years of stress. It was the arrival of the boys. They reminded her of her lost sons, as Mia's baby had conjured memories of my infant.

"Did Mia leave early?"

"She must have. I didn't see her this morning. The girl is barely here anymore."

I poured a cup of coffee. It was watery and bitter, but the heat warmed my body. "She has had a lot of work to catch up on at the shop since her summer absence."

Signora Fontana nodded slowly. "It's good to see her growing up and taking responsibility."

"Yes." I kissed the signora on the cheek. "Do not spoil those boys too badly today."

"The poor things are half-starved. They'll love the cheese for breakfast."

"I'll see what else I can find today for them to eat."

She pinched my cheek. "That's a good girl. With the money you gave me, I'll check the black markets for meat."

As I hurried to work, the streets were shrouded in a grayish light and were already filling with Italian and German soldiers as shopkeepers opened their doors along the piazzas. I was careful not to make eye contact with the soldiers, fearful of attracting their attention. Several whistled at me, and some made rather rude suggestions, but I pretended not to understand and quickened my pace.

Relieved to see the familiar red door of Sebastian's salon, I rushed to the side-alley entrance. I discovered the door was locked, so I pulled the bell cord three times, feeling the chime resonating in my chest.

The door came equipped with a small peephole, and I sensed a scrutinizing eye angled close to it on the other side. Straightening my shoulders, I lifted my chin, looking slightly annoyed.

When the door opened to Sebastian, I asked brusquely, "Now you lock me out?"

"I'm taking precautions. I don't want any uninvited guests to surprise us. This city is becoming too dangerous."

"Perhaps that is wise."

"You look like you haven't slept."

"I did not sleep well." Which was the truth. My sleep had been troubled with dreams of bombs, of the boys hidden within our house, Mia's absences, and her troubled brother who had visited.

"Mia again beat you to work."

Perhaps I had been wrong about Mia. Maybe she had slipped out early. "Good."

I darted around him, hurried down the narrow hallway toward the sewing room and the chatter of women. In the sewing room, I passed by each machine, nodding politely to each woman. At the end of the row, I slid on my well-worn smock, which smelled faintly of lye soap. Mia was working at her station, her head bowed as she eased the sleeve of a blue dress under the needle. This was not the time to talk to her about Riccardo or let her know about the additional houseguests. That would wait for our lunch break.

Sebastian brought me a skirt made of thick wool, dyed a deep, rich navy blue. "Frau Brenner's maid dropped it off for her. Frau Brenner believes the hot Italian summer must have shrunk the garment."

"So it needs to be let out."

"Yes."

"Before the war, many women complained of the same problem. No more, thanks to the food shortages. I'll have one of the girls use the measurements I took at her dress fitting."

"The original seams are generous, and I suggest the seamstress steal every quarter inch of fabric she can. Better to make her feel a little too small for the garment."

"Of course."

After waving Maria over, I watched as she laid the skirt out on my table. The process of tearing out the seams was more tedious than I had imagined, but I wanted the girl to go slowly and not make any mistakes. The original seamstress, perhaps the Jewess the frau had mentioned, had constructed the garment with small stitches that did not wish to be dislodged.

Though I moved to the next project, a tea dress for an Italian princess, I kept a watchful eye on Maria. By ten she had the skirt deconstructed and laid out on the table behind me. By our lunch break, she had sewn half the expanded seams back together.

"You look like you had a terrible night's sleep," Mia said.

"Perhaps I was worried about you," I whispered.

"Don't worry about me," she said lightly. "I can take care of myself. Come into the alley, and we can take a break. I have the best cheese and sausage."

Ration cards offered limited quantities of meats and cheeses, if they could be found, so unless she had raided Sebastian's stash as I had, she could have received it only from Hauptmann Brenner.

"I can see your thoughts churning," Mia said as we climbed the stairs to the alley entrance. "There's nothing wrong with a man being generous to a woman he likes."

Outside a warm breeze swirled. I followed her to a bench, and we sat. "Frau Brenner sent her maid to the shop this morning with a skirt," I said. "Do you think she knows about you and her husband?"

She seemed uninterested as she laid the cloth on top of a barrel and unwrapped it. "He says she's the jealous sort."

"She has the right, don't you think?" I snapped.

"It's up to her to keep her husband interested."

"Foolish girl. Do you think this will end well?"

"I don't care how it ends," she said.

"What do you know of Dannecker?"

"Tall, rather vicious looking. Why?"

"Frau Brenner, your lover's wife, is hoping to impress her husband's business associates, who are SS. Do you really think it's wise to get close to a man like that?"

"I am not worried about being wise, Isabella. I want to have fun, and so does he. Don't worry. I'll be fine."

"And what will happen when this war ends? The Americans have taken Naples. Some say they'll be in Rome by January."

"Karl does not think the Allies will win. He's confident the German defenses will hold them off."

"He's SS. He's married," I said. "There is no happy ending."

"He plans to divorce his wife." She opened the muslin cloth, spread it out over the stone bench between us, and arranged the pieces in neat rows. "When he's free, he's going to marry me. He assures me she won't be a problem much longer."

"Frau Brenner does not act like a woman getting a divorce."

"She's very clever," Mia said. "They have not been in love for years."

"How many times have we dressed women who have said the same thing? And how many of their lives have ended in despair?"

"This is different." She chose a piece of cheese and nibbled the edges. "Do not worry about me, Isabella. I know what I'm doing."

"I don't think you do."

"Enough about me."

"Have you seen Aldo again? He watched you closely that night at the café."

"No, I haven't seen him."

"I saw you two arguing the day of the bombing."

She sighed. "He wants what he cannot have. Now do not spoil my lunch with a lecture."

I looked into her brown eyes. "Your brother stopped by the house last night."

Her mild expression hardened. "Riccardo. What did he want?"

"He wanted to see you."

"The time to see me has passed."

"Why? He's your brother."

"We had a falling-out when I told him about the baby. We have not spoken since." She dropped the piece of cheese on the muslin and slowly brushed her fingers clean. "He's the past."

"He will always be your brother."

"I don't want to talk about him anymore. What matters to me now is enjoying what little fun we can." She selected a thick sausage. "Now we must eat before Sebastian calls."

"I'm not hungry."

"Of course you are. I've seen how little you eat. You'll do no one any good if you faint."

I accepted the slice of sausage. It had been weeks since I had eaten meat and was surprised how good it tasted.

We ate in silence for several minutes, and I was amazed at the rich flavors. Karl Brenner, like many of his kind, was enjoying the sweet fruits of the city.

"Can you teach me some German?" Mia asked.

"I speak just a little."

"I thought you were quite fluent. Didn't your father teach you many languages?"

"No, not really." I loved Mia and would do what I could for her, but I did not trust her, given her attachment to the captain. We would have to be very careful with the boys hiding at the signora's house. We had been lucky that Mia had not returned with her lover last night. "My father was."

"What other languages do you speak?"

"A little French and English."

"I don't think there'll be much call for English. Right now, most Romans hate the English and Americans. And it won't be long before they are turned away from Italy's shores."

Given the destruction the Allies were willing to dispense, it seemed they were not ready to give up on Italy.

"You must see Riccardo," I said.

"It's better for us both if we do not." She wiped her hands. "Now I must get back to work."

Mia left the food behind, so I quickly rewrapped it, knowing the boys would gladly eat it. Mia returned to the blue cocktail dress she was hemming, and I checked on Maria's progress. At ten minutes to two, the garment was complete, and I was ironing out the final wrinkles.

"Frau Brenner is here," Sebastian said.

"Is there a problem?" I asked. "She does not have an appointment."

"She has brought a friend, and she would like to introduce you to her. This is good, Isabella. It could be more money for the shop. It's important that we make a good impression. Hurry up."

"I have finished her skirt."

"This is bigger than a skirt," he said quickly. "These women cannot wait. Now go on. Get upstairs."

I hurried up the back staircase, the skirt draped over my arm, and, pausing at the curtains, listened as the women spoke to each other in German.

"It's a pretty city even with the bombing. I love my apartment and would hate to see my view of the Colosseum ruined," Frau Brenner said.

"We live near the Vatican, so we should be fine," another said. "The Americans are soft, which is why we will win."

"I'll feel better when the roundups are complete. Karl won't be gone from home as much, and perhaps we can enjoy the city."

"Stop fretting over the roundups," the second woman said. "And be careful. Your sympathy for the Jews still shows from time to time."

I had no love lost for the Americans. They had killed thousands and left twice as many homeless. However, the Germans posed a greater, longer-lasting problem.

Summoning a smile, I pushed through the curtains. "Ladies," I said in Italian. "Frau Brenner. A pleasure."

Frau Brenner's expression brightened. "Isabella, you look well."

"I am indeed."

"May I introduce Frau Schultz. She has only recently moved to Rome with her husband."

Frau Schultz regarded me with some skepticism, as if judging me as too Italian looking. Hair too dark, skin not ivory white, a figure of curves. "How wonderful," I said in Italian. "What is it I can do for you ladies?"

"I'm hoping that is my skirt and it's ready."

"It is. Would you like to try it on?"

"Yes."

I motioned to the dressing room. As Frau Brenner passed, she moved with more confidence. "When will my dress be ready?"

"The first fitting is Monday as planned."

"Are you personally sewing the dress?"

Frau Schultz sat as Frau Brenner set her purse down and unbuttoned her jacket.

"I am overseeing its construction," I said.

"How many girls do you have here?" Frau Brenner asked.

"Eight. Plus me."

"I hear there is a girl named Mia here," Frau Brenner said.

"Yes."

"I would like to meet her," she said.

The purpose of this visit was not for a skirt or dress but to see Mia. "It can be arranged."

She slid off her skirt. I took it and held up the mended garment so she could step inside. It slid up over her silk slip, and I fastened the button in the back and smoothed the sides over her full hips. "You like?"

"It fits much better," she said.

"Good."

"What do you think, Elke?" she asked.

"Very nice. The workmanship is excellent."

"I told you these girls were talented."

"Frau Schultz would like you to make her a dress," Frau Brenner said in Italian. "And I would like another as well. There's going to be several parties coming up very soon."

"How very exciting. When are these parties?"

"Early November at the German embassy," Frau Brenner said.

As tempted as I was to ask more, to do so could lead to trouble. "Can you come with Frau Brenner on Monday? We will look at new fashions after your fitting."

"So long?" Frau Schultz asked. "I was hoping for today."

"The Romans move at a slower pace," Frau Brenner said in German. "But the wait should be worth it."

"I certainly hope so," Frau Schultz said. "I want a dress no later than November first. My husband has assured me the roundups will be finished by then, and he will have more time for me. Who would have thought there was so much work involved in transporting Jews?"

I smiled blankly, as if their words buzzed past my head like a breeze.

"Now, Mia," Frau Brenner said.

"Of course."

Down the back staircase, I hurried to Mia's station. "She wants to see you."

"Why?"

"Why do you think?" I said.

Mia rose from her machine. "Then I suppose we will meet."

"This is trouble," I said.

"I'll play nice. I swear."

We climbed the stairs together and found the two women standing in the center of the room. Frau Brenner regarded Mia closely. "This is Mia?"

Mia nodded. "Yes."

"She's a pretty little thing," she said.

"She'll be easily forgotten," Frau Schultz said in German. "You have lowered yourself enough. Now we will go."

Frau Brenner stared at Mia a little longer. "He will never divorce me, girl. I know too much, and he knows it."

Mia was silent.

Finally, the women turned and left the store, and we stood, watching the ladies get into the waiting Mercedes. "This is not good," I whispered.

"It'll be fine."

Sebastian rushed into the room. "What is Mia doing up here?"

"The ladies wanted to meet one of the seamstresses," I said.

"But they are returning?" he asked.

"Yes."

"Excellent."

Hours later, when it came time to leave the store, I gathered up my hat and purse as Mia approached. "Are you headed home?"

"Yes. And you?"

"To a nearby apartment. It's a very fancy after-curfew party. There will be wine, and my friend has a record player. Wouldn't you love to dance?"

"Perhaps another night."

Mia regarded me. "I can see there is a young woman trapped inside you, Isabella. She wants to get out and have fun."

"Another time."

"Suit yourself. But I'll tell you all about it in the morning and do my best to make you regret missing the party."

Her cheer prompted a smile. "I am so warned."

The streets were busy, as they always were in Rome. It struck me that there were helmeted Germans everywhere. Their presence was a stark reminder that Italy's former friend now controlled her every move.

I stopped by the church, anxious to tell Padre Pietro what I had heard today, but when I could not find him in his office, I stopped a nun passing in the hallway. "Have you seen the priest?"

"He's out making rounds and will not be available until morning. Can I tell him who wants to see him?"

"Not necessary. I'll return in the morning."

As I walked out on the street past a busy café filled with music and laughter, memories of a happier time came alive. When I was eight, my mother and I had taken the train into the city, hired a car, and ridden to the Hotel Pincio near the Trevi Fountain. Our first night in the city we had dined in a café and then spent several glorious days in the fashionable Via Veneto area, studying the garments in the tiny shop windows. Mama had laughed a lot in those days. Papa had still held his teaching job at the university, and none of us had seen the troubles beyond the horizon.

After losing my Enzo and our child, I was more attuned to the shifting winds. There had been a sudden cooling of the air in Rome, and we were about to be hit with a storm.

As the sun dipped lower and the people on the streets thinned, I made my way to the signora's house. The front door was locked, so I knocked.

The signora opened the door, smiling. "Ah, Isabella. I always worry. You're late."

"I was looking for Padre Pietro."

She took my coat and hung it up. "Confession again?"

"Yes."

"Ah, your soul must be light. Hurry and put your things away. I've heated dinner with the evening's ration of gas. Best to eat while it's still warm."

"I brought food for the boys." I handed her the muslin-wrapped cheese and sausage.

"Their bellies are fed, and they're already to bed. Now you must eat."

Dinner was a simple fare of lentil soup and warm rustic bread. We ate in silence, the flickering light of a bulb swaying gently over our heads. The tension simmering between us was no different than the worry sweeping the residents of Rome.

After supper, we sat in the kitchen, each of us mending garments for the children on the streets. Winter would come soon enough, and many were homeless. "I heard rumors of roundups today," I said.

"That is not good," she said as she hemmed a pant leg.

"No."

"Can you warn that woman you know?" Signora Fontana said.

"I already have."

"And when you deliver these clothes to the ghetto, can you spread the word?"

"I will try. But most don't believe the Germans will harm them. For the most part, the Germans are good customers in their shops and polite."

"Then what more is there to do?"

"I don't know. It doesn't feel like it's enough."

"We do what we can, Isabella." She clipped a piece of thread and held up the small pair of pants. "Did Riccardo show up at the shop?"

"No. Why do you ask?"

"He will return. Men like him only come around when they have good reason."

"Maybe he wants to make peace with her. She said he was angry when she told him about the baby."

"People are rarely as simple as they appear."

CHAPTER ELEVEN

ZARA

Richmond, Virginia
Sunday, June 6, 2:00 p.m.

Nonna slept all afternoon, giving Zara time to pay all the outstanding bills. She then went through every box in the garage, making sure there were no other items that might have been valuable to her grandmother. She was fairly certain the light-up snowman that did not work, the Easter wreath that had faded, and the threadbare yard flags were not that valuable. These items, along with the old artificial Christmas trees, broken chairs, and stacks of magazines from the eighties, were hauled away by a local junk-collection service. She had taken the man's card, promising him there would be more calls in the coming days.

Zara confirmed that Nonna was still sleeping and, after walking the dogs, decided to make another run into the attic. She could at least move around at the top landing and had a space to pull the items closer toward the stairs. This layer of the attic archaeology dig included many of the items that had belonged to Gina and her.

By the time she returned to the kitchen, sweat dripped from her face and puddled between her breasts. She grabbed a soda from the refrigerator and drank greedily. The cool liquid soothed her dry throat, and the sugar replaced some of the electrolytes she had lost.

As Zara sat in her lawn chair in the garage, a red sports car pulled up in front of the house. Gina leaned over and kissed the man behind the wheel. She lingered, said something to him, and then climbed out. As the car drove off, Gina waved goodbye.

Her sister wore a bright-lemon dress with soft-white polka dots. Her short hair was brushed back, and she wore large white Jackie O–style sunglasses. Red heels stood three inches tall, and the straw purse matched the shoes.

Gina tipped her sunglasses forward and peeked over the tops. "Looks like you've been busy."

"Never a dull moment. Who's the dude in the sports car?" Zara asked.

"Jeff."

"Looks like you had a good time." Her sister had a boneless, dewy quality that screamed of great sex.

"I did. Jeff knows his way around—"

Zara held up her hand. "I don't need the details."

"Jealous?"

"You bet. It's been a while since I've been around a man who knows his way around." Hell, *a while* did not cover it. Had it been two or three years?

"If you don't use it, you lose it."

"I hope not." Zara rose from her chair and drank the last of her soda.

"You've made progress."

"I've already had a load taken away. This is round two. If there's anything you want saved, let me know. Otherwise, if it can't be donated, it's off to the dump."

Gina removed her sunglasses, then dangled them between her red manicured fingertips. Heels clicked as she approached an old table painted a bright purple and decorated with sparkles. "Remember the weekend we painted it?"

"The summer of 2004. How could I forget? I was the new kid on the block. Nonna gave me a job because she said I needed a task."

"And she voted me your number one helper. She always believes the best cure for sadness is work." Gina ran her finger over the table.

"We both ended up covered in paint, and Nonna, practical as ever, sprayed us with the garden hose."

"That water was so cold." Gina shook her head. "All I could remember was that I was twenty-four and my grandmother was hosing me down. But you started giggling, and that made it worth it."

"Remember how Nonna laughed at us that day? Said we looked like drowned rats."

Gina cocked her head. "Do you really want to travel to that summer your mother died?"

"I wonder how it would all be different if she hadn't. I'm not sure I'd have made it to college, let alone nursing school. Mom wasn't the most consistent."

"When Dad married her, he had less and less time for me."

"He wasn't around much for Mom or me either."

"I think he's why I never had children. I didn't want to screw them up like my parents did me."

"Everyone, no matter how old, has some complaint about their parents."

"I don't want to waste another minute thinking about it."

"We've never really talked about Dad. I mean, as adults."

"There's not much to say. He was always searching, never content. When he shined his attention on you, there was no better feeling. And when he turned it off, there was nothing worse."

"I remember."

"Not a perfect upbringing, but I've been okay with my life," Gina said. "Not conventional, but that's what makes it interesting."

"Maybe."

"No more armchair psychology. You're here to take care of Nonna and give me a break. No more digging into my past."

"No worries. I've never been a fan of dark and scary places."

"Funny."

"I did find the hat that Nonna wore on her wedding day. She seemed pretty touched by it."

"Really? Who was the maker?"

"No idea. But you should ask her. You two speak in that twin fashion language that I don't understand."

"Are there more clothes in the attic?"

"I don't know. There are large trunks, but there's too much stuff on top of them. I've layers to peel before I can get to them."

"Why is Nonna hell bent on cleaning out the attic?" Gina asked. "She's never cared before."

"There's something up there she wants us to see before she passes."

"Such as?"

"I have no idea."

"Nonna always did like her secrets." Gina's gaze scanned the garage one last time. "Let me know if you find any clothes. I'd be curious to see them."

As her sister slowly rose, Zara noticed the dark circles under her eyes. "And where are you going?"

"To work. I need to check in with my store managers. We're gearing up for a summer clearance sale."

"Already?"

"We're actually behind. By Fourth of July it's moving out the door."

"For the fall fashions."

"Maybe."

"What's that mean?"

Gina was silent for a moment. "I'm thinking about closing the shop."

"I thought you loved it."

"It's a lot to take care of. And it might be time for a change."

"Such as?"

"Your guess is as good as mine," Gina said. "But be prepared for me to be MIA for the next week or so. With you here, I must make hay, as the saying goes."

"You do remember the part about Nonna dying, right? Two weeks is a lot of time for her."

"She and I have bonded a lot over the last couple of years, and now it's your turn. Remember, she asked for you."

"You'll check in here, right?"

"Sure. I'm not heartless. But I'll be busy. If anyone would understand, it's Nonna. She put a lot into that business."

"When was the last time Nonna worked in the shop?"

"The day before Papa died was her last full day."

"That was seven years ago. What's she been doing?"

"Hanging out. Sometimes she has lunch with Mr. Harper. And sometimes Amanda will drive her to the shop, but she never stays long."

"Mr. Harper came by here last night."

"I think he's sweet on her. I think whatever they had goes way back."

"She adored Papa."

Gina shrugged. "A girl can love two men."

CHAPTER TWELVE

ISABELLA

Rome, Italy
Saturday, October 9, 1943, 5:30 a.m.

I rose before dawn, washed my face, and dressed in my white blouse and black suit. I took the stairs down to the second floor and knocked on Mia's door. When I did not hear her quick breathing, I opened it, expecting not to see her. But she lay curled on her side.

"Yes, yes," Mia said. "I am awake."

"We must go to work."

"I know."

On the main level, I discovered Signora Fontana in the kitchen, kneading her daily bread dough.

"Good morning, Signora Fontana."

"Coffee is ready. Get yourself a cup. There's no sugar, and I wonder if we'll ever see cream again."

After pouring a cup, I sipped. It was remarkably strong and bitter. "You found coffee at the black market?"

The old woman grinned. "A luxury, I know, but sometimes one must splurge."

"Can I help you with breakfast?" I asked.

"Sit at the table." She wiped off her hands with a towel, ladled watery oats into a blue bowl, and set it in front of me. I ate, finding the mixture flavored with a touch of honey and a pinch of salt. Another luxury. When I had finished, Signora Fontana took the bowl. "I am going back to the market today. I might be able to get more flour. That will allow me to bake bread for some of the neighborhood children."

"That is very kind of you."

"The money goes fast at today's prices."

"You'll spend it wisely. It's good to know the children will get warm bread."

"I almost forgot. Carlo came by early. Padre Pietro would like to speak to you."

"Of course." I wiped my hands and reached for my purse. "Mia can meet me at the shop. Make sure she does not fall asleep."

"I didn't hear her come in last night."

I slid on my coat and wrapped a blue silk scarf around my neck. "Do you think she saw the boys?"

"If she did, she won't say. She's silly but not cruel."

"I hope you're right."

Out the door, I hurried along the cobbled alley toward the church. As I climbed the side steps, the clock tower chimed six times.

The church's interior was dimly lit with candles and small gas lamps. I drew my scarf over my head, and as I passed in front of the crucifix, I crossed myself and hurried up the side aisle toward the priest's office.

I knocked on the door. "Padre, it's Isabella."

"Just a moment."

Papers rustled, and a curtain drew back before he stepped outside. "You came by last night. Are the boys doing well?"

"Sleeping and eating."

"I'll have someone come for them this afternoon. There's a farm in Tuscany that's willing to take them. Because they're Jewish, it'll be better for them out of the city."

"Signora Fontana will be sad to see them go." I leaned closer. "Padre, if you have connections in the Jewish community, tell them roundups are planned any day. If people are going to escape, it has to be now."

"Have you spoken to Signora Bianco about this?"

"How do you know about her?"

He regarded me in the dim light. "I received a young couple here late last night. Signora Bianco mentioned they should come to me if they needed help."

"It's her grandson and his wife."

"They did not know where you live?"

"No. I thought your church would be easier to find."

"I can house them in the church today, but they cannot stay beyond that. You'll have to hide them."

"Mia is spending more time with a German officer, Hauptmann Karl Brenner. I'm not sure I truly trust her. She came home last night but with luck will not venture upstairs toward the boys' room."

"She's too clever for her own good."

"Since the baby died, she's been running from party to party. I know how grief can change your life." I stood straighter. "Signora Fontana and I will find a way for the Biancos. I'll come for the couple this evening before curfew."

"Given this new development, you understand the consequences for hiding Jews will be more severe."

"So be it."

He stared at me with an intensity that suggested there was another request, but he said nothing. "Go with God."

Out the door I noticed the man across the street immediately. He was turned away from me, but I could see he wore the uniform of the Italian police. When I closed the door behind me, he turned. The uniform had thrown me, but now I could see it was Riccardo. He smiled and crossed the street toward me, his strut sensual and full of confidence.

"I missed you at Signora Fontana's house. She said you came here for confession."

My growing bundle of secrets suddenly grew heavier. "I didn't know you were with the police."

"It's a recent appointment. An army friend had connections."

"Did you see Mia?" I asked.

"Yes, we spoke for several minutes. All is well between us."

That I doubted. "What are you doing here?" Even the simplest questions were dangerous, considering the conversation I had just had with Padre Pietro.

"I came to walk you to work," he said.

I looked around, half expecting to see more police ready to arrest me. When I saw no one, I began walking. He fell in step beside me, as if I had openly accepted his invitation for company. "Why are you here?"

"You were kind to me, and I appreciated it."

Aware that several people had taken note of me with a police officer, I dropped my voice a notch. "This is not necessary."

"I am going to take you to dinner tonight. It's the least I can do."

"Perhaps another night."

"There is a small café I know. I'll meet you at your shop. When will you be finished for the day?"

"I cannot tonight."

"Then perhaps another night."

"Yes, of course." I hoped he would take my yes and leave me be until the Biancos were safely tucked away.

We strolled the road, and I could not shake the feeling that he had another motive. He was either using me to get to Mia, which would have been a relief, or he had heard that Signora Bianco was sending her money and grandson away. The family was worth a fortune, and the Roman officials would not want so much gold and treasure to escape them.

"Mia said you're very talented," he said.

"Did she?"

"She also told me what you did for her child."

"I see."

His face lost the last traces of humor. "We have forgiven each other, as blood does."

"Good."

"I visited the child's grave and saw Padre Pietro." He glanced at me, regarding me closely. "You took a chance forcing the priest's hand."

"I simply do what must be done."

"Which in these times requires risk."

When I saw the red door of Sebastian's, I was relieved to be rid of him. "This is where I work."

"Ah, too soon," he said. "I'll see you again. Maybe tonight. We can walk together, and you can tell me more about your story." He bowed.

"I look forward to it," I lied.

I waited for him to vanish around the corner and then hurried along the alley toward Rene's hair salon several doors down from Sebastian's. Though I had never had the luxury of having my hair done here, many of my clients had in recent weeks.

When I entered, the manager, Giorgio, approached me. In his early fifties, he was a tall, thin man who wore a gray suit with a white shirt and a red tie. He and Sebastian had been close friends for years.

"Isabella?" he said. "What brings you here?"

"I need a bit of acetone. I have a blue ink stain I need to remove."

"Ah, blue is a very persistent color." He moved to a small station, where one of his ladies would soon be doing the nails of a wealthy woman. He plucked one of the vials off the stand and handed it to me. "There seems to be an epidemic of blue stains in the last few weeks."

Though tempted to ask him what he knew, trusting anyone now could cost me my life. "I wouldn't know about that."

Giorgio heard all the secrets in Rome. Just as in the dress shop, women chatted when they had their hair and nails done. "Well, good luck with your stain removal."

"Thank you, Giorgio."

I arrived at Sebastian's minutes after seven. Sebastian stood by the door, waiting for me. "Isabella, Mia has once again beaten you to work. Should I be worried about you?"

"The damage from the bombings delayed me."

"Ah, the bombs. That excuse will not work for me on Monday. Isabella, I have work for you that must be done immediately."

"Always an emergency."

"Rush orders mean more money."

In the sewing room, I hung up my coat and scarf and slid on my clean white smock. As I secured the tie at my waist, Sebastian brought me a black evening dress made of beaded silk. "That dress belongs to Frau Brenner. She's coming for a fitting on Monday. Maria was going to handle it."

"Maria is sick, and the Frau has changed her mind. She wants the dress this afternoon. I told her if she could pay her balance, we could accommodate her."

"This isn't how we do things, Sebastian. There's no way of judging if the dress will fit properly."

"You will see that it does."

I ran my fingers over the fine fabric. "I only took her measurements once. I cannot make guarantees."

"Yes you will. That's why I adore you."

"Very well. I'll get to work."

As he left, Mia walked up to me. She looked thinner, and I could see she had used powder to cover dark circles under her eyes. "The dress is for a party at the German embassy on Monday night."

"Is there a reason for the party?"

"Does there need to be?" Mia shrugged. "And Sebastian is softening the truth as he always does. Maria is not sick. Her husband was shot yesterday. He's expected to live, but the poor fellow is ailing."

"Who shot him?"

"A soldier, I suppose. I don't know."

"Your brother was waiting for me outside the church this morning," I said. "He wants to take me to dinner. I said no, but he won't hear of it."

"He can be very insistent." Mia's voice held a slight hint of bitterness.

"I'll not go with him. I'll make an excuse."

"No, you should go out. If there was ever a woman who needed a man's attention, it's you."

"What does that mean?"

"The virginal Isabella. So chaste."

The way she said it suggested it was wrong. Irritated, I snapped, "My late husband never thought I was that pure when we were alone in bed."

Mia regarded me with surprise. "You were married?"

"It was a long time ago."

"How come I never heard of it?"

"He died on the Albanian front soon after we wed."

Mia regarded me closely. "So you're even better at keeping secrets than I thought. Very wise." She nodded to the dress. "Better get to work."

I barely looked up from my machine over the next few hours. The dress was nearly complete, but what remained was the fine finishing details that would silhouette Frau Brenner's body perfectly. When the lunch bell rang, I watched Mia and the other girls stroll outside as I kept working.

Three hours later, when I came upstairs with the dress, I found Sebastian speaking to Frau Brenner and Frau Schultz. Sebastian summoned me forward, and I entered the room with the dress draped over my arms. "Frau Brenner, Frau Schultz, you, of course, know Isabella."

"And you have finished my dress?" Frau Brenner asked. She motioned toward the dress, as if signals would take care of the language barrier.

"Yes."

"Would you like to try it on?" Sebastian asked in German.

Frau Brenner nodded, and I stepped into the large changing room with her and Frau Schultz. My gaze downcast, I accepted her blouse and skirt and laid both on a chaise to my right.

Wearing just her silk slip, Frau Brenner waited as I lifted the dress and held it while she stepped into it. I pulled it up, and then, as she faced the floor-to-ceiling mirror, I fastened the twenty individually covered buttons.

Frau Brenner regarded the dress with a critical eye, smoothing her hands over the fabric. The garment hugged her full waist and rounded hips exactly as it should.

She turned sideways and glanced at the dress's high back. She frowned.

"Problem?" I asked.

"The dress is lovely. But not quite right. It makes me feel . . . old."

"You look quite respectable," Frau Schultz said.

"But is it the kind of dress that will catch Karl's attention?" Frau Brenner asked. "He has ignored me too long."

"Do not blame him. My Heinrich is the same."

"They are both busy with the pending roundup," Frau Schultz said. "And Karl with his Mia."

"I assure you he's not had time for the girl. I would wager he's already losing interest."

I kept my gaze averted, but my first thought was for the Biancos.

"You're right, of course. Karl is worried the Jews will cause him trouble."

"Once that is cleared up, he'll settle down, and your lives will return to normal. Don't worry. No more families will evade the police," Frau Schultz said. "They'll finally all be swept away."

Frau Brenner regarded her reflection with the wary expression of a woman who understood her husband too well. "So many families."

"Don't be soft again, Greta. Your sympathy will get you in trouble again."

As Frau Brenner smoothed her hand over the fabric, she regarded her reflection before she quickly looked away. "Yes, of course. I'm just moody because the dress does not feel right."

"The party is Monday, Frau Brenner?" I asked in Italian.

"Yes."

I removed scissors from my pocket and carefully raised it to the back's top center seam.

"What are you doing?" Frau Brenner said.

"Nothing that can't be fixed, but I would like to try something," I said in Italian.

"This dress is costing my husband a fortune," she said.

I ran the scissors through the fabric, splitting the dress open to her waist. Either way, Frau Brenner would have to return on Monday morning for another fitting. Perhaps she would have more to say about her husband.

I peeled the seams open, creating a dramatic plunge. "See?"

Frau Brenner looked at me and then into the mirror. "It's striking. You said the back should be more dramatic."

I nodded. "It looks good, no?"

"You have very good instincts, Isabella."

"Every time you move around the room, you'll be noticed," I said.

Her shoulders straightened, as if she was proud of her reflection. "It's rather daring."

"I can put it back as it was," I said.

"No, no." Off the dais, she walked around the room, glancing at her likeness. "This would not do in Munich."

"What shall I do?" I asked.

"Keep the back open. I'll return on Monday morning to pick it up."

"It'll be ready," I said.

"Good. I need a bit of brightness." Frau Brenner dressed, gathered her purse, and donned her red hat. She nodded her thanks and, with Frau Schultz, left the shop.

Barely seconds passed before Sebastian burst into the salon. "That was a daring risk, Isabella. Very dangerous."

It was a dress. A seam. And in light of the true losses this city had and would endure this weekend, it did not feel daring. "She was happy."

"Thank God." He crossed himself and looked toward the heavens. "We want her to spread the word about Sebastian's. Her kind will keep us in business."

Outside, a car horn blared, and a woman screamed. I crossed to the window and saw a crowd gathering around someone who had been struck by a car. "There's been an accident."

I hurried out the door and raced to the growing circle of people. Several women had turned their faces, and the men looked grim.

"Who is it?" I asked.

No one seemed to know, but one man stepped forward and announced he was a doctor. When the crowds parted slightly to make room for him, I saw the woman's face. It was Frau Brenner.

Mia's words returned, and I remembered how she had said the woman would not be a problem much longer.

CHAPTER THIRTEEN
NICOLAS

Richmond, Virginia
Sunday, June 6, 3:30 p.m.

Nicolas drove around the city, trying to calm the restlessness seeing Zara had stirred up. Finally, when he felt settled, he drove to his hotel and parked in the lot. He didn't get out right away but listened to a ZZ Top song and out of his pocket fished the crumpled paper that detailed Catherine's bucket list. As he traced her handwriting with his finger, he remembered she had written the list shortly after the doctors had suspended chemo in May 2019, but she had not given it to him until July, a few days before she'd died.

Two years ago, he could have smelled her perfumed scent on the ivory paper, and if he'd closed his eyes, he could have pictured her sitting right next to him.

"Why're you looking so serious?" she would tease.

"You know me. I worry about all the details."

"It's all going to work out." She traced his jawline with her finger. "Don't worry."

But now when he studied the list and raised it to his nose, he did not see Catherine or hear her. All the images he now recalled were not from memory but from pictures. She was drifting away. He had lost her once to cancer, and now time was stealing her memory.

He had meticulously worked his way through her list in the requested order. It had cost him a damn fortune in flights, and some trips had required days of travel time. She had sent him on crazy, too-damn-expensive excursions that he would never in his life have attempted if she had not asked.

He traced Zara's name, wondering when Catherine had added this last tidbit. "Why did she save you for last?"

He had asked Zara out for dinner, but she had refused him, so technically he had accomplished his task. Though technicalities were good enough for a court of law, they would not have flown with Catherine. Asking was not the same as doing, and the last box to check would not happen until he and Zara broke bread in some fashion. He dropped his head against the headrest. "Shit, Catherine. I need to move on, but I'm stuck."

His phone rang. "Dad."

"Where are you?" The old man's voice grew gruff when he was worried.

"I'm in Richmond."

"What are you doing there, son?"

"Catching up with a friend."

"You have a job interview here in three days. You haven't forgotten, have you?"

The interview was with his father's law partner, who ran the firm's day-to-day operations now. The plan had been for Nicolas to take over the firm, but when Catherine had died, Nicolas had quit his job, cashed out his investments, and started traveling. His old man had not said much initially, but when he'd come home for that first Christmas, both his parents had suggested he settle. With only one item completed on the list, he could not stop. So they had given him a pass for another year.

Now the gloves were off, and both his folks were pressing him toward a normal existence.

Only he was not sure what normal was or if he cared about practicing law. But out of respect for his father, he had agreed. "I'll be there."

"Your mother had your suit cleaned. And my barber said he'd see you at a moment's notice."

He stabbed his fingers through his long hair. His parents loved him, and they wanted their boy back. They wanted their normal again.

"Thanks, Dad. I'll be there."

"When will you be home?"

"It'll be a couple of days."

"That's cutting it close."

"It's only a two-hour drive."

Silence echoed over the line. "Catherine wouldn't want you drifting like this."

But she had wanted him to wander. That was the purpose of the list. "I'm getting the last of it out of my system. Don't worry, Dad. I'm not the crazed man I was two years ago."

"Call me if you need anything."

"I will."

"I love you, son."

"I love you, too, Dad." He ended the call, entered the hotel, and rode the elevator to the ninth floor. Walking to the picture window, he looked out toward the still waters of the James River. A kayaker slowly passed, and as much as he wished he were on that river now, he could not outrun his life anymore.

He looked at Zara's name on the list. Images of her sweat-stained shirt clinging to her breasts and the wild curls framing her face made him hard. His attraction surprised him because he had never thought of her this way.

He had weathered the loss of his wife, endured the worst of that horrific storm, and in some way, shape, or form had survived. And without the fear of crushing pain, there was now room for desire. He just hadn't expected to feel it when Zara had bent over to pick up a random piece of junk in the garage.

"Shit, you're going to hell, Nicolas. Catherine didn't send you here to screw Zara. She sent you here to say thank you."

He carefully folded the paper up and tucked it in his pocket. He was having tea with Zara and her grandmother tomorrow. That technically was breaking bread. But it was not a legit dinner.

Besides, they were dining with Nonna. Which really wasn't bad at all. He liked the old woman. She was nobody's fool, and like him, she understood the kind of loss that changed your life forever.

Nicolas braced for the sadness, expecting a right hook, but this time it did not sucker punch him.

As he turned from the window, he started whistling. And for the first time he was looking forward to tomorrow.

CHAPTER FOURTEEN

ISABELLA

Rome, Italy
Saturday, October 9, 1943, 5:00 p.m.

I left the shop at twilight. The sun had already dipped below the distant hills, and the few working streetlamps flickered on. I assumed Riccardo had found himself a more willing woman. To my surprise, I was disappointed. I had enjoyed his dark, sensual stare. Not since Enzo had a man really looked at me as if I mattered.

On our wedding night Enzo had kissed me with such raw passion my body had radiated with hope and joy. We'd had two blissful days together in a mountain cottage near Assisi, and then the war had taken him, and he was gone. When I'd learned of the baby, my reason to continue had revived. And then God had taken her, and I'd been left with only work and duty.

Holding a bundle filled with sausage and cheese I had taken from the storeroom, I continued along the main street, careful to avoid the soldiers. As I rounded the final corner near the church, Riccardo was there waiting. He leaned against a stone wall, a cigarette in his hand. He took one last drag, dropped it, and ground out the embers with his shoe. "Isabella, you look lovely."

"I cannot have dinner with you tonight." Heat warmed my face, and I sounded a little breathless.

"I could not resist seeing you." He grinned, even white teeth flashing, as he moved toward me. "Working late making dresses for the German ladies?"

"I don't discuss my clients." My pace quickened.

"I bet you hear a lot of gossip from the fine ladies of Rome."

"What are you fishing for?" I asked.

His laugh was deep and throaty. "You're so serious, Isabella. I'm simply trying to make conversation."

"I have nothing to say tonight."

He took my arm in his hand and gently pulled me into the growing shadows of an alley. "I like you, Isabella. You're kind. And quite lovely in your own way."

His intensity diluted my annoyance. "I must go. I really do have to get home tonight."

"I understand. You take responsibility very seriously. I like that about you." He leaned a little closer, and the smell of his tobacco, clinging to his jacket, mingled with his own scent. "I want to kiss you."

"I have to go."

"One kiss, and I'll release you tonight."

"I don't know you."

"Of course you do." His face was merely inches from mine, and his warm breath brushed my skin.

God would strike me down as a liar if I said I did not want him to kiss me. I had enjoyed kissing Enzo very much, but there was something dangerous and exciting about Riccardo.

I did not speak or move, and he took that as consent. He leaned in and pressed his lips to mine. The sensations that swirled through me set my body ablaze. My hand came up to his chest as he pressed me closer to the stone wall. He was pure fire, anticipation condensed to its essence, and I feared he was as dangerous as Signora Fontana had warned.

But as his lips pressed harder against mine, I forgot about the world around me, and for a moment, I was a young girl again without a care in the world.

A slight smile curled Riccardo's lips, and he made no effort to distance himself. "You'd better get going, Isabella. Responsibility awaits."

Padre Pietro, Signora Bianco's grandson, and her granddaughter-in-law were waiting for me. "I must go."

"Hurry on, then."

He retreated a fraction, allowing me to slide my body along the wall, my breasts brushing his chest as I put distance between us.

"I'll see you again, Isabella," he said. "We'll have that dinner."

"That's rather forward."

"It's war. Nothing is guaranteed, so we should have fun while we can."

"Perhaps."

His grin widened, and when we reached the street, he strode away, arrogant and so self-assured. So like my Enzo it warmed my heart.

I arrived at the church as agreed upon and found Padre Pietro waiting for me in his office. He removed his glasses and rubbed the bridge of his nose. "Isabella, I worried you were not coming."

"I was forced to work late," I lied. "The roundups are going to be this weekend, I think."

"How do you know this?" the priest asked.

"Two women in the shop spoke about it today. And I can assure you it was not idle gossip. Can you speak with someone and send out another notice?"

His frown deepened. "I have already done so. Many heeded my warning but not all. Now we must get your couple into hiding." He opened a side door that led to a small sitting room.

The moment the door opened, the young man and woman rose. The young man looked very much like his grandmother. He had olive skin, a true Roman nose, and a strong jaw. His dark eyes were leery. The woman was petite, and she had light-brown hair with porcelain skin. She stood close to her husband, her fingers intertwining in his.

"This is Isabella," Padre Pietro said. "She'll take you to a safe space. And I will arrange transport out of the city as soon as I can."

"You're the woman my grandmother mentioned," the man said.

"You must be Edoardo, no?" I asked. "And your bride is Eva?"

Hearing their names did not set them at ease. "That is correct."

"Your grandmother told me much about you," I said. I knew the young man's parents had died when he was a child and his grandmother had raised him. "I hope your wedding was all that you dreamed of."

Eva nodded. "And the signora looked radiant."

"Where is she?" I asked. "She should be with you."

"She won't come," Edoardo said. "We sent word again today, but no matter how much I've begged, she refuses to leave her memories in her apartment."

"She won't be allowed to stay there long," I said. "The climate in the city is changing fast. There's talk now of roundups soon."

"We begged her," Eva said.

"She can be stubborn," I said.

"Where are we going?" Eva asked.

"To the house of a friend. There's a room on the third floor. It's small, but you can hide there until Padre Pietro arranges transport out of the city. Do you know where you'll be going?"

"We have friends in Switzerland," Edoardo said. "But there's a problem with our papers."

"Your grandmother mentioned there might be."

He opened his identification card, and stamped across the bottom was the letter *J* in blue ink. "The authorities will know immediately we're Jewish."

I took the papers and traced my finger over the faint letter. It looked as if the administrator stamping it had not been wholly committed. "Leave your papers to me," I said. "I might be able to alter them."

"They are both stamped with *J*," Edoardo said.

"There's a little trick I learned about removing ink stains. I think if it works with fabric, it might work with paper."

"You all must go now," Padre Pietro said. "The longer you linger, the more likely someone is to notice."

"Of course." I guided the couple outside, and we wove through the alleys to Signora Fontana's house. I knocked on the door, and Signora Fontana opened it immediately, broom in hand and a white apron wrapped around her round body.

"Who are these people, Isabella?" she asked.

"Friends of Padre Pietro," I said. "They'll be here only a few weeks."

She regarded them closely. "Of course."

"Where are the boys?" I asked.

"Padre Pietro sent a man this morning to take Marco and Gino to the country. It is safer." Her disappointment was palpable.

"He did tell me," I said. "I forgot to tell you."

"He knows best, of course." She looked at the couple. "Come with me. Once you're settled, I'll bring you up soup."

"Thank you," Eva said.

Signora Fontana waved away her comment.

We climbed the stairs to the room by the attic, where there were two cots covered in quilts. "Signora uses the room for the occasional visitor coming to Rome for holiday. It's not fancy but serviceable. There is also a false panel in the wall here." I pressed, and the wall shifted. "The space is not large but enough for two people, if necessary."

"Do you think it'll come to that in Rome?" Edoardo asked.

"I believe it might," I said.

Edoardo's frown deepened, but for his wife's sake he drew back his shoulders. "Thank you."

"Get some sleep, eat, and I'll work on the rest."

CHAPTER FIFTEEN
ZARA

Richmond, Virginia
Monday, June 7, 8:45 a.m.

Gina popped in for a half hour in the morning, sipping tea, chatting, and leaving Zara to feed and bathe Nonna. After Amanda arrived, Zara took her dogs for a long morning walk and then geared herself up for the early-morning attic expedition.

"Your grandmother is glad to have you here," Amanda said as she unloaded the dishwasher.

Zara raised her coffee cup to her lips as she stared toward the attic stairs. "How can you tell?"

"She's been in such a good mood."

"This is a good mood?" Zara asked.

"She's been really fretful the last few weeks. I've asked her over and over what's bothering her, but she won't say. She's barely come out of her room. But you're here, and she's her normal feisty self."

"Do you think she's been worried about her latest medical report?" Zara asked.

"Could be. But she's not been fretful about dying since your granddaddy passed."

"Maybe she'll tell me."

"I hope so. I like your grandmother a lot. She's always been good to me, and I want to see her happy."

"Well, if I'm going to keep her happy, I need to get into that attic. That junk isn't going to clear itself out."

Zara drank the last of her coffee and climbed up the stairs to the attic. This third layer took her past her own childhood, to the days when her mother was younger. Of her two parents, Zara favored her father's appearance the most. They both shared dark curly hair and an olive skin tone. Gina favored her mother and, like Nonna, had blonde curls and pale skin.

She found boxes of clothes that had belonged to Nonna. Each box was carefully marked by the year, and when she peeked inside, she saw that the clothes were wrapped in tissue.

It took seven trips up and down the attic stairs to retrieve boxes that she set in the garage. In the attic, she found a white box that was meticulously labeled: *Anna Mitchell's wedding dress, 1991*.

Her mother had been twenty-two when she had married her father, who had been in his midforties. He had been the dedicated heart surgeon, and she had been the new young administrative assistant. It was a classic tale. Older man, younger woman. Zara had been born eight months after the wedding. Her mother had never claimed the dress after the ceremony, which likely hinted of a marriage that had begun failing almost immediately. Richard and Anna Mitchell had been married only five years.

As Nonna told it, Richard had seen Zara's mother as a pleasant distraction, a bright light in a world of green scrubs, masks, and gloves. However, as much as he'd loved the frivolity Anna had brought to his life, his true love had been his work.

Zara carried the dress to the garage. Curious about the garment she had never seen, she quickly washed her hands and returned to the box with a pair of scissors. Carefully, she unsealed the yellowing tape and pried open the cardboard.

Inside, there was a thick layer of tissue, which she carefully peeled like the petals of a flower. When she reached the soft satin dress slightly yellowed by time, she lifted it and held it up to the light.

Nonna had designed and made the dress in the 1950s glam style of Ava Gardner and Sophia Loren. As Zara studied the dozens of covered buttons that ran up the bodice and the lace-trimmed neckline designed to skim across the chest and shoulders, she could not imagine her mother wearing this. The woman she remembered had worn primarily pink and baby blue, her hair always blown out, curled, and smelling of jasmine shampoo.

Nonna's bell rang, and Zara quickly tucked the dress in the box and carried it with her. Nonna was sitting in her bed, her legs swung over the side. "Do you not hear well? Should we call a doctor and have your ears checked?"

"I hear fine," Zara said. "But you could exercise a bit more patience." She set the box down and helped her stand and settle her hands on the walker.

"At my age, patience is a luxury I cannot afford."

Many of her clients joked about the ticking clock that grew louder and louder each day. She never took the jests at face value but understood it was their way of venting their fears and perhaps trying to convince themselves that they were not worried.

After Nonna's morning bath routine was complete, Zara helped her into a loose-fitting light-blue dress that skimmed her calves. She unraveled her thin white hair.

Nonna regarded the image looking back in the mirror. "Where is Gina? She knows how to do my hair properly."

"She was here early this morning. Drank coffee and promised to return. Apparently, she's preparing for the summer clearance sale at the shop. But I called your hairdresser, and Delores will be here at three."

"My normal time is nine. And Nicolas is coming at eleven. I can't have him see me like this."

"We're basically homebound now, Delores is working you in, and I'll do your hair."

Nonna shook her head. "Can Gina do it?"

"She's not here."

"Then I will make the best of it."

Zara shifted the conversation. "I found several boxes of old dresses in the attic and Mom's wedding dress. I know Gina would love to have them."

"They should all be in perfect condition."

"They are."

Nonna regarded Zara for a long moment, as if, again, she had slipped into the past. "Is she still seeing Jeff?"

"Yeah. What is his story?" Zara brushed out Nonna's thinning white hair until it was smooth.

"He's much like your father. He has given his heart to his work and sees your sister as a pleasant distraction."

"How can you tell by looking at him?"

"Some men are consumed by a hunger no one else can fulfill. This desire is what fuels their soul and gives them a reason to breathe. The woman is merely an object to bed."

"But it wasn't like that with you and Papa, was it?"

"He was a very loyal man. He put his own needs aside for family. But he was very driven."

"You never really explained how you met Papa."

"It was a long time ago." She looked in the mirror past herself to the white box. "I hoped for your father's sake that he had found someone to love. Anna was pleasant enough, whereas Gina's mother, Brenda, was more demanding. I rather liked Brenda and was sad when she passed."

"Were you sad when my mother died?"

"She was young, and it's always a tragedy when the young die. And I was sad for you."

"You didn't like her."

"I hoped having you would help her grow up. But it did not."

"If I close my eyes, I can imagine my mother's perfume and how soft her skin was."

"She wore an Italian perfume on the day she married your father. They had a lovely garden wedding here at the house. Last minute, of course. The gown was a dress I'd already made, and I quickly tailored it for Anna's body."

"Did you know Mom was pregnant with me?"

"No."

"You didn't question the quick wedding?"

"Your father was impulsive." Nonna nodded to her dressing table. "There, the vial with the dove on top. Get it for me."

Zara picked up the bottle and removed the stopper. Inhaling deeply, she closed her eyes and was immediately transported to a sunny afternoon when she was in her mother's lap, sitting in a rocking chair. "I can almost see her." Tears tightened her throat. "Most days I can't remember what she looked like."

"You have pictures."

"A few, but for some reason they never really captured her. But this scent does."

"Keep it."

"Why do you have it?"

"I was the one who introduced your mother to the perfume. I stopped wearing it when your grandfather died."

"This bottle is fairly new."

"I still buy it from time to time. Scents help me remember the better days."

"Mama never seemed settled or content. Neither did Daddy."

"Ultimately, they were not a good match. I hoped for the best, but Gina, even at eleven, saw their problems from the start. I assumed it was because she didn't want such a young stepmother. She bet your papa they'd be split in a year. He did not take the bet."

"Gina is so much like Daddy in temperament," Zara said.

"Yes, they're two peas in the pod."

"In a pod."

Nonna shrugged. "It's a ridiculous saying anyway."

"You and Papa were so steady. Were you ever young and silly?"

"Very much so. But I grew up when your father was born."

"You're being unusually forthcoming."

"I'm trying to fill in all the blanks. It's not always easy to speak of the past." Nonna fingered the lace detailing on the dress. "The hours I put into this gown. The dreams I had for your mother and father. Perhaps it was a bad omen that I altered another woman's dress for her. A more independent woman might have handled your father better, but he wasn't attracted to reasonable women."

"I'm reasonable to a fault. It makes me boring."

"It makes you strong. It makes you the person no one has to worry about because they know you'll be fine. I've found there are few people who are as steady as you and your grandfather."

Zara stared at her grandmother. "Is that a compliment?"

Nonna sniffed. "Don't let it go to your head."

Zara smiled. "What would you like me to do with the dress? I can wrap it up."

"You can keep it."

"I don't see me wearing a dress like this if I ever get married."

"You make it sound like you won't get married."

"I move around so much."

"Then stop moving. There are plenty of patients in Richmond."

She fingered the satin fabric and then let it slip through her fingers. "Tell Gina to sell it in her shop."

"You want to sell it?"

"Perhaps the next bride will find the joy and hope woven into it. How much time did you put into altering this?"

"Fifty hours, if you include the added beadwork." She spoke as if she regretted the lost hours.

"Okay, I'll repackage it for Gina. Maybe she'll wear it one day."

Nonna's face grew sullen. "No, I would rather you girls not wear the dress."

"Why not?"

Nonna raised her brow. "As you said, it's not your style, and Gina would want a different dress."

"What is my style?"

Nonna arched a brow. "At the moment I would say hobo."

"No, seriously. What should I wear? Do you see me in a dress like this?"

"No." She reclined and regarded me. "I see you in simple lines. Perhaps a halter top and an A-line skirt. No veil. But flowers in your hair."

"That might work." Zara laughed. "I never inherited the fashion gene from you or Dad."

"There is still hope for you. Though it'll take work."

"What should the dogs wear at my wedding?" Zara teased.

"Tuxes for the boys, and pink ribbons for the little girl."

"Seriously?"

"They're your family, and you'll want your family with you."

"What will you or Gina wear to my wedding?"

Nonna dropped her gaze and fussed with the folds of her gown. "Isn't Mr. Bernard coming by today? Didn't you say something about taking a shower and putting on lipstick?"

"I'm not so sure he's coming," Zara said.

"Why would he not? He strikes me as a man who keeps his word."

"He's also a very polite man. He was being kind."

"I don't agree. That is why you must bring me my coffee and take a shower. Then Delores will do your hair properly when she arrives, but for now do the best you can."

Zara ran her fingers through her hair. "It's thick and coarse, and I've never been able to do much with it. I blame my Italian heritage."

Nonna shrugged. "Would you rather be balding like me?"

Zara leaned forward and kissed Nonna on her cheek. "I think you're beautiful."

The old woman took Zara's face in her hands, staring into her eyes. "Whenever I look at you, so many memories are stirred."

"What kind of memories?"

"The old days. In Rome. When I was young."

"What memories?"

"Keep digging in the attic, Zara. You might find some."

Thirty minutes later Zara was trying to arrange Nonna's hair. She never could fix it to Nonna's satisfaction, but finally the older woman pushed her hands away and demanded her coffee. Zara, for all her fashion faults, could make a great cup of coffee, and even the old woman could not resist a nod of approval as she sipped from a porcelain cup.

"It's a bit weak, though," Nonna said.

"You don't need a rush of caffeine. It's bad for your heart."

"Before I go to my grave, I'll have one more proper cup of espresso."

"Let's hope that's a long time."

"We must make a pact right now. No more talk of the future. I find it irritating. Today is busy enough."

"Could we talk more about the past?"

She raised the rose-rimmed cup to her lips and paused. "Take your shower, wash your hair, and please shave your legs."

Zara glanced at the bristle on her knees. "It's been a few days."

Nonna raised her hand. "A few days too many."

"I've been pretty busy here."

"That is no excuse. Clean yourself properly and then return to me, and we will find you a lipstick."

CHAPTER SIXTEEN

ZARA

Richmond, Virginia
Monday, June 7, 10:15 a.m.

Zara returned to Nonna's room with clean hair and freshly shaved legs. She had first chosen shorts and a T-shirt, but Nonna had insisted on a dress. The only one Zara had, other than the one she wore to funerals, was a cotton sleeveless frock that skimmed her knees and doubled as a bathing suit cover-up.

"Your sandals are very sensible," Nonna said.

"You don't sound thrilled."

"Don't you own a wedge?" she asked. "Any shoe to elongate your leg?"

"Sorry, no."

"Rome was not fashioned in a day." Nonna selected a light-cranberry lipstick from the collection on her dressing table. "This will suit your skin tone."

Zara applied the lipstick and was pleasantly surprised. "Not bad."

"I've always had an eye for this. Now run your fingers through your hair so you can fluff it up a little. It's all but plastered to your head. Too bad the hairdresser is coming to the house so late. There is a reason I always see her in the mornings."

"The good thing about your old-world directness is that it cuts out the guesswork."

Zara reached for a brush and carefully ran it through Nonna's hair. Using a little hair gel stolen from Gina's room, she worked it into Nonna's hair until the curls fell into place. Not bad, if Zara were to judge.

Nonna regarded her hair and then asked, "Did you make tea?"

No critique of the hairstyle was endorsement enough for her. "Before Amanda left for the grocery store, she set out tea bags and a tin of Italian cookies from the pantry."

"Hardly a king's feast, but it'll have to do."

Zara rolled the wheelchair close to her chair. "Your ride is here."

"I want my walker."

"Today is the day we get serious about using that wheelchair."

"I can walk."

"I feel the tremble in your legs every step you take. You're too much of a fall risk," Zara said.

"I do not intend to fall."

"No one does."

Zara helped Nonna stand, steadied her, and settled her in the wheelchair. "See, that wasn't so bad."

"Such an ugly device."

"Maybe we can decorate it."

"I might set it on fire."

"Funny."

The two reached the kitchen and spent the next half hour chatting as Zara boiled water and set out the cookies on a tray, which Nonna promptly rearranged. At two minutes to eleven, the black Jeep pulled up in front of the house. Zara glanced out the kitchen window, a thrill of excitement running through her.

Nonna arranged her loose-fitting bodice. "Stop gawking out the window. He'll think you're anxious."

Zara turned from the window. "About what?"

Nonna arched a brow. "It's better the boy chases the girl and not the other way around."

"He's not chasing any women anytime soon."

"Even broken hearts must mend eventually."

"But aren't they forever scarred?"

"Scars are where we are most durable."

Zara poured hot water into the teapot as the dogs barked and clamored around her. She had hoped for a moment with him alone before the tea, but the three jumping bundles of fur, who had never been this excited to see her, refused to share him.

She opened the door a crack. "The hordes are about to descend."

He grinned. "Ready."

Gus was the first out the door, rushing to Nicolas as if time did not matter. Nicolas was holding a dozen yellow roses, and he quickly handed those to Zara as he dropped to a knee and allowed the dogs to circle him.

Zara raised the roses to her nose. Their fragrance was as soft as the petals.

When he stood, he said, "Those are for Nonna."

The hit of disappointment surprised her as she handed the bouquet to him. "She'll love them. It's been a long time since a man brought her flowers."

"She's practical and direct, but she strikes me as a woman accustomed to being spoiled."

"That is Nonna."

Zara led him to the kitchen, where Nonna was sitting very straight and smiling. "Mr. Bernard."

"I thought we agreed you'd call me Nicolas."

"Nicolas." When the name glided off her tongue, her faint accent added an exotic air. "Tell me those roses are not for me."

He grinned and handed them to her. "They are."

"And how did you know yellow was my favorite color?"

"You were wearing yellow yesterday."

"Ah, a man who notices the details. That's rare indeed." She sniffed the roses and touched several of the petals. "Zara, would you put these in water?"

"Sure." Zara took the roses as the teakettle whistled. She set the kettle aside and rooted in the cabinet above until she found a crystal vase. She carefully arranged the flowers, filled it with water, and set the arrangement on the table close to her grandmother.

"They're lovely, Nicolas." She extended her hand. "Please sit. Zara will bring us our tea."

Whatever disappointment Zara harbored was pushed aside as she saw the hints of color rise in her grandmother's cheeks. Zara was pleased to recognize faint clues that Nonna still enjoyed the attention of a handsome man.

At Nonna's request, Zara filled the china cups rimmed with red roses with tea and carried the tray to the table.

She served tea and then retrieved the plate of cookies. Sitting across the table, she savored the smile on her grandmother's face.

"You remind me of my late husband," Nonna said.

"And what did he do?" Nicolas asked.

"He ran a law firm. He practiced international law, but before that he was a spy."

Zara's cup paused by her lips. "A spy?"

"Yes. This was all before your father was born."

She thought about the quiet well-read man who washed his car weekly, loved the Sunday paper crossword puzzle, and fell asleep in his chair during the evening news. "Papa was a spook?"

"I don't like that term. He was in intelligence, and he gathered information. He was always a very good listener and knew the right questions to ask to get people to talk." She smiled at Nicolas.

"What about his partner, Mr. Harper?" Zara asked. "Was he a spy too?"

"No. Mr. Harper was never good at secrets," Nonna said. "My husband was a very likable man, as you are, Nicolas. Are you a spy?"

"I'm not a spy," Nicolas said easily.

"And what is it you do?" Nonna tucked a strand of hair behind her ear.

"Corporate law."

"You don't look like a lawyer, and I mean that in the kindest of ways," Nonna said. "I always found my husband's peers rather stuffy."

"No offense taken," Nicolas said.

"How do you like this work you do?" Nonna asked.

"It was lucrative," he said. "I never really thought much about it until my wife died."

"And now?" A keenness sharpened Nonna's gaze in a way Zara had not seen in years. She always had a way of seeing behind expressions and reading an individual's true feelings.

"I'm not that excited about it," he said. "I wonder how I'll spend the rest of my life now that I've finished my late wife's bucket list."

"You appear to be a bright young man. What else would you want to do?"

White teeth flashed. "I don't know."

Nonna sipped her tea and then carefully set the cup in the saucer. "I suspect that you do know what you want. But you refuse to acknowledge it."

He arched a brow. "Really?"

"We all know what we really want. The trick is to strip off all the trappings, shut out the noise, and get to the heart of it. Take Zara, for example."

"Don't pull me into this," Zara said.

And as if she had not spoken: "Zara wants a family. She wants to find a home, settle down, marry, and have children. But she's afraid of that, so she travels around and surrounds herself with dogs."

Color warmed her face. "I like my job."

"I know you do," Nonna said. "But you don't need to travel to do it." Nonna raised a hand, silencing Zara's next comment. "We're not talking about you now, dear; we're talking about Nicolas and what he wants."

"That's the thing, Renata. I don't know what I want," he said. "There's a lot I loved about my old job, but I don't want to get back into the grind."

Zara swirled her tea, glaring at it, wishing it were a strong coffee. "Apparently, I have no clue either."

"Tell me about this list your wife made for you, Nicolas," Nonna said.

"Catherine put the bucket list together one day while she and Zara were waiting for her chemo treatment," Nicolas said.

"Zara, how did you and Catherine choose?" Nonna asked.

"We started brainstorming the wildest ideas. I told her I'd always dreamed of seeing the volcanoes in Hawaii, and she wrote it down. She laughed, said it was outrageous, but she quickly started coming up with suggestions of her own."

Zara remembered that afternoon.

"I've been making a bucket list since I was twelve," Catherine said. "All kinds of crazy adventures. I thought there would be plenty of time, but there isn't."

"What would you like me to do?" Zara asked.

"Which items do you think Nicolas would enjoy the most? We need at least five, maybe ten adventures. I want him to stay very busy the next couple of years."

"I can help you with that."

"Good. Without a list, he'll be working fifteen hours a day at the law practice, and it'll eat him alive."

"I think we came up with a dozen items, and then the nurse came for her."

"There were eight items by the time she finished it," he said.

"I never saw the last draft. I thought whatever she was writing or planning for you was personal, so I didn't pry."

"Was it your idea for me to hang glide off the Hawaiian volcano?"

Zara smiled, shaking her head. "She kept hang gliding?"

"I was sure I was going to die during that one and thought maybe it was Catherine's way of reuniting us." His lips curled at the thought. "I still think about that day."

"Life never feels more real than when we are close to death. This I learned during the war," Nonna said.

"You never talk about the war, Nonna," Zara said.

"I'll bet she has some stories to tell."

Nonna set her cup down. "I do. But perhaps we'll discuss it another day. For now, I must retire and rest. But do not leave, Nicolas. As soon as Zara gets me tucked in my bed, then you two can visit."

Zara pushed Nonna's wheelchair to her room, tugged off her shoes, and helped her into bed. As Zara pulled the covers up, she said, "Nonna, you've stories to tell me about your life in Rome, don't you?"

"Perhaps a few," she said. "Invite that handsome young man of yours back, and maybe I'll share one."

"He's not my young man," she said. "He's a friend who lost the love of his life."

"Again, one love in a lifetime is not enough."

"Are you telling me there was someone before Papa?" Zara fluffed Nonna's pillows and dispensed her meds for the afternoon.

Nonna dutifully took her pills. "Keep working on that attic. There are items I must see before I die."

"If you'll tell me what I'm looking for, it might help."

"It's been so long, and I put it away decades ago because I didn't have the courage to handle it properly."

"What is it?"

Nonna's eyes drifted closed. "Just keep looking. I'll know when you find it."

Zara left her grandmother sleeping and was pleased Nicolas had stayed. He had cleared the dishes and rinsed them out in the sink.

"She's asleep. Thank you. I haven't seen her that engaged in a long time. She might have a crush on you."

He leaned against the counter as he slowly dried his hands with a dish towel. His gold wedding band glinted in the morning light. "I bet back in the day she had the men chasing her. What has she told you about living in Rome?"

"Nothing. She never talked about it. Neither did my grandfather. Whenever they had an issue to discuss they didn't want us to know about, they spoke to each other in Italian."

"Your grandfather was Italian?"

"No, he was born in Virginia, but his family moved to Italy in the early 1930s, and when the depression hit, they decided to stay. They didn't return to the States until 1939, and by then he was fluent in Italian. Spoke it like a native." She shrugged. "I've never been much into family history, so I never really asked many questions. Now that my connection to my grandparents is dissolving, I really need to figure this out."

"It's back to the attic?"

"Either way, it'll have to be cleaned out. And I hope there's more up there that'll spark Nonna's memory."

"I'm available to help," he offered.

"That's very kind but not necessary."

"I think it is. You were there for me when Catherine was sick. I can help you carry a few boxes out of the attic."

"Well, the help would be nice. I cleaned out the light stuff, and now it's the big pieces of furniture and the trunks."

"If brawn is what you need, then I'm your man."

"Thanks, Nicolas. That really is a help."

"What time?"

"Early morning. About eight."

"I'll be here."

"It's going to be hot."

"Heat never scared me." He pushed off the counter, scratched the dogs on their heads, and waved goodbye.

She stood in the kitchen, watching through the window as he climbed in his Jeep and drove off. Gus rose up and looked out the window, wagging his tail slowly.

"He's coming back," she said, walking toward the flowers and then inhaling the scent. "But neither of us can get our hopes up, okay? He's a great guy; he's just not our guy."

By three in the afternoon, the hairdresser had arrived, and Nonna, refreshed from her nap, was ready to have her hair properly done. Delores was in her late forties and sported a thick mane of very blonde hair. She wore rings on all her fingers and a blue T-shirt that read **BLONDE IS BETTER.**

Zara helped Nonna lean over the sink while Delores washed her hair. After, Delores towel dried her hair, and they set her in a kitchen chair.

"Not the most relaxing," Nonna said. "But the beggars cannot choose."

Zara watched as Delores clipped and snipped Nonna's stark-white hair. "In the pictures I've seen of you in your younger days, your hair was always styled."

"I always took good care of myself. A woman's best asset in my day was her looks."

"Not her brains?" Zara asked.

"A smart girl looked her best, and if she was clever, then all the better. I was not so clever as a young woman. I could be impulsive."

"I don't believe that, Renata," Delores said. "You give out the best advice."

"Years of experience," Nonna said. "I was foolish in my early days."

"Who isn't?" Delores asked.

"Zara has never been a silly girl," Nonna said. "An old soul, as her grandfather used to say."

"Gina said I was a stick-in-the-mud."

Nonna shrugged. "She was too distracted to see the value."

Zara waited for a zinger to follow, and when none came, she absorbed the touching compliment.

By the time Delores was finished, Nonna's hair was styled into a lovely twist, held in place by what must have been a can of Aqua Net.

"Now you must rescue Zara's hair," Nonna said.

"I don't need a cut," Zara said.

"When's the last time you cut it?" Delores asked.

"A year."

"Hon, it's time," Delores said. "Have a seat."

While Nonna watched with some satisfaction, Delores combed out Zara's curly hair and studied the ends. "Split ends," she said.

"I keep it in a ponytail most days," Zara said.

"I could cut five inches off, and you'd still have plenty for a ponytail. You'll be amazed at the lighter weight."

"Have at it," Zara said.

Delores clipped quickly, not only trimming the ends but adding a few long layers. By the time she was finished, Zara was rather pleased with the results. "Thanks, Delores. What do you think, Nonna?"

She regarded Zara for a long moment. "Very nice."

Two compliments in one day from Nonna were enough to make her wonder if Jesus was calling her home.

After Delores packed up, Zara paid her and walked her to the door. "Thanks for coming."

"Anytime Renata needs her hair done, you call me. That woman saved me more than once, and I'd do anything for her."

"I will, thanks."

"I feel half-human," Nonna said as she glanced in the mirror, scrutinizing herself with a critical eye.

"You look wonderful. Now we need to go to your doctor's appointment."

"I don't see why. I'm ninety-seven. What could they do for me?"

Zara unlocked the brake on Nonna's wheelchair. "Do you need to powder your nose?"

"No."

"Then here we go."

"A waste of time."

"Think of it as a bonding moment for the two of us."

Out in the garage, she opted to take the Mercedes for Nonna's comfort. Gina had again taken an Uber to work, most likely because she had another date with Jeff tonight.

Twenty minutes later, Zara and her grandmother were sitting in the doctor's office for her scheduled appointment.

"You should have reapplied your lipstick," Nonna said. "You don't look as sickly when you have a little color."

"I put on a clean shirt and showered today. And I had my hair done."

"The shirt was hours ago. And I don't smell a hint of perfume."

"A clean shirt and shower is a win. Hair done is bonus points."

"You must raise your standards, Zara."

"I'd rather talk about when you met Papa. Tell me about Rome during the war," Zara said. "Now that I know Papa was a spy, I'm beyond curious."

Nonna was silent for a long while, and Zara was not sure she would answer. But then, "When I first moved to Rome, it was so lovely. Untouched by the war. Very exciting."

"What year was that?"

"1942. I came to work in a dress shop."

"Really? Which one?"

"It was a small couture shop. I arrived, and the manager tested my skills. He was happy with my work and told me to start the next day."

"Sounds exciting."

"Not really. There were eight of us girls, and we sat in a small room in the basement sewing garments for customers ten hours a day. It could be very tedious. And then there were times when it could be very exciting. The fabrics were finer than any material I had seen in Assisi."

"Assisi? As in Saint Francis of?"

"It's a small town in Umbria, north of Rome."

"What were your parents like?"

Her brow knotted. "Papa could be a hard man, but he was smart. He hated the Fascists, and when he drank too much, he complained about them publicly. It wasn't long before he lost his job and was jailed several times. We had to rely on the farm. Mama taught me the basics of sewing."

"You also spoke English. Wasn't that unusual?"

"My English was very basic until I moved to the United States."

"You didn't have brothers or sisters?"

"Two brothers. They died very young."

"How awful."

"Yes, it was," she said softly.

"How does an educated girl end up sewing clothes?"

Her eyes met mine. "You make it sound as if it were a step down."

"You could read and write and spoke some English. Most of Italy was illiterate at the start of the war."

"It was a legitimate way for a woman to make a living. And it was a reason to stay in Rome. My parents said I could only stay a year, and then I was to return to Assisi and find a proper husband."

"What happened?"

"The war, of course. First the Italian army swept up the men and sent them to fight. And then the Resistance came and took more men. Then the Germans took more for forced labor in the factories. The Americans began bombing Rome. Talk of marriage was forgotten."

"What did you do?"

She shrugged. "Nothing of great consequence, as it turned out. I passed on the occasional secrets to the Allies."

"Nonna, you were a spy too?"

"You make it sound dramatic. I passed on information."

"To who? How do you figure out who wants to hear this kind of intel?"

"There was a man. He was passionate about helping Italy in any way he could."

"What happened to him?"

Nonna raised a brow. "You ask a lot of questions, Zara."

"That's the kind of answer someone gives when they don't want to answer."

"Then perhaps you should accept my hint and not ask."

"You know me. It'll be the only question I ask."

The door to the waiting area opened, and a nurse appeared. She glanced at the file in her hand. "Mrs. Mitchell."

Zara tossed her *People* magazine on the table, stood, and pushed Nonna's wheelchair past the waiting nurse.

The nurse looked at Nonna with appreciation. "I love your hair. Did you just have it done?"

Nonna gently touched her hair. "Yes, I did. Thank you."

Once in the exam room, Nonna removed her top, and Zara helped her slip on a gown. "These are the most lifeless garments. I always feel sicker when I must wear a gown."

"It'll be easier for the doctor to hear your heart."

"And what will he hear? That it's more broken than it was last month. I could save us all a lot of time and confirm that over the phone."

"He might be able to prescribe a medication to make you more comfortable."

"I'm growing tired of the pills."

"If you could do anything in this world, what would it be?"

"Are you making one of your bucket lists for me?"

"It's good for us all to think about what we want."

"What do you want?" Nonna asked.

"I asked you first."

Nonna retied the cotton ribbon fastener on her gown. "There is a church in Rome that I would like to visit."

"What church?"

"The church of Saint Luca," she said. "There's a graveyard there, and I would like to see it again."

"What's special about this graveyard?"

"It's one of the most peaceful places on this earth," she said. "There was a time I thought I would be buried in that small cemetery. But it's not to be the way."

"Is that where you want to be buried?"

"No, your grandfather gave me a country and a life, and I'll forever be grateful. I'll be buried by him, as I've already planned."

"You said you wanted to be cremated. I could take some of your ashes to that little graveyard."

She looked at me with her pointed gaze. "You could do that?"

"Sure. I've never seen Italy."

"Perhaps you could take a small part of me, but leave the bulk here with your grandfather and father."

"Do you really want me to do that?" Zara asked.

"Yes, I think that I do."

"Then I'll figure it out. We can plan it together if you like."

"I would like that."

The door opened, and the doctor entered. She was tall, lean, and in her late thirties. She held out her hand to Nonna. "Mrs. Mitchell. As always, you look stunning."

"I do what I can. Dr. Douglas, this is my granddaughter, Zara Mitchell. She's a nurse practitioner now, and she's caring for me."

Dr. Douglas shook Zara's hand. "Good to meet you. Will Gina be joining us?"

"She's preparing for a big summer sale," Nonna said proudly.

"Good for her. She said at your last appointment she was thinking about closing the shop. I should tell my friends to get by and see her."

"She has a keen eye for clothes. She can dress anyone. Zara, as you can see, is a work in progress."

Zara regarded her clothes. "And here I was impressed that I didn't have stains on my shirt."

"She needs to wear more color," Nonna said.

"At least I'm not wearing scrubs," Zara said.

"Amen." Dr. Douglas gave her a smile, but it dimmed as she glanced at the file likely filled with test results.

"I have my work cut out for me," Nonna said. "Now, Dr. Douglas, tell me how much time I have to make a difference in Zara's life."

"How's your energy holding up?" Dr. Douglas asked.

"It's fine," Nonna said.

"She sleeps about twelve hours a day."

"I take naps from time to time," Nonna said. "Any woman my age who says she doesn't is a liar."

"She's easily winded," Zara added. "She's now using the wheelchair at home."

"The wheelchair is a good idea," Dr. Douglas said. "At almost ninety-eight, you're doing pretty darn well. You might outlive us all."

Zara looked at her grandmother, who suddenly seemed more interested in the flower pattern on her gown. "She's not dying any minute?"

"There's no end date, as far as I know," Dr. Douglas said.

"Well, then if that's all you have to say, we must go," Nonna said. "The good doctor has kindly confirmed that I am old. Let's leave."

"Do we have any new meds to take?" Zara asked.

"Stick with what you have," Dr. Douglas said.

"Pills. So much trouble," Nonna said. "Zara, we must get home, and you need to finish that attic."

Zara helped her grandmother dress and pushed her wheelchair to the car. "You have some explaining to do, Nonna."

"I am too old to explain myself."

Zara helped her grandmother into the front seat and clicked her seat belt in place. She quickly closed the wheelchair and put it in the trunk of the car. Behind the wheel, she started the engine and the air conditioner. "Why the red alert from Gina? If you wanted me home, I'd have come. No need to tell me you were dying."

"I would like to get ice cream," Nonna said. "The place you and Gina and I went when you were so young."

"Ice cream. You're always counting calories. And for you to eat ice cream in the middle of the week tells me you're dying or there's another shoe to drop."

"I have a craving for the strawberry. It reminds me of when I was a little girl."

Zara drove to the ice cream shop and pulled up to the drive-through-window menu. Memories stirred of her sitting under the shop's candy-striped umbrella with her very pristine grandmother eating strawberry ice cream. Her grandmother rarely had much to say. She was a quiet, steady presence that made Zara feel like all her problems would solve themselves.

"We came here a lot that first summer I moved in with you," Zara said.

"I gained seven pounds that summer."

"I'm a little shocked you consumed so many calories. You had more that summer than you have had in your whole life." She pulled up to the speaker and ordered a medium vanilla and a small strawberry shake.

"Creatures of habit."

"Yes." She paid the woman at the window, set both shakes in the cup holders, and pulled into an empty parking spot. She handed Nonna her strawberry shake. "Go on; live a little."

Her grandmother swirled the straw in her shake before she tasted it. "It's sweet."

Zara sucked on her straw. "It's fantastic. These shakes are my weakness."

"They are rather tasty."

"Better than Wasa crackers and cheese?" She took another taste and closed her eyes, as if she were transported to her childhood.

"Wasa crackers have their place."

"What am I looking for in the attic? This isn't about Christmas trees and old rockers."

Nonna settled the shake in the cup holder. "There's a wooden box I need to find."

"How big is it?"

Nonna held up her hands, indicating a box that might be about a foot long.

"What's in it?"

"When you find it, we'll go through it together. And then I'll explain."

"Explain what?"

"Why I keep so many secrets."

"As in present tense."

Nonna was silent for a moment. "I'm old, and yes, I'll die in the near future. But that's the natural course of life."

"What are you saying?" Zara asked.

She stared out the window over the fast-food parking lot. "Gina is the one that's sick."

Zara stopped sucking on her straw. "Gina? Sick how?"

"She has cancer. It's pancreatic cancer. Stage four."

The blood drained from Zara's head, leaving her dizzy. "What?"

"She does not want you to know. She wants to live her life as fully as she can."

"That's a very aggressive form of cancer. How long has she known?"

"I've known a few weeks. But I think she's kept it a secret longer."

Zara leaned against the headrest. "How did you find out?"

"By accident when I overheard her on the phone. She thought I was asleep."

"Why didn't you call me?"

"Gina called you first."

"To say you were dying. She never said a word about herself. Why didn't she tell me the truth?"

"Your sister doesn't want to be babied. She doesn't want to be seen as weak, especially in front of you. She always took care of you."

Zara had met this kind of resistance from patients before. There were five stages of grief, and the first was denial. "She will be weak very soon."

"I see it myself, and I know she must realize it as well. We three don't have much time; that's why finding the box is so important. You and Gina must see it together."

CHAPTER SEVENTEEN

ZARA

Richmond, Virginia
Monday, June 7, 10:00 p.m.

Zara settled Nonna into her bed, walked her dogs, and made herself a cup of coffee. Gina's illness made it impossible for her to think, to read, or to sit for long periods. She used the energy to clear more boxes from the attic, allowing the heat to burn all the thoughts from her mind as she dragged the larger trunks to the edge of the stairs, hoping among them was the small wooden box. Zara found only old pairs of shoes, purses, small mementos from a trip to Paris in the 1970s, and all manner of junk that had lost its value a long time ago.

Finally, exhausted and soaked in sweat, she showered and changed into clean clothes and walked her dogs again.

When the headlights of a car swiped over the garage, Zara was sitting in her lawn chair by the attic items. She raised a cold beer to her lips and took a long drink.

With her clients she had always suggested balancing honesty with kindness, but right now she prayed she would not cry or scream. She took another pull on her beer.

Gina rose out of the back seat of the car, and when the security lights clicked, they caught the silhouette of her painfully thin figure. How was it that she had not noticed this before? She was a nurse, for God's sake.

"What are you doing up so late?" Gina asked. "I can't remember a time when you weren't in bed by nine."

"I was waiting up for you." Zara raised the beer to her lips and finished the dregs.

"Why? Is Nonna all right?"

"She's doing well. Her doctor was impressed."

"Good." Gina opened a red purse and dropped her keys inside.

Zara tipped her beer toward the empty lawn chair beside her. "Gina, she told me about you."

Gina lowered into the chair. For a moment she barely drew in a breath. "What did she tell you?"

Zara set her beer down. "You have pancreatic cancer." She stared at her sister, praying she would laugh and chalk up their grandmother's story to old age and dementia.

"I didn't think she knew," Gina said. "But I should have known better. Very little gets by that woman. I was going to tell you, but I didn't know how. Then last Saturday she insisted she needed your help, so I called you."

All the hope Zara had pieced together scattered. "So it's true."

Gina fiddled with a shoe charm on her bracelet. "Yes it is."

"How long have you known?"

"A few months at best. The symptoms are managed, but it's a matter of time before the treatment won't work. I'm already losing energy."

Little Sister rose up from her bed and walked to Gina and licked her leg. Gina picked her up, and the dog settled in her lap.

"That guy I saw you with, is he your boyfriend?" Zara asked.

She looked amused. "No. I was hoping mindless sex would make me feel better."

"Did it?"

She shrugged. "It wasn't bad. But to say I saw stars would have been an overstatement."

Zara drew in a breath. She had traveled this road with a dozen clients, but this time she was out of her depth. "Can you still work?"

"Barely. Business had trailed off at the shop this year anyway. My manager has no desire to take over the store, and I can't see you running it, so I let the lease run out. What inventory is not shoved in the spare rooms here was sold. June thirtieth we are closed for good."

"You haven't been going into the shop, then."

"I booked a motel room and slept. I've not done much of that in the last few months, and it felt terrific. I didn't want you or Nonna to know how tired I was."

"You can start sleeping here now. Nonna and I can take care of you here."

"I know you're being kind, but the idea of you and Nonna bossing me feels like the fourth degree of hell."

"How so?"

"I was the one that took care of the problems. I took care of my mother when she was sick, and I took care of you when you arrived on Nonna's doorstep. I looked after Nonna when Papa died." She shook her head. "I was expecting once Nonna went over the rainbow bridge that I would sell the shop. My big plan was to travel. Drink great wine, laugh, and have wonderful sex. I was really going to live a little before I figured out the next chapter. So much for that plan." She looked around the crowded garage. "What's with all this shit?"

"There's something she wants us to see."

"What?"

"A small wooden box somewhere in the attic. I've yet to find it, but it can't take much longer."

"Good. I'm running out of time," Gina quipped. "Don't take too long."

Zara's throat tightened. "I should have the last of it out by tomorrow."

"And then?"

"I don't know."

"I thought you were the one with all the answers."

"Nope, I take it a day at a time like you do."

Gina's blank expression crumpled, and she buried her face in her hands. "I was hoping for more days, Zara. More time. Nonna is almost ninety-eight years old. I'm forty-one, for Christ's sake. That's a fifty-seven-year difference."

Zara rose from her chair and draped her arm around Gina's thin shoulder. "I'll be with you every step of the way."

"I don't want to take this journey. I know there are stages of grief, but I'm stuck in denial with the occasional shift to anger. Acceptance is nowhere near in sight."

Tears welled in Zara's eyes. She had held countless clients as they had wept and begged God for more time. She had cried her share of tears with them. But there had always been a sliver of distance that had allowed her to keep going. Now there was no barrier separating her from the knife edge of pain.

"I'm going to find the box," Zara said.

"And then?"

"We'll find out what Nonna's hiding. And maybe have a party. We can invite George. And a few of the neighbors."

"Nonna's lost interest in her neighbors. But it would be nice to see George again."

"Then I'll make it happen."

"Invite your friend Nicolas," she said finally. "Nonna's rather sweet on him."

"How do you know?"

"She called me and told me so."

Zara brushed away her tears. "I'll even dress up for the party."

Gina's lips tipped into a half smile. "Now I know Jesus is calling me home."

Tears welled in Zara's eyes, but she forced them back and crammed them in a box with her anger and frustration.

CHAPTER EIGHTEEN
ISABELLA

Rome, Italy
Saturday, October 16, 1943, 7:00 p.m.

"Signor Bianco is very angry," Signora Fontana said. "He has worried all week about his grandmother. The wife insists the grandmother is staying so they can escape with their unborn child. Poor thing can only stomach bread, but she's strong and determined to get to Switzerland."

"A child, so soon?" I sat at the kitchen table with the Biancos' identity papers, the acetone, and scraps of muslin. "Of course. These are more modern times."

I opened the first set of papers, which were Edoardo Bianco's. "This trick works on fabric, and I've heard it removes ink from paper."

"How will this work?" the signora said.

"Let us see." I twisted the muslin into a fine point, unscrewed the top of the acetone jar, and dipped the tip inside. Very carefully, I blotted only where the blue stained the page. "We are lucky the clerk didn't stamp over the picture."

"Maybe he hoped someone like you would come along."

"Maybe." I carefully rubbed the blue ink in tiny increments until slowly the letter was gone. While I left the first set of papers out to dry,

I worked on the second. It took an hour, but in the end, both identity cards were passable as long as they were not scrutinized too closely.

The front door opened, and the signora and I quickly hid the papers. As I was closing up the jar, Mia entered the kitchen. She held up a bagful of eggs. "I come bearing gifts."

"What are you doing here?" I asked.

"I live here," she said brightly.

"I thought you lived with Hauptmann Brenner." No effort was made to hide my displeasure.

"He's too busy tonight." She yawned. "It smells like Rene's in here."

"I borrowed some acetone. I have a stain in my white blouse."

"Ah," she said, peering toward the table. "I hope you removed your stain."

"Yes."

She set her eggs on the counter, kissed the signora on the cheek, and left. Listening to her footsteps, I prayed the Biancos were very quiet.

"What will we do with Mia?" the signora whispered.

"There is nothing we can do. We need another two days, and the Biancos will be gone."

"I love that girl, but I don't know if I trust her anymore."

"We'll pray for her silence if she does see something." I kissed her on the cheek. "Go to bed. I'll lock up."

I waited until the signora vanished into her room, and she finally turned off the light. As I climbed the stairs, my legs were wooden and so heavy. Just a couple of days and the young couple would be safely on their way.

I woke to the sound of a fist pounding on the door of the house. After rising from my bed, I rushed to the window and saw the military truck parked in front of the building. The Italian policeman stood at the door as another pounded again. I grabbed my robe and, shrugging it on, hurried to the Biancos' door and rapidly knocked. Edoardo opened it immediately. He stood in his socks but otherwise was dressed. "You must hide behind the wall. Do you remember?"

"Yes," he said.

"It's the police, isn't it?" Eva came to his side, clinging to her husband's arm. "Have they come for us?"

"I don't know," I said, hurrying across the room. "But you must hide." I pressed the panel in the wall, and it opened to the darkened space. "Gather your things."

They had kept all their belongings in their satchels, and it was a matter of picking up their shoes. I quickly made their bed, and when they were in the secret room, I closed the door behind them.

I found Signora Fontana standing in the entryway, staring at her front door. "What do we do?" she asked.

"Let me speak to them."

She stood behind me, her body looking more fragile and thinner in her nightclothes. I unlatched the lock and opened the door a fraction.

Standing on the step were several Italian policemen. The man who took the lead was tall, midtwenties, and broad shouldered. I recognized him from the neighborhood.

"You're Sergio," I said.

Hearing his name softened his stern features a fraction. "Yes."

"How is your mother?" I asked. "Is her back better?"

"Yes." Few Italian men were immune to references to their mothers. "I am not here to talk about that."

"What can I do for you, then?"

His attempt to harden his features did not quite erase the hints of the gentler young man I had seen in church with his mother from time to time. "We are here for the Jews."

"What Jews?"

"The ones living in this house," he said brusquely.

"There's no one here but the signora, Mia, and me."

Sergio pushed past me. "We need to search every room. Stand aside, or you'll be arrested."

His two men hurried up the stairs toward my room on the third floor. "We've received a report that you've been hiding people here."

"Who would spread such gossip?" There were many in Rome who whispered secrets for extra ration cards. "We have hidden no one. We rented a room to a couple, but they have left. Their papers did not indicate they were Jewish."

"What were their names?" Sergio asked.

"Gomez," I lied. "Estella and Mario Gomez."

The two other officers descended the stairs with Mia on their heels. Their faces were flushed, and they looked a little put out. "We didn't find anyone."

Mia wore a thin silk robe that clung to the contours of her supple body. Barefoot, her red-painted toes peeked out from under the gown. "Sergio, is that you? Why on earth are you here?"

"We're carrying out orders," Sergio said. "The Jews are being rounded up in the city tonight."

My heart sank as I thought of the hundreds of police and soldiers banging on doors, waking families who had refused to believe they were in grave danger.

"So why are you here?" Mia asked.

"Some said they saw a couple enter."

Mia rearranged her robe, and in the process, she showed off a sizable portion of her breasts. The action did not go unnoticed by any of the men, especially Sergio. For good measure, she ran her fingers through her hair, arched slightly, and gave them one more glimpse. "We are alone here, Sergio."

"They are looking for a couple," I said. "I told them they left last week."

"Ah, I remember them. They kept to themselves," Mia said. "Whoever was here is gone, but if you insist on making this an issue, I can contact my good friend Hauptmann Karl Brenner and see what he has to say about it."

The policemen looked at each other, and, judging by their frowns, they recognized the name. "If you harbor any Jews, you'll be arrested."

The three of us stood silent, doing our best to look dazed and confused.

When they left, I closed the door behind them and slid the lock into place. "The roundup has begun."

Mia yawned. "Are there Jews hiding here? I guessed you were up to something when I saw you taking food from Sebastian's storeroom. Does he realize you're feeding runaways and Jews?"

"The food was for me."

Mia grinned. "You never steal for yourself. But you would steal for others. If I had to guess, your stowaways are Signora Bianco, her grandson, and his new bride."

"Why are you here tonight?"

"Does it matter? I helped save your friends. Be grateful it was Sergio and not Dannecker. He would have set fire to this house for sport. And you would be in the Gestapo's Via Tasso prison, a very ugly place." When I didn't answer, she added, "I won't tell Karl. He has bigger problems."

"I need two more days before transport is ready for Edoardo and Eva," I said.

"Where is Signora Bianco?"

"She would not come."

"That is unfortunate," Mia said. "Her apartment will be one of the first raided. They'll strip it bare. I would suggest your guests leave sooner than later, Isabella."

"Why would the police come here?" I asked.

"There are so many spies in this city, Isabella. You cannot trust anyone. Your neighbors aren't your friends, as you now know."

"But Signora Bianco . . . ," I said.

"You tried to help her, and now that time has passed. You did what she wanted. You've shielded her grandson."

"It's not enough."

"It'll have to be enough," Mia said. "If you go now looking for her after curfew, you'll be arrested."

"I'm not afraid of jail."

"You need to be afraid of it, because they'll make you confess to everything by the time they've finished with you. The Germans do not waste their breath with pretty pleases."

"And what of your lover Karl? Why do you continue to see him?"

"For now, he's very useful."

"What does that mean?" I demanded. "You're playing a very dangerous game with that man. I saw his wife struck by a car in front of our shop."

Mia's frown deepened. "When?"

"Today. Didn't you tell me she wouldn't be much more trouble?"

"Karl said he was sending her to Munich. He says she talks too much."

"And he kills her for talking too much?"

"When she drinks, she discusses details of his work. There have been leaks. Suspects escaping the police one time too many."

"If he killed her, what will he do to you if he finds out you were here tonight?"

"Don't worry about me, Isabella. Worry about getting your Jews out of the city."

After spending most of Sunday packing and worrying, at first light on Monday, I was dressed and out the door. Despite Mia's warnings I went to Signora Bianco's apartment. The building was quiet, but at the corner several German soldiers stood guard by an armored truck. Most of the roundups would not have happened here but in the ghetto near the Tiber River. I knocked on the porter's door.

When he finally opened his door, he was dressed in a collarless shirt, suspenders, and black pleated pants encircling his belly. "What is it?"

"I've come to see Signora Bianco."

He shook his head. "She's gone."

"Gone where?"

"They arrived last night and found her dead in her bed. They said sleeping pills."

"Do you believe them?"

"It's not my place to question them. After they took her body away, they spent the rest of the night stripping her apartment bare. They took every stick of furniture, work of art, and even the drapes." He looked past me to a collection of Nazi soldiers marching in a straight line. "You should not be here."

"Did you see them take her body out?"

"I stayed in my rooms and minded my own business. There was nothing I could do."

I curled my fingers into fists, feeling more frustrated than I could have imagined.

"Return to your life," he said. "Forget her. And the others like her."

I left, moving in the direction of Sebastian's, but I had not forgotten the signora, and I would not ever forget her. And I would not look the other way.

When I arrived at the shop, I saw my calendar was fully booked with names such as Mueller, Hoffman, and Wetzel. There were no Italian names.

"They are customers," Sebastian said. "And we are no good to anyone if we do not survive."

I didn't speak.

"You must smile and make the customers happy," he said. "We must survive."

"Of course," I said.

Mia arrived and shrugged off her coat. Her cheeks had a rosy glow, and she looked happy. "You left early this morning."

"I wanted to walk and clear my head."

"We had a bit of drama last night," she said to Sebastian. "Roman police looking for Jews at Signora Fontana's. Of course, there was no one there for them to find."

Sebastian regarded me. "That is good. Now off to help your clients. Appearances matter."

I did as I was told. I smiled, did my work, kept the customers happy, but now I listened more closely as they chatted in German to each other. There was much talk of Saturday night's raids. More Jews had already escaped than they'd anticipated, and many Roman policemen had done a poor job of arresting Jews.

I was the last to leave the sewing room, and as I shrugged on my coat, Sebastian appeared, carrying a cloth sack. "I waited until everyone was gone."

"Why?"

He handed me the satchel. "To give you this. It'll be easier than taking it piecemeal."

I looked in the bag at the sausages and cheeses. "I never took anything for myself."

"I know. Go home, and feed your guests, and if you should have more, take what you need."

My gaze rose to his watery dark eyes. "Thank you."

He tugged at his cuff. "We do what we must."

CHAPTER NINETEEN
ZARA

Richmond, Virginia
Tuesday, June 8, 9:00 a.m.

Gina's doctor's appointment was scheduled for nine in the morning. She had thought she would go alone, but Nonna had insisted on accompanying her, so after walking the dogs, texting Nicolas, and rescheduling his visit for the afternoon, Zara pushed Nonna's wheelchair to the car while Gina trailed slowly behind. Since her confession about her illness, the walls of pretense had crumbled, and her body had seemed to wither overnight.

How had she not seen Gina's illness earlier or heard it in her voice when they'd spoken on the phone? She had been distracted by the illness of her last patient and had not had the energy to peer beyond the surface. Perhaps she simply had not wanted to hear it.

Zara followed Gina, pushing Nonna's wheelchair into the waiting room, which was thankfully empty. As tempted as she was to speak to the receptionist for Gina, she hesitated, allowing her sister as many dignities as life still offered her.

She parked Nonna's wheelchair by a stack of magazines and handed her the latest *People*.

"Who are these people?" Nonna asked, waving her hand over the starlets on the cover. "They look like children."

"They're singers."

"They must not be so good if I have not heard of them," Nonna said as she leafed through the pages. "These women are half-naked. Nothing left to the imagination."

Gina sat beside Zara. "I can go in alone."

"No," Nonna said. "I did not come all this way to see half-naked ladies in *People* magazine. I want to hear your doctor."

"Nonna's right," Zara said. "Like it or not, you need extra sets of ears now."

"I'm aware of my condition," Gina said.

"And now we all will be," Nonna said.

Gina shook her head. "Okay, you can come, but do not make a thing of this."

"A thing?" Zara asked.

"You're dying," Nonna said. "We do not have to make it a thing. It's a thing all unto itself."

When the nurse opened the door, Gina and Zara stood, and Nonna set her magazine aside. The nurse was a young woman with long brown hair tied back into a ponytail. "We normally only let one family member back."

"I can't leave my ninety-eight-year-old grandmother here alone."

"I am not ninety-eight until next month," Nonna said.

"You get the point," Zara said.

The nurse studied them all and finally waved them back. "Just this once."

And so the three Mitchell women walked to the exam room and waited while the nurse weighed Gina, noted she had lost eight pounds, and then escorted them to an exam room. "Change into a dressing gown, but you can keep your underwear on."

"I know the drill," Gina said.

When the door closed, Zara settled Nonna's chair in the room's corner.

Gina pulled off her shirt, revealing her thin torso and the red lace bra. "Basically, I'm a very fit person. It's my pancreas that's going to hell."

It was easy for Zara to treat patients as if they were not sick. She had never known them before their illnesses. But with Gina, she had to concentrate on not crying. "I like your bra."

Gina glanced at the red lace. "Thanks. I love this shade of red. Note the panties match, Zara. Keep that in mind. Always makes a statement when you're pulled together in the places most don't see. Gives you confidence." Gina slid on the white paper gown, which immediately drained the remaining color from her face. Gowns had a way of making the healthiest among us look sick.

Nonna reached in her purse and pulled out two shades of lipstick. "To brighten your face." Gina selected a shade and began to apply. "You too, Zara. You look the sickest of us all."

Zara glanced at her reflection in the stainless steel paper-towel dispenser. "Really?"

"Pick one," Gina said.

To keep the peace, she selected a red and applied it, and when she glanced in the reflection again, she was a little surprised it suited. "Thanks, Nonna."

"We must look our best," she said.

A knock at the door, and when they all said, "Enter," it opened to the nurse practitioner. She was a young woman in her early thirties and wore her hair short. It was hard to see much of her face behind the mask, but her eyes were bright and alert. "Gina, it's good you have your team with you today." She introduced herself to Zara and Nonna. "Debra Winchester."

"I'm Zara Mitchell, and this is our grandmother, Renata Mitchell."

"They wouldn't let me leave home without them," Gina said.

"That's a good thing," Debra said. "You need your family."

"So what's the deal?" Gina adjusted the folds of her gown. "What's the time left on the clock?"

"Let me get your vitals first," Debra said. She listened to Gina's heart, took her blood pressure, and then palpated her belly. "How's the pain?"

"Manageable."

"And the appetite?" Debra asked.

"Fair."

"Can I ask what tests she's had done?" Zara asked.

When Gina nodded, Debra ran through the list. "We're trying to keep the swelling in her belly to a minimum so she will be comfortable."

"It seems to work pretty well," Gina said, adjusting the folds of her gown again. "But the chemo pills make me sick."

"It's the lesser of the two evils." Debra wound her stethoscope around her neck. "The tests confirm that the cancer is spreading."

"How much?" Gina asked.

"It's about thirty percent bigger," Debra said. "And it's migrated to your right lung."

"That's one hell of a jump. I'd hoped the chemo might slow it more," Gina said.

"We knew from the original diagnosis we were going to focus on quality of life. Have you been slowing down?" Debra asked.

"Burning the candle at both ends," Gina said. "I'm trying to squeeze in what I can."

"I can appreciate that," Debra said. "But you have to rest more. Your body needs it."

"Why?" Gina asked. "It's going to be dead pretty soon."

"Will rest halt the progression of the disease?" Nonna asked.

"Not really," Debra said. "But rest will help her feel a little better. She doesn't have the reserves for extra anything, and that'll become more pronounced very soon."

"You never answered Gina's question. How much time?" Nonna asked.

Debra looked shocked by the direct question, and when she glanced at Gina, she simply nodded for her approval to answer. "You know we don't like to talk in time."

Nonna glanced at Zara. "What does that mean?"

"It means they really don't know," Zara said. It also meant Gina did not have much time left on the clock. "I'll make sure she keeps up with her meds and rests."

"She's sitting right here," Gina said.

"I don't mean to talk over you," Zara said.

"Then don't." Then softening her tone, she said, "The downside is I'm going to be spending the summer binge-watching movies. But on the bright side, I won't have to worry about Christmas gifts."

"You could make a bucket list," Zara said.

"Bucket list?" Gina asked. "My bucket has overflowed the last twenty years. I have nothing else I need to do."

"Make one for Zara," Nonna said.

When they both looked at Nonna, she shrugged. "You did it for Catherine and Nicolas. Why can't Gina do one for you? No time like the present."

They were a somber trio when they arrived at Nonna's house. Nonna was exhausted and decided to take a nap, and Gina also looked pale and drawn. However, when Zara returned to the kitchen after putting Nonna to bed, she found her sister pouring a glass of bourbon.

The time for lectures about eating clean were long past for Gina. This was about quality, not quantity.

"I need to run the dogs," Zara said. "Pour one for me."

"Will do."

She took her trio outside, and to her relief they did their business and were ready to return to the air-conditioning. While each lapped water, Zara reached for her glass of bourbon and sipped. "This is smooth."

"It was Papa's. I found it a few months ago. It's thirty years old and never been opened. Seemed a shame to waste."

Zara held up the glass to the light, admiring the play of ambers and golds. "He loved his bourbon."

"There's another dozen bottles like this one in his study. I plan to finish them all off before I go."

Zara pulled out a piece of paper and scribbled *#1*. "Number one on the bucket list: drink bourbon. You see, lists often make themselves."

Gina took a liberal sip. "Do you do bucket lists for all your clients?"

"Those who want one."

"What did they want to do for themselves?"

"For themselves, not that much. My last client was worried about his dog, Little Sister. I wasn't his first choice, but it seems to be working out."

"The runt is better off with you," Gina said. "If I had a dog or a kid, I'd want you to have it."

"Thanks."

"What about Catherine, Nicolas's wife? What was on her list?"

"Mostly travel experiences. She was worried that he would drown himself in work after she died. She didn't want him to become his father and thought seeing the world might open his eyes up to a different life."

"Has it worked?"

"He's interviewing with his father's firm later this week. Looks like he's returning to his old life."

She finished off her glass and poured another. "Did Catherine want anything for herself?"

"Time. But when that was running out fast, she wanted Nicolas to live for them both."

Gina regarded Zara over the rim of her glass. "I could make a list for you?"

Zara sipped her bourbon. "Yeah, you could."

"And would you do it?"

Zara nodded slowly. "For you, yes. Though I'm not doing all the work. You have to participate as well."

Gina raised her finger. "Flip that paper over. We can put your list on the other side."

Zara turned the paper over and wrote the number *one*.

Gina grinned. "Zara will bang Nicolas Bernard."

Her pencil froze. "What?"

Gina grinned, much as she had as a teenager when she and Zara had skipped out on their father's funeral reception to get ice cream. "Come on; you know you want to. Nonna said you blushed around him."

Heat rose in Zara's cheeks, but she blamed it on the bourbon. "I did not."

"Like a ten-year-old schoolgirl. Tell me, have you been practicing kissing on your hand or the bathroom mirror like you did when you were fourteen?"

Zara stared into the depths of her glass. "He's a good-looking man."

"And there's nothing wrong with you wanting him sexually."

"He was in love with his wife. He'll never love another woman."

"We're not talking about marriage and a picket fence. We're talking about good old red-blooded sex. When's the last time you had mind-blowing sex?"

"I don't know."

"You don't know?" Gina glanced at the clock. "It's been less than forty-eight hours for me."

"A few years ago." And *mind blowing* would not be the correct adjective. Pleasant. Comforting. Forgettable.

"No wonder you're so uptight." Gina swirled her bourbon but was not drinking.

"I have a high-stress job," Zara said. "I move around a lot. I have dogs."

"You're on your way to being the dog lady who lives in a van. Please tell me you're still shaving your legs."

"Yeah, of course. I only missed today. And I like the pups."

"So do I, but there has to be balance. We're both out of balance. I have too much fun, and you have none. Somewhere between us is a normal person."

Zara shook her head. "Do either one of us know what normal looks like?"

"I'm not so sure it really exists."

"You're turning into quite the philosopher."

"Dying has a way of focusing life, Zara. You've worked with the dying, but you've never seen it from my side. It's different."

As Zara regarded her sister, anger, frustration, and sorrow mashed up inside her. "You're right. I don't know what it feels like."

"Enough about me. Let's get back to you. I'll go through my contact list and see if we can get you waxed and manicured so Nicolas won't see you as just nurse Zara."

"I had my hair cut."

"No doubt that was Nonna's doing."

"You can dress me up all you want, but Nicolas won't go for it."

"Don't underestimate yourself, Zara. Or me. Or Nonna."

"Any other item you want to add to my bucket list?"

"That should do it for now." Gina rose and poured the remains of her glass down the sink. "Sorry, Papa. I don't have the tolerance I once had."

"I'm sure he'll forgive you," Zara said. "He's probably sorry he saved all that good bourbon and never drank it."

"Finish yours," Gina said.

"I intend to. Are you going to rest?"

"Just for a few minutes."

"I'm cleaning out the last of the attic later this afternoon with Nicolas, and maybe finally I'll find the trunk Nonna wants."

"What trunk?"

"Wooden and about a foot long. That's all I know."

"Well, that's something to look forward to."

"She has more secrets than the two of us put together."

"You know it."

Zara waved to Gina and then sat in the quiet of the house, listening to a clock tick in Papa's study. She sat in the chair, drained the contents of her glass, and then refilled it. Zara thought about the attic, hoping if she cleaned it out, the world would right itself in some way. Maybe if she were organized enough, worked hard enough, or prayed hard enough, it would all correct itself.

And then she realized what she was doing. Like many of her clients, she was striking a bargain with God. I do this; you keep my family alive.

Tears welled and spilled as she drank half the glass, savoring the smooth burn in her throat. She was wholly unprepared to lose the two most important people in her life.

It was not fair. She had lost her parents, her grandfather, and soon her sister and grandmother. "Shit, what the hell am I going to do when they're gone?"

CHAPTER TWENTY
ZARA

Richmond, Virginia
Tuesday June 8, 1:00 p.m.

Zara had walked the pups, fed them, and opened the garage door when Nicolas arrived at precisely one o'clock. He was dressed in a clean brewery T-shirt, shorts, and athletic shoes. He was carrying a bag of doughnuts and two coffees. "I come bearing sustenance."

The dogs barked, hurrying toward him, tails wagging. She accepted the coffee. "Bless you. I could really use an afternoon pick-me-up."

"The doughnuts are the simple glazed kind. I thought about getting you one of the flavored ones but had no idea if you liked chocolate, strawberry, or bacon flavored. You used to bring Catherine and me the cake doughnuts."

"It's hard to be sad around doughnuts," Zara said.

"You're right. I've had three and feel pretty good."

"It's the sugar surging through your system." She selected a doughnut that looked a little fatter than the others and took a bite. "Thanks, I needed this."

"How's it going?"

"It's going." She was enjoying this moment and did not want to talk about Gina. There would be plenty of time for that. For now, she wanted a normal moment or two.

"This is good," she said.

Nicolas pinched off a small piece of doughnut and gave each dog a bite.

"They're going to get fat if you do that," she said.

Nicolas looked at Gus. "What's that, boy? Zara doesn't know what she's saying?"

"She does."

"It's a treat. Let the old guy live a little."

She could detail all the medical reasons why this was a bad idea but let it go. "Ready to tackle the attic?"

"Ready and willing."

"Follow me." She took him down the hallway past her bedroom with the unmade blow-up mattress and a beige bra strung across the pillow. She quickly closed the door.

"Not the first time you've slept on a floor mattress," he said.

She had pulled a twin mattress into Catherine's room during her last few days. "They turned my room into a sewing room, and the floor mattress is as comfortable as the van and way roomier."

She opened the attic door at the end of the hallway and clicked on the lights. "We shouldn't have more than a couple of hours' work left, which is good. This space gives hell a run for its money."

He rubbed his hands together. "If I can climb a mountain, I can work in an attic."

At the top he surveyed the nearly empty space. All that remained were several large dressers and a steamer trunk.

"Let's start with the dressers," he said.

"Will do."

Each grabbed an end of a Queen Anne dresser and tried to lift it but found it unmovable. They removed the drawers, all filled with clothes, shoes, baseball cards, and several boxes of old coins. They carried each to the garage and, when they returned to the dresser, found its weight a bit unwieldy but manageable.

"I'll go first," Nicolas said. "Any time the weight is too much, let me know."

"Will do."

She made it as far as the bottom of the attic steps before she had to stop, shake out her cramped fingers, and catch her breath. They continued down the hallway and then out to the garage. The steamer trunk was more of a challenge, and she had to stop a few times to catch her breath. Nicolas was patient, waiting for her to shake the cramps out of her fingers before they continued to the garage.

It took another forty-five minutes to get the remaining two dressers. By two thirty, they were both covered in sweat, but the attic was empty and the garage full.

Zara dug two cold waters out of the refrigerator. She handed one to Nicolas and kept the second for herself. Both drained their bottles.

"What else do you need?" Sweat beaded his brow, but he barely looked winded.

"Nothing more to do until Nonna sees the trunks and furniture. She has to decide what she wants to keep, which will be all of it; then she'll take a nap, and then I'll have the movers take away most of it."

"You don't want any of it?"

"Most of this goes back to my grandfather's mother. I only met her once, and she was not thrilled with me."

"How do you know that?"

"She asked my grandfather at my dad's funeral why I looked so Italian and then asked if he really believed my father was his child."

He grimaced. "That's really low."

"Papa told me his mother was old and senile. And she confused the past and present. Apparently, she lost a lot of good friends in World War

II on the beaches of Anzio, Italy, and her brother's plane crashed over the Mediterranean Sea."

"That's not your fault."

"That's basically what Papa told his mother. I never saw her again."

"Funerals."

"Tell me about it."

"Nonna lived in Rome during the war, right?" he asked.

"She did, though she doesn't like to talk about it. I'm hoping one of these boxes solves this mystery. She has something to tell us but doesn't have the words."

Nicolas's phone alarm rang. "It's the witching hour for me. I need to shower and get up the road to my father's office for the big interview tomorrow."

"Your father is making you interview?"

"He doesn't want to play favorites."

"I don't believe that. He wants you in that office more than anything."

"He's trying to be cool about it."

"Is it what you want?"

"I've missed the brainwork. And I am excited to get back in the game. The trick this time is not to let the work take over my life."

"You'll figure it out."

"Thanks. And keep me posted on what's in the trunks. I'm very curious now."

"You'll be the first."

She and the pups watched him drive off, and then after another walk with her trio, she filled water bowls for them all. As they lapped water, she stared at the dusty trunks and furniture. This was the last of it, and if Nonna could not find her wooden box, she would expand the search to the closets and spaces under the beds.

As tempted as Zara was to open Nonna's steamer trunk, she opted to wait. They needed to savor all the moments they had left together, and the box was going to be important to them all.

She showered, and then downstairs she rummaged through the refrigerator and found fixings for a minestrone soup. Using the recipe Nonna had showed her dozens of times, she started chopping onions, garlic, and carrots. The kitchen quickly filled with the savory garlic flavors, and when the pot was simmering, she shifted her attention to the pantry and dug out ingredients for bread.

"A dear friend of mine used to make a loaf of bread and a pot of soup daily," Nonna said to twelve-year-old Zara. "She used whatever she could find, but it was always delicious."

Zara mixed yeast, sugar, and salt into the flour and then heated the water in the microwave for twenty seconds.

"Warm, not hot." Nonna was sipping her coffee as she watched Zara combine the ingredients with her hands. "It's all about touch."

"Who taught you to do this?" Zara asked.

"Signora Fontana. A dear friend. Dead many years now."

Zara had been proud when she'd pulled her first, somewhat-flat loaf out of the oven. Both Nonna and Papa had eaten a slice, and her grandfather had assured Zara she was a far better cook than Nonna.

Nonna had simply shrugged. "My talents lie elsewhere."

Papa had grinned slightly, but thinking back, Zara blushed when she considered the implications of the comment.

She turned her sights to deep cleaning the kitchen. After wiping the counters and cabinets, she opened the junk drawer. A purgatory for odd items, it was chock-full of all the odds and ends that were not quite ready for the trash bin.

She emptied the drawer, dumping the contents on the kitchen table. She pulled the trash can over and picked through the pile, throwing out manuals for devices that had not been sold in a decade, old batteries, broken sunglasses, single earrings, and menus for restaurants that had gone out of business years ago.

It was not until she reached the bottom of the pile that she found a photo of Gina, Nonna, Papa, her, and her father. The image had been taken nearly twenty-five years ago, when she had been five and Gina seventeen. She remembered the trip to Washington because it had been a rare moment when they had all been together. Papa was smiling proudly, and his arm was slung around her father's neck. Nonna had a hand on each of her granddaughters' shoulders, and she, too, was grinning. Gina looked bored, and Zara squinted into the sun.

The five of them had driven to Washington, DC, to see Papa receive an award from the government. She recalled her father had pressed Papa for details afterward.

"Dad, it's a big deal," her father said. "It's a citation. You've tracked war criminals."

"It wasn't anything. I'm good with data," he said.

"Sounds like it's out of a spy novel."

Her grandfather laughed. "Nothing like it, son."

Her father skillfully maneuvered the car through the streets of Washington, DC. "Not many men have an award like that."

"What did you do, Papa?" Zara asked.

"Nothing important, honey."

"Zara looks like she could use an ice cream and a trip to the zoo," Nonna said.

"Excellent idea, Zara," Papa said. "What do you all say?"

Gina grinned. "I love the idea."

Her father had not been happy about the change of subject. "You two never answer my questions."

Nothing more had been said, the five of them had gone to the zoo, and if there had been any underlying tension between her father and her grandparents, she had been too young and too fascinated by the hippos to care.

Two weeks later, her father had died in a car accident, and Papa's mysterious award had been forgotten as easily as the questions about Nonna's and Papa's pasts.

She taped the picture on the refrigerator and swept most of the junk-drawer contents into the trash. By the time she was finished, the dough needed shaping. She washed her hands, kneaded the dough, and formed it into a flat focaccia. By the time she pressed dimples into the flat dough and placed it in a warm spot, the dogs required a walk. Little Sister raced to the door with Gus and Billy. It was good to see the three were working as a pack.

"I might be a crazy dog lady," she mumbled to herself as she hooked the leash on Billy's collar. "But there are worse lives to live."

As soon as Zara returned from her walk, Gina strolled into the kitchen. Her coloring was better, and she seemed more alert. "It's been a long time since I smelled homemade soup. It's Nonna's recipe."

"No, it's Signora Fontana's recipe," Zara corrected.

"Who is Signora Fontana?" Gina asked.

"I have no idea. Nonna once said she was the greatest cook in Italy."

Gina dug a tasting spoon from the drawer and sampled the broth. "This tastes great. Thankfully, you have not inherited the Nonna cooking gene."

Zara laughed. "I didn't think we had any of those in the family. Nonna only did it out of necessity."

"She taught you."

"To keep me from crying."

"Maybe. Someone along the way must have been good at it. I certainly am not." Gina filled a small bowl with soup and, after grabbing her spoon, she sat at the table. "Do you cook for your patients?"

"Sure, if they require it. Sometimes there's family around to do it."

"What's the weirdest dish you've made?"

"I had one client who liked ice cream and pickles, and no, he was not pregnant. Another only ate banana cream pies, and another loved this vegetable soup. Whatever gives comfort."

"Keep making this soup for me. And if that bread is as good as it smells, then you'll have a special place in heaven."

"I do try."

Gina paused. "Hey, thanks."

"For the soup?"

"For treating me like me."

Zara found it in her to casually arch a brow. "Who else would you be?"

"Sick invalid girl. I don't want to be her. Even when my body fails me. Or, God forbid, my mind."

"You'll always be you."

"Thanks."

Nonna's bell rang, saving Zara from tears. "The boss calls."

"If I had a nickel for all the times I answered that bell in the last couple of years."

"You should have told me. I would have come home sooner."

"I never minded taking care of Nonna. And I didn't know I was sick until after Christmas. I attributed the fatigue to too much booze. When I did the unthinkable and slowed the drinking and didn't feel better, I went to the doctor."

"You'll feel better if you eat healthy and drink less booze."

"Maybe." As Zara turned to leave the room, Gina said, "I'm still in charge."

"We'll see about that." Her light tone belied the terrible ache in her chest as she found her way to her grandmother's room.

Nonna was sitting up and swinging her legs over the side of the bed. "I thought you left the house. I've been ringing for hours."

"Thirty seconds at best."

Nonna shook her head. "At least five minutes."

Zara helped Nonna into her wheelchair. "I'm here now, and that is all that counts."

"Where is Gina?"

"In the kitchen eating minestrone soup."

"You cooked?"

"Don't look so shocked."

"I thought you forgot."

Zara was starting to understand Nonna's little jabs were an expression of fear as well as appreciation and love. "I did not."

Five minutes later Nonna had powdered her nose, smoothed out her chignon, and applied lipstick. Zara pushed her wheelchair into the kitchen beside Gina.

"So we meet again," Gina said. "How is Nurse Ratchet treating you?"

"She's rather tough at times," Nonna said.

"And bossy," Gina said.

"And right here," Zara added.

Her phone dinged with a text. It was Nicolas Bernard. Sitting a little taller, she carefully read:

Nicolas: Hair officially cut off. Suit picked up from the dry cleaner.

Zara: Knock 'em dead in the interview.

Nicolas: Keep me posted on the garage finds. I've got sweat invested.

Zara: Will do.

Zara slid the phone in her back pocket. "When you ladies are finished, we can open the steamer trunk in the garage."

"What can I do to help?" Gina asked.

"You can sit, comment, and point. I'll do all the heavy lifting."

"I'm not an invalid," Gina said. "I'm capable of helping."

Without her makeup, Gina looked painfully pale, and her eyes were sunken.

"That was the deal. You two watch; I hold up items. Consider me your Vanna White of attic junk."

"Vanna turns letters," Nonna said. "And this is not junk. It's my life."

"You get the point," Zara said.

After they finished their meal, Zara loaded the dishwasher while Gina wiped the table. Ten minutes later Nonna and Gina were sitting in lawn chairs in the garage.

"Ready, ladies?" Zara asked.

"Let's get the show on the road," Nonna said.

"Time's a wasting," Gina remarked.

Zara held up several items, including pictures, chairs, and tables that Nonna said all belonged to Papa's family.

"They never liked me," Nonna said.

"Why is that?" Gina said.

"I was always the Italian girl who appeared out of nowhere with their son and grandson."

"Weren't they excited about their grandson?" Zara remembered the words her great-grandmother had whispered to her grandfather. *"Are you sure Richard is your son?"*

"Not really. He looked too Italian for their tastes."

"That's not cool," Gina said.

"No, it was not. His mother and I nearly came to blows at your father's funeral, but Papa intervened, gave Gina forty dollars and keys to my car, and told her to take Zara for ice cream. I would gladly have gone with you girls that day, but I would not disrespect my son by running."

When Zara pushed the trunk closer, Nonna's eyes lit up. "That's my trunk. The one I packed before my trip to America."

"You said I was looking for a wooden chest," Zara said.

"It's inside," Nonna said, leaning forward in her chair.

Zara dragged the trunk across the garage's concrete floor and pried open the lid. She carefully peeled away the brittle tissue paper. On top was a blue dress that was torn and stained.

"What's with the dress?" Zara asked as she laid it in her grandmother's lap.

"I wore that dress the day the Americans entered Rome." She gently touched the light-blue fabric and smoothed her fingers along the frayed collar and skirt marred with dark stains.

"What's the stain?" Zara asked.

"Blood." She smoothed her hands over the fold marks left over the decades. "I never wore it again after that night, but I could not let it go. I could not forget all the people who died."

"Whose blood is it?" Gina asked.

"Find the box," Nonna said.

Zara continued to dig through layers of baby clothes, fabric, threads, and shoes until her fingers brushed the smooth surface of a box. "Is this it?"

"Yes," Nonna said.

"It's locked," Zara said.

"There's a key in the kitchen taped under the drawer by the stove."

"Very James Bond, Nonna," Zara said.

"A need-to-know basis," Nonna said.

Zara returned to the kitchen and skimmed her fingers under the drawer until it brushed a metal key. "Looks like you've kept more than a few secrets from us."

She returned to the garage with the key and worked it into the lock, then twisted it until the latch released.

The lid opened to a thin layer of muslin. As Zara lifted the cloth, Gina leaned forward, whereas Nonna sat still, as if afraid of the contents. Zara removed the muslin.

On the top of the pile was a small infant's gown made of a soft cotton and trimmed with embroidered flowers. Meticulous stitches joined the tiny seams.

"Did you make this?" Zara asked as she laid the gown on her grandmother's lap.

"I did. I made it for my firstborn."

"It's beautiful," Gina said as she ran her fingers over the delicate stitching and then handed the gown to Nonna. "A lot of love went into that gown."

Nonna's finger skimmed the yellowing fabric with reverence. "A child always brings the hope for a brighter future."

Zara's gaze went next to a black-and-white picture of a young man. He was dressed in an Italian uniform, had deep-set eyes that peered directly into the camera, and wore a slight smile that hinted he might know a secret no one else did.

"Who is that?" Zara handed the picture to Nonna.

"He's very handsome," Gina said.

"That is Riccardo," she said softly as she traced the line of his lips and then his eyes with a bent finger.

Gina looked at Zara, her eyes bright with curiosity. "He looks a lot like Daddy."

CHAPTER TWENTY-ONE
ISABELLA

Rome, Italy
Friday, November 5, 1943, 5:00 p.m.

The streets were filled with patrols as police searched for any Jews in hiding. As the days and weeks passed, Edoardo and Eva Bianco kept to themselves and rarely said much to me when I brought them food. Finally, in the first week of November Padre Pietro sent word he had arranged for a car at the church. My job was to guide the couple to a waiting car.

I would have preferred to wait until the sun set, but Padre Pietro said it was too risky. The nighttime patrols had doubled, and anyone caught without a pass would be taken to prison. Our best defense was to travel by day.

I knocked on the Biancos' apartment door. "It's me, Isabella."

On the other side, I heard the heavy dresser being dragged away from the door, a habit Edoardo had developed since the police had shown up at the front door.

When he opened the door, he stood erect, his gaze filled with a mixture of anger, frustration, and fear. Eva stood behind him, her hand on his arm, as if she were ready to fight.

"Take this suitcase, put on the garments inside, and then pack what you're wearing inside the case. I'll return in fifteen minutes, and we'll leave immediately."

Edoardo opened the case and removed a priest's black cassock and a nun's habit. "We are to be a priest and a nun?"

"Yes. There's still respect among some of the Fascist and German soldiers for the clergy, so we must hope they don't look past the vestments." I reached in my pocket and removed their papers. "They're not perfect, but they'll do if no one looks closely."

"What if they do?" Eva asked.

I hoped my slight smile hid my worries. "I don't think they will if you're dressed like holy people."

"I don't know how to put this on," Eva said.

"Put on the tunic, and I'll help you with the cowl," I said.

"Go on, Eva," Edoardo said. "It's a good idea. Who would think to look for Jews dressed as a priest and a nun?"

"Exactly," I said.

"Was there any other word of my grandmother?" Edoardo asked as he shrugged off his jacket.

"No."

"Have you been by the apartment again?" he asked.

"There is a German couple living there now."

His jaw tightened as he unfastened his tie and unbuttoned his shirt. "Thank you for checking."

I faced Eva and took the young woman's garments as I would for a client in the shop. When she removed her shirt, I saw that her belly was indeed rounding nicely. "A tunic hides a great deal."

Eva's hands went to her belly. "I'll die to protect him."

"I know. I would do the same." Threading my hands through the tunic, I held it high so she could slip her head and arms through it. Carefully, as I straightened the lines of the garment, my gaze dropped to her fine leather heels. "The shoes will not do. A nun would not own footwear so nice."

"I have no other shoes," Eva said.

I slipped off my worn brown leather shoes. "Try these. They're quite comfortable and will serve you well if you find you must walk a long way."

Eva slipped her foot into the shoe. "They are a little big, but they'll work."

"I'll take that as a good sign." I slipped the white cowl over her head and centered it. To finish the look, I produced a large cross and a gold chain. "To sell an outfit, you must have the right accessories."

Next, I attached the white Roman collar around Edoardo's neck and then buttoned the front of the cassock. The two stood side by side. "You're now two proper Catholics on a mission to help refugee children in Tuscany."

When we came downstairs, Signora Fontana was waiting for us with a muslin bundle made up of supplies provided by Sebastian. "It's enough to keep you for a couple of days."

"We can't thank you enough," Edoardo said.

The old woman waved away his thanks. "Go on with you now. The streets are fairly quiet, but soon there'll be more comings and goings from people who've been at work."

I slipped on a pair of older shoes and retrieved my Bible. I handed it to Eva. "Take this. Think of it as another accessory."

She smoothed her hand over it. "It looks very old."

"It is. But one day we'll see each other again, and you'll return it to me."

Eva's eyes glistened. "I swear I'll return it."

"Good."

We hurried out the back door and took the series of alleys to the church. When I saw the black Mercedes parked at the side entrance, I paused.

"Walk slowly with me, but let me get ahead of you so I can see who's in the car."

The two dutifully followed behind and paused as I walked to the vehicle's door. When I saw the driver, my heart nearly stopped. It was Riccardo.

I thought perhaps we had been caught. I took a step back, but as I did, he turned and saw me. He rose out of the car, his gaze lingering on me, and then it shifted to the priest and nun. "Good, they're here. Now we'll go."

He opened the rear passenger door. "Padre, Sister, if you please."

The couple looked at each other.

"Please," Riccardo said. "We must go now."

The couple sat in the rear seat, and he closed the door.

"Where are you taking them?" I asked.

"That is for me and Padre Pietro to know. It's better that way."

"How do I know you aren't working for the police?"

"I do work for the police. And sometimes I help the priest when he needs a special favor."

"What kinds of favors?"

He shrugged and leaned a little closer. "You do favors for him, too, no? Otherwise we both would not be here. There are many Romans very happy to help Padre Pietro."

"When will you return?"

He arched a brow. "Are you worried about me?"

I was. And for the Biancos. The consequences for us all if we were caught were quite grave. "Be careful."

He grinned. "And when I return, will you go out to dinner with me?"

I shook my head. "No."

He opened his door and looked at me unabashed. "I think you will."

CHAPTER TWENTY-TWO

ISABELLA

Rome, Italy
Friday, March 17, 1944, 5:00 p.m.

The winter was long and bleak as the Allies pushed closer to Rome. According to the BBC, the Allies had landed on the beaches of Anzio, thirty-three miles to the south; had broken the German lines; and were nearing Rome. Rumors swirled that the Allies would arrive any day, but we had been hearing that for months.

In January, there had been a mass roundup of able-bodied men, who had been trucked off to forced labor camps. Mia was rarely here. I supposed she was with her German lover, but she always refused to say what she was doing when I interrogated her at the shop.

By February, she had quit her job and had vanished into the city. And there was no sign of Riccardo, who had once again disappeared without even a word of the Biancos' fate.

I continued to meet with Padre Pietro every evening, and though most of what I told him about my clients was women's gossip, he dutifully listened to it all and said that in the right hands, it could make sense.

The sun hung low on the warm March evening as I walked toward Signora Fontana's home. As I crossed in front of a narrow alley, I heard my name whispered from the shadows. "Isabella."

Stopping, I turned and saw a tall lean man standing in the shadows. I hesitated.

"Isabella, it's me. Riccardo."

His voice sounded rough, strained. Riccardo stepped out of the shadows, and for a moment I did not recognize him. He had swapped his police uniform for peasant's clothes, and his beard had grown in full and thick.

"Riccardo?"

"I told you I would return."

I rushed to him, wrapping my arms around him, grateful to see a friendly face. "What happened? The Biancos?"

"Delivered to a contact in the north. No doubt sipping wine in Zürich now."

"Where have you been?" I took his hand in mine and felt the rough calluses on his palm.

He pulled me into the shadows. "Doing more favors for the priest. You must know the SS are looking for me."

"Why?"

"Those favors have created some troubles for the Nazis and the Fascists." A car drove by, and he tensed and pulled me closer. "It isn't wise for us to be on the street."

"Of course." I took his hand, we hurried the remaining steps to the front door, and I pulled him inside. He watched me wrestle with the iron bolt, and he did not visibly relax until it was firmly in place.

"Let me get you something to eat."

"Where is Signora Fontana?"

"She isn't well. She takes to her bed early most winter evenings, but there's always food in the kitchen."

"I could eat anything."

As he sat at the hand-hewn kitchen table, I sliced off a piece of crusty bread and placed it with a precious jar of olive oil in front of him. He took a bite, and his eyes closed with such pleasure it made my heart ache. He quickly ate the slice and the next three along with a bowl of lentil soup I ladled out.

I could eat only half my serving, and when I pushed it aside, he took it and finished it off. "I'll never leave food on a plate again."

"When is the last time you ate?" I asked.

"A meal like this? Months."

I poured him a glass of wine from a bottle Sebastian had given me from his storeroom. "I've missed you. I thought perhaps you had left Rome for good."

He laid his hand over mine. "Never. I've stayed away because the SS could cause you trouble. But I needed to see someone with a kind face. Call it a weakness. Loneliness."

Feeling isolated had become a familiar sensation. Each night I went to bed alone, I craved the touch of my Enzo so much I wept. "I have not seen Mia in months."

"I spoke to her days ago. She's fine."

"Is she still with her German?"

"Yes."

"There has been a great deal of sabotage in the city. Tires slashed, buildings burned, four-pointed nails tossed in front of German trucks, people killed. Is that what you've been doing?"

"Let's not waste our time talking about the war. I came to see you because I needed to see your face. But I'll have to leave in the morning. It's not safe."

"I'm not worried about me."

He leaned over and kissed my lips. "I am."

Tears glistened as I leaned into the kiss and cupped the side of his face with my hand. Neither of us spoke of the future or what was to come as we rose, and I led him upstairs to my bedroom.

When he shrugged off his shirt, I saw that his skin was marred with bruises and deep gashes barely healed. I ran trembling fingers over his skin, trying not to imagine the pain.

I kissed him, and he wrapped one hand around my waist and the other up to the curve of my breast. We moved slow, each savoring the raw power of touch. Though I did not want to believe this was the last time I would see him, I had witnessed too much death to fool myself with stories.

He kissed my neck, the rough hair of his beard sending delicious sensations through my body. My need to touch him built quickly, and I fumbled with the buttons on my blouse until I popped one. After I shrugged off my blouse, he stared at my slip and my breasts rising over the top.

He kissed each gently. "I have wanted to do this since the day I met you."

Later, when we lay in bed, naked and huddled close, I traced an old scar on his biceps.

"That's from the war in Greece," he said lazily.

"What happened?"

Eyes still closed, he said, "I was shot, of course. I was lucky; the bullet went right through my arm." He sighed. "I was a different man in those days. I believed in the Fascist government and its promises. And then on the battlefield it failed us, and I knew I had to make changes."

"My husband died on those battlefields. Enzo Mancuso."

His jaw tightened. "I knew him."

I rose up on my elbow. "You knew Enzo."

He nodded slowly. "He spoke of you so often I felt as if I knew you. In some ways I began to think of you as mine."

"Were you near him when he died?"

He wiped a tear from my face. "I didn't see him fall. But I was in the same battle, and later I saw him buried."

My breath caught in my chest, and for a moment I was certain my heart had stopped. "Did he suffer?"

"I don't believe he did." He drew in a breath and released it. "I sent Mia to you. I knew from what Enzo said about you she would be in good hands."

When I looked into his eyes, I saw fear. He was afraid I would turn on him for his confession. "I failed her."

He threaded his fingers through my hair. "No. She is headstrong, and she might have died if not for you."

I laid my head against his chest, listening to the beating of his heart. When the sun rose, he would rejoin whatever group he was now a part of, and there was a good chance I would never see him again.

"Isabella, if you ever see a collection of German soldiers, I want you to stay away from them," he warned.

I traced small circles on his chest. "I always cross the street."

"In the future, get off the street. Hide. Put distance between you and them."

Rising and meeting his gaze, I asked, "What are you going to do?"

"It doesn't matter. Just stay clear." He rose up on his elbow and looked at me. "Promise me."

"I will."

He kissed me on the lips, and soon he again slipped inside of me. This time our lovemaking was slower and more thoughtful, as if we believed our lives were ordinary and we had all the time in the world.

As the sun's orange light filtered through the shutters on my window, I followed him to the kitchen and made him a strong coffee, which we shared with sliced bread. I walked him to the door, my fingers intertwined with his.

"You'll return to me," I said. "You owe me dinner."

He brushed my cheek with his fingertips. "Yes."

My statement was as foolish as his answer was false. Neither of us expected he would return, but it was nice to hope.

When he left through the rear entrance, I stood in the doorway, watching his tall frame move with a sensual strut that made me smile. He believed he could conquer the world, and I needed to trust he would.

He vanished around the corner without a glance back, but I still waited, half hoping he would return.

"Close the door, Isabella," Signora Fontana said. "He won't return."

I closed the door on the dark street and what felt like my future. "He's doing something dangerous. He wouldn't say, but I know he's risking it all."

"He's a passionate man who loves his country. Men like that cannot watch what is happening to Rome."

I slid the bolt in place and then wiped the tears from my cheeks. "I must get to work."

"Yes. It's best to stay busy."

After washing my face, I took extra care with my hair and made sure my dark skirt and white blouse were neatly pressed. In the kitchen, I kissed Signora Fontana on the cheek. "There's some lovely ribbon and fabric at the shop. I'll bring it to you."

"What will I do with that?"

"You will sew for the children. So many need clothes."

Signora nodded slowly. "There were several babies born last week in the district."

"Then we'll make clothes for them and visit their mothers."

"You're a good girl, Isabella."

"I'm not sure *good* is what I should be now," I said.

"What else would you be?"

"Tougher, like the women in the Resistance."

"Choosing death is easy. Choosing life is far more dangerous."

CHAPTER TWENTY-THREE

ZARA

Richmond, Virginia
Tuesday, June 8, 6:00 p.m.

Zara's great-grandmother's words came to mind. *"Are you sure Richard is your son?"*

"Did Papa know about Riccardo?" Zara asked.

"Of course, he and I never kept secrets from each other," Nonna said.

"Did he ever see this box?" Zara asked.

"Your grandfather knew about it, but I never showed it to your father. There were times when Papa wanted me to, but I could never bring myself."

Next in the box was an identification card from the Italian police dated 1939. The man pictured had dark eyes and a slight smile that hinted at secrets. The name read Enzo Mancuso. "Who is Enzo?"

"He was a young idealist who honored his duty for Italy above all else." Nonna's voice grew tight. "There were so many men like him on all sides. So passionate, so sure."

"Where is Enzo now?" Gina asked.

"He died in 1940 in a battle on the Albanian and Greek border. Italy had taken Albania and was trying to swallow up Greece."

"Who was he to you?" Zara asked.

"I hardly know anymore," she said quietly.

Gina and Zara looked at each other. Gina shrugged.

"You have never once mentioned him," Zara said.

"Enzo fits in a lifetime that does not belong to me anymore."

"Papa was your great love, then?" Gina asked.

Nonna shrugged as she set the identification card aside. "Yes."

"You said the gown was for your firstborn," Zara said. "Was that Daddy?"

"No. I lost my first child." She dropped her gaze to bent fingers as she plucked imaginary lint.

"You never said a word," Gina said.

"I was so young, but in many ways a woman in full. We all grew up faster then. Most of us lost children. Some of us died giving birth. It was the way then."

"When was the baby born?" Zara asked.

Nonna shook her head slowly as she stared at Riccardo's face. "It's been so long."

Nonna had always been good at avoiding questions she did not want to answer, and this one was no different. For whatever reason, she was not ready to talk about the lost baby. "But you were a seamstress when you lived in Rome?" Zara asked.

"Yes, that is true."

"You dressed the Italian royalty," Gina said.

"And movie stars and very rich women. We served the wealthiest in Rome. Even wives of the Nazi officers."

"Is Sebastian's still in Rome?" Zara asked.

"No. It went out of business years ago after Sebastian passed."

"What was it like dressing the wives of Nazi officers?" Zara asked.

"They were no different in some ways."

"But . . . ," Gina prompted.

"They didn't think much of us," Nonna said. "Which made it easy for them to underestimate us."

Zara studied Riccardo's direct gaze, high cheekbones, and full lips. "What happened to Riccardo? What's his story?"

"Like Enzo he fought on the Albanian front. He was badly injured and sent back to Rome, but he was a changed man. Riccardo became passionate about ridding Italy of the Fascists and then the Nazis. He believed to regain Italy's honor, he needed to take on the most dangerous work."

Zara dug below another layer of muslin and found a picture of a young woman. Her eyes were bright and her smile vivid.

"Is that you?" Gina asked.

With pride Nonna said, "It's me. I had the picture taken shortly after I arrived in Rome."

"Gina, you and Nonna could have been twins," Zara said.

"I have always thought so," Nonna said.

Gina regarded the picture closely. "Wow, it does look like me."

"You said Riccardo took dangerous jobs," Zara said. "What did he do?"

"He became a radio operator for the Allies. In essence he was a spy."

"You said the Nazi wives underestimated you," Zara said.

"Yes, they did."

CHAPTER TWENTY-FOUR
ISABELLA

Rome, Italy
Wednesday, March 22, 1944, 6:15 p.m.

I had not seen Riccardo in days, and given what he had said, I suspected I would not see him again. I continued to work, seeing clients ten to twelve hours a day. With the twentieth anniversary of the Fascist Party's formation approaching, wives of the German and Fascist officials were anxious to find the right dress. They understood that maintaining the best image would help protect their standing as they all maneuvered through the shifting sands.

I arrived in our neighborhood, feeling overly tired as I walked toward the signora's house. My gaze down, I nearly walked headlong into Mia and her lover, Karl, who were standing on the street corner. They were sharing a wanton embrace. I cleared my throat as I approached.

"Isabella," Mia said, drawing out of Brenner's arms.

Careful not to look too scolding in front of the captain, I nodded. "Mia. Hauptmann Brenner."

The Hauptmann regarded me with a steady gaze. "I have not seen you in some time, Isabella."

"No, sir. I have been working." Sounding respectful was important, but the words all but caught in my throat.

"I understand you've spent time with Riccardo Ferraro."

His casual comment sent a chill skimming along my spine. Had he been watching me? "That was months ago. We had dinner, and then he was gone."

Hauptmann Brenner studied me closely, and I sensed he did not believe me. Mia leaned closer, pressing her breast against his arm, but he was not distracted. "When you see him, let me know. I want to talk to him."

"Why?" I asked.

"I have questions," he said easily. "And I still might have a few for you if I can't find him soon."

Questions from a Nazi officer never boded well. Riccardo's warning to stay clear of the soldiers rang clear. "I'll let you know if I see him."

Mia grinned and stuck out her hand to display a diamond. "You should congratulate us. We're to be married."

As I stared at the glistening gem, my heart sank. If we were alone, I would have grabbed the young woman by the shoulders and shaken her. Instead, I smiled, aware that Hauptmann Brenner watched closely. "How nice for you both."

"You'll help my Mia make her wedding dress," Hauptmann Brenner said. "She tells me you're one of the best."

It did not sit well that they had been discussing me. "Thank you. I would be honored."

"You were coming from the church?" Hauptmann said. "You spend a lot of time with Padre Pietro?"

"I was not at the church tonight, but I am there often. The bombings have displaced many, and the people need help."

"I hear you're fond of confession." He grinned. "They say confession is good for the soul. But I don't see you as a sinner, or am I wrong?"

"Have you been watching me?" I asked.

"I've kept my eye on the priest. There are rumors many of the priests help the enemies of the state."

The comment suggested terrifying consequences for the priest. The Nazis respected the Vatican's boundaries, but parish priests might not be so lucky. "Padre Pietro is dedicated to his flock. There are many prayers that need to be said these days. Many lost friends."

"To the American bombs," Hauptmann Brenner said.

"Yes. And to the labor camps and the Gestapo prison on the Via Tasso."

His eyes narrowed. "What are you doing this evening?"

"Dinner with Signora Fontana and then to bed. The curfew approaches."

"Come with us," Hauptmann Brenner said. "We're going to a party."

"I don't think that I should. It has been a long day, and I am tired."

"I insist," he said. "It'll be fun."

"Yes, fun," Mia said brightly.

"But I am not dressed for a party."

"You look good to me," Hauptmann Brenner said. "Again, I insist."

He was being polite, but I was pushing his limits, and soon he would not be so nice. "Of course."

"My car is right here. Let us go. You'll be glad, Isabella."

Hauptmann Brenner opened the door to the black Mercedes, and I slid in first, then Mia and the captain. He ordered the driver to take us to the Excelsior Hotel, which took me toward Sebastian's and the German commandant's headquarters.

In the rear seat I scooted to the door and pressed my body against it. My hand grazed the handle as a precaution. I did not trust that we were going to the hotel, and I wanted to be ready to escape the car quickly.

As the car moved through the streets, we did not head north as expected but south. The car slowed and then stopped in front of the gray building that housed the Gestapo's prison on the Via Tasso. Two soldiers exited the building and paused to light up cigarettes. They were laughing, as if exchanging a private joke.

"It's where I work," Hauptmann Brenner said.

Sitting straighter, I tightened my grip on the door handle. Could I open the door and pull Mia out with me? Would she come? How far would we run before one of the laughing guards shot us?

"So many arrests in the last month," he said easily. "It barely gives me time for Mia." He laid his hand on her leg and rubbed it possessively.

"Darling," Mia said sweetly. "I want to dance. You promised no work tonight."

"I did promise," he said finally. He tapped on the front seat and ordered the driver to the Excelsior.

As we pulled away, a heaviness settled in my chest as I pictured Riccardo in that building. Hauptmann Brenner was a precise man, and this little side trip had a purpose I could not even guess.

The car moved quickly now, and the transition from the San Lorenzo district to the Via Veneto was quick and a little startling. Normally, when I walked the distance, my mind had time to gradually grow accustomed to the shift. But tonight, it was fast and jarring, and I was struck that there were two very different Romes existing side by side.

We arrived at the Excelsior Hotel, a block-long alabaster building that had once been a palace. A doorman dressed in a red jacket opened the gilded front door, and immediately we were greeted by lively music drifting from a ballroom. The three of us walked across the black-and-white-tiled floor toward the ballroom, where an impressive party was underway. A five-piece band played as a tall blonde wearing red lipstick sang a German song into a microphone.

I was hit by the noise and the laughter and wondered how anyone could celebrate knowing the Via Tasso was less than a mile away.

"Darling," Mia said. "I must powder my nose. I'll be right back."

"You're a butterfly, Mia," he said. "Always flitting about."

She kissed him on the lips. "But I always return to you."

Mia vanished into the crowd and left me alone with the captain. Gripping my purse tighter, I felt trapped.

"Let me get you a drink," he said. "You're as nervous as a cat."

"I'm not nervous."

Laughter rumbled in his chest. "Of course you are, but I find it very charming." He guided me toward the bar, ordered a red wine for me and a beer for himself. Ever the gentleman, he raised his glass to me in a toast. "To an end to this war."

"Yes," I said.

"It was very astute of you not to mention my late wife. It upsets Mia to hear such a sad story."

"I suppose it's very troubling. Did the police find out who hit her?"

"The driver sped away and escaped. It was tragic."

"Your wife was a lovely woman."

"Yes, Greta was a good wife, if not a bit too softhearted. Did she ever gossip with you at the shop?"

"I don't speak German that well. I wouldn't know."

He sipped his beer. "Did she ever talk about the Jews?"

"I don't know."

"Too many slipped out of the city last year."

"I wouldn't know."

He regarded me closely. "I think you know more than you let on, Isabella."

"What does that mean?"

"Nothing." Mia's laughter drew his attention. "Mia is a simple creature, like most of you Italians. It's refreshing. Though at times tricky."

"I'm glad you're happy with her." Sipping the wine, I discovered it was delicious. Of course, only the best for this party.

"Are you certain you have not seen Riccardo?" he asked.

The wine was cool to the tongue, and it helped ease some of my nerves. "I have not seen him."

"And you'll tell me when you do."

"Of course."

"See that you do, Isabella. I'm generous with you because of Mia. But even she cannot keep me from doing my duty. If you found the outside of the Via Tasso upsetting, I can assure you the inside is far worse."

When Mia returned, she had checked her coat, and she was smiling. I noticed the broach pinned to her dress immediately. It was the emerald that had been Signora Bianco's.

"You like the little gift I gave Mia?" Hauptmann Brenner asked.

Grief and fury stole my voice.

"Quite stunning," he said.

"Where did you get it?" I asked.

"I don't remember," he said.

He remembered. What was the purpose of this game? Was it to scare me?

Mia slipped her arm into Brenner's and snuggled close. "I would love to dance."

"And what will people say? I must maintain a respectable image." He kissed her gently on the cheek.

"I must have wine, darling. Can we abandon you for a moment, Isabella?" Mia asked.

"Of course." As they walked away, I turned toward the crowd of strangers all laughing, as if bombs had not dropped on the city or the prisons were not full of good men and women suffering at the hands of the SS.

"You look pensive."

The familiar voice had me turning. Aldo. I'd not seen him since last fall. The lines in his face had grown deeper and his gaze sharper.

"Do I?" Suddenly I did not have the reserves to pretend.

"Your friend, Mia, looks like she's quite attached to Karl Brenner."

"Yes, she is." I looked past him and watched as Mia nuzzled close to her fiancé while he spoke to several men. "They are engaged."

"I saw the ring." As he watched the couple closely, he pressed his lips together. Finally, all traces of emotion vanished. "And you're here alone."

"Hauptmann Brenner insisted I attend."

"Would you like to dance?"

"I would rather not. I want to leave, but the curfew has passed, and Hauptmann Brenner knows I'm trapped here."

"I have a pass," Aldo said. "I would be happy to escort you home."

"Why would you do that?"

"Why wouldn't I? These parties are very redundant. All the same people."

"You really have a pass?"

"We can leave now."

I took a liberal sip of wine. "Then let us go."

He grabbed his hat from the coat checker and, pressing his hand into the small of my back, led me out a side door. When we were away from the music and laughter, I felt as if I had escaped a tiger's cage.

Across the glittering hotel foyer, we stepped out into the evening air, and he settled his hat on his head. "You live in the same place."

"Yes. In the Monti district."

"Lead the way."

The clip of our shoes fell in step as we walked the cobblestone street. The wine had relaxed me enough to ask, "What business are you doing these days?"

"Again, a little of this and that."

"And it's treating you well?" More and more men worked in the shadows of Rome, either in the growing black markets or for the SS.

"I can't complain." From his breast pocket he drew out a cigarette, offered me one, which I declined, and with a silver lighter lit the tip. "You still work at Sebastian's, no?"

"You have quite the memory."

"It pays to remember details."

Under the flickering light of a streetlamp, his expression was relaxed, but his presence suggested he was very alert.

"Have you seen Padre Pietro lately?" she asked.

"We have lunch from time to time."

"Hauptmann Brenner asked about the priest," I said. "It would be wise for him, and those who know him, to be careful."

"I'll keep that in mind. But how do you know I am not forwarding your warning on to the Gestapo?"

The question silenced my response. He was right. I did not know him. Perhaps if I was not so tired or the wine had not hit me especially hard, I would not have been so forthright.

"I've seen you at the church," he said. "Though I doubt you noticed me."

"I take confession daily. I pray for all the lost souls."

"You're a good woman."

"Is that a question?" I asked.

"An assessment." He inhaled and let the smoke trickle out over his lips.

"I'll let God decide if I am good or not."

From the alley came the sound of young boys. When they crossed the sidewalk in front of us, we could see they were roughly dressed, their faces smudged with dirt. They were from the *borgate*, the slums, and were searching for food or trouble. They stopped, and several held up crossed fingers to Aldo, who regarded each with cautious concern. Even the young could be dangerous. Finally, the boys, sensing he could be trouble, laughed and ran off.

"What was that?" I asked.

"Their pockets are likely full of the four-pointed nails."

"For the German tires. But why taunt you? Unless they think you're German."

He laughed and inhaled his cigarette. "They're half-wild with no sense, so they challenge anyone."

"In their own way patriotic."

"Perhaps." We continued on down the street as a German armored truck passed. "Have you seen my friend Riccardo lately?" he asked.

Twice in one night two men had asked about Riccardo. And because I did not believe in innocent questions, my worries for Riccardo doubled. "No, I have not. The captain is also looking for him."

"Are you sure you have not seen him?" He stared at the glowing cigarette tip.

"Very."

"You're the kind of woman who knows more than she lets on."

"I don't know what you mean."

Even white teeth flashed in the moonlight. "Of course not."

"What is it you want, Aldo?"

"Nothing more than to enjoy a walk with a beautiful woman."

Nothing in Rome was that simple.

We approached a building that had been hit by a bomb. Built during the Renaissance, its ancient beauty had crumbled like dried bread into an unwieldy pile of stones.

"There are better times ahead," he said.

"Is that so?"

He inhaled deeply. "The Americans are pushing closer to Rome."

They were the devil we did not know. But I was willing to take a chance if it meant ridding us of the Nazis. "The Germans will not surrender this city easily."

"No. They won't."

We reached my building, and I paused at the front step. "Thank you for the escort."

"My pleasure. Perhaps we'll see each other again."

"Perhaps."

He flicked an ash from his cigarette. "If you should find Riccardo, could you get word to me?"

There was no reason to trust this man, but for Riccardo I would take the chance. "Hauptmann Brenner drove Mia and me to the Via Tasso tonight. We didn't enter, but the message was clear."

"Did he threaten you and Mia?" he asked carefully.

"Seeing the prison was threat enough."

"Be very careful, Isabella. And if I should find Riccardo, I'll send word to you."

"Thank you."

"I'll see you again."

"It's a large city."

"That can be surprisingly small at times, no?"

The next day I was in the dress shop when I heard the explosion that rocked walls and shattered glass for several blocks. At first, we thought it was the Allies and another bombing raid. But gunfire followed the explosion, and the German trucks parked near the shop quickly started moving in the direction of the commotion.

By the next morning I learned it had not been the Allies but the Resistance. They had set off a bomb in a trash bin on the Via Rasella. When it had exploded, at least twenty German soldiers had been killed, and during the gunfire that followed, another thirteen had died. In all, thirty-three German soldiers had been killed.

Within twenty-four hours the deaths of these SS troops would unleash a new kind of vengeance on Rome.

CHAPTER TWENTY-FIVE

ZARA

Richmond, Virginia
Tuesday, June 8, 6:30 p.m.

"What happened to Riccardo?" Gina asked.

Nonna sat quiet for a long moment as she stared into the young man's smiling eyes. If he were alive today, he would have been over one hundred. "He was betrayed."

"By who?" Zara asked.

"I have chosen to forget so much," Nonna said. "I don't think that I could bear to speak it out loud even after all this time."

"Okay," Zara said. "You don't have to talk."

"There is a journal in that box," she said finally. "Read it. It contains answers both you girls should know. I should have shared this with your father long ago. But I was too afraid to speak of the secrets."

Zara dug in the box and fished through stacks of letters, old rumpled lira banknotes and coins that must have dated to the war, a small black jewelry box, and a leather-bound journal. Zara gently thumbed through the book, noting the even, precise handwriting. "It's written in English."

"To maintain privacy. Few read Italian in those days, let alone read English."

The alarm on Zara's phone rang, sending her into the kitchen. She selected three pill bottles from the counter, doled out one of each, and handed them to Gina, along with a glass of water. "Evening regimen."

"It's only six thirty," Gina said.

"Making it the evening."

"I always considered this early afternoon."

"Instructions say evening. You're now on Zara time."

"You read the instructions?" Gina stared at the white and pink pills.

"Cover to cover. Have you?" Zara asked.

"I skimmed them." Gina popped the pills in her mouth and chased them with water. "I see them as general guidelines."

"Well, not anymore."

"And what if I don't want to follow all the rules? Life is short, literally, so why do I want to fill it with rules?"

"Rules are a fact of life," Nonna said. "Some can be bent, but in your case, they must be followed."

"You never followed any," Gina said. "You took a pretty radical path."

"Because I had no other choice," Nonna said.

"And you stepped up and became very brave," Gina half joked.

"I was not brave, Gina. I did what I had to do to survive, and that's what you must do now. I didn't like all the choices I made. I was young, a little desperate, and afraid."

Gina finished the last of her water.

Nonna motioned to Zara. "I am ready for dinner. And so is Gina. If she's going to thrive, then she must eat good food."

"Nonna, I'm not going to thrive," Gina said.

Nonna shrugged. “You don’t know what the future holds. None of us do. Now return these items to the box, and let us eat. I have a very strong appetite tonight. Zara, I hope you didn’t put too much pepper in the soup.”

“I never do,” Zara protested.

“You always do. In fact, get me a glass of water. I must be ready when the great fires of hell consume my mouth.”

Zara sat in the open garage with her pups, sipping a beer and staring at the sky filled with stars. She was on her third bottle, and if she had her way, she would finish the twelve-pack tonight. The hangover tomorrow was a fair trade-off for peace tonight.

The rumble of a Jeep in the distance had Gus sitting straighter. It sounded like Nicolas’s. “It can’t be him, fella,” she said. “He’s up in Washington, DC.”

The dog, however, did not relax, and so they all waited until Nicolas’s black Jeep rounded their corner and parked in front of the house. “Well, you were right.”

Nicolas rose out of the vehicle and came around, keys in hand, his hair now freshly cut.

“Don’t you have an interview tomorrow?”

“They moved it up to today. We did it via Zoom. One of the partners had to travel.”

“Well, then, how did the job interview go?” she asked.

He ran his hand over his shorn hair. “Great. They want me to start next week.”

“That’s terrific. You going to take it?”

“Yes.” He pulled up another lawn chair and sat beside her.

“Congratulations. There’s beer in the cooler,” she said. “Grab one.”

He reached in, twisted off the top, and took a swig. "Why the celebration?"

"Not a celebration," she said before she finished off her bottle and reached for another.

"Did you find what Nonna was looking for?" he asked.

"I did. It's a box of memories and a journal. I'll start reading it in the morning."

He regarded her. "Is Nonna okay?"

"She's great, as it turns out. She has no life-threatening illness other than she's old."

He waited, as if sensing the other shoe dangled, ready to drop. "That's good news."

She twisted off the bottle top with a hard turn. "Gina is sick."

"Gina?"

"Pancreatic cancer. The red alert from Gina wasn't for Nonna but her."

"Shit, Zara. I'm sorry."

"Shit is right," she said. "She's forty-one years old."

He took a long swig, as if sudden memories were clawing up from the shadows. "That cancer is pretty aggressive?"

"Her case is particularly fast moving. Her symptoms are manageable for now but not fixable."

He released a long, stilted sigh. "I'm sorry, Zara. I really am."

"Thanks." She had heard these words spoken to her patients so many times. Usually, the words were awkward and rushed, but in rare times, like now, they carried the heaviness of understanding.

"What can I do? And I mean that. It's not just words."

"No, there's nothing. But thank you for asking." She pressed the cold bottle to her temple. "Tell me about your job interview."

He took a long pull on his beer. "It doesn't seem that important."

"Don't underestimate the ordinary."

"Seriously? Because I never wanted to hear anyone else's good news when Catherine was sick."

"I do. It would be nice. You deserve all the good news you can grab."

"I get the corner office that has a view of the Potomac."

"You sound underwhelmed."

"I'm not. I'm grateful my old life was willing to wait for me. There was a time when I really loved it."

"But . . ."

He dug his thumbnail into the label. "No buts. It's all good."

"But?"

"It doesn't fit anymore. Like an old shirt that's shrunk."

"Because . . ."

A half smile tipped the edges of his lips. "Because I'm not the same guy, Dr. Zara."

"My parents' and grandfather's deaths changed me," she said. "I'm stronger than I was. So are you."

"Could you go back to your old life?"

"I've lived this one so long I don't remember what it was like before. And I rarely look back."

"Do you look forward?" he asked.

She smiled. "Not like I should. My parents' and grandfather's deaths made me a little afraid of living. Loving. I thought keeping Gina and Nonna at arm's distance would save me from that kind of pain again, but it didn't work. When they die, it's going to hurt like hell." She was already starting to question if she could keep doing hospice work.

"I know how much it sucks to be the one left behind."

"I thought I was suitably armored up so it wouldn't really hurt again. But the plain truth is hurting is a part of living. No risk, no reward."

He stared into his bottle. "Would you like to go out to dinner with me? You always said it was good to take care of the caregiver."

"I have said that."

"Did you know Catherine put you on the bucket list? She wanted us to have dinner."

"Really? I didn't know that." Zara was surprised and a little disappointed the list had brought him here.

"Dinner with you was the last item."

"You're here because of Catherine's bucket list."

"I am. But it's more than that. This is the first item on the list that doesn't feel like a chore."

"It was a chore for you to go to Hawaii and Key West?"

"It was lonely, to be frank. Dinner with you feels natural. Like reconnecting with an old friend."

She took another long swig, really wishing she did not like this guy so much. "In full disclosure, Gina has started a bucket list for me."

"That so? What's top of the list?" He raised the bottle to his lips.

"Sex with you."

He coughed. "Really?"

Zara shrugged, enjoying his discomfort. "She says I need to live a little. Or maybe she needs to live a little through me."

He arched a brow. "That so?"

"I'm not saying we will, of course."

His thumb dug into the label on the bottle. "Of course."

"But I'm all about honesty. If this is too much information, just say so."

Gus rose and put his head on Nicolas's lap. He leaned forward and scratched the dog between the ears. "How about we start with dinner?"

"Dinner sounds good." She was not sure why Catherine had put her on the list. Maybe it was because Zara and Nicolas had cared for Catherine, and this was his final act of closure. Whatever the reason, she wanted to spend time with him. "A little fun is very appealing."

"Have fun? That's a novel concept."

She laughed. She had been working nonstop since her grandfather's death and realized she was suddenly very tired. "I know."

"Where do you want to go?" he asked.

"I haven't been out on a date in this town for a decade. I couldn't even tell you what's still open. But I want a hearty meal. No salad or vegetables."

"A woman after my own heart." He drank from his beer. "You'll come out on the other side of all this," he said.

"I told you that when Catherine was sick."

"And I didn't believe you. I thought it was a stupid platitude. But you were right. I'm here. I'm breathing. And you will be too."

"We need to promise each other right now that we can't talk about death or dying on this date."

"Fair enough."

She was not sure what they would talk about, but nothing ventured, nothing gained. "Should I meet you?"

"No, we'll do this old school. I'll pick you up at six. Can you dress up in something fancy?"

"I live with two style icons. They'll take great pleasure remaking me."

He nodded slowly as he rose and tossed his beer bottle in the trash bin. "Good, I'll see you tomorrow evening."

"It's a date." She stood, sliding her hands in her pockets because she was not sure what to do with them.

"Okay." He grinned, patted all the pups on their heads, and headed toward his Jeep. He walked with an easy confidence, but his demeanor had changed. Before Catherine had died, he had been arrogant, believing he could will anything into happening. He'd been the captain of the ship. Period.

He remained the captain, but he seemed to understand that even the best seaman was no match for Mother Nature's gale-force winds. And like any good sailor after a storm, he had gathered the fragments of his ship and forged them into a new vessel that was not as sleek or perfect but was more resilient.

And a hell of a lot sexier.

CHAPTER TWENTY-SIX

ZARA

Richmond, Virginia
Wednesday, June 9, 7:00 a.m.

Zara sat at the breakfast table, staring at the leather-bound journal. Several times she had been tempted to open it, but Nonna had asked her to read it with Gina.

She was refilling her second cup of coffee, wondering why the fourth beer had seemed like such a good idea last night, when Gina appeared in the doorway. She had applied some makeup and brushed her hair, but her pallor was still evident. Zara smiled even as she wondered how she was going to get through all this.

"Good morning," Zara said, rising. "Have a seat, and I'll get you your tea."

"I can make my own tea." Gina moved to the electric kettle. "No need to baby me yet. I'm sure the time will come soon enough."

No pithy platitudes came to mind to counter her sister's claim or the realization it was going to get rougher. "While you're there, can you refresh my coffee?"

"Be my pleasure." Gina carried the coffeepot to the table and refilled Zara's cup. "I've never known how you could stomach coffee this strong. It's like drinking battery acid."

"Breakfast of champions."

Gina returned the pot to the coffee maker. "If you say so."

"I've been waiting for you to get up. I want to read this journal."

"I figured you'd have it all read by now."

"Nonna said to wait for you."

"Since when did you listen?"

"Even an old dog can learn new tricks." She sipped her coffee. "I haven't read any of it. Get your tea, come sit with me, and I'll read."

The kettle boiled. Gina carefully filled her mug and walked to the table. "Let's hear some of it."

"Okay."

The pages were dry and brittle under Zara's fingertips, and she was mindful as she turned to the front page. There was no name on the inside flap, simply a date: 1943. Rome.

"I wonder why she chose to journal?" Gina asked.

"According to my internet search, it was a crazy time in Rome. The government was collapsing, the Germans took over, and the Americans were bombing and advancing on the city. Writing might have been a way to destress."

Gina sipped her tea, staring out the window. "That makes sense."

For the next hour, Zara read aloud from the journal, which appeared to be written by a young woman named Isabella. She and Gina followed Isabella through the streets of Rome, into the couture shop on the Via Veneto, past the stark exterior of the Gestapo prison, inside the glittering Excelsior Hotel, and through the Resistance attack in March 1944 on the Via Rasella.

"Isabella is Nonna, right?" Gina asked.

"I suppose she is. I'm starting to understand why she never talked about living in Rome."

"I never saw Nonna as anyone other than Nonna. I'm trying to picture her doing all this as a young woman."

"She never talked about her life before America. I asked a couple of times, but she always blew me off."

"So why is she telling us now?" Gina asked. "Is it because I'm sick?"

"That's part of it. She's also at the end of her life. I don't think she ever told Daddy about all this, but Papa must have known."

"Why wouldn't she tell? Daddy was conceived around this time."

"Maybe she was afraid," Zara said. "Maybe she feared hurting Daddy."

"What could hurt Dad?"

Zara thumbed through the remaining pages. "It must have been big."

The bell rang, and Zara rose. "Speaking of Nonna."

She found her grandmother sitting up in bed, looking impatient and ready to go. "Good morning."

"You're very slow this morning. Are you feeling all right?" Nonna asked.

"I'm fine." She raised the blinds. "Too much beer last night. Ready to get dressed?"

"Yes. And I think I would like oatmeal for breakfast. With brown sugar and raisins."

"That's a lot of carbs, Nonna."

"One must live dangerously from time to time." She swung her legs to the side of the bed, and Zara settled her in the wheelchair. Nonna's dressing routine had been moving faster as Zara had learned how to maneuver her and wash her hair in the way she liked best.

Within a half hour they were in the kitchen, and Zara was cooking oatmeal for all three of them. When she set a bowl in front of Gina, her sister grimaced. "I never eat this stuff."

Zara placed Nonna's bowl in front of her. "You do now. It'll settle your stomach."

"My stomach is fine," Gina said.

"No, it's not," Zara said. "I looked up your meds and know the side effects. Eat the oatmeal."

"Go on," Nonna said. "We'll all get fat together."

"It won't make you fat, ladies," Zara said. "Very good for you. Fiber."

Both regarded Zara with annoyance and then began to eat. Satisfied, she sat and dug into hers, sprinkling extra brown sugar and raisins on top.

"We've been reading Isabella's journal," Zara said.

"Ah, I do love brown sugar," Nonna said.

"Code for 'Not going to talk about it now,'" Gina said.

"It's not a code," Nonna said. "I'm hungry and would rather not talk with my mouth full."

"I have a date," Zara said to Gina and Nonna. "With Nicolas, tonight. And he asked me to dress up."

Nonna stared at Zara across the kitchen table. "What does that mean?"

"I don't know. I was hoping you two would be able to suggest an outfit. If not, I can run up to the mall. There are tons of summer sales now."

Gina set her spoon down hard. "Nonna and I have enough clothes between us to dress half this city. You'll not be going anywhere."

"I don't want to be dressed up like a fashion model. I'll be uncomfortable and feel weird," Zara said.

"You cannot dress like you normally do," Gina said.

"I get it. We've established that I don't dress well," Zara said. "Let us accept that and move on to stylish but comfortable."

Nonna pointed her spoon at Zara. "Sometimes you have to choose."

"Not me, ladies," Zara said. But maybe she might bend the rule a little for Nicolas.

"When we finish our gruel," Gina said, "the real work will begin."

Two hours later Nonna's bed was covered in dresses. Sheaths, A-lines, smocks, minis, and maxis had been pulled from the shop inventory crammed in the spare room. Zara had, to her grandmother's and sister's delights, tried them all on. She finally settled on a black sheath dress, a long silver chain, and teardrop earrings. She could not fit her size 9 feet into Gina's or Nonna's size 8 shoes, which were all stunning but might as well have been metal vise grips. Gina finally called a friend who worked in a shoe store and had a size 9 pair of black sandals sent to the house.

After the morning fashion expedition, both her patients were exhausted, and both needed rest, leaving Zara alone to walk her dogs and then make herself a fresh cup of coffee.

Zara went to Nonna's chest and opened it. As promised, Zara did not continue to read the journal and dutifully set it aside. But she had made no promises about digging into the box's other contents.

In the box there was a christening gown, Riccardo's picture, Enzo's identification card, a small cloth satchel, and a black velvet box. She leaned Riccardo's image against the sugar bowl and reached for the black box.

Carefully, she unhooked the gold latch and pushed open the lid. Nestled inside was a large emerald broach mounted in a gold setting.

Zara held it up to the light and marveled at the play of shades in the stone's multiple surfaces. "This has to be worth a fortune. And you stowed it in the attic."

She carefully wiped the vivid green surface with the hem of her T-shirt. Never once in her life had she seen her grandmother wear this. She turned it over and saw a jeweler's mark.

Inside the muslin pouch was a gold locket and a slim wedding band strung side by side on a chain. There were also baby-soft strands of hair bound by a ribbon.

She held the locket in her hand and, seeing the hinge on the side, opened it. Inside was a picture of a very young woman and a man. The woman wore a white wedding dress and the man a black suit, and each stared at the camera with the shocked expression of a couple who had no idea what marriage meant.

Engraved on the back in a flowing script were two names. "Enzo and Isabella, 1940," she said softly. They had been married over eighty years ago, and Enzo would have been dead most of those years.

Everyone thought they had all the time in the world, but, she realized, they were all passing through.

The strands of hair were the kind of keepsake a mother saved to remember her child. At first, she assumed the hair had been her father's, taken shortly after his birth. But as she held the ribbon up, traces of pink caught the light. Nonna had said she had lost a child. "A girl."

Zara carefully slipped the locket, ring, and hair back into the muslin and closed the satchel. People responded to grief in so many ways. For a young woman who had lost her husband and a child, perhaps the only way she could survive was to lock the memories away. They were too precious to throw away but too painful to revisit. It explained why her grandmother had been so stoic after her father's and grandfather's deaths.

"So much loss, Nonna," Zara whispered.

Zara picked up the emerald broach and smoothed her thumb over the hard, glittering stone. Nonna was ready to tell her story, but that did not mean that she would do so easily. A lifetime of secrets was a hard burden to release.

CHAPTER TWENTY-SEVEN

ISABELLA

Rome, Italy
Saturday, March 25, 1944, 7:00 a.m.

Riccardo had warned me to stay clear of patrolling German soldiers. Now I understood why. He had known the bombing was imminent. That explained Hauptmann Brenner's and Aldo's interest in him.

I hurried to the church and went directly to Padre Pietro's office. I knocked, and when he told me to enter, I closed the door behind me.

"Isabella, what's wrong?" Padre Pietro asked.

"What have you heard about the reprisals? With so many Germans killed, there has to be retribution."

He removed his glasses, and slowly he rubbed the lenses with a linen cloth. "I've only heard rumors. The SS is being very quiet. But they have emptied out the prisons and took a busload of men out of the city."

"They've done this before and used them for forced labor."

"There is talk the men were shot," he said quietly.

"Shot?"

"For every one German killed in the Via Rasella attack, ten Romans were shot."

My knees suddenly went weak, and I lowered into a chair. "Have you heard from Riccardo? I know he's been in contact with you. Could he have left the city?"

"There are whispers that he has been arrested."

Obviously, the trip to the Via Tasso had not been by chance. "Is he among those that were taken from the prisons?"

The priest put his glasses back on. "I don't know."

"What aren't you telling me?" I begged.

"I fear the Gestapo have him, and if he's not dead, it's a matter of time," he said quietly.

"Because of this bombing?"

"He operated a radio for the Americans," Padre Pietro said. "He has been passing along information to the Allied troops via radio for almost a year. That's why he was gone for long periods of time."

"Hauptmann Brenner was asking me about Riccardo just days ago."

"Maybe he doesn't know where he is. Or maybe he's testing you. Men like him play games."

"Mia has some influence on the captain. Perhaps she knows where her brother is."

"Be very careful, Isabella. Asking anyone about Riccardo could get you arrested."

"She's also in grave danger."

"She has been for some time," he said.

"What game is she playing?"

"I don't know," he said.

"I have to know what happened to Riccardo."

"No good will come of you getting involved."

"I don't care."

I left the church and went directly to Hauptmann Brenner's rooms overlooking the Spanish Steps. The doorman regarded me with a mixture of interest and skepticism as I approached.

"I am here to see Mia Ferraro." I smiled. "She's a guest of Hauptmann Karl Brenner."

"The blonde," he said.

"Yes. I am her cousin, and I've come to visit. I am Isabella Mancuso."

"Your papers?"

Given the recent attack, it was not surprising that the doorman was extra vigilant in protecting his German residents. If harm came to a German here, it would mean a death sentence.

After handing him my identification card, I waited as he studied it and then me. He turned away and scribbled my name and address before returning the card.

"You can see her, but don't dally. Room 302. The soldiers residing here are particular about who visits since the bombing."

"Of course."

I climbed the marble stairs to the third floor and located number 302. After knocking, I stepped back.

"Who is it?" Mia asked.

"It's me, Isabella. Signora Fontana wanted me to check in on you."

"I am fine."

"Can you open the door so I can see with my own eyes?" I glanced side to side and then lowered my voice. "I'm not leaving until you do."

A chain scraped across the lock, and the door opened. She wore a hunter-green suit that skimmed above her knees and nipped at her waist. Her hair was curled into soft ringlets that framed her face and accentuated her red bow lips. "As you can see, I am fine."

"May I come in for a visit?" I did my best not to look anxious.

"Karl would rather I not have visitors right now. The city is very tense since the attack."

"Where is Hauptmann Brenner?"

"He was called away immediately after the bombing. There was an emergency order issued."

"The Germans are clearing out the prisons, and there are rumors they are shooting the men. Nazis, we all have learned, can be vengeful. Mia, I have not seen Riccardo, and I am worried about him."

She touched the diamond ring on her finger. "I asked Karl about Riccardo after we returned from the Excelsior. I pressed him for an answer, but he wouldn't tell me. He has many informants in the city. I told him Riccardo was a nobody, but he wasn't convinced."

"I know there was bad blood between you and Riccardo," I said. "He should have been there for you and the baby."

Mia raised her chin, as if warding off a blow. "I don't think about that," she said softly. "He's my brother, regardless. Many men have made the same sacrifice for this war."

"We both know he's in the Resistance," I whispered. "He knew about plans for yesterday's bombing."

"He would not be so foolish," she said carefully.

"A man who is driven does not always care about consequences."

"Why do you care about him?" Mia asked. "He's of no importance to you."

"He's a good man. He's missing. Someone needs to care."

"Do you love him?" Mia asked.

"What?"

"Early last year, I was you. I was drawn to the intensity of a man who made me feel so alive. But then he vanished, and I found out I was pregnant. To this day he doesn't know what he lost while he was gone. And I'm glad our child is with God, for he will be a better father than my former lover."

"You don't mean that."

"This life is turning into a curse for us all. I couldn't bear to see my child suffer. And thanks to you, she lies in consecrated land, and her soul is at peace."

I reached for her arm, but she flinched and withdrew. "Did I hurt you?"

She rubbed manicured fingers over her arm. "It's nothing."

"Let me see your arm."

Mia shook her head. "No."

"He's hurting you."

"I'll be fine."

For a long moment, I could not speak as unshed tears tightened my throat. "Come away with me now. We will hide you."

"Karl will find me. It's safer for us both if I stay right here."

"Rome is a big city. There are many places to hide."

"Not nearly enough."

"Mia, you're with a very dangerous man. His wife was killed outside the shop."

"It was an accident," she said. "It was no one's fault."

I thought I knew the girl she had been, but I did not recognize this woman now. "There is nothing stopping him from hurting you."

"I'm not worried about dying."

"Mia, please come with me to Signora Fontana's house."

She retreated a step and reached for a silver cigarette case. "If I told Karl what you knew about Riccardo, he would have you inside the Via Tasso prison by nightfall."

"Is Riccardo there?"

"I don't know. And I have tried to find out." Her cool expression flickered, and I glimpsed the pain she was hiding. "I would be careful, Isabella. Karl is watching you."

"Are you coming to Signora Fontana's home?"

"No. My life is here now." She regarded me. "Do you love my brother?"

Love was too strong a word. What I felt for Riccardo was affection, and I wanted him to be safe. "I didn't say that."

A sad smile tipped the edges of her lips. "I hope he does not break your heart. Or give you a child that has no chance of surviving in this world. At least Karl won't break my heart."

"You deserve better," I said.

"I deserve what I have. Now, our paths are taking us in different directions, and it's wiser if we keep our distance. Have a good day, Isabella."

She closed the door, leaving me standing alone in the hallway. Gripping my purse, I left the building more worried than ever about Mia and most especially Riccardo.

Two days later, I received word from Padre Pietro that Riccardo's body had been dumped in a side alley by his church. I left the shop, leaving behind unfinished projects and Sebastian demanding I return. I ran through the noonday streets, past the trams, rubble, and the crowds of soldiers and Romans.

Breathless, I raced in the side door of the church and was immediately intercepted by the priest. "Isabella."

"Where is he?" I asked. "I want to see him."

"It's best you do not," he said. "I have sent for friends to tend to the body."

"No, I'll see to him. He was my responsibility."

"Isabella, it's not a pretty sight," the priest warned.

"I don't care!" Fear rushed me because I knew what I was going to find would be horrific. But I would not be a coward and turn away from Riccardo's last suffering.

The priest led me into the dimly lit room in the basement, and before he opened the door, he paused. "Remember, he's with God now, and his suffering has passed."

My eyes filled with tears. "Let me see him."

He opened the door and turned up the gas light to reveal a draped body lying on the table in the center of the room. I walked slowly toward it as I studied the form and prayed it was not Riccardo. Perhaps a terrible mistake had been made, and he was alive and well and living in the mountains with the Resistance fighters. Riccardo was a smart man, a skilled fighter, and he would not have been captured by the SS.

I reached for the bloody cloth covering on his body and slowly pulled it back. When I saw his face, I didn't recognize it for a moment. It was so swollen and battered it was easy to convince myself that a mistake had been made. But then I looked closer and saw the strong jaw, the curve of Riccardo's ear, and the scar he had earned on the Albanian front.

I drew the sheet past his torso and saw the red burn marks that looked as if they had been made with a torch. His fingers, his lovely long fingers, were twisted and broken, and several of his fingernails were missing.

"Animals," I whispered. "Who would do this?"

"The SS. They knew he wasn't working alone, and they wanted names."

"How did they find out about him?"

"Someone betrayed him."

Raising my chin, I ran a finger along a deep burn. "He did not tell them any information, did he?"

"We won't know for certain, but I have not been arrested. So that is a good sign."

"You?"

"There are several of us, including you, who have been helping the Allies."

"I have been helping Italy."

"Which means you have sided with the Allies," he said.

Riccardo had endured this pain for his sister's and my benefit as well as those men he had sworn an allegiance to. "Do you know who the others are?"

"No," he said. "It's safest if each of us knows as little as possible about the others' work."

"Mia said they had no other family. Is that true?"

"I don't know."

The sound of hurried footsteps echoed in the hallway, and the door opened. Mia stood in the entryway, her breathing labored and her face pale. With a cry of anguish, she rushed across the room to Riccardo. For a long moment she was silent as she studied his devastated flesh. She gently traced the line of his brow over his bruised eyes and then leaned forward and kissed him.

"I told him he would die like this," she said. "I told him so many times. I begged him to be careful."

"You knew?" I asked.

"Yes."

"Mia." I moved to put my arm around her, but she jerked away.

"I do not deserve your kindness. I do not deserve anything."

"This is not your fault," I said.

"I could not convince him," she said.

"Let Padre Pietro take you away, and I'll see to his body," I asked.

"That is my responsibility. I am his family. I'll prepare his body for burial."

"We will do it together," I said.

Mia looked at me and nodded. "Thank you."

The priest was silent for several seconds before he cleared his throat. "We cannot linger. It won't be wise. I'll bring you water and rags and then clothes for him to wear."

When he left us alone, I leaned forward and kissed Riccardo on the forehead. I could summon no tears. "I am so sorry."

Mia and I prepared the body, washing away the dried blood that quickly soaked the muslin cloths and stained the water basin red.

The damage broke my heart, and we forced ourselves to touch each wound and gently clean every one. I thought by washing his body, I could somehow erase the damage, but without the dried blood to obscure the wounds, they looked all the more savage. His screams echoed in my head, and though I begged God to silence them, I was sure they would follow me forever.

We dressed him in a simple dark suit and a white shirt, and I took time to fasten the tie. I removed the small scarf around my neck, arranged it into a triangle, and tucked it in his coat pocket.

Two young men came into the chamber with an empty coffin and set it on the floor. Carefully, they lifted his body and laid it inside the box.

As they reached for the lid, I knelt beside the coffin and said my prayers. Mia kissed him one last time, and I did the same.

I held Mia's hand, and we rose and watched the men seal the coffin and carry it to the small cemetery behind the church to a hole dug next to the small grave I had covered with dirt myself seven months before.

"We will need to move quickly," Padre Pietro said. "I don't know if and when the Nazis will come. Word has surely reached them that Riccardo's body was taken from the alley."

Of course they cared about who had the body, because they wanted Riccardo's pain and suffering to extend beyond his physical remains to the ones he loved. How many times had his interrogator threatened his family? Did they know about me or Mia?

Hauptmann Brenner's trip to the Via Tasso took on a more ominous meaning. Had Riccardo been there all along? Had we been brought by so Riccardo could see us? The Nazis could have threatened our safety if he did not talk. And yet he did not.

For the first time I regretted being with him, knowing that it could have cost him more pain than he had endured.

Padre Pietro stood at the head of the coffin and said the words of the last sacrament. Mia gripped my fingers tightly.

And then the men tossed the tilled dirt onto the simple wood, slowly covering it bit by bit. Soon the coffin was buried and the hole filled. All traces of Riccardo were gone. When the men were finished, the priest sent them away, and together we stood silent in the growing darkness.

"You must leave now, Isabella and Mia," Padre Pietro said. "The less you're seen here, the better."

Mia pulled her hand from mine and, raising her chin, walked out of the courtyard.

"Mia, stay," I said.

She stopped but didn't turn around. "I can't."

"Please. He will kill you."

"My work is not finished," she whispered.

"What work?"

Shaking her head, she vanished down the darkened corridor.

I did not move. "What work is she doing?"

"I cannot say."

"Riccardo *was* helping the Allies."

"Yes, I know you're not fond of them," the priest said.

I lifted my chin. "His work will now be my work."

"It's too dangerous," he said quickly.

"For a woman?" I asked. "The women of Rome are already suffering. I see how they struggle to feed their children and hide from the Allied bombs. It's not too dangerous for me." I met his gaze. "And I have nothing to lose now. I am alone in the world. You'll come to me and let me know what I can do to help."

"You've kept us informed of the gossip in the dress shop. It's been very helpful."

"It's not enough, and you and I both know there will be less requests for dresses if the violence escalates. The women already are more careful with their words, or their husbands tell them less and less thanks to Greta Brenner's death."

"Isabella . . ."

"Swear to me that you'll give me work to do. Swear it to me as we stand by Riccardo's grave."

He stood silent, the wind rustling the folds of his black vestments. "I'll find you when you're needed. I swear to God that I'll do whatever is required of me."

"I understand."

It would be less than three weeks before the priest asked for my help. And when he informed me of my task, I nearly denied him. And then I remembered the wounds on my lover's body and the vow I had made to God.

CHAPTER TWENTY-EIGHT
ZARA

Richmond, Virginia
Wednesday, June 9, 5:55 p.m.

"The heels feel weird. I feel weird," Zara said as she stared at her grandmother and sister, who both grinned at her like proud parents sending their only child off into the world.

"Finally, you look like a real woman," Nonna said.

"We knew she was under there somewhere," Gina said. "She was just buried alive."

Zara glanced at the sleek black dress and would never admit it but liked the way it skimmed her legs. And the dress accentuated her breasts in a seductive but not obvious kind of way. Her hair hung loose around her shoulders in soft curls, and her makeup, thanks to Gina's expert application, highlighted her eyes. "I have to admit, you ladies know your stuff."

"Of course," Nonna said. "We have done this before."

Gina glanced at the clock. "He said he'd be here at six?"

"Yes."

"It's five minutes to six. Is he going to be late?" Gina asked. "Because no creation of mine waits for a man. Ever."

"He's always been very punctual," Zara said. "He's never early or late."

"He will come to the door," Nonna said. "No honking of the horn, no?"

"Correct," Zara said. "He said we'd do this old school."

"Excellent," Gina said.

A car pulled up at one minute to six, triggering the dogs into a barking frenzy. No one was going to sneak up on her ever again.

Gus led the charge to the front door with his tail wagging. The other two followed, as if between the three they'd had a meeting and decided he ran their pack.

"I've walked the dogs, and they should be good for several hours. I'll return in time to walk them before bedtime."

"I'm still capable of walking dogs," Gina said. "I'm not an invalid."

"I didn't say you were."

Gina shrugged. "Good. Don't ever."

"The big dogs are old and slow," Zara said. "And Little Sister is pretty easy, though she's starting to pull on her leash more."

"The girl has sass. I like it," Gina said.

"We'll be fine," Nonna said.

The front doorbell rang, and Nonna and Gina both sat a little straighter. Zara turned to hurry, but it was Nonna who said, "A lady does not rush."

"Make him wait," Gina said.

"Why?"

Both Nonna and Gina shook their heads.

"Because no man gets excited when he hears a herd of buffalo racing toward him," Gina said. "Anticipation, darling."

Zara smoothed her hands over her skirt and straightened her shoulders as she walked slowly in the new sandals. The chances of her making it an entire evening in the shoes were slim, but she had already tucked a pair of flip-flops in her purse.

Eagerness bubbled as she reached for the door. It reminded her a little of prom night fourteen years before, only when she opened the door, the man standing there looked nothing like Ron Tolliver, who'd had acne and long greasy hair.

Nicolas was dressed in a dark suit, crisp white shirt, and no tie. His hair was slightly damp around the edges, as if he had just stepped out of the shower. She tried not to imagine him standing naked under a hot spray of water. He was holding a large bouquet of flowers.

When his gaze swept over her, appreciation flared. "You look lovely."

"You look pretty handsome yourself," Zara said.

The dogs clamored on the other side of the door. "No one is going to let you get away without saying hi."

"I want to see them."

She thought he would hand her the flowers but to cover her bets asked, "Are those for me or Nonna?"

"Sorry, they're for Nonna."

"Don't be sorry. She'll love you for it." If she could have fallen for a guy, it would have been one like Nicolas Bernard. Christ, if only he had not given his heart to Catherine.

He petted all the dogs, who circled around him as if they had not seen him in years, and then made his way to the living room, where Gina stood behind Nonna.

He moved directly to Nonna, kissed her on the cheek, and gave the flowers to her. "For you."

Nonna's face softened, and she blushed. "You are quite the charmer."

Gina smelled the flowers. "Yes, you are."

Nicolas looked at Gina and gave no hint that he knew she was so ill. "Which of you dressed Zara?"

"It took a village," Gina said. "But Nonna and I led the effort."

"Excellent job, ladies," he said.

"Nonna," Gina said. "Can I put those in water?"

"In the blue vase this time." She referenced the vase she had purchased weeks after moving to the United States. *"Flowers in a vase makes a house a home,"* Nonna always said.

"I know the one," Gina said.

Nicolas glanced at Zara, looking at her in a way that was so sweet and charming it scared her.

Gina reentered the room with roses artfully arranged in the vase that Zara had seen so many times filled with flowers. Gina set the vase on the coffee table in front of Nonna, who leaned forward and gently touched a petal.

"If you two don't leave now, Nonna is going to steal Nicolas away," Gina said.

"Are you two sure you'll be okay with the dogs?" Zara asked.

"Yes, we'll be fine," Gina said. "Go."

Zara picked up a sleek black purse borrowed from Gina. "See you soon."

"Not too soon," Gina said.

Nicolas walked Zara outside, the dogs following. When she closed the screened door behind her, they stared as if they had been abandoned. "Such drama."

Nicolas opened her car door and waited as she gathered her skirt and climbed into the Jeep's front seat. He carefully closed the door. Quickly, he moved around the car and slid behind the wheel. Zara looked toward the house and saw Gina and Nonna staring at them through the open window.

"Thanks for giving Nonna the flowers," Zara said. "That was sweet."

"She's a lovely woman."

"With a very fascinating past."

"Really?"

"I'll share over dinner."

"Now that'll be a conversation starter. I was wondering if I should begin with current events, the weather, or apartment hunting in DC."

"If not for Nonna's fascinating history, my fallback would have been the dogs. Always the dogs."

He grinned. "Then we can thank Nonna for conversation and also the way you look. You really do look fantastic."

"Thank you."

"I mean it, Zara." His voice turned husky. "Really terrific."

Zara fussed with the folds of her skirt. "Where are we going for dinner?"

"There's an Italian restaurant in Church Hill. Seemed fitting."

"I love Italian."

"I thought you might. Tell me about Nonna's history. I'm not sure I can wait until dinner."

"You'll have to rely on the weather until we get to the restaurant. This story is show-and-tell."

"Now there's an opener." He turned on the radio, and they chatted about the dogs, the weather, and Nonna until a silence settled between them. "Gina looked good."

"That's Gina. She'll always want to look her best. I've asked her to get a second opinion."

"Wise. You never know what you'll learn." He had done the same with Catherine. In fact, they had gotten several opinions that had reaffirmed the grim prognosis.

"I always admired how you handled yourself with Catherine," he said. "You treated her like she was normal to the very end. Not everyone was able to do that."

"Lots of practice." How many times had she been alone with her patients in the middle of the night with no family or friends around? She became their family, their link to the living, and in those moments they confessed their darkest fears.

He slowly shook his head. "I feel like I failed her at every turn."

"You didn't. She said so often enough."

His fingers tightened on the steering wheel, and again the silence settled.

"I've broken my rule of keeping it light," she said.

He held up a hand. "I'm the one that brought Gina up."

"It's hard to ignore."

"We made it all of six miles, and we're almost at the restaurant."

She forced her body to relax into the seat. When she had worked for Nicolas and cared for Catherine, she'd had an easy camaraderie with him. They had joked about sports, the best brand of chicken nuggets, and whether bourbon should be served with or without ice. A layer of professionalism had been a constant and in some ways had allowed each to be themselves.

Now that the layer was gone, she was not sure how to act around him.

Relief washed over her as he pulled into the parking lot of the Italian restaurant. They walked in together, side by side, not holding hands or brushing shoulders as lovers might but close enough to suggest some kind of connection.

The host showed them to a table in the corner, and they were soon sipping a very nice bottle of red. Anxious to fill the space with non-cancer-bucket-list stuff, she reached into her purse and pulled out the small black box. She set it on the table between them. "Have a look."

Interest sparked in his gaze, and he opened the lid. Inside the emerald broach sparkled. "Wow. Where did you get this?"

"It was in a wooden box buried in the steamer trunk. It contained a journal, identity papers for Enzo Mancuso, a picture of Riccardo Ferraro, and this broach."

"Damn, Zara. The emerald is massive. Do you have any idea who this belonged to?"

"The journal was kept by a woman named Isabella Mancuso, Enzo's widow. According to Isabella, the broach belonged to Signora Bianco, a wealthy Jewish woman. Signora Bianco refused to leave the city even after Isabella warned her about possible roundups in October 1943."

"Do you know what happened to Signora Bianco?"

"She was found dead in her bed the morning after the roundup of the Jews on October 16, 1943."

"Suicide?"

"I think so. She had heard tales of the concentration camps."

"Shit. What a hell of a choice."

"Isabella also hid Signora Bianco's grandson and granddaughter-in-law, and she helped them escape Rome. That broach belongs to the Bianco family, but I have no way of finding them."

"I might be able to help you with that," he said as he turned the broach over in his hands. "Dad's firm has many international connections. I've also read that there were records kept of the roundups, and it might be possible to discover if the family survived the war."

"That would be fantastic. It would mean a lot to me to finally know what happened to them. I'm starting to feel as if I know Isabella."

"Has Nonna talked about any of this?" he asked.

"No. I've asked her straight up if she's Isabella, but she always deflects. Telling me about the journal was a huge step for her. She never once talked about her time in Rome or how she met my grandfather. Gina said our father always knew there was more to his story than they were telling him."

"What did Isabella do in Rome in the mid-1940s?"

"She worked in a dress shop on the Via Veneto."

"Very fancy area. Still very expensive."

"The shop was called Sebastian's, and it was a couture shop that served many wives and mistresses of the Italian royalty and the German elite. Isabella spoke three languages, including German. And she made it clear she was handing off information to a priest connected to the Resistance."

"Damn. Are you sure Isabella and Nonna are one and the same?"

"She won't confirm or deny."

From her purse, Zara removed the picture taken of her, Gina, and her father and grandparents. "I found this in the junk drawer in the kitchen."

He studied the picture. "You were a cute kid."

She rolled her eyes. "Curly hair and glasses. There were talent scouts that wanted Gina to model for them when she was a kid, but not me."

"You were cute then, and you look fantastic tonight."

When his eyes rose to hers, warmth slid through her body. "Thanks."

"What was the occasion for the picture?" he asked.

"It's the day my grandfather received a medal from the government for his service. Nonna said he was a spy."

"Wow. Do you know what he did?"

"No. And Nonna is still very hesitant to talk about it."

"It's that generation. They did what they had to do and then moved on and never talked about it. I could also ask around about your grandfather," he said. "My father has connections that extend to the OSS days, the precursor of the CIA."

"That would be great."

"Happy to do it."

She leaned forward. "I think my grandparents were badasses."

He grinned. "You might be right."

Dinner of handmade pasta with a rich tomato sauce, freshly baked bread and butter, and a side salad calmed more of the nerves fluttering her belly. Nicolas and she regained the easiness they had once shared, and talk shifted to sports, living in Virginia, and the work Nicolas would do for the law firm.

When he escorted her out of the restaurant two hours later, she was smiling, more relaxed than she had been in years. In the car, as she clicked her seat belt in place, she turned to him and said, "Thank you. This was really fun."

"It was fun," Nicolas said, sounding amazed.

"Surprised?"

He chuckled. "I wasn't sure how it would go."

"Me either." Pent-up energy rolled under her skin, leaving her restless. "I don't want this to get weird between us."

"How so?"

"I want to kiss you."

"A kiss won't make it weird."

Instead of giving voice to all the reasons she should not follow her feelings, she leaned forward and pressed her lips to his. He tasted of wine, tiramisu, and the extra something that made her heart beat faster.

He raised his hand and cupped the side of her face, threading his fingers through the soft curls of her hair. "You taste great."

"You too." She deepened the kiss. Her hand pressed to his chest, and his heart beat rapidly under her fingertips.

"Is this for Gina's bucket list?" he asked softly.

"No. Just for me."

"My hotel is close by," he said carefully.

"That's the best news I've had in weeks."

He drove the half-dozen blocks to the downtown high-rise hotel, valet parked, and led her across the lobby's tiled floor. They rode the elevator in silence, and when the doors opened, he took her hand in his and escorted her to his room. A swipe of the key, and they were inside. The large window overlooked the city lights that glowed softly on the James River, meandering through the city.

She dropped her purse on the small desk and kicked off her shoes as he shrugged off his jacket and draped it over a chair. She moved toward him and wrapped her arms around his neck. He pulled her toward him.

Energy pulsed desire through her body, blocking out the outside world. Her problems would be waiting as they always did, but for now they were quiet.

Still kissing her, he unbuttoned his shirt as she reached for the hem of her dress and pulled it over her head. His attention shifted to the red lace bra and panties, and his gaze darkened. "This night is full of surprises."

"Good ones, I hope."

"Yes."

"Thank you, Gina," she said, more to herself.

"What?"

"Never mind."

The moon glistened over their bodies as he lowered her to the bed and carefully pushed down the straps of her bra. He kissed her jaw, neck, and the tops of her breasts.

She slid her arms along his shoulders and his back, amazed at how sculpted his muscles had become over the last two years.

As he kissed the valley between her breasts, she arched toward him and threaded her fingers through his thick hair.

An inner voice reminded her that he would never really love her. This night was going to be amazing, but it would be fleeting. No expectations. But that was okay. She had now. And that was enough.

CHAPTER TWENTY-NINE

ZARA

Richmond, Virginia
Thursday, June 10, 4:00 a.m.

When Zara woke, she did not move, fearing Nicolas would stir and this perfect evening would end. On her side, she faced the window and the view of the river, and she savored the warmth of his body nestled close. The older folks called it *spooning*, and it felt like the kind of moment real couples shared.

He rubbed his hand over the curve of her thigh and down her leg. His erection pressed against her, and she rolled on her back and moved under him. His eyes were half-closed when he cupped her breast and slid into her, and she arched against him. Their lovemaking was as fevered as it had been the first time, and both found their release.

"Catherine," he whispered.

"Zara," she said quietly.

His eyes opened. Desire knotted with confusion and then disappointment. He rolled off her and lay on his back, staring at the ceiling.

He must have been imagining that the woman in his arms had been his late wife, and now he was faced with the reality that he was with Zara.

Zara waited for him to speak. She half expected a hurried apology, but instead he sat up and swung his legs over to the side of the bed.

"Zara," he said roughly.

"Yes. Are you okay?" She ran her fingers over the tense muscles along his shoulders.

He flinched and cleared his throat. "Yeah, I'm fine. I'm sorry. I need a second. I'm a little thrown off."

"I can see that." Last night, his focus had been on her; of that she was sure. But somewhere in the twilight, Catherine had stepped between them. "I'm the one that's sorry."

He glanced over his shoulder at her. "For what?"

"That I'm not her," she said. "That's what you want, what you thought you had."

He shook his head, stabbing fingers through his hair. "No. That's not it. I was confused. It happens sometimes. I dream about her and think she's still alive."

"That's very natural, Nicolas. Feelings don't just switch off." She sat up. "I'm here if you want to talk about it."

He looked at his hands, keying in on his left hand and the wedding band he still wore. "There's nothing to say."

"It's okay to miss her. I don't expect her to vanish from your memories."

"Sometimes I wish she would," he said. "If she left me alone, maybe I would have some peace. And then I realize what I've wished for, and I feel like a real shit."

"You're not a shit, Nicolas. She's a big part of who you are, and her dying created a wound. We all get tired of the pain sometimes."

"She was the best part of me," he whispered.

She stood and gathered her clothes. "You've always been a kind man, Nicolas."

"What happened here wasn't kind."

"It wasn't intentional." She vanished into the bathroom and shut the door, turned on the water, and stared at her reflection in the mirror. Splashing water on her face, she did her best to wash away the disappointment. When she came out, she was dressed, as was Nicolas.

"I'm sorry," he said. "Really. This was supposed to be a special night, and I was really looking forward to it."

"It was a great night. And like I said, it's okay. I understand."

"Really? Because I don't. I don't know why I can't get on with my life."

"You will." She reached for her phone. "I'll call for a car."

"No, I'll drive you. Damn. This is not how I wanted this night to end." He stood rigid but did not reach for her.

"Not necessary. It was a really lovely night."

"I'll drive you."

"No, seriously. I appreciate the offer, but it's easier this way. We both needed to prove to ourselves we're alive. And we did. And it was amazing." She moved toward him, took his clenched fist in her hands. "Now you've finished your bucket list with our dinner—you'll be free." She had believed for a moment she was more than an item to be checked off Catherine's to-do list.

"What if I'm not free? What if I'm stuck here forever?"

"Talk to Nonna about losing people. She's lost more than her fair share."

Zara had never thought about the life her grandmother had lived, but the more she learned, the stronger her admiration grew. She remembered how her grandparents would turn on the stereo and dance alone. They would whisper to each other in Italian and kiss as Zara hid on the stairs, watching. She had always thought it quaint but now realized it was a rare love indeed.

She might not ever have that for herself, but that was the gold standard, and she would not settle for second place in someone's life.

Zara squeezed Nicolas's hand gently and kissed him softly on the lips. He had been up front about the list. And he had always been clear how much he loved Catherine. She was the one who had read more into this night.

Zara left the hotel, caught a car, and within twenty minutes was in her grandmother's driveway, staring at the silent old house. Inside the front door, the pups ran toward her, and she quickly put a leash on them, slid on her flip-flops, and took them for a walk.

As she listened to Little Sister's excited gait and looked up at the clear sky, she realized this was her life. And it was okay. There were people and pets who needed her, and if this was where the universe wanted her now, then so be it.

GINA

Gina was sitting in her grandfather's study when she heard the car pull up. Moving to the window, she saw Zara get out of an Uber. Prince Charming had not driven Zara home. Not the end of the world but also not the best sign.

In the foyer, Zara quietly kicked off her heels, trading them for flip-flops; collected her three dogs; and went back outside.

Gina turned from the window, wincing as her stomach tightened. It ached with every step into the kitchen, and when she reached the counter, she had to pause.

Finally, the pain passed, and she turned on the coffee maker. As it gurgled, Gina sat in a kitchen chair, staring at the rising sun, feeling an odd sense of hope. Life was going to go on; maybe not hers, but Nonna's and Zara's would go on.

Zara.

When Zara had spent summers with them, everyone had been on their best behavior. Always reserved and quiet, the kid clearly did not feel like a part of the family but a guest. Papa always planned multiple adventures that kept the four of them on the move during Zara's two-week annual stays.

Once twelve-year-old Zara moved in, carrying a Spice Girls backpack and a suitcase, the transition was not perfect. Zara was tense that year, still unsure of her place in this new family. One thing to vacation together but another to live together. Zara spent a great deal of time in her room, reading. Papa was the only one who could lure her out, and together they played chess or checkers or read books.

But that kid had become Gina's the day her family position here had become permanent. They'd never had much in common, but they were family. And she'd felt oddly complete.

Maybe that was why Gina had never felt compelled to marry and make her own family. She'd had her own little person to raise and mold. Though that little person had a strong mind of her own, and the two sisters had rarely agreed on much.

She rose, moved toward the coffeepot, and poured a half cup and, because she was dying, filled the rest with whole milk and a tablespoon of sugar. She took a sip, savoring the taste, praying she never lost this simple pleasure.

She walked into the living room to the bookcases on either side of the fireplace, filled with pictures. One of her favorites had been taken in the early 1950s of her grandparents. They had been dancing at some event she could not recall. Her nonna and papa looked so young. He was tall, with broad shoulders and a thick shock of black hair. Nonna was petite and slim, and her light hair curled around her shoulders. What was so sweet was how their bodies leaned into each other, as if there were no one else in the world but them.

In all the years, Gina had never heard her grandparents mention Isabella, Riccardo, Mia, or Aldo. The only remnant of Italy was Signora Fontana's soup and her father.

"Why didn't you ever tell us?" she asked.

The front door opened, and she heard Zara chatting quietly with her dogs, cautioning them all to be quiet. "No barking hounds. Nonna is asleep."

"But Gina is awake," she said.

CHAPTER THIRTY
ISABELLA

Rome, Italy
Thursday, April 13, 1944

In the month after Riccardo's death, I was numb to the world around me. I kept working, sending the crumbs of gossip I heard from the ladies in my shop to Padre Pietro as the Germans tightened their grip on the city with more roundups, looting, and shootings. The Allies continued to drop their bombs, but for the most part the airports were the sole targets. There were fewer casualties in Rome, and for that we were grateful.

Mia spent all her time with her German lover, and I did not see her once. I was glad for the distance, because I could not deal with more sorrow. Signora Fontana's health was failing, and she spent more of her days in bed. She finally taught me some of her recipes, though with the city all but starving for food, there was little to cook. The minutes, hours, days, and weeks blurred.

As I climbed the steps to the church, fatigue weighed heavily on my limbs, and I took one stair at a time. When I paused midway, I noticed a flicker of movement in the alley and spotted the form of a man walking away, his head turned so that I could not see his face.

Standing still, I watched him hurry away, but I had the overwhelming sense he had been watching me. I was not naive enough to believe that my comings and goings had gone unnoticed.

As I entered the church, my eyes adjusted to the dim light, and the cool stones fostered a sense of calm. I understood this space was not safe from the bombings. No place was these days. But in here I could almost convince myself that God protected me.

I found Padre Pietro in his office, talking to two other priests. As soon as he saw me, he sent the priests away and beckoned me inside. "Isabella, thank you for coming."

"You said it was urgent."

He rose and closed the office door. "It's a matter that must be dealt with quickly."

"Of course."

"Are the rooms at Signora Fontana's house still empty?" he asked.

"They are now. We've had several people come and go. Most are homeless now, but all have moved on."

"Does Mia still live in the house?"

"No, she's living with Hauptmann Brenner," I said. "After Riccardo, there was no talking reason into her."

"Perhaps that is for the best," he said carefully.

"Why?"

"I have someone who will need those rooms for the foreseeable future."

"Who?" She knew there were still Jews hiding in the city, moving from hideout to hideout. "Another family?"

"Two men," he said. Under his glasses, I could see the dark circles rimming his eyes. "American airmen."

"What?" I asked.

"Their planes were shot down outside of Rome over a month ago. It's taken them this long to make their way here."

"The Vatican will take them, won't they?"

"The pope won't jeopardize the church's tenuous relationship with the Germans by helping the airmen. If the Vatican is invaded, many more will suffer as a result. The pope, through his emissaries, has discreetly reached out to the churches to take men like this."

"Have you hidden other Allies?"

"Other priests have airmen under their care, but I have not had the opportunity."

"You need me to hide them? Signora Fontana has been very clear that she does not like the bombs. She has seen too many friends killed."

"This is war, Isabella. It's not pretty, and it's fraught with evils. But we must try to find the mercy in the chaos when we can."

"And you expect me to find mercy for these two men?" The anger, buried so deep since the bombs, roundups, and Riccardo's death, rose up within me like a great wild beast.

"God does."

Bitterness soured my mouth. "Where was God when Riccardo's fingernails were pulled out and his skin burned? Where was he then, Padre?"

"I cannot speak to the higher purpose. I cannot. But you have a chance now to be kind. If you do not, these men will be captured and sent to the camps."

"They are soldiers. They understood the risks."

"Isabella," he said softly. "So was Riccardo."

Tears welled in my eyes.

"I wish you and I had the time to sit and pray on this. But there's no time. You'll have to decide now. Though the Vatican is momentarily safe from raids, this church is not."

My fingers curled into tight fists as outrage wrapped around my chest and throat. How much more would I be expected to give? And even as I asked the question, I thought about the boys hiding from forced labor, Signora Bianco, her children, and Riccardo. They had given everything. And I was simply being asked to put aside anger.

"Very well, I'll take them," I said. "Where are they?"

"In the church basement. They're going through donated clothing so that I can bury their uniforms."

"How long will they be with me?"

"The Allies are advancing on Rome. They say it's a matter of days or weeks before they're at the gates of the city."

I had heard as much since the fall. Everyone thought the Americans were days away from saving us, but there was no guarantee the Americans would march through the city gates soon. "Show me these men."

His expression was a mixture of worry and acceptance as he led me through a side door and down a narrow set of stairs. As we descended, my sight grew accustomed to the dimmer light, and when we reached the small rooms, I could see well enough.

Padre Pietro removed a metal key from his pocket, then unlocked and opened the door. Inside, the two men sitting immediately stood and faced us, fingers clenched and ready to fight.

The man on the right was tall and lean, with short blond hair and sharp blue eyes telegraphing his wariness. He looked young, not more than twenty, but his eyes were war sharpened beyond his years. He guarded his right arm.

The other airman had a thick crop of dark curly hair, olive skin, and a large nose. He looked as Italian as any man born in Rome.

"I do not speak English," Padre Pietro said. "And their Italian is terrible."

On cue, the blond man spoke in such broken Italian it was impossible to understand. It had been some time since I had spoken English, but I used it often in my diary and listened to the BBC nightly.

"I am Isabella," I said carefully. "What are your names?"

The two men looked at each other. "You speak English?" the blond asked.

I shrugged. "Better than your Italian."

The shorter man glared at the blond. "You said you could speak Italian."

"I can," the blond said.

"No, he cannot," Isabella said. "What are your names?"

The tall man said, "Lieutenant George Harper."

"Sergeant Ben Martinelli," the shorter man said.

The threadbare pants Harper wore were too short and skimmed his ankles, and Martinelli's pants were too tight. They looked like men wearing castoffs. That was often the case in this city now and not a real problem, but they knew so little about Rome it was a matter of time before they gave themselves away.

"There was a man watching the church," I said to Padre Pietro.

"There is always someone watching."

"They'll need hats to hide their hair," I said to Padre Pietro. "The curfew is minutes away. But there's enough light remaining to draw attention to them."

"What are you saying?" Harper asked.

"That you look too American," I replied in English. "But if we wait for dark, we risk arrest."

"What's the plan?" Harper demanded.

"We get you hats, scarves, and we leave now. I know the alleys between the church and my house. And then I'll hide you until your army collects you."

"How can we trust you? I don't know you from Adam, lady," Harper said.

"If that means I am a stranger to you, then I could say the same. If it were up to me, I would leave you here. But because the priest has asked, I'll keep you safe, despite my better judgment."

"What's that mean?" Harper demanded.

I snatched up two hats from the bin and handed one to each. "It means I have little patience for Allied bombers right now. But I have less patience for the Germans, and I cannot refuse any of the priest's requests." Turning to the priest, who had been watching the exchange, I could see he had picked up enough of our tones and expressions to realize the exchange was not cordial.

Switching to Italian, I said, "Is there any way we can get longer pants for that one? His white ankles reflect like a beacon."

"I can get him socks," the priest said.

"Better than nothing. I don't have much food at the house."

"I'll send some with you. Are you sure Signora Fontana will be okay?"

"I'll make it okay," I said.

"Can you speak in English?" Harper demanded.

"I was speaking of your glowing white ankles that I am sure can be seen from your American planes. The priest is getting socks for you."

Harper glanced at his ankles. "They're not that white."

"They are." I looked at the other man. "You look Italian."

"I'm from New York. My family came over from the old country before I was born."

"Where?"

"Turin."

"Why didn't your parents teach you Italian?"

"They wanted me to be an American," Martinelli said.

"You'll blend well enough, but you both must be careful. Men are still being rounded up for the labor camps. Do exactly as I say. Keep your gaze averted, and do not speak to anyone."

The priest returned with socks and handed them to Harper. "It's quiet outside now," he said.

"Then as soon as the ankles are covered, we will go."

Padre Pietro handed me a satchel of food. "Bread, some cheese, but no meat."

Harper sat and toed off his shoes and pulled on the socks, using only his left arm.

"No one in the city has meat or milk now," I said. "The cheese is a luxury."

"Thank you, Isabella," Padre Pietro said.

"I told you I would honor any request of yours, and I will." I turned to the men waiting for instructions like little boys from a nanny. "Remember, do exactly as I say. Stay close, and do not speak, especially Italian, Signor Harper."

Martinelli nudged Harper.

They left by the narrow staircase and exited through the church's side door. On the darkening streets, the men ducked their heads and stayed close as we hurried down the side alley. Ahead, a German patrol passed the alley's opening, and we all stopped and pressed against the wall. Above, an old man stepped out onto his balcony as the soldiers passed. As he retreated inside his apartment, he saw me. Our gazes locked for a moment. I was not sure if he saw the men, but he knew I was on the verge of breaking curfew, which was cause enough to contact the police. One shout from him, and the patrolling soldiers would stop. Instead, he nodded and then closed his shutters.

I led the men to the rear entrance of Signora Fontana's house, and we entered. There was a pot simmering on the stove, and both men paused, as if the scents were too much.

"I'll bring you up food as soon as you're settled," I said. "For now, to your room."

Without a word, they followed me up the stairs to the third floor and the tiny room the Biancos had inhabited. As I'd told the priest, we'd had several homeless women who'd stayed a night or two and then found transport to the country. Signora Fontana had cleaned the space with soap, water, and scrub brushes, as if she could wash away the city's suffering.

There were two small beds for two tall men, but we were all making do. "Stay here, and lock the door behind me. Do not let anyone in until I return."

"We appreciate this," Harper said in his terrible Italian.

"What is wrong with your arm?" I asked.

"I dislocated it when I hit the ground."

"Take your shirt off."

"Are you a doctor?"

Arching a brow, I waited until he unfastened his shirt and slid it off. I could see the joint was swollen and terribly misaligned. "Sit in that chair."

"What are you going to do?"

"I grew up on a farm. The men who worked there suffered accidents from time to time, and I helped my mother minister to them."

I ran my hand over the misaligned joint, and he flinched. "Signor Martinelli, can you hand me that metal pitcher?"

"What are you going to do with that?" Harper asked.

"I have a trick."

As Martinelli approached, Harper eyed him warily. I slid my hand down his arm and pressed my other palm to his shoulder. "On the count of three, Mr. Martinelli, I want you to hit Mr. Harper in the head."

"What!" Harper shouted.

I pulled up on his arm and pressed my palm. He screamed, and the joint slid into alignment. "There, it's fixed."

"Jesus, lady. That hurt like hell," Harper said.

Martinelli laughed. "Try your shoulder."

Harper rolled it gingerly. "It's sore, but it doesn't hurt like it did. You fixed it."

"I did."

"Thanks, ma'am. I mean that sincerely," Harper said.

I replied with a nod. "Of course."

Down in the kitchen, I dished polenta out of the signora's cast-iron pot.

"Isabella," the signora said from the doorway. "Who have you hidden upstairs this time? I heard a man scream."

There was no easy way, so I spoke directly. "Two Allied airmen."

"What?" She hurried toward me, mumbling prayers. "Have you lost your mind?"

"I am certain that I have," I said. "But the priest asked."

"And you promised," she said with a sigh. "Perhaps this is too much. Even if the Germans don't find them, anyone in this area would gladly take them apart and incinerate this house."

"I know. And I am sorry for the risk to you. Truly."

The signora moved toward an earthenware pitcher, filled two cups with water, and set them on the tray. "They'll be thirsty."

I kissed her on the cheek. "Thank you."

"We are both mad."

"Yes, we are."

I climbed the stairs and knocked on the door. Martinelli answered. Harper stood by the shuttered window, cradling his arm and staring out the cracks.

"Where are we?" Harper asked. "I can't get my bearings."

I set the tray on a small table. "In the Monti district. Ten blocks west of the train station."

"The station in the San Lorenzo district?" Harper asked.

"I'm sure you've flown over this area many times." I stepped away from the table. "Eat. There's a lavatory down the hallway. It should be fine to use, as we three are the only ones on this floor. The owner of this house is a kind lady, and she's graciously allowing you to stay. Please do not go outside, and if you hear anyone downstairs, remain up here."

Martinelli sat at the table and tore off a piece of bread with trembling hands. "Thank you."

Harper looked at the food, but he stayed by the window. "What's outside?"

"Homes, apartment buildings, and beyond that rubble. Did you know two thousand people died in the July bombing?"

Harper's gaze shifted to me, but he gave no hint of his emotions. "You sided with Hitler, lady, not me," he said in English.

"I did not side with that butcher or his man Mussolini," I said. "My family lost a great deal because my father stood up to the Fascist government. My husband died on a battlefield, and the Germans are bleeding us dry. I'll be grateful when all you men have forgotten about Rome. Eat your food." I turned. "For now, we must get along. And hope that your bombers don't end up killing us all."

I closed and locked the door behind me.

CHAPTER THIRTY-ONE
ZARA

Richmond, Virginia
Thursday, June 10, 5:15 a.m.

"Look what the cat dragged in," Gina said.

Zara closed the front door and saw her sister sitting in the floral chair in the living room. She had wrapped a large blue afghan blanket around her body and wore pink footies with the nonskid pads on the bottom. The dogs hurried into the kitchen to lap up water.

"What are you doing up?" Zara asked.

"I don't sleep well lately," Gina said.

"You never did." She kicked off her flip-flops and set them by her discarded heels near the front door as the dogs settled on their beds. "I was hoping the medicines might help you sleep."

"I'm afraid to close my eyes. I'm not ready for it to be the last time."

Her sister looked thin and pale, and her hands trembled very slightly. "Can I get you anything?"

"Just made coffee. There's a fresh pot if you want some."

"Bless you." Zara filled a cup and sat on the couch next to her sister's chair.

"How did your evening go?" Gina asked.

"Great, until he called me Catherine." There was no other person on the planet she would have admitted this to, and she wondered how she would cope when Gina was gone.

Gina winced as she sipped her coffee. "I'm guessing it was postsex."

"Yes."

Gina's eyes sparked. "Before the name mix-up, how was the sex?"

Zara cradled the cup in her hands. "Great. Terrific."

"Not a total waste of a night, then?"

"No, it was a terrific night. And honestly, I don't blame him. Catherine was a wonderful woman. And you can't flip a switch and end your feelings for someone when they die."

"You're a reasonable woman, Zara," Gina said. "Maybe too reasonable. I would have had a minor meltdown."

Zara rubbed her feet and then propped them on the coffee table. "I've never been good with meltdowns."

Gina sipped her coffee. "I'm going to have to add a meltdown to your bucket list. You're too self-contained. You would be well served if you lost your shit with a real temper tantrum once in a while."

"They don't work."

"I beg to differ."

Laughter rumbled in Zara's chest, but when she imagined losing Gina and Nonna, she realized an outburst was very possible. "Does my meltdown have to be in public?"

"Well, public displays leave a lasting impression, but no. You can sit in your van and scream to the heavens. Beat on the steering wheel, and honk the horn."

"That would make quite the show," Zara said.

Gina traced the rim of her cup. "By the way, I've had a will drawn up. It's all going to you."

Thoughts of Nicolas and their evening vanished. "I do fine on my own, Gina. I don't need money."

"You live in a van, Zara."

"A tricked-out van that allows me to save a lot of money."

"You cannot live in a van forever, Zara."

The third dog would make a tight squeeze, but for now she would not worry. "I'd rather talk about you seeing a friend of mine who is a cancer specialist."

"That was a shift in gears. I'm offering you money, and you're talking about doctors. And I've seen too many doctors."

"Humor me, and see one more, Gina. It'll give me some peace to know we've done all we can."

"I'm so tired of paper gowns, needles, and MRIs, Zara. I want the last weeks or months to be here, chilling."

"He's a great doctor, and he has a decent bedside manner. He's already agreed to work you in, so there'll be no waiting."

"It's not going to change anything," Gina said.

"We don't know that."

"I do, but for your sake, I'll see this guy. Tell me he's cute."

"Not bad looking, and thanks."

"Enough about cancer. Where does this name debacle leave you with Nicolas?" Gina asked.

"Nowhere. But that's okay. I think we both needed this night, and now it's time to move on."

"That's very Zen of you."

Zara smiled as she rose. "I do try."

"Have you noticed how your tone of voice changes when you talk about him? It gets all girlie and soft."

"It does not."

"Say his name," Gina dared.

"What?"

"Say his name."

"Nicolas." Zara kept her voice even, but color warmed her cheeks.

"I knew it," Gina said.

"Let's get you to bed. You need the sleep."

"Yes, Doctor."

Gina rose gingerly, and when she stood, it took a moment for her to steady herself.

"You okay?"

Gina grinned. "Sure. Sometimes the room spins a little. Like the merry-go-round we rode at the zoo that time."

"I almost threw up."

"That about sums it up."

Zara settled Gina in her bed. "Remember when Nonna used to tuck us in?"

Gina laughed. "She never tucked us into bed."

"I know. Just testing your memory."

"I'm still in here," Gina said.

"Good."

Gina gripped Zara's hand. "There might come a day when I'm not all here. That scares me the most."

"I'll be right here."

"You won't leave, will you?"

"No. Remember, we're the steady-as-you-go sisters."

"Me? No way."

"You've stuck by Nonna all your life. We aren't that different." Zara kissed her sister on the forehead.

Gina gripped Zara's arm, squeezing her eyes closed before she released her. "I'm not going to cry."

"Good."

Zara closed the door behind her and stood in the hallway as tears pooled in her eyes. Several slid down her cheeks, and she quickly wiped them away.

She looked in on Nonna, found her sleeping, and then in her room tugged off her dress and swapped the lacy undergarments for a big T-shirt and cotton pants. She collected her dogs, who all settled on the mattress in her room, and slid under the blankets. Gus curled at the end of the bed, Little Sister crawled under the blankets and settled her head on Zara's pillow, and Billy stretched out beside her.

She loved her pups, her work, and her family. A week ago, she would have told anyone she was content. But the foundation under her feet was crumbling, and she did not know how she was going to move forward.

Zara woke to the buzz of her cell phone and looked at the display. It was eight o'clock and time to give Gina her morning meds. Her back and neck were stiff as she disengaged from the dogs. They were slow to wake and did not spring from the air mattress, which gave her about fifteen minutes to hit the bathroom and dress. She put on her glasses, checked her medicine chart for Gina, and doled out the pills.

Down the hallway, she crept into Gina's room and found her sitting with her head cradled in her hands.

"What's going on?" Zara asked as she hurried to the bed.

"My gut is on fire. It feels like I've been hit with a two-by-four."

"Take these," she said. "And if the pain doesn't settle in half an hour, we're going to the hospital."

"I don't want to go. It'll mean hours and hours of waiting for doctors and then more time before a discharge. Let's see how the meds do."

Nonna's bell rang, and Zara muttered, "She's never up this early."

"I've always said she's part witch. Nothing happens around here without her knowing it."

"Stay put. I'll check on her."

"I'm not going anywhere."

Zara hurried to her grandmother's room and found her trying to sit up. "Are you okay?"

"You have a heavy foot strike, and I hear you when you're moving about the house."

"Duly noted."

"What is happening with Gina?"

"Gina has a bellyache. I've given her morning meds, but if it doesn't work, I'm calling the doctor."

"You have this under control?"

"Yes. Don't worry."

Nonna softly said, "You're a blessing, Zara."

"Even with big feet?"

"Especially with big feet."

Zara took her dogs on a quick walk, and as they headed back inside, they barked as if complaining they had been shortchanged. "You know the drill, guys. Sometimes the patients come first. It's what we do."

After breakfast, the bigger dogs settled with chew sticks, but Little Sister whined when Zara moved toward the kitchen door. Getting left still did not sit well with the dog.

Zara scooped her up and carried her to Gina's room, where her sister lay on the pillows with her eyes closed. She set Little Sister on the bed, and as she reached for her sister's wrist to check her pulse, the little dog nestled next to Gina.

"There's a dog in my bed," Gina said.

"Little Sister is worried about you," Zara said.

"How can she be worried? She barely knows me."

"Dogs are very intuitive. She more so than the other two. She knows you aren't feeling well."

Eyes closed, Gina fumbled around until her fingers brushed the top of the dog's head. She gently scratched. "Tell her I'll be fine."

"How's your stomach?" Zara asked.

"Better. And my heart isn't racing."

"That's good. It means the medicine is working." The day would come when the medicine might not work, and then they would have to find other care options.

Little Sister licked Gina on the hand. "She's sweet."

"The dog seal of approval," Zara said as she wrapped a blood pressure cuff around Gina's thin arm. She took her blood pressure and found it high. "I want you to stay still. I'll check on you every fifteen or twenty minutes." She reached for Little Sister, who scurried away. "Looks like she likes you better than me."

"She knows a fashionista when she sees one."

Zara reached for the dog. Little Sister growled.

"Let her stay," Gina said. "I don't mind the company."

"If the dog wants to get down, call me, and I'll get her."

Zara smoothed her hand gently over Gina's damp scalp before she petted the dog. Emotions rose up and tightened around her throat as she stepped into the hallway. Finally, she drew in a breath and reached for her phone. She cleared her throat and called Mr. Harper. He answered on the second ring.

"Zara, how are you?" he said.

"Doing well. Wondered if you'd like to come here for dinner tonight. Nonna and Gina were saying how nice it would be to see you." It would have been a true statement if she had asked.

"I'd love to. What can I bring?"

"Just yourself. Thought I'd make pasta with tomato sauce. It's a recipe Nonna learned in Rome."

"I'd love that. Been a long while since I had a home-cooked meal."

"How about five thirty?" It was early, but considering the crowd, earlier was better.

"I'll be there, kiddo."

"Terrific." She hung up the phone. "We're going to make the best of the time that's left, even if it kills me."

CHAPTER THIRTY-TWO
ZARA

Richmond, Virginia
Thursday, June 10, 5:00 p.m.

"I don't see why you invited Mr. Harper to dinner tonight. I really needed more advance notice," Nonna said as she stared into the mirror. "My hair is a mess."

"It looks terrific. Delores just did it, and I've perked it up."

As Nonna stared at her reflection, she whispered to herself, "I look so old. There was a time when I thought I would live forever. That I would always be fresh and lovely."

"You're lovely. And Mr. Harper will think so as well." Maybe the timing of this dinner was not perfect, but time was slipping away too fast to waste any of it.

"The first time we met, we were so young."

"Where did you meet?"

"In Rome."

"How?"

"It's in the journal. You will see."

Her grandmother's tone suggested that was all she would say on the matter. "What was he like when you first met him?"

"Brave. Bold. Daring."

"And then he moved to Richmond?"

"Yes."

"You and Papa were good friends with the Harpers. Do you see him much these days?"

"We used to have lunch from time to time after Papa died, but lately we haven't seen much of each other."

"I'm looking forward to talking to him about Rome."

"I doubt he remembers much," Nonna said as she fingered a diamond teardrop earring.

"I bet he remembers it all. Guys his age are usually dialed in to the memories from their twenties."

Zara pushed Nonna's wheelchair into the kitchen, where Gina held a match to a set of candles in the center of four place settings. Zara had set out the good china and polished the silver, and she had made handmade pasta and Signora Fontana's sauce. It seemed fitting that they share the meal that Nonna and Harper might have enjoyed over seventy-five years ago.

When the doorbell rang, Nonna fiddled with her hair, trying to tuck the soft white wisps behind her ear. "I should have worn the blue dress."

"This one is perfect," Gina said. "You look stunning, Nonna."

"Are you sure?" Nonna asked.

"Yes," Gina said.

"Well, then okay," Nonna said.

"I said you looked great too," Zara said. "Why do you believe Gina over me?"

Gina and Nonna exchanged glances and then chuckled.

"Okay, I get it. Fashionably challenged Zara."

Zara went to the door and opened it to Mr. Harper. He was dressed in a dark suit and had combed what remained of his thinning white hair. He held a bouquet of roses. "Zara. Am I early?"

"Right on time. Nonna and Gina are in the kitchen." Zara leaned in and kissed him on the cheek. "Did you Uber?"

"Of course."

"Come on inside."

He stepped over the threshold and was greeted by her three dogs. "This is the crew you brought with you."

"Billy, Gus, and Little Sister."

He patted each on the head and then dug three dog bones from his pocket. "Can I give these to them?"

"You sure can. But I warn you—they'll be looking for treats each time they see you."

"So warned is so armed," he said easily.

When they entered the kitchen, Nonna sat a little taller and absently straightened the knife and spoon at her place setting. "George," she said.

He crossed the room and kissed her on the cheek. "How are you, Renata?"

"I am good."

"I think you look younger every time I see you," he said.

"You're a liar but a very sweet one," Nonna said. "Are those for me?"

"They are." He handed her the bundle of roses.

"You know my weakness."

Zara took the flowers and reached for the blue vase she had cleaned out this morning. It had saddened her to throw out Nicolas's flowers, but they had wilted as quickly as their romance or whatever it was called. She arranged the new roses. "Can I get you a drink?"

"A beer would be great," Mr. Harper said. "My doc doesn't like me drinking, but I'm not driving, and I feel like celebrating."

Gina kissed him on the cheek. "What are you celebrating?"

"Seeing you lovely ladies. It's been a while since I had such fine company."

Zara set the flowers on the table while Gina poured a bottled beer into a glass. "Nonna, would you like a glass of wine?"

"Yes," Nonna said. "It's a night for wine."

Zara served Nonna, herself, and Gina wine, though she deliberately poured a little less in Gina's glass. The move did not go unnoticed by Gina, who arched an eyebrow as she studied the diminished portion. She said nothing.

They all settled in the living room. Gina chose what was now her favorite overstuffed chair, while Mr. Harper and Zara took the couch beside Nonna's wheelchair. The dogs sat near Mr. Harper.

"We've had a really interesting discovery," Zara said. "Nonna had me in the attic looking for a wooden box. It held Isabella's journal and a rather large emerald broach."

Mr. Harper paused with the beer glass close to his lips. "That so, Renata?"

"I sent them looking for it," Nonna said. "I thought it was time they knew."

"We're convinced Nonna is Isabella, but she isn't giving us any details beyond the journal," Zara said.

Nonna sipped her wine but remained silent.

Mr. Harper regarded Nonna. "I remember Isabella well. She didn't like me when we first met. But looking back, I can't much blame her, given what our bombs did to her neighborhood."

"You were a pilot?" Gina asked.

"Yeah, I'd been piloting a B-17 out of Sicily and later Foggia Airfield. We had targeted lots of the Italian towns. We did the best we could not to hit homes, but it was a war."

"How did you get shot down?" Gina asked.

"I was copilot on the crew that day. It was a beautiful day. Not a cloud in the sky, and winds were almost nonexistent."

"We called days like that *una giornata da B-17*. A B-17 day," Nonna said.

"I didn't know that." He sipped his beer. "On the run to Rome that day, the pilot was Lieutenant Bill Lyndhurst. He and I never got along too well. He was an arrogant son of a bitch. Excuse the language."

Gina winked. "We've all heard worse. Go on with your story."

"Lyndhurst and I always put our differences aside on the missions. Saved our fights for later in the barracks. Anyway, our mission date was March eighteenth, and our target was Rome. We dropped our bombs and hit the city pretty good and were returning to Foggia in southeast Italy when we got hit by antiaircraft shrapnel. It tore us up. Killed our nose gunner immediately." He was silent for a moment. "Our hydraulics system was shot up good, and the flight controls became really heavy. It took both Lyndhurst and me to keep the plane up."

"That must have been terrifying," Zara said.

"Yeah, it was humbling as hell. Our flight crew had made it the last eight months without getting shot up, and suddenly we were going down."

Nonna sipped her wine. "I've never heard this story before."

"Like you, I'm not always anxious to talk about it," Mr. Harper said.

Gina shifted in her seat, as if trying to get comfortable. "How did you get out of the plane?"

"Lyndhurst ordered the guys to jump. One after the other, the men spilled out of the back of the plane. The yoke was getting heavier, and my arms were on fire, and I knew neither one of us was going to make it much longer. When all the guys were off, Lyndhurst ordered me to go next. He said he would be right behind me."

Silence settled over the four of them.

"I argued with him, but he made it an order, so I went. Last I saw him, he had both his feet on the control panel and was pulling on the yoke for all he was worth. I jumped and hit the ground hard and looked up in time to see the plane crash into the mountainside."

"Did Lyndhurst jump?" Gina asked.

"Naw. No way he could have let go and made it out the door in time. And I know he figured if he crashed into the mountains, he'd not be taking out any farmers. We were always told to look out for the farmers because they usually hid downed airmen."

"Was Lyndhurst ever found?" Nonna asked.

"His body was recovered by farmers and buried until he could be moved home."

"How did you get to Rome?" Zara asked.

"I found Martinelli, our tail gunner. He had landed on his feet, but that crazy bastard always did. We ditched our parachutes, took off the flight suits, and stripped to white T-shirts and pants. Even then we didn't blend in so well. Anyone who saw us would have pegged us as Americans. I'm not proud to say it, but I took a couple of old jackets two farmers had left behind while they worked in the fields. We knew Rome was due west, so we started hoofing it."

"How did you get into Rome?" Nonna asked.

"Luck. A farmer spotted us, and he motioned for us to hide in the bed of his truck under sacks of potatoes. Neither one of us was sure about him, but my arm was hurting so bad I couldn't walk much farther, so we took the chance. The old farmer kept smiling, saying something like, 'Don't worry.' He hid us in caves near his farm for weeks and then one day loaded us up back in his wagon. He said we were going to Rome. We were stopped at Rome's city limits, and one of the Germans poked around the bags with a bayonet. Missed my leg by a half inch. When we arrived into the city, he dropped us off at Padre Pietro's church. Told us to find him."

"Padre Pietro seems to have hidden a lot of people," Zara said.

"He was a quiet guy and didn't look like the type to take the chances he did," Mr. Harper said. "But in my book that old priest was a badass."

"You just walked in the church?" Gina asked.

"We went in a side door. A priest saw us, took one look, and hid us in the church basement. We cooled our heels there for a couple of hours, and Padre Pietro came and introduced us to Isabella that night. I can tell you she was none too happy to see us. Argued with Padre Pietro, waved her arms, and looked like she'd storm out and then made a crack about my ankles."

"Too white," Gina said.

He grinned. "And she said my Italian was lousy. We ended up hiding at her place until the Allies came a couple of months later. The rest, as they say, is history."

"What was Isabella like?" Zara said.

"A real sharp lady. Pretty too. Not in a classic kind of way, but she had a bearing that made her hard to ignore. Like I said, she wasn't too fond of us, I'll tell you that, but she looked out for us better than anyone."

"And you ended up in Richmond working for Papa," Zara said.

"Funny how the world works." He was silent for a moment, and Zara sensed he had said all he wanted to about Rome. "I smell something good on the stove."

"It's Signora Fontana's recipe," Nonna said.

"Hell, I remember her. Whatever happened to her?"

"She died in a bombing," Nonna said quietly. "She was a very kind and patient woman."

A silence settled over the room as Zara stood. "If you'll follow me into the kitchen, we can eat."

"Don't have to tell me twice," Mr. Harper said.

When Gina rose out of her chair, her face tightened a fraction, but when her gaze met Zara's, she smiled and held up her wineglass. "I hope there's more of this. It's a great red."

"There's more," Zara said, studying her like a nurse would a patient.

Zara pushed Nonna to the head of the table, and Mr. Harper took the seat to her right. Zara waved Gina away from the stove. "Gina, sit. This is my show."

"I adore being waited on," she said.

"I hope you all like it," Zara said.

"It's home cooked, so it must be great," Mr. Harper said.

Zara set out a large bowl of pasta along with her red sauce, bread, and salad. They all accepted large portions and marveled at the rich garlic-roasted-tomato smell of the sauce.

The four spent two hours laughing about stories involving Papa and Nonna when they'd first arrived in Richmond with their infant son. And there were stories about Mr. Harper's wife, Stacey, who had been a friend to Nonna.

Papa, they learned from Nonna, had had enough money to put himself through law school, but because his parents had not approved of Nonna, they'd given him no extra money. He'd been two years into law school when Harper had reconnected with him. Papa had helped him get set up in Richmond and connected at the law school.

Zara mentioned Isabella several times, but Mr. Harper, though always polite, avoided her questions.

Gina had done a good job of pushing her food around her plate, but she had not eaten much or drunk her refilled glass of wine. Gina was getting tired, and as much as Zara wanted to continue, her sister had hit her limit.

Mr. Harper seemed to notice the change as well, and he reached for his phone. "Ladies, it's been wonderful, but it's time for the Uber to take me home. I can't go all night like I used to."

"It's been lovely, George," Nonna said.

"Anytime you need me, Renata, I'll be there for you." He kissed her on the cheek. "Gina, always good to see you. You get prettier every day."

She smiled and stood slowly. "And you're the perfect southern gentleman."

Zara walked Mr. Harper to the curb and waited with him for his car. "Thanks for coming. That was fun."

"Sure. Anytime." He glanced at his phone and checked on the car's status. "What's going on with Gina?"

"You noticed?"

"She looked okay at first, but she was pale as a ghost by the end of dinner."

"She has pancreatic cancer, Mr. Harper." Saying the words out loud still sounded foreign. "I've got an appointment for her to see a second doctor on Monday, but I'm not too hopeful."

"Damn it," he said. "I'm sorry as hell to hear that, Zara. What can I do?"

"Be a friend to Nonna. It's going to be a rough couple of months."

"I can do that. Your nonna saved my life once, so that is the least I can do."

"That's a story I would like to hear."

"She'll have to tell it to you." A black four-door sedan pulled up. "My ride."

Zara walked him to the car and opened the back door. "You take care, Mr. Harper."

"Don't you worry about me; worry about yourself, Zara. I've seen all my friends die and my wife. It's hard being the last man standing."

"How do you do it?" she said.

"Some of us are meant to endure, sweetie."

CHAPTER THIRTY-THREE
NICOLAS

Alexandria, Virginia
Friday, June 11, 7:00 a.m.

Nicolas sat in his hotel room, staring at the image of the emerald broach on his phone, and wondered who on this planet could have been a bigger asshole than him. It was not like he and Zara had made any big promises to each other about the future, but the way it had ended was not great.

What really stung was that she had been so understanding. Hell, in those moments when he was half-awake, he had felt Catherine, and all the unsteadiness he had endured had vanished. He had had a few women in the last couple of years, but not once had he confused them with Catherine. Not once had he woken up feeling like the world had finally righted itself. Shit, it had been bound to happen sooner or later. The past and present were not as separate as everyone thought, and Catherine would always thread through his life.

Given all this logic, why was he riddled with guilt? Why did he feel like he'd hurt the one person who had stood by him during the worst days of his life?

"Jesus, Catherine, how did I turn into such a moron?"

Her imagined laughter surrounded him. And he sensed her taking a seat next to him, as she had done so many times in the last two years.

"Cut yourself some slack, cowboy. It wasn't the worst screwup." She leaned so close he could feel her breath on his ear. "Remember our first date?"

The memory made him chuckle. He had been working late at the office on a corporate merger. His father had put him in charge of the project, and he had been determined not to screw it up, even though he'd known he was in over his head. He had totally forgotten they had a date.

Instead of getting angry, Catherine showed up at his office, dressed to the nines and looking so hot he nearly melted. She produced a bag of burgers and a six-pack of beer. "Hope you're a fast-talker, cowboy."

They had eaten burgers in the conference room, but all he could remember was how she had licked the salt from her fingertips each time she'd eaten a french fry. She had wanted him to know what he was missing. He had never forgotten a date with her again.

"You're the one that saved me," he whispered. "But you're not here now. I'm on my own, and I don't know how to figure this mess out."

"You're smart, cowboy. And you can fix this, if you want to."

He twirled the wedding band on his ring finger. "I don't know, Catherine. Fixing it with Zara means losing you."

"I'll always be close," she said softly. "But she's alive. Don't give up on living. No one likes a quitter."

And she sure as hell had never stopped fighting the cancer that had consumed her body. She had left this world kicking and screaming.

A simple *I'm sorry* was not going to cut it. He needed a grand gesture to show Zara she mattered.

He paused. Zara did matter to him. She mattered a lot.

If he had a superpower, it was sifting through mountains of data and tracing a trail to its source. He could find out what happened to the Biancos. And there was Zara's grandfather, John Mitchell. Nicolas's father had connections in the army, and finding his service record during World War II might also give Zara another missing puzzle piece to her family history.

He could give Zara, Gina, and Nonna answers and maybe some kind of peace.

Peace.

It sure as hell had been in short supply the last three years. He had moved from fire to fire, trying to put out one before the next ignited.

When he had been with Zara in bed, he had experienced peace. Perhaps that was why he'd thought Catherine had returned to him.

Whatever he had shared with Zara was strong, and he wanted to feel it again.

CHAPTER THIRTY-FOUR
ZARA

Richmond, Virginia
Monday, June 14, 8:00 a.m.

"We need to finish the journal," Gina said as they sat in lounge chairs in the open garage, having morning coffee. Coffee with the dogs was becoming their morning routine. As they speculated on Isabella, the pups chewed their new rawhide sticks.

"I wish Nonna would just come clean," Zara said.

"She's not saying a word until we finish the journal," Gina said. "And she's a very stubborn lady."

"I have thought about Isabella a lot." Zara had lain awake the last few nights, rereading the pages she and her sister had covered during the day. Isabella's story gave her a sense of connection, and right now, given the latest very grim doctor's report, she needed to feel attached to someone.

"She has to be Nonna," Gina said.

"It stands to reason. Otherwise why would she have the journal?"

"Why use the name Isabella?"

"It could have been a way to protect herself. I found a few other journals written in the same time frame, and the diarists all used pseudonyms. Imprisonment was a real danger if the diaries were discovered."

"It would have been proof that she had broken the law."

"Exactly."

Gina rubbed Little Sister's head as the dog nestled in her lap. "Why do you think she never mentioned all that?"

"Like Mr. Harper said, it was the generation. None of them ever mentioned Isabella. Nonna only just admitted to the journal, and it's been over seventy-five years. It's hard to think about the guy that wore black socks with his sandals at the beach and washed his car every Sunday as a spy."

"And don't forget those plaid pants he favored. God, I'm amazed Nonna let him out of the house." Gina started humming the tune to "Secret Agent Man," and they both laughed.

"He was really good at blending in and looking like he was kind of clueless. But he had a sharp mind, and he didn't miss much."

"Tell me about it," Gina said. "I tried to sneak out of the house the summer I stayed here when I was sixteen so I could go to a party, and I didn't make it past the front door before he called me out. The guy was the lightest sleeper I knew."

"I'll get the journal."

"Good. Maybe if we can figure out what happened to Isabella, we'll know about Nonna and maybe Papa."

Zara rose. "Be right back."

As she moved upstairs, she heard her grandmother stir and moan. She found her sleeping, but it was a restless slumber, and she seemed to be calling out to someone.

Zara sat on the edge of the bed and took her grandmother's hand. "It's okay, Nonna. You're safe."

Her grandmother responded, but she spoke in Italian, a habit that surfaced when she was stressed or angry. Nonna kept repeating the same words over and over. *Scusa, scusa, scusa.* Zara knew enough Italian to know the word meant *sorry*.

"It's okay, Nonna," she said. "We're all still here."

Finally, her grandmother stopped mumbling and sighed as she seemed to reluctantly slip into a deep sleep. "Ah, Nonna, too much loss."

Zara rose, retrieved the journal, and found Gina in the garage, staring at the clouds. "Sorry. Nonna was having a nightmare."

"Was she speaking Italian?" Gina asked.

"Yeah."

"She started doing that after Papa died. Those two were always a team. It began again in earnest a few weeks ago. I didn't realize she'd figured out what was going on with me."

"Sounds like she's saying 'I am sorry.'"

"What is she sorry for?" Gina asked.

"Nonna never explains."

Zara opened the journal to the last page they had read. "I showed the emerald broach to Nicolas. He took a picture of it and said he'd look into it, but that was before our date ended." She opened the black velvet box and marveled at the play of light against the hard angles. "It really is a stunning piece."

"It's one of a kind."

"It must have cost a fortune."

"And today, God only knows," Zara said.

"If Mia had the broach, how did Isabella end up with it?"

"I don't know. Isabella hasn't mentioned receiving the broach so far, and she's been pretty detailed about what happened."

"Why didn't Nonna ever wear it? Why hide it in the attic all these years?" Gina asked.

"Too many bad memories?" Zara suggested.

"I don't know."

Zara passed the broach back to Gina. "The Bianco family might still be alive, and it would be nice to return the broach. Nonna's already said she would like me to spread some of her ashes in Rome."

"Wow, that's saying something for Nonna." Gina fingered the broach. "Could you take some of me to Rome as well?"

Zara's throat tightened as she struggled with the reminder that her family would soon be dust. "Sure, of course."

"Thanks. I like the idea of spending eternity under the Italian sun."

"I'll find the church Isabella mentioned."

"Perfect."

Zara refocused on the broach to push aside thoughts of dying. "If we could find out who made the broach, we might be able to trace the family."

"There are jewelers in town that can help us." Gina turned it over. "There's a maker's mark. It looks distinctive, which might make it more traceable."

"We can go today when Amanda shows up."

"Now the day is interesting," Gina said.

CHAPTER THIRTY-FIVE

GINA

Richmond, Virginia
Monday, June 14, 10:00 a.m.

Gina texted a picture of the broach to a jeweler friend of hers and then showered and dressed. Hair and makeup always made the day brighter. But as she stood, pain in her belly twisted, and she froze.

She regularly graded the pain on a scale of one to ten. Until the last week, it had hovered around a five. Irritating but manageable. But today it was at least a ten plus and enough to take her breath away.

She had dreaded her last days, fearing they would be filled with pain and, worse, pity. She had caught Zara's lips tightening when she was upset or worried, but for the most part her sister had kept her sadness hidden. Perhaps it was selfish, but she was grateful that this had not turned into lots of drama and tears.

She pushed into a sitting position and reached for the two painkillers Zara had left out for her. Her baby sister was doling out the pills now because she worried it was too easy for Gina to get confused and take too much.

Maybe she was also worried that Gina would swallow the entire lot and end this slow slide to the finish line. She had considered it once or twice in the early days but had decided she was too stubborn to quit.

But that was when the pain had been a four or five.

She swallowed the two extra pain pills and lay back, breathing deeply. "Christ, this illness really sucks."

Finally, she was able to rise up, square her shoulders, and move toward the bathroom and turn on the steaming spray. She stepped inside and ducked her head under the hot water that beaded on her neck and shoulders. Slowly the meds kicked in, and she finally drew in a deep breath.

She stayed in the shower until she drained the hot-water tank, then toweled off, ran her fingers through her hair, and sat at her makeup table. She stared at her skinny, gaunt reflection. How many times had she dieted to get off the elusive last five pounds? Now those pounds and a few of their friends were gone, and she would give anything to have them back.

"Buck up, girl," Gina said. She spent the next twenty minutes applying makeup, and though she was not red-carpet ready, she looked decent when Zara knocked on her door.

"Come in."

Zara carried a steaming glass of herbal tea, which she set on the dressing table. "Are you feeling okay?"

Gina cradled the cup and inhaled the herbal scents. "And why would I not?"

"The long hot shower is the usual tip-off. How are your pain levels?"

"Manageable since I took the two emergency pills. Pain and I are getting to be good friends."

Gina's phone rang. "That's my jeweler friend," she said. "I sent him pictures of the broach this morning."

"That was fast."

"I still have some moves," she said proudly.

"More than some," Zara said.

Grinning, she accepted the call. "Tony. What do you have for me?"

"I have information on your broach." Tony's southern drawl drew out the words in a slow, easy way. He was never rushed, never frazzled. "But I would really love to see it in person."

"I could bring it by today," Gina said, ignoring Zara's raised brow.

"That would be fantastic," Tony said. "I'm here all morning."

"Great. See you in a few."

Zara shook her head. "If your blood pressure is too high, you can't go. I don't need you blacking out on me because the pain is so bad."

"It's not that bad. And I'm going. This is the one adventure that truly interests me."

Zara wrapped the blood pressure cuff on Gina's thin arm and pressed the button. Gina waited, watched the numbers like a game show contestant. Too low: you don't go. Too high: same deal. But just right . . .

"It's a little elevated," Zara said.

"But not too high?"

"Close, but you pass."

"Bingo. We go to the jeweler. I'll get my purse, and we're off. What about Nonna?"

"Still not talking about the broach or journal. Amanda is here, so she'll be fine."

Gina followed Zara downstairs and paused to scratch each dog's head. The little creatures were underfoot a lot, but they had a charm she was growing accustomed to. "We'll take Nonna's Mercedes. I'm not crazy about the van experience."

"Don't knock it. It's a great way to see the country."

"No, dear, five-star hotels are the way to go. By the way, I haven't seen you sleeping in it since you arrived. Nice having running water and toilets, isn't it?"

"I'm not complaining."

Gina slid on her darkest sunglasses and ducked her head a little so the bright sunshine did not smack her square in the face and trigger another headache. She texted Zara the address. "This is where we're going."

"Got it." She opened her maps app, turned the radio to a soft-rock station, and kept the volume low.

Gina settled into the passenger-side seat against the warm leather, and she actually felt better. Baby sister was a good nurse and knew all the little tricks to make life easier. "We haven't talked much about your bucket list."

"I tackled it, remember?"

"It was just one item, if you don't count a meltdown."

"Number one was a fairly large ask. And I've already agreed to take you and Nonna to Italy."

"That won't count unless you spend at least a week, hopefully two, in Rome. You'll have the money to do it, and I expect you to spend it," Gina said.

"A pet sitter will cost more than the trip."

Gina grinned. "So you'll go for a couple of weeks?"

"I would like to walk in Isabella's shoes, and as long as the trip doesn't involve me sleeping with another man, I'm open to suggestions."

"Have you heard from Nicolas? It's been a couple of days."

"No, I haven't heard from him."

"Have you called him?" Gina asked.

"He's the one that has to work it out. Calls from me aren't going to help. If he wants me, he knows where to find me."

"Do you think he'll reach out?" Gina asked.

"I don't think so. Like I've said, Catherine was his one and only."

"That doesn't mean he can't love again."

"Nobody likes to play second fiddle," Zara said.

"I don't think it works that way."

"Have you ever been in love?" Zara asked. She pulled out of their neighborhood and onto Forest Hill Avenue toward the Nickel Bridge, which fed into the city.

"When have I not?" Gina asked.

"No, I mean really in love." Her brow wrinkled as it had when she was a kid and she had been pondering a problem.

"There was a guy in my midtwenties. I thought he was the one."

"Was that Bob or Mark?"

Gina grinned. "It was Simon."

"The doctor?"

"That's right."

"He was a nice guy. Good looking, and he had the best stories about working in the hospital. He's part of the reason I became a nurse."

"I figured you inherited your medical talent from Dad."

"Remember the stethoscope Simon gave me? Big hit."

"How old were you? Fourteen?"

"Give or take. Why didn't you marry him?"

"He was into his work. Like Daddy was. I loved him for his dedication, but I saw myself taking the same path as my mother. I suddenly pictured myself at forty with kids and a husband chasing a woman half his age. I didn't want to go there, so I broke up with him."

"How did Simon take it?"

"Not well. I broke his heart." In her worst moments, she traveled to the day she left him and how shattered he had looked. "He eventually married about ten years later, and I hear he has a couple of kids."

To Zara's credit, she did not ask how it made Gina feel. It had never felt good, not even after all these years.

They rode into the town, the silence only broken up with the mechanical voice that dished out their directions. She pulled into a handicap parking spot in front of the store.

"I don't have a tag," Gina said.

Zara pulled one from her purse. "I have Nonna's. You're going to need it too."

Gina stared at the blue-and-white tag now hanging from the rear-view mirror. Though it was another indignity, she was grateful the car was close to the shop, and she was spared crossing the hot parking lot.

Out of the car, she moved toward the door and pulled it open. Overhead bells rang.

Standing behind the counter was a tall, lean man in his late forties. His dark hair and olive skin, coupled with a quick, smooth smile, had Gina grinning. "Tony," she said.

"Gina." He came around the counter and kissed her on each cheek. "I've not seen you in a while. Where have you been? And is it true you're closing your shop?"

"On to a new adventure." Gina did her best to sound breathless and unbothered. "I've missed you. This is my sister, Zara."

He greeted Zara and only betrayed a flicker of curiosity over the sister who did not resemble her at all. "And now you reappear with the most fascinating mystery for me."

"Never boring, darling," Gina said.

"Were you able to find any information about the broach?" Zara asked.

Tony reached for his black, chunky glasses. "Of course."

"Tony is a miracle worker when it comes to old pieces of jewelry. Now tell my sister what you found before she busts."

Grinning proudly, he moved around the counter and produced a manila folder. He opened it to the large-scale picture Gina had sent him. "I was intrigued the moment I saw it," he said. "And if you have not sold it, do not accept any offer without talking to me first."

Gina moved to the glass case and glanced at the sparkly diamonds. God, but she loved them. She was going to miss dressing to the nines. "It's not for sale. Can you tell me what you found?"

"The maker's mark was very distinct. I started in Rome, as you suggested, and though it took a few calls, I found the jeweler who made the piece."

"You found the shop? How is that possible?" Zara asked.

"It's very easy. It's still in business. It was made by a Marcello Conti, who was the original shop owner. He opened his doors in 1920 on the Via Veneto. He ran his shop until the early 1960s and then turned it over to his son, and now his grandson operates the business. I sent them a picture of the piece and inquired about Signora Margherita Bianco. They still have their original sales records."

After all this time, Gina thought.

"It's not uncommon for stores in Rome to be passed from generation to generation and to stay in business for centuries," Tony said.

Again, the universe had allocated time in a disproportionate way.

"The broach was purchased in 1921 by Ferdinando Bianco, who was a general in the First World War. Apparently quite the war hero and businessman. He bought many pieces over the years, but no one had ever inquired with the jeweler about them."

"Isabella's diary said the Bianco apartment had been completely looted. Whoever took her jewels kept them," Zara said.

"When an item as unique as this one is stolen, it's often divided into smaller stones. It becomes untraceable very quickly," Tony said.

"We know who bought the broach, but the original owners are long dead," Zara said.

"Signor Conti looked through his records to see if any of the other Biancos had been a client. The signora's grandson, Edoardo, bought an engagement ring in 1943, and then there were no purchases until 1950, when Edoardo Bianco returned to the shop to buy a necklace for his wife. The Biancos continue to frequent the store to this day."

"How can you be sure it's the same family?" Gina asked.

"The store keeps careful records, always creating files for wealthy families. Edoardo was filed under his grandfather's original account, and the store manager confirmed that the elder Bianco had purchased an emerald broach in 1921 for his wife."

"Signora Bianco's grandson and granddaughter-in-law survived the war," Zara said. "They made it out of Italy."

"The couple spent the remainder of the war in Switzerland and returned to Italy in 1946. Edoardo worked hard to rebuild his family's fortune, and the family now owns extensive properties in Rome, Umbria, and Tuscany," Tony said. When they both looked at him a little surprised, he shrugged.

"My goodness, you've been busy," Gina said.

"I became quite fascinated and did a little detective work on the family this morning."

"We can contact the family through the jeweler?" Gina asked.

"He said he would be more than happy to set up a meeting," Tony said.

"Nonna will be interested to know this," Gina said.

"Maybe she can finally tell us how she came to own the broach," Zara said.

CHAPTER THIRTY-SIX
ISABELLA

Rome, Italy
Saturday, June 3, 1944, 7:15 a.m.

I was more tired than I should have been as I hurried toward the Monti district. The whispers on the streets carried rumors that the Americans were within a mile of Rome. In days, many said, they would march into the city.

Though we had been disappointed many times before, I began to see changes in the German soldiers. They were assembling their vehicles at the outskirts of the city, ready to push north. All were on edge, and there were reports of shootings and more arrests for anyone helping the Allies. This gave me more hope. If the Germans were nervous, then the Allies were as close as the rumors suggested.

The lack of food and water had claimed many lives. The church overflowed with women and children seeking protection, and every waking moment I was not at the shop or attending the Americans, I was at the church.

As I approached Signora Fontana's house, I saw a man standing across the street, dressed in a German SS officer's uniform. His head was turned, but there was something familiar about him that reminded me of the man I'd seen outside the church the night I had collected the Americans. If the Germans knew about the pilots, why had they not arrested me? Was this another game masterminded by Karl Brenner?

I circled the block and entered through Signora Fontana's back entrance, carrying a bag of bread and a few precious eggs that I'd taken from the storeroom at the dress shop. Sebastian was now adept at looking the other way. He was practical enough to know the Americans were coming, and if he could win some favored status with them, he would take it.

Inside the house, I found the signora in the kitchen, sipping hot, weak tea. "How are you?"

"Your Americans are restless," she said slowly. "They pace all the time."

"They are not my Americans." I set my bundle on the kitchen table and shrugged off my dark suit jacket.

"They have a certain charm when they try to speak Italian," she said. "It's awful but amusing. The one named Harper tries to ask questions about you. He likes you."

I grimaced. "He does not care for me in the least. I am a means to an end."

The signora's smile was slight. "You could do worse, Isabella."

"What's that mean?" I asked.

"You'll need a husband. One of them might suit. I hear the Americans are rich."

Shaking my head, I smiled. "I don't need a husband."

The signora drew in a deep breath. "Your child will need a father, Isabella."

My smile faded. "What child?"

The signora rose and pressed her wrinkled hand to my belly. "I am old, but I see. Everyone else is getting skinny, and you grow fat."

My hand slid to my slightly rounded belly. I counted back to my night with Riccardo and realized it had been some months since my monthly flow. But this had happened to me before when I'd been under stress. "You're mistaken."

She shrugged and rinsed her cup in the sink. "I'm going to the church. I need to pray for you to find a good husband."

"I don't need a husband." I kissed her on top of her head. "But I'll take all the prayers you have for me."

When she left, my hands slid to my belly. The doctor in Perugia had said I might not ever conceive again. There'd been damage when my daughter had been born. She had died, and I had nearly bled to death.

A child.

The idea of another baby should have scared me, given these times. But I was not the least bit frightened. This child was a blessing.

I found the Americans sitting at the table in their room, playing cards. When I entered, they stood immediately, as if braced to fight their way out of an ambush.

"It's only me," I said as I set my parcel by the hot plate. "And I have eggs for you."

"Bless you. I'm starving," Martinelli said.

"Where did you find them?" Harper asked.

"More and more customers are paying us in goods. No one has gold."

Harper took the eggs and moved toward the small stove. He had learned gas was scarce, and he had to cook as quickly as possible. He cracked the eggs into a bowl and with a wooden spoon mixed them until they were blended.

"We appreciate what you're doing," Martinelli said.

He was the friendlier of the two, and he liked to talk. She had learned he had five brothers and sisters, and after the war his father wanted him to join the family restaurant business. He also wanted to know what was happening on the streets, what areas the bombs had damaged, and any news of the American troops. I told him what I knew, realizing there was no point hiding the city's suffering.

"The Germans are moving their trucks north," I said. "Your Americans might arrive here soon after all."

"Any news on the BBC?" Harper asked as he scrambled the eggs.

Harper never talked about himself, but Martinelli had hinted he came from a farming family, and he said he was one of the smartest guys he knew.

"There's talk the Allies might land in France soon," I said. "But no one knows when."

"There's been no bombings here since we arrived," Harper said.

"Consider yourself lucky," I said.

Harper pulled out three plates and doled out the scrambled eggs.

"None for me," I said.

"Why not?" Harper demanded. "You need to eat."

"Everyone needs to eat in Rome." My stomach had been unsettled for weeks and could only be satisfied by bits of bread.

Harper did not say much, but he was always watching and keeping a close eye. "You don't look well."

As I smelled the eggs cooking, my belly tightened. I had blamed feeling poorly, as I had my missing flow, on the weeks of stress, knowing if the airmen were found, we would all be shot on sight. "I am tired. Everyone is tired." I tore a piece of bread and ate it, knowing it could calm my stomach.

Harper picked up the plate with my portion of the eggs and scraped half onto Ben's dish and half onto his own. "Enjoy."

Martinelli bit into the eggs and closed his eyes in a moment of pure pleasure. "God, this tastes good."

"We'll need a plan to get out of here when the Allies arrive," Harper said.

"And go where?" I asked. "I can assure you there are still enough Germans in the city to shoot you on sight. A shame to die when you're so close to freedom."

Harper stabbed an egg. "The boys are coming, and we need to greet them, let them know we are here. Hell, kill Nazis if we can."

My stomach tumbled. "Do that now, and you'll get shot, if not by the Germans, then by the Italian police, desperate to avoid more reprisals. There have been many roundups in the last few days. You look too American."

"I'm proud to be American," Harper said.

"It's not a matter of pride but of living or dying. We do what we must. Now if you gentlemen will excuse me, I have to retire to my room."

"You sure you're okay?" Harper asked.

"I'm doing very well given that my city is a battleground."

But when I closed their door behind me, I allowed my shoulders to slump. My stomach rumbled, and I realized I was going to be sick, so I ran to the lavatory at the end of the hall. The lavatory's smell alone was enough to upend the meager contents of my stomach.

I had no idea how long I sat there, but when I rose, I was as weak as a kitten. As I reached my door, the Americans' door opened, and Harper looked out at me. He did not speak but simply shook his head as he closed the door behind him and walked toward me.

"You're pregnant."

"I don't know," I said.

"Who's the father?"

"Killed by the Nazis," I said.

"No Nazi is going to get you while I'm here," he said.

"Very kind."

"Kindness ain't got nothing to do with it. I owe you."

"Thank you, Mr. Harper."

After moving toward my room, I closed the door behind me. I kicked off my shoes and sat on my mattress. I reclined and closed my eyes, willing my stomach to settle.

I must have drifted off.

A sharp, desperate banging on the front door woke me with a start. I feared it was the Nazis, and they had come for the Americans and me, as they had come for the Biancos.

I put on my shoes and hurried into the hallway. Harper appeared, fists clenched and ready to fight.

"Stay where you are. I'll handle this," I said.

"Not alone."

"Yes, alone," I said.

A muscle pulsed in his jaw. "I'll be listening."

"Just be quiet."

I hurried down the stairs to the entryway but slowed as I approached. "Who is it?"

"Mia," she said. "Please, let me in."

"Mia, what are you doing here?"

"Please, Isabella, let me in. If you don't, he'll kill me."

I pushed back the bolt but kept the chain latched. Through the cracked door, I saw Mia standing there, a small knife gripped in her hands, her eyes red from crying and a large growing bruise on her face.

"Who did that to you?" I asked.

Mia looked over her shoulder and then back at me. "Karl. You were right about him."

I thought about the German watching the house and wondered if Karl had sent his spies to find Mia, knowing she would come here.

"How do I know this isn't a trick?" I said. "You've been close to that Nazi for months." Thinking of the airmen, I was tempted to leave Mia to the fate she'd chosen.

"It's not what you think," she said. "Let me in, and I'll explain."

"There's a Nazi watching the house."

"I didn't see anyone," she said.

I looked past her and searched the surroundings, and there was no sign of him on the darkened, shadowy street. Mia's bloodshot, watery eyes softened my heart, and I unlatched the door.

She hurried inside the house. "Close the door quickly. I don't want anyone to see."

"Did he follow you here?" I asked.

"I don't think so, but he has spies all over the city. You're the only one that I could trust."

I quickly looked from left to right and could still see no sign of the SS officer. After closing the door, I locked it behind me.

"Thank you, Isabella."

"Have you eaten?" I asked.

"No. I'm not hungry."

"You look like you haven't eaten in days."

"I've been moving around the city since yesterday."

I strode toward the small stove, where Signora Fontana kept small pieces of cheese and a half loaf of day-old bread. I sliced a section of bread and cut off a wedge of cheese. Behind me, the chair scraped against the floor as Mia sat.

When I turned, she set her knife on the table.

"Where did you get that?"

"I took it from our apartment. I've been sleeping with it close by for weeks." She removed her overcoat.

My gaze went immediately to the emerald broach pinned to the center of her white lace collar. "You should not be wearing that," I said. "There is blood on it."

"Karl insisted I wear it all the time," she said.

"It's a reminder that they can take whatever they want." I stared at Mia, wondering if I had ever known her. I had always wanted to believe goodness would grow out of the immaturity, but now I was not sure.

Mia swiped a strand of hair from her eyes. "I didn't take it from her. I swear. But when he gave it to me, what was I to do?"

"You could have thrown it in his face," I hissed.

With trembling fingers, she quickly unfastened the broach from her collar. "And then what? End up dead like his wife? Take it. I never liked it."

I didn't dare touch the broach, feeling if I touched it, I would be a party to the evil that had stolen it.

Impatient, Mia set it on the table. "She would have wanted you to have it anyway. She adored you."

"She wanted to pass it to her granddaughter one day. She wanted it to stay in the family she was so very proud of."

"I helped you save them, you know." When I looked surprised, a bitter smile curled the edges of Mia's lips. "I knew Karl suspected you when he could not find the Biancos. That's why I came here that night. Do you think I bared my breasts to those policemen by accident? I thought Sergio would faint when he saw me."

"Why did Karl hurt you?"

"It doesn't matter."

There was more she wasn't saying, and I was now very tired of secrets. "It does."

"When the Americans enter the city, then I'll tell you."

"Tell me now." When she simply stared at me, I walked toward the front door. "Go to Padre Pietro. He will give you shelter."

She followed me, catching up quickly. "I cannot go out there now. I must stay here."

I thought about the Americans upstairs. "No. You must go."

Mia's finger curled into fists as she looked toward the stairs. "Who are you hiding in the house now?"

"Why did Karl hit you?" I demanded.

"You take all the broken birds under your wing. And I'm here to tell you now I'm one of them. I need a few days. The Americans will be here soon. As soon as they arrive, Karl will run, and I'll be safe."

She was young and selfish. "Your lover killed Riccardo. It was no accident that he took us to the Via Tasso that night."

Tears pooled in her eyes. "Don't you think I know that?"

"Then why stay with such a monster! You saw how they mutilated Riccardo's body."

The pounding of a fist on the door shocked me into silence. As I stepped away, I turned toward the window overlooking the street and saw the black Mercedes bearing the Nazi flags. "Did you bring him here? Did you set a trap for me?"

Mia shrank back. "I went out of my way for hours, hoping to lose anyone that might be following me."

"Isabella Mancuso!" The captain's deep, gruff voice cut through me. "Open up immediately."

"I was spying on him," Mia whispered. "He knew someone close to him was whispering his secrets when so many Jews escaped arrest. He assumed his wife had betrayed him, because she was sympathetic to the Jews and jealous of me."

"Who were you giving secrets to?"

"The Americans."

"How?"

The fist pounded against the door, thundering through the house. Mia's heeled shoes clicked on the stone floor as she ran toward the kitchen.

"What do you want, Hauptmann Brenner?" I asked.

"Open up this instant."

"Do it," Mia said from behind me. "If you don't, he'll summon his men. I'll go with him. Then he might leave you alone."

"I won't give you to him," I said.

Shaking her head, Mia rushed past me and opened the door. Karl stood on the doorstep, his feet braced, his hand on his sidearm. He appeared to be alone. "I'm here, Karl."

He smiled, but there was no joy. "I knew you would run to her. I'm taking you in for police questioning, along with Isabella."

"She had nothing to do with this," Mia said.

"We'll see. I would bet she's a spy like you, my darling Mia," he said.

"Mia is no spy," I said, laughing. "She's a silly girl who chooses men who are no good for her."

Mia put herself between Karl and me. "Karl, this isn't necessary. I'll go with you. I'll answer all your questions."

Karl stared at his young lover, his eyes softening with sadness. "Do you have any idea how you have humiliated me? When Dannecker came to me about possible leaks, it never occurred to me it was you. Sweet, silly Mia. I was certain it was Greta. I believed her death would put an end to it."

"I didn't fool you," Mia said, reaching out for his hand. "I love you."

"And why should I believe you? All you do is lie."

"I have not lied," Mia said, dropping to her knees. "I really love you. I swear."

He ran a hand over her soft hair. "Sweet Mia."

"Let's go now," she said. "Please."

He drew back his hand and struck her hard across the face. "You both are spies, and you both will be punished."

I dropped to her side, shielding her body from his next blow. "She's not a spy!"

Hauptmann Brenner's lips curled into a mirthless smile. "My little Mia has been going through my papers. Who did you tell my secrets to?"

Mia wiped the blood from the corner of her mouth. "I told no one. I was looking for money."

Hauptmann Brenner grabbed her by the hair and pulled her to her feet. "You were working with Riccardo. He was kind enough to tell me that when we had a very candid conversation at the Via Tasso prison."

I stilled my mind, returning to the devastation on Riccardo's body.

"That's right, Isabella. Every cut and every burn on his body was done by me," Karl said. "I especially enjoyed when he cried for God to take him."

Mia's gaze grew dark. "Why would you do such horrors to him?"

"At first I wanted to find out about the radio. But men who are as tough as he and who confess so quickly often have something more precious to protect. I wondered who he was protecting. That's when I found out you were his sister. And Isabella his lover."

"Monster," Mia whispered as she rose, her hand slipping into her dress pocket.

My restraint snapped, and I was filled with a white rage I had never experienced before. I lunged toward him, hoping I could scrape out his eyes and hurt him as badly as he had Riccardo.

Hauptmann Brenner shoved Mia hard against the stone wall and then struck me across the face. Pain radiated through my body and stunned me as I staggered back. Without hesitating, he again slapped me with such force my teeth rattled. I dropped to my knees and could not breathe as the pain spread through my body.

Hauptmann Brenner grabbed my chin and angled my face up to his. "Where are they?"

"Who?" I whispered.

He hit me again. "The Americans. The Jews. Whoever it is you're hiding illegally."

The taste of copper filled my mouth, and when I swiped my hand, it was smeared in blood. "I don't know."

"Isabella doesn't know anything," Mia screamed. "I'm the one you want!"

"You both are liars." He put his face so close to mine I could see the bursts of blue in his irises. "I'll do to you and Mia exactly as I did to Riccardo. You will leave this world in as much pain."

He hauled me to my feet, and fingers bit into my arm as he dragged me toward the front door. Hauptmann Brenner would take me to the Gestapo prison, and by the time the Americans reached the city, I would be long dead.

Floorboards creaked above, and we all turned to see Harper and Martinelli rush down the stairs. The captain pulled me in front of him and pressed his sidearm to my temple. "That wasn't so hard after all."

Harper and Martinelli paused midstep, and then each held up their hands. "We'll go. Just leave her."

Hauptmann Brenner dragged the tip of the gun along my cheekbone, sending a chill through my body. "I'll take you all," he said. "I'll kill each and every one of you, starting with Isabella."

"Karl," Mia said, her bruised lips forming a grotesque smile. "You and I will leave the city. Before the Allies. You have enough gold now to live a life of luxury. You said yourself you must be gone before they arrive."

"I will be."

Mia raised her hands and slowly moved closer, as if approaching a wild boar. "Please, Karl, let's leave. If we go to jail, your commanders will know you were responsible for the leaks to the Americans."

My heart thrummed in my chest as I looked at Mia, hoping she could talk some sense into the captain. As she inched closer, her hand lowered to her side. Her smile was constant, and I began to believe she might love this man. I thought about the knife on the kitchen table and wondered if she had retrieved it and intended to use it. But she gave no sign. Either way, we would all die here today if I did not at least try.

Drawing in a breath, I jammed my elbow into the captain's belly, twisting my torso to add extra force. I connected with his gut, and tension rippled through him briefly before he recovered. "You stupid woman."

His attention shift to me was brief. But Mia drew her knife, rushed toward him, and plunged the blade into his throat. He turned, and the sharp point sliced the corner of his neck. Howling in pain, he retreated, pressing his hand to the blood spewing from the wound.

Harper took the last of the steps two at a time and dived on the captain. He grabbed the gun, and the two wrestled with it. Martinelli jumped into the fray and started kicking and punching Brenner until he finally was forced to release the weapon.

Harper steadied himself, drew the gun, and pointed it at Brenner's head.

"Don't," I said. "There will be reprisals."

"The Allies are coming," Harper said.

"What if they fail again? Many will die if you shoot him before they arrive."

Hauptmann Brenner struggled to sit up, cupping his hand to his neck. "You will all be punished for this."

"Do you have rope, Isabella?" Harper asked, as if Brenner had not spoken. "We'll keep him locked up until the Allies arrive."

"Nothing strong enough," I said.

Martinelli pulled Karl's black leather belt from its loop, rolled him on his belly, and dragged his hands behind his back. He fastened Brenner's arms together and lashed them in place. "Isabella, is there a basement or root cellar?" Harper asked.

"Yes. Through the kitchen. I'll show you the way."

"We'll lock him in the cellar and wait on the Allies," Harper said.

"That could be days or weeks," Martinelli said.

"So be it," I said.

Outside the building, several trucks pulled up in front of the house, and when I looked out, I saw German tank cars.

"Did you think I came alone?" the captain asked. "They are under orders to burn this house to the ground if I do not come out immediately."

"There is a rear exit," I said. "I know a place where we can hide."

"Holy Christ," Martinelli said. "They have grenades."

"They are good, loyal soldiers," Hauptmann Brenner said.

I grabbed Mia as a soldier tossed the first grenade toward the door. Seconds ticked, and then another hit the front of the house and exploded. Rubble from the ceiling fell as the walls crumbled. My ears rang, and I could barely breathe as I stumbled with Mia.

Hauptmann Brenner lay on his side, several large rocks and beams pinning him down. He was still, and then he jerked his legs forward. It was too much to hope he had died.

Harper lifted me to my feet while Martinelli steadied Mia.

Coughing, I turned. "The back exit."

As we ran, Mia rushed toward Hauptmann Brenner. Gripping her knife, she dragged it across his neck, slicing his throat. "That is for Riccardo."

"Mia," I shouted.

She stared at his body, her chest rising and falling, and then ran after us. Another grenade exploded.

My head was spinning as we four raced through the alley and two more grenades landed in the foyer and detonated in the house. The windows blew out, and fire ignited inside. Dizzy, I caught my foot on the cobblestones. I tripped and fell hard.

I thought about my unborn child, the babies I had buried, Riccardo, and Enzo. It seemed my child and I were soon to cross over. My world went black.

I opened my eyes, and as they focused, I saw the SS insignia on the gray uniform. Raising my arms, I lashed out. Strong hands grabbed my hands.

"Isabella!"

Aldo's familiar voice shocked me to stillness. "Don't fight."

"You are German?"

He was frowning as he ran his hands over my body in a clinical, quick way and searched for broken bones. "Can you stand?"

"Yes, I think so." I shoved a thick lock of hair off my face.

"Then get up," he ordered.

"Where are the others?" I asked.

"I've sent Harper and Martinelli on with Mia," he said gruffly.

My vision refocused on the SS insignia on his collar. "How do you know their names?"

"It doesn't matter now," Aldo said as he pulled me to my feet. I staggered, bumping into him. Firm hands wrapped around my waist and gripped my arm. "We need to get out of here."

Glancing over my shoulder, I saw flames roar and consume Signora Fontana's house. "Karl Brenner was in that building. Mia killed him."

"Good," Aldo said. "Good riddance."

My arms were scratched, and my body ached as I lurched forward. "Where are we going?"

"You told Mia you knew a place."

"The shop. In the Via Veneto. They've not bombed that area so far."

"Right. Then we will go there."

CHAPTER THIRTY-SEVEN
ZARA

Richmond, Virginia
Monday, June 14, 5:00 p.m.

The weather had grown oppressively hot as the three Mitchell women gathered at the kitchen table. After they finished a light supper, Zara read the last of Isabella's journal.

Gina pushed around her untouched pasta and sipped sparingly on her glass of rosé wine. "Nonna, how did you escape Rome?"

Nonna dabbed her napkin to her face. "I don't remember. It was so long ago."

"Nonna, you don't forget," Gina said. "You can still recite each grade I earned my senior year of high school."

"They weren't the best grades," Nonna said. "I was worried."

"If you didn't want to talk about Rome, you wouldn't have told us about the wooden box. I would have found it after you passed and been left to speculate," Zara said. "And you know how I hate unanswered questions."

"Who was Aldo?" Gina asked. "And do not say you don't remember. Neither one of us has a lot of time left, so you'll have to spill soon."

Nonna regarded Gina for a long moment and then in a quiet voice, as if she were revealing a dangerous secret, said, "He was your grandfather."

"You mean Papa?" Gina said.

"Of course. As you know, he spent some of his youth in Italy, and he spoke Italian fluently, like a native. When the war broke out, like many men, he signed up. He told anyone who would listen that he spoke Italian and that he should be placed in Italy as a spy. Which of course is what they did in early 1942."

"Was he working with Padre Pietro?" Zara asked.

"Not at first. When he arrived, he had to build a network of men and women he could trust. Riccardo was one of his first recruits."

"How did you meet him?" Zara asked.

"I met him at a café party that Riccardo took me to. He asked me to dance."

"Was it love at first sight?" Zara asked.

"He said it was for him, but for me, no." She drew in a deep breath and exhaled slowly. "As you say, one kiss led to another."

"I never remember you two saying a word about the war."

"We did some in the early days, when your father was a baby. But as he grew and time stretched on, we chose not to think about it. It was easier to forget."

"Wait. Are you Isabella?" Zara asked.

Nonna carefully set down her fork and reached for her glass of wine. She took a liberal sip. "No, I am not Isabella."

Gina and Zara sat in stunned silence, staring at their grandmother.

"Then who are you?" Zara asked. "How did you get her journal?"

"I found it at Sebastian's," Nonna said. "She had taken to hiding it there in those last weeks."

"What happened to her?" Zara asked.

"Signora Fontana died the night her house came down. She had been returning to her home when the explosions occurred. It would be days before her body was found in the rubble. Isabella and Mia left Rome for Umbria because there was more food, and the air was cleaner. In many ways, the two of them were like sisters and all each other had." She was silent for a long moment as she moved her bent fingers along the wineglass stem.

"So how do you fit into all this?" Zara asked.

"I am Mia."

Both Gina and Zara exchanged glances. Of all the theories they had had about Isabella, they had never once assumed their grandmother was Mia.

"Wait a minute," Zara said. "Your name is Renata, not Mia."

"Mia was a family nickname that stuck. I stopped using it when I came to America."

"If you're Mia, that means you lost a baby in the summer of 1943. How did Papa figure into this? The way Isabella wrote about him, I thought maybe he had a thing for her."

"No 'thing,' as you said. But he respected Isabella. And he appreciated what she had done for our child."

"The baby you had, Gina, was Papa's?"

"Yes. We met at the café, as I said, and he kept finding a way to see me. We began a secret affair, and I fell deeply in love with him. I knew he was involved in some part of the Resistance, but I had no idea he was an American. He and my brother shared a passion for freeing Italy, and the two left Rome shortly before I found out I was pregnant."

"Where did they go?" Zara asked.

"Naples. They were trying to set up networks to help the Allies when they landed in Italy."

"And then you had the baby alone," Zara said. "When did he find out about the baby?"

"When he saw Isabella in Padre Pietro's office, and she told the priest the baby was mine."

"Had he come back for you?" Gina asked.

"Yes, but I didn't know that. And he could not make himself known to me. It was far too dangerous at that time. The Germans and the Fascist police were arresting people for no reason, and if anyone were to dig into his background, they would have known his papers were forgeries."

"You became Karl Brenner's lover," Zara said.

"Grief and anger make us foolish. I thought I could not only hurt Aldo but I, too, might earn my brother's respect and be a source of information for the Allies."

"That night after the bombings. You insisted on seeing Brenner. Aldo told Isabella he would escort you. Why?"

"It was his chance to see me alone," she said.

"You have lost your mind." Aldo spoke quietly as he gripped her arm.

"Maybe I have," she said. "What difference does it make to you?"

"Brenner will kill you."

"Not if I'm careful."

"We need to talk properly."

She tried to yank her arm out of his grip, but it was unbreakable. "We're done."

"We are far from finished," he said.

He approached a parked car and opened the front passenger door. "Get in. We will talk before I deliver you to that monster."

"No."

"Get in the car."

As she considered running, several Roman police dressed in black uniforms strolled along the sidewalk. She knew they were part of Italy's secret police, so she got in the car as Aldo waved to them casually, smiled, and got behind the wheel. He turned to her as a lover might. They both sat in tense silence as the police passed.

"I know about the baby," he said quietly.

All the fight and anger melted from her body. "How?"

"I was at the church when Isabella brought her to Padre Pietro."

Her body had shed so many tears she was certain there were none left to give, but they still came, spilling down her cheek.

He took her hand in his and said quietly, "I am so sorry."

"There is nothing to be done about it," she said softly.

"I love you, Mia," he said. "I have since the moment I saw you laughing at that party."

She closed her eyes, and the pain gripping her heart eased. When he touched her face, she looked into his. "Now is not the time for love."

Shaking his head slowly, he kissed her on the lips. She had missed his touch and hungered for it more than she had realized.

They drove to his small apartment and that night made love. It was as endearing as it was passionate. When she rose before dawn to dress, he sat propped on the bed pillows, staring at her. "You can't go back to him," he said.

"I have to. I can learn so much."

He rose out of bed and laid his hands on her shoulders. "There will be another way."

"Not until this war ends. We both know that."

His face grim, he reached in his coat pocket and removed a knife. "Keep this close. Promise me you'll use it if you have to."

She ran her fingers over the worn black handle. "I promise."

Snatching up her purse, she hurried from the room, fearful if she lingered, she would lose courage. She went straight to Sebastian's.

"And then Brenner caught you going through his papers?" Gina said.

"Yes."

"Where is Isabella?" Gina asked.

Nonna closed her eyes and again lapsed into silence. Zara thought she might not answer, but when she opened her eyes, they reflected raw pain. "After the Americans arrived, Isabella and I left Rome, as I said."

Neither Gina nor Zara spoke as they waited for her to continue. Nonna took a moment to rearrange the folds of her skirt. "Isabella died giving birth to her son. I was with her, holding her hands as the midwife helped with the delivery. I thought she was going to be fine. And then she started to bleed, and before I realized it, she was gone."

Zara studied the deepening lines in her grandmother's face. "And the baby?"

"Your father, of course."

"You and Papa weren't Daddy's biological parents?" Gina asked.

"The boy was my nephew and the child of a woman I respected greatly. I took him to raise as my own without a second thought."

"Did you ever tell Daddy?" Zara asked.

"No," she said. "There were times your grandfather and I wished we had, but our generation didn't talk about the past. We moved forward. We tried to give him his best life, but as you girls know, he was never settled or content. So like Riccardo."

"How did Papa find you?" Gina asked.

"He came looking for Isabella and me in Assisi. By then your father was four or five months old, and I was supporting us, taking work from anyone who needed mending or a new dress made. We were barely getting by, but I was content. I was where I belonged."

"And Papa showed up," Zara said.

"And you two made up?" Gina asked.

Nonna laughed softly. "No. Not at all. But he felt an obligation to Isabella and Riccardo's son. He saw to it we had extra food rations, and then he left. I thought he would never return, but a week later there he was. These visits went on for several weeks until finally he told me he was returning to the United States. He asked me to marry him. Our love had never died, and we shut the door on the past. God did not bless us with more children, but we had your father, and he gave us you two girls. Our lives were full."

They all sat in silence.

"In my heart your father was my son, and I didn't want him to think less of me," Nonna said. "I should have shown him Isabella's journal when he was a young man. Papa wanted me to tell him, but I begged him to remain silent. I thought no good would come from the truth."

"What about the broach?" Zara asked. "How did you get it?"

"When I returned to the kitchen to get the knife, I took it as well. I thought it could be of use."

"You recognized the broach when Brenner gave it to you?" Zara asked.

"Yes. But I could not speak for fear Brenner would kill me. He already suspected me by then."

"You were spying on him?" Zara said.

"Yes. I was able to track who Karl was hunting and able to tip off many. As I told Isabella, my arrival the night the police showed up for the Biancos was not an accident. I would like to find the Biancos," Nonna said. "The emerald belongs to them. I am too old to find them, but you girls are clever."

"We actually have a little news about them," Zara said. "Finding them might not be so hard."

CHAPTER THIRTY-EIGHT
ZARA

Richmond, Virginia
Wednesday, July 7, 3:00 p.m.

Zara sat in the garage, enjoying the afternoon warmth. It was good to be in the fresh air and out of the air-conditioning, which always had an antiseptic quality to it. Both her patients were asleep, as was becoming the afternoon routine. Gina was getting worse. Despite all her best efforts to follow the drug protocols to the letter, her sister's body was failing.

Zara stared at the garage ceiling, letting the tears slide. She was not going into any long spiel with God about unfairness or the lack of time. She had seen so many patients' families promise the moon *if only* . . .

But if she were honest, if she knew what God or the universe wanted in exchange for Gina, she would have given it. But the magic words would always be a mystery.

A Jeep pulled up, and Gus stood. His deep-throated bark echoed in the open garage. She rose, and when she saw Nicolas emerge from the car, she stilled.

Nicolas was wearing khakis and a button-down, looking as preppy as he had two years before. The clock was turning back in time, and his old life was pulling on him. Instinctively, she glanced to his left hand, expecting to see a wedding band, and was surprised when she did not.

"How's the job going?" Zara asked.

He smoothed his hand over his shorn hair, as if he were still getting used to it. "It's not bad. I haven't forgotten as much as I thought."

"I have no doubt you'll thrive. You're one of the smartest guys I know."

He strode toward her with purpose. "I'm sorry for being such an ass."

She shook her head. "You have nothing to apologize for, Nicolas. Seriously."

He stopped within inches of her, slid his hands into his pockets. The scent of expensive aftershave drifted toward her. "I should have been here earlier, but I wasn't sure I could be around death again. And then I realized I needed to man up and see you. How is it going here?"

"Not great. Gina is getting worse. She can barely get out of bed now, and we're talking about hospice care."

"I'm sorry as hell, Zara. I know how this sucks."

"She's a lot like Catherine. She's not afraid, has maintained her sense of humor, and still insists on wearing lipstick. I wear it in solidarity."

"I noticed," he said. "It looks good."

"Thanks."

"Did she ever add more to your bucket list?"

"You mean like sleep with another guy?" When he tensed, she enjoyed a moment of satisfaction. "Nothing like that. Gina and Nonna want me to take some of their ashes to Rome. They want me to find the Biancos and give them the broach. I suppose that's on the bucket list as well."

"Any luck with the Biancos?"

"The jeweler who made the broach said he would reach out, but I haven't heard back."

"I did drop a few lines in the water regarding your grandfather. A buddy of my dad's thinks he might be able to get his intelligence reports. They are declassified now, so it's a matter of getting them."

"Wow. That would be terrific."

"The first item on the list was pretty great. Inspired," he said. "And a trip to Italy will be nice."

Zara could feel the pull toward him and resisted. "Yeah, so far, item number one was pretty good."

"Pretty good?" He arched a brow.

"Great."

He reached out and took her hands in his. "I know your life is upside down now. And this is not the time for anything other than what you have on your plate. But I want you to know I'm here if you need any help."

"What does that mean?" she asked.

"Anything."

"Anything? Again, a word that means everything and nothing."

"I don't make promises I can't keep," he said. "But I would like to keep seeing you."

"Why?"

"You make me feel alive. No one else has done that since Catherine. I've seen other women, but none ever made me feel whole, like you did."

Her resolve to be cool disintegrated. "Kiss me."

Without hesitation he cupped her face and kissed her on the lips. She closed her eyes, savoring the beat of her heart and the full-on sensation that she was alive. Guilt edged close, but she pushed it away. She needed this to keep going.

"That was nice," he said.

"Nice?"

He smiled. "Great." He kissed her gently on the lips. "I want you to know I'm here, and I'm not going anywhere."

"Why are you saying all this?" she asked.

"I care a lot about you. I want to see you happy. And I missed the hell out of you."

"I've tried really hard not to miss you," she said.

"Did it work?"

"No."

She wanted him to stay and take her in his arms. But now was not the time. She had witnessed this moment so many times in her career. Families faced with death allowed their emotions to soar high only to see them quickly crash to the ground.

"I wish I could make it all go away," he said.

"I know."

This transition was only hers to travel; no matter how much people wanted to help, they could not. And if anyone understood this, it was him.

"I'll call soon," she said.

"I'm less than two hours away. I'll come anytime you need me."

She would not put that burden on him. She laid her head against his chest, listening to the beating of his heart. "Nice to have a friendly ear."

He kissed her again, and they sat together for a long time before he finally rose. "I'm here for you."

"I know."

He left her standing in the garage with her dogs, watching him drive off.

Two weeks later, Gina passed in the early morning hours. Zara lay beside her in the bed, Little Sister tucked between them. Nonna's face was still and stoic as she sat holding Gina's hand. Gus and Billy slept on the floor beside the bed. They had all seen death, but when the moment came and Gina drew her last breath, it was no less painful.

Zara and Nonna both kissed Gina's forehead, and then Zara called the police and then the mortuary to collect her sister's body. There were no tears, no words as she spoke to the police officer about her sister. He filled out a form, she signed it, and then the mortuary team, a man and woman dressed in black suits, arrived, and she escorted them to Gina. They moved Gina's body to a stretcher, but when they readied to cover her with a quilt, Zara said, "Wait."

She grabbed a satin blanket that had been Gina's favorite for years. "Use this. She never liked quilts and would be appalled to be seen in one."

"We can't return it," the woman said.

"That's fine."

Zara kissed her sister on the head and then helped Nonna up from her wheelchair. Her grandmother kissed her and whispered soft words in Italian. "I'll see you soon."

Zara escorted Nonna out of the room, and the two waited in the living room. The team took Gina away, and Zara and her grandmother sat in the silence, listening to a clock tick.

"I could use a whiskey," Zara said.

"Get the fifty-year-old Scotch whisky from your grandfather's study. And pour me a glass."

Minutes later they both stared into empty glasses. "Thank you," Nonna said.

Zara refilled her glass and downed it, knowing her grandfather would understand why she had guzzled and not sipped. Experience told her the gut punch of emotions was coming—maybe not today or tomorrow, but it was a matter of time. For now, she was blissfully numb. "Thank me for what?"

"For escorting your sister to the light. I could not have done it alone again. And for helping me speak the truth. I will go to my grave with a clear mind."

"You should never have had to do it alone." She considered refilling her tumbler. "We are family, Nonna."

"Do you forgive me for my lies?"

Zara squeezed her hand. "We would not be here now if not for you."

"Your father might have been a better father if I had been honest."

"You don't know that," she said. "We all make choices, including him."

Zara had imagined the funeral would be a small, private, and, of course, tasteful affair, as Gina had requested. But her sister's life had touched the lives of so many the small graveside service commanded a circle of mourners that numbered at least one hundred people.

Nonna, dressed in all black, was silent through most of the ceremony. Stoic, she shook hands for over an hour as each of the well-wishers spoke to her.

Finally, when the last person left and the funeral director told Zara it was time to lower the casket into the ground, she pushed Nonna's wheelchair to her van. She opened the front door and ducked so Nonna could put her hand on her shoulder and shift her body inside.

"You did good for your sister," Nonna said.

"We did it together."

"No, it was you."

Zara clicked her grandmother's seat belt in place, and as she stood, she saw Nicolas walking toward them. He was dressed in a charcoal-gray suit, his hair was brushed back, and dark aviator sunglasses covered his eyes. He moved with a steady confidence, filled with the strength she needed. She had not seen him during the service and had done her best not to search for him.

"Your man is here," Nonna said.

"He's not my man," Zara replied.

Nonna chuckled. "Sometimes, Zara, you're very smart and sometimes not."

She had not seen Nicolas since the afternoon in the garage, but they had spoken on the phone many times, and last week, she had texted him and told him about the funeral.

"Hey," she said.

"I'm sorry I was late. Traffic on I-95." He leaned past Zara to Nonna. "My sincere condolences."

"That means something coming from you," Nonna said. "I'm glad you're here."

He reached into his breast pocket and removed a piece of white paper neatly creased. "I have information for you ladies," he said. "About the Biancos."

Nonna regarded him with sharp curiosity. "How did you know about them?"

"Zara told me what her jeweler friend said about the shop in Rome."

"I haven't had time to follow up," Zara said.

"I did. I took it a step forward and tracked down Edoardo Bianco's grandson, Roberto. Edoardo's been ill the last month, and Roberto had not had a chance to tell his grandfather about the broach." He handed the slip of paper to Nonna, and she regarded his neat, precise handwriting. "I remember this area."

"It's not far from the Via Veneto." He grinned. "I had to look it up on Google Maps to be sure."

"Good," Nonna said. "This is good. You two will return the broach for me. And I'll write a note for you to deliver to Signor and Signora Bianco. I would take it myself, but my days of long-distance travel have ended."

"Nonna, I said I would take care of it. It's not exactly fair to ask Nicolas. He's just restarted his job."

"Put it on my bucket list," Nonna said.

Nicolas looked at Zara. "I'm in if you want me."

"I would love for you to come," Zara said.

"Good, then, Nonna, you may consider it done."

"Excellent. Now we must return home. The caterers will be waiting for us, and Amanda will need us to greet Gina's friends. Gina would be quite disappointed if her party was not a success."

EPILOGUE

ZARA

One Year Later
Monday, May 2
Rome, Italy

Nonna had passed in her sleep eight weeks ago with Zara and the pups at her side. She had been watching her favorite game show, *The Price Is Right*, with Little Sister sitting by her side. Nonna and Zara had been arguing about the price of a catamaran on the show when Nonna had closed her eyes. She had sucked in a breath, and just like that she was gone.

Her funeral had been a private affair. She had not wanted the fanfare of Gina's funeral but had asked that George Harper attend. So, only Zara, Nicolas, Mr. Harper, and the pups had been at her service. Afterward, they had returned to her house, eaten pasta, and toasted with John Mitchell's best bourbon.

By the end of April, Nicolas's plans for their trip were in place. Zara had wondered if they should wait, but he had insisted Nonna would have wanted them to go immediately.

Zara had paid a king's ransom to Mr. Harper's great-granddaughter to babysit the pups, and she and Nicolas had left for Europe.

It had been a cool spring day when they'd landed in Rome, carrying the broach, a letter from Nonna, and two small containers holding Nonna's and Gina's ashes.

They arrived at the church of Saint Luca in the Monti district Isabella had written about in her journal. In the digital age, it had been easy enough to reach out to the church staff and speak to them about burial protocol. Of course, there was an endless amount of paperwork, red tape, and a donation to the church.

When they stood at the gravestones of Riccardo Ferraro and Isabella Mancuso, both of them did not speak for a long time. Isabella had been alive and vibrant in Zara's mind. She had walked side by side with Isabella in Rome in 1943 and 1944 and had shared her triumphs and losses. It had taken her time to reconcile that Isabella had unfairly died at the age of twenty-one.

Isabella was Zara and Gina's biological grandmother and Riccardo their grandfather. The lives of two people who had died more than seventy-five years ago had given them so much. She was equally grateful to Nonna and Papa, who had taken Isabella's infant son into their lives and loved him like he was their own.

The funeral service was conducted in Italian, but it shared the same melodic tones that Zara remembered from Gina's and Nonna's funerals. She had thought this time around she would not feel such sadness, but the weight of the losses hit her with an equal punch.

They thanked the priest and remained by the graves, staring at the two new headstones next to the two older ones bracketing the tiny infant's unmarked grave.

Nicolas threaded his fingers into Zara's. "I can hear your thoughts."

Zara tightened her grip. "Nonna had two lives. And now she'll rest forever in both worlds."

"She lived a long and full life. And Gina packed so much into every second of hers."

"Gina was gone before her time, like Isabella and Catherine."

"Life is fragile," Nicolas said. "We're here one day and gone the next. Which is all the more reason to make the most of what we have while we're here."

"Thank you for coming," she said.

"I wouldn't have missed it."

In the last ten months, he had settled into his job in the law firm but had chosen to spend several days a week working remotely from Richmond in Nonna's house. Zara had spent much of the last year cleaning out her grandparents' closets and desk drawers. The house was too big for her, and she had already met with a real estate agent. Selling the house that had been her home for most of her life was strange and unsettling. But life was changing. Which it always did, like it or not.

"We have to get moving if we're to meet the Biancos at the jeweler's at one," Nicolas said.

"Right."

"We can come back here if you like," he offered.

"No, neither one of them would want us to linger."

They walked hand in hand through the busy streets of Rome, making their way until they found the small shop.

Inside, there was an older, immaculately dressed man behind the counter. His thick graying hair was combed back, and a red silk handkerchief peeked out of his breast pocket. "You're the Americans?"

Zara was not sure what the telltale signs were, but she was grateful for the icebreaker. "Yes, my name is Zara Mitchell. This is my friend Nicolas Bernard."

"You've come about the broach?" he asked.

"Yes."

"I am Marcello Conti." His stern face softened with a smile as he motioned to an older couple sitting to the side. Standing behind them was a much-younger man, who must have been the couple's grandson.

"I would like you to meet the Biancos," he said. He introduced Edoardo, Eva, and their grandson, Roberto.

The old man took her hand and stared into her eyes, as if he were glimpsing the past. "Zara Mitchell?"

"Yes, sir. My grandmother was Isabella Mancuso," she said. "I was raised by her friend, Mia Ferraro."

"I was sorry to hear about Mia's passing," the older man said. "You will excuse me, but you look so much like your grandmother. I feel as if she's standing right here."

Eva reached out a fragile hand. "Isabella."

The older man turned to Roberto, who removed a black-and-white picture from his pocket. The image was of a young woman standing in front of Sebastian's. "This is Isabella."

"How did you get this?" Zara asked.

"After the war my grandparents wanted to find her. To thank her. They went to Sebastian's, and after some convincing, the old man who owned the shop produced this picture."

Zara stared at the smile that mirrored her own. "I've never seen this. Nonna said I looked like her, but this is uncanny."

Seeing Isabella's smiling face triggered a swell of emotions. She handed the picture back to Edoardo. "Thank you."

"That is for you," Edoardo said. "If not for her, Eva and I might not be here now. My wife was pregnant with our first son while we hid out with Isabella."

"She was so kind," Eva said in heavily accented English.

"It's nice to have a small piece of her," Zara said.

Roberto reached in a bag and pulled out a very old pair of shoes. Eva looked at her grandson and spoke quickly in Italian.

"My grandmother says that Isabella gave her these shoes."

"She was afraid your grandmother's shoes would give her away," Zara said.

Again, Eva spoke to her grandson, and he translated. "These shoes carried my grandmother over the Alps as she and my grandfather hiked to Switzerland and freedom."

Zara traced her finger over the worn, scuffed shoes. "Thank you."

"My grandmother used to speak to the schools each October sixteenth, the anniversary of the roundups. She always took the shoes and told the children about the woman who had given them to her."

Tears welled in Zara's eyes. She offered the shoes to Eva, but the woman shook her head. "They are yours now."

Roberto next handed her a worn Bible. "Isabella's."

Zara smoothed her hand over the cracked leather. She opened the front cover and saw the names of family members that dated back over a hundred years. "Thank you."

"It's my pleasure," Eva said.

Zara reached in her purse and removed the small jeweler's box. "My nonna's last wish was that I give you this."

Edoardo opened the box and smoothed his hand over the emerald's hard edges. He produced another picture, this one of an elderly woman elegantly dressed. She was standing in front of a marble fireplace, and she was wearing the broach. "This is Margherita Bianco, and this was taken shortly before we were married."

Zara stared at the face of the woman proudly looking into the camera. Again, she sensed she was visiting an old friend. "She's lovely."

"She was a great lady," Edoardo said. "She gave up everything for Eva, me, and our child."

"According to Isabella's diary, Signora Bianco wanted the broach passed on to her first female great-grandchild," Zara said.

"I had only sons. Roberto is my youngest grandson, and he and his wife are expecting their third child. She'll be the first girl in generations."

"Then I've arrived just in time," Zara said.

"Yes," Edoardo said.

"Your grandmother stayed behind to buy time for you, didn't she?"

"The Germans wanted more than the art they looted from Margherita's apartment," Roberto said. "They wanted my grandfather to sign over the estates and the lands so they could claim they obtained it all legally." Emotion tightened his voice. "When my grandfather returned to Rome, it was his mission to find out what happened to his grandmother's body. The right money in the right hands bought him the location of her grave on the outskirts of town. He had her reburied in Rome."

"She was a brave woman," Zara said.

"We cannot thank you enough," Roberto said.

Eva took Zara's hand and kissed it. "Thank you."

Edoardo insisted on taking them to lunch, and the five spent several hours eating at the Ritz overlooking the streets that Isabella, Riccardo, Mia, and Margherita had walked. At the end of the meal, they hugged and went their separate ways.

"You did good," Nicolas said.

"I hope it gives both Isabella and Mia peace."

Nicolas wrapped his arm around her shoulders. "I know that it does. I'd also like to think Catherine is at peace, knowing that her to-do list brought me back to life."

Zara kissed him on the lips. "You make me very happy, and if I haven't told you lately, I love you."

He deepened the kiss, and when he drew back, he had removed a ring from his pocket. "It seemed only fair if you gave up the broach, you should get a gift in return."

She looked at the ring with a single emerald bracketed by two diamonds. "It's lovely."

"Will you marry me?" he asked.

She cupped her hands on the sides of his face. "I will."

He slid the ring on her finger. “I love you. I think I have from the moment I saw you in that garage surrounded by all the contents of Nonna’s attic and your three dogs.”

She arched a brow, grinning. “And to think I wasn’t wearing lipstick.”

He laughed and hugged her close. “Lipstick or no, you’re perfect to me.”

John Mitchell: Last Report, June 2, 1945

We're closing up shop in Rome. The brass has asked me to stay behind and help with the transition, but I have had my fill of this war. I'll stick around a couple more months, because there is a matter I need to fix.

A buddy lent me a jeep from the army pool, and with a basket of canned foods from the commissary, I drove east toward the town of Assisi. I had heard Isabella and Mia had moved there midsummer of last year, and I had stayed in touch with local contacts. When I'd learned of Isabella's death, it had taken me aback. And when my commander would not release me to see Mia, I'd spent the rest of that afternoon drinking rotgut bourbon.

The drive east was filled with rolling hillsides, olive trees, and dusty roads that cut through small villages. When I arrived in Assisi, I already had the address for Mia, who I had been told was raising Isabella and Riccardo's baby.

I parked in front of the ancient stone building on the edge of town, and after several inquiries I found Mia's room. The basket of canned goods tucked under my arm, I approached her door, wondering if she would be glad to see me, or if she would hurl the cans at my head. If she did, I cannot say I would have blamed her.

From inside, I heard a baby cooing and a young woman singing to the child.

I knocked. Seconds later, determined footsteps crossed the floor, and the door opened. Mia stood before me with the baby tucked comfortably in her arms. At first, I did not recognize her. Gone were traces of the carefree girl I had fallen in love with and then lost to the German officer.

Her face was scrubbed clean of makeup, but it had a healthy warm glow from living in the country. Soft blonde curls framed her face, and she wore a simple blue cotton dress and an apron.

"Aldo?" She stood still, staring at me, as if she did not believe her eyes.

"Mia," I said softly.

"You have heard about Isabella?"

"I have." I cleared my throat. "I came to see the baby."

Mia tightened her hand on the child, as any protective mother might. "Of course. This is Riccardo. He's four months old."

The baby had red rosy cheeks and the chubby legs of a healthy child. "He's a fine-looking boy."

"Would you like to come in? I have just fed him, and he's in a particularly good mood today."

I held up my basket. "I brought you a few things."

She glanced at the canned corn, beef, beans, coffee, cheese, and crackers. "That's very kind, Aldo. Thank you."

I set the basket on a small wooden table. Beside it was a cigar box filled with needles and thread. "You're sewing?"

"Of course," she said easily. "I am very good at it. And we must eat." She sat by the table, balancing the baby on her knee, and I took the chair beside her.

"Are you getting by okay?"

"Yes, better than most. A far cry from Sebastian's, but it suits. We are happy."

"I should tell you my name is not Aldo Rossi."

She raised a brow. "Who are you, then?"

"John Mitchell," I said. It felt good to say my real name to her out loud.

"You are an American?"

"Yes."

She sat silent for a moment, smoothed her hand over the thick curls on the baby's head. "He ran his radio for you."

"Yes. He was very brave. And I'm sorry for how he died."

I braced for tears or the scene the Mia I had known would have made. Instead she nodded slowly. "Riccardo wanted to save Italy. And if he had not found you to help him, he would have found someone else." The baby cooed. "Would you like to hold the baby?"

"I've never held a baby."

"Neither had I until four months ago." She drew in a steady breath. "To my shame, I never held our child. Only Isabella looked into her pretty face."

"I'm sorry as hell I wasn't there for you."

"We both made difficult choices."

I accepted the baby and balanced the boy on my knee. "He's strong."

"Yes. He eats enough for two." The baby's head flopped, and she raised my hand to steady it.

"Sorry."

"I was terrified for the first month. Always worried that I would feed him milk that would make him sick or swaddle his blanket too tight."

"You look like a natural to me."

"We all must grow up and learn." She sat and crossed her legs.

Christ, I had forgotten how beautiful she was. "You look good, Mia."

"So do you, John."

The baby looked up at me and grinned. "He looks like Riccardo."

"Yes, he does. But I also see Isabella in him as well. He will be a handsome man." Mia watched me settle the kid in the crook of my arm.

"He's heavy."

"Yes. I suspect as he grows, he'll eat everything in sight, as my brother did when we were children. Can I get you coffee, Mr. John Mitchell, the American?"

"Yeah, sure, if it's no trouble."

"It's nice to have someone to talk to. Most days it's me and the baby and my needle and thread." She set the coffeepot on the small burner and lit the gas. "It's coffee from this morning, so it'll be strong now."

"That's fine."

She rummaged through the basket of food and found a sleeve of cookies. Carefully she opened them and set them on a plate by the cups before she filled each with coffee.

"You should save all that for yourself," I said.

"Ah, what fun is it if I do not share?" Mia said. "Tell me, where are Mr. Harper and Mr. Martinelli?"

"They're stateside now," he said. "Back home."

"That's good." Her brow knotted. "My foolishness nearly got them both killed."

"Harper said you stuck up for him when it counted."

She stared into her cup. "Better late than never, no?"

"I heard about what you did when you were with Brenner. You saved many families."

"The least I could do."

The baby settled in my arms, and soon he drifted to sleep. It took balancing to hang on to the kid and reach for the cup, and Mia seemed amused as she watched me.

"That is also an acquired talent. Most days he sleeps in a sling across my chest as I sew."

"You're doing a good job with him, Mia," I said.

"Who would have thought that Mia Ferraro would be such a devoted mother." She tucked a blonde curl behind her ear and smiled. "I pray Isabella doesn't mind that I think of her son as mine now."

"She took care of our child, Gina, so I know she would be glad to know you care so much for her boy."

"Gina? I don't understand."

"Isabella named the baby Gina."

"I didn't know that," she said softly. "She never told me. I should have named her, but I was too upset to think of such things."

My throat tightened, and it took a moment before I could speak. "I didn't mean to be gone so long. Maybe if I stayed, the baby would have lived."

"I've played that game for two years. If I only . . . I have discovered there is no answer that changes the past. I am grateful for what I have now."

I smoothed my hand over the baby's thick hair.

"He seems to like you," she said.

Sitting there, a sense of calm I had not felt since I'd left Rome for Naples two years ago settled over me. It was a feeling that life would go on, and that it would be good again. "I've got to return to the base. But I'd like to come back."

Mia regarded me. "Of course, John Mitchell. I would like that very much."

ABOUT THE AUTHOR

Photo © 2017 Studio FBJ

A southerner by birth, Mary Ellen Taylor has a love for her home state of Virginia that is evident in her contemporary women's fiction. When she's not writing, she spends time baking; hiking; and spoiling her miniature dachshunds, Buddy, Bella, and Tiki.